ALSO BY JESSICA LOTT

Osin

THE Rest *of* Us

JESSICA LOTT

SIMON & SCHUSTER
New York London Toronto Sydney New Delhi

Simon & Schuster
1230 Avenue of the Americas
New York, NY 10020

First Simon & Schuster hardcover edition July 2013

For information about special discounts for bulk purchases, please contact Simon & Schuster Special Sales at 1-866-506-1949 or business@simonandschuster.com.

The Simon & Schuster Speakers Bureau can bring authors to your live event. For more information or to book an event, contact the Simon & Schuster Speakers Bureau at 1-866-248-3049 or visit our website at www.simonspeakers.com.

Designed by Jill Putorti

Manufactured in the United States of America

10 9 8 7 6 5 4 3 2 1

Library of Congress Cataloging-in-Publication Data
Lott, Jessica, date.
The rest of us / Jessica Lott.
p. cm.
1. Self-realization in women—Fiction. 2. Man-woman relationships—Fiction.
I. Title.
PS3612.O777R47 2013
813'.6—dc23 2012028667
ISBN 978-1-4516-4587-3
ISBN 978-1-4516-4589-7 (ebook)

In Loving Memory of

Dorothy Lott *1910–1996*	*Ann Oshmiansky* *1940–2006*
	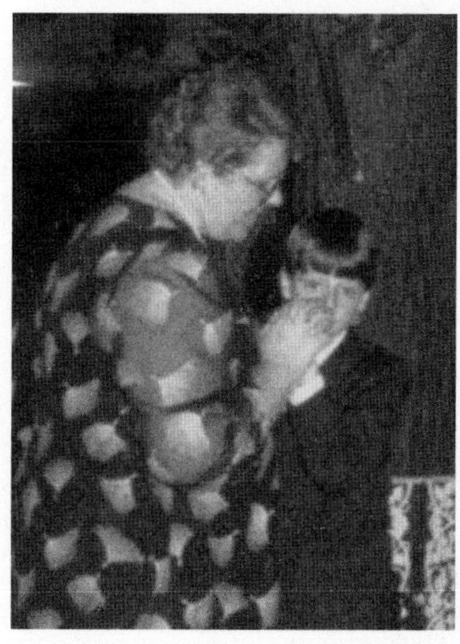

THE
Rest *of* Us

CHAPTER ONE

From *The New York Times*:

Rudolf N. Rhinehart, Pulitzer Prize–Winning Writer, Dies at 56

Rudolf N. Rhinehart, a noted cultural critic, literary scholar and poet, was the author of six books of poetry, including the acclaimed "Midnight, Spring," published in 1999 and winner of the Pulitzer Prize and the National Book Award. "Midnight, Spring," which the New York Review of Books praised for "creating an entirely new idiomatic register," was widely lauded, claiming numerous international prizes and achieving a level of commercial success rare for a book of poetry. A profile on Mr. Rhinehart for The New York Times Magazine in 1999 attributed the book's bestseller status to its "finding portals of transcendence in the unceasing repetition of our daily lives."

Mr. Rhinehart described his own working life as "alternating periods of grandiosity and self-sabotage." Although a prolific poet throughout the 1980s and '90s, he stopped writing poetry in the late 1990s, and was later known for his nonfiction and essays. He was a frequent contributor to the New Yorker, Harper's, and the Atlantic, and was the editor of seven poetry anthologies, and four critical volumes. The recipient of many literary awards and fellowships, Mr. Rhinehart was a member of the American Academy and Institute of Arts and Letters. He held honorary degrees from seven universities, as well as a Chair in Poetry at Columbia University.

Mr. Rhinehart is survived by his wife, Laura Constable, and two stepdaughters, Cindy Mithins of Asheville, N.C., and

Annabelle Mithins Ross of Durham, N.H. About his early life, little is known: Born in Ukraine, he immigrated to the United States with his mother at the age of five . . .

It was the beginning of November. Exactly fifteen years ago, I'd been nineteen, and in my junior year of college in upstate New York. I drove a rattling Nissan and wore the same pair of maroon corduroys every day—they were split in the left knee, and in the cold, the wind would slip in and deaden the skin. I sort of liked the sensation, but Rhinehart feared frostbite, and bought me thermals I refused to wear, and a bright green beret that he styled perched on the back of my head. I pulled it down, like the droopy cap of a straw mushroom, so that it covered my ears. My ears were a source of embarrassment to me, the way the tips protruded from between the strands of hair, which was a nice brown and long but too straight. I mostly wore it up with bobby pins that dislodged and were scattered around the house, he said, "like feathers from a rare bird. They let me know where you've been."

"You keep it too neat here. Otherwise you wouldn't notice." Except when he was writing, the only mess was stacks of newspapers and journals, the occasional used coffee cup, or jelly jars stained red in the bottom from wine—the living room of the house he rented for the duration of his time as a visiting writer at my college. This was what he had chosen—an old house with creaking doors and a bathroom under the staircase. He'd brought some of his furniture, striped low-back couches and an enormous featherbed that he'd dragged his library into, so that we often kicked books onto the floor when making love. He was working on the collection of poetry that would win him the Pulitzer, through miserable fits of self-doubt and manic intensity that made life even more exciting for me than it already was.

I'd met him at an artist lecture in town that summer, two months before he'd started his appointment at the school. We'd started talking about our mothers, both of whom had died when we were young. Slightly embarrassed, he'd revealed that he'd just attended a séance in Manhattan, and described the cramped, overheated room into which his mother didn't appear. I reached into my pocket and showed him pebbles that my mother had collected from the beach near our house. It was bizarre and superstitious but sometimes, if I was feeling nervous, I'd carry them around, knowing she had once touched them. She had died when I was three. Unlike other people, Rhinehart didn't assume that because I couldn't remember her, I didn't miss her.

Afterwards, I knew he was someone I wanted to be around. If I hadn't been in the grip of some sort of magical thinking, I would have recognized that he was in his forties, nearing the height of his career, and a professor. I would have been intimidated, rightly. I would never have had the guts to pursue him. I told myself, I'll just try and get to know him better. But it wasn't as easy as all that. It took me weeks to distinguish myself from the other young people milling around town that summer. We did become friends, but by then I felt we should be together and said so. He had discovered that I was a college student and was reluctant.

I plowed ahead, too confident in the connection between us to be dissuaded, and in the end I was right. Once he'd overcome his own objections, we'd moved very quickly from dating, to falling in love, to being in a relationship. He was continually amazed by how visual I was—it made his powers of observation "crude by comparison." When he'd said this, I'd been crouched down on his floor, studying a spiderweb spun between two storm windows, and the shadow it cast. I was a photographer, or an aspiring one. That fall, I was often at his house, shooting—the slim white birches just beyond the porch, sun on the floor, Rhinehart's fingers gripping a pen, the blond stubble on his face. I had almost too many ideas. In the morning, I'd disappear on my bike to take pictures in the woods, returning to a large, silent afternoon indoors, steam hissing up from the radiators. We'd sit on opposite ends of the couch, Rhinehart crossing out lines in a yellow memo pad, while I sketched future projects, and the fickle sun moved back and forth in the doorway. Occasionally, when he wasn't looking, I'd watch him. I had been excruciatingly happy. For months, I walked around with a foolish smile on my face. Everywhere, even in the bathroom.

The obituary had appeared online, and I printed it out to show Hallie. She'd been my roommate throughout college and after, when we first moved to Manhattan. I still lived in the apartment we had shared for years.

She was already waiting for me in a café on Jane Street. "What's the big mystery?" I took the obituary out of my purse and passed it to her.

"No way." Both of us stared at his photo. He was in profile, looking at someone out of the frame and smiling. "When was the last time you saw him? College?"

I nodded. Rhinehart and I had been together less than a year. He took a job at Columbia University the fall I was a senior and moved to the city. After I graduated, I moved here, too, but we'd never met.

I watched her read, her lip pinched between her fingers, her floating green irises like planets. Next to hers, my face had always seemed plain—like a farm girl's I used to think when feeling down. We'd grown up together on the North Fork of Long Island, but while my father had greenhouses, hers worked in Manhattan. She had spent overnights in the city, knew how to make us sexy ripped T-shirts, and sneak on the Orient Point ferry without paying.

She put the paper down. "How are you taking this?"

After the shock of it, I was depressed. Also incredibly disillusioned. "I was so sure we would see each other again. I can't believe how wrong I was." But then again, I'd been wrong about other things. My future as an artist. I'd basically stopped shooting, if you didn't count my job at Marty's portrait studio. I hadn't even noticed until about a year ago. Where had all that time gone? It was as if New York had swallowed it, along with my twenties. I'd revolved through possible solutions—sketch out some ideas, take a class at the ICP, buy a new camera. Instead I agonized and then did nothing. How effortless making my own work used to be. That's what I remembered of that time. That and what it had felt like to be lying on Rhinehart's bed, shirtless, in my corduroys, giggling.

Hallie was revisiting my relationship history. She'd often said she couldn't understand why anyone would bother to get married. Until she had her own lavish wedding and bought a house out in New Jersey with her husband, Adán, last year. Now she was bent on converting me.

After ticking through a list that included my boxing instructor, several bartenders, as well as a guy I'd made cupcakes for, slept with, and never heard from again, she concluded, "You haven't had a serious relationship since Rhinehart."

"You left out Lawrence. We dated for over a year." We'd even discussed living together, and in a roundabout way, marriage. I was white and he was African American and some people, including his parents, were convinced the relationship would fail because of this. It was not something we were ever actively concerned with. We were fixated on other, more pressing differences—such as our career ambitions, or his law-school-trained style of argumentation that used to make me flounder around in a self-incriminating way, or how each of us felt about living in New Jersey.

"I knew that wasn't going anywhere," Hallie said. "You were too much like pals." Maybe she was right. I hadn't felt the same type of passion, that soul-bearing intimacy that I'd felt with Rhinehart. Towards the end, I was also beginning to feel some pressure. He had wanted reasonable things, things that most women my age wanted—children, a nice home in the suburbs. I wanted to want those things, too. But I didn't. Instead I began to feel claustrophobic.

"Terry, you're coming up on thirty-five. Not a good age to be single."

I wanted to point out that statistically, in New York, I was likely in the majority, but Hallie had developed a theory. "I think this entire time, in some subconscious way, you've been comparing men to Rhinehart."

"But I haven't even been thinking about him. Until recently."

"I said *subconscious.* You need to have a little ceremony. Write down what you would have said to him if he were alive, a goodbye speech to the relationship, and then bury the piece of paper."

What would I say? How there existed a time that whenever I saw him, I'd want to touch him affectionately, encouragingly squeeze his arm. That even though he was older than me, I felt that protectiveness. That I still remembered the sweetness of being with him. I hadn't even been invited to the service. If I did memorialize Rhinehart, I would have to perform some private, self-serving ritual in front of my apartment building. I imagined myself dressed in black, trying to bury a piece of paper with my feelings on it in that strip of dirt between the sidewalk and a tree.

But then, two days later, for the first time in a couple of years, I got out my old Minolta and two rolls of black-and-white film and took the train up to 116th, Columbia University, and stood outside the gates, where I used to linger, hoping to run into him. The camera felt heavy and foreign in my hands. The light fading, I shot the route I had walked, ending up at the bookstore. The bar where I'd once sat and had a beer, looking hopefully out the window, longing to see him, or for a future in which I no longer cared about him as much as I did.

The second part of Hallie's advice entailed buying new clothes, and then, Internet dating, which I didn't plan on doing. But I thought she might be right about the shopping, and a couple of weeks later, on impulse, I decided to go into the Bloomingdale's in SoHo. Once inside, I remembered why I avoided department stores, especially in late November, their atmosphere of repressed panic and desperation, the overheated crush of people and sale signs and mirrored lights and the heavy, artificial odor that hung over all of it. As a teenager, I would spend several agonizing hours circling the racks clutching the Christmas money my father had pressed into my hand before dropping me off, saying "treat yourself." I longed for a mother the most then, for her to prevent me from making the mistakes I always made, buying something overpriced and too trendy, so that when it went out of fashion two months later, I'd have to lie to my father when he asked why I wasn't wearing "the pretty new top."

After scanning the floor and checking out the price tags, I decided to try my luck elsewhere. I was in the cosmetics department, headed for the doors, when I saw Rhinehart. He was standing in front of the Estée Lauder counter.

My entire body began trembling. I recognized him instinctively, the way I know desire or fear or my own face when passing a mirror. And he looked exactly as I expected him to look, but older than he had been in the obituary photo. His hair had gone completely white and he'd grown a short, academic-looking beard. I was hallucinating. I'd been far more affected by his death than I was able to admit. I willed him to vanish. But he didn't, and I stood there gaping. When he started to move off, I followed, targeting his wide back, taking in details. His coat was cashmere, expensive. He was carrying three bags, one was awkwardly shaped like it contained electronics. I circled around a counter to get a better angle, but he kept himself half-turned away, as a celebrity would.

I had moved in close enough to smell him, even in this olfactorily confusing place. He wore the same aftershave. Reaching out, I grabbed him as he approached the escalator.

He turned, squinting slightly, and looked at me.

"Tatie!" He dropped the bags and pulled me towards him, kissing me on the face. "How are you!"

I returned the embrace, shyly at first, and then with force. I clung to him for an embarrassing length of time. And then, out of nowhere, I started sobbing. Once I started, I couldn't stop. As if with other ears, I heard myself—I sounded like a large drowning mammal. I was wetting the front of his coat, hauling in my breath, conscious of him rubbing the back of my head in a soothing, concerned way. A woman came up and asked if I was all right. "I think I've just surprised her," Rhinehart said. "It's what she does sometimes. When startled."

I laughed and began apologizing, trying to disentangle myself. I was fishing around in my pockets for a tissue. Rhinehart was peering into my face, holding it in both his hands so that I couldn't clean it.

In my defense, I said, "I thought you were dead! I read it . . ."

"I know—it was released by mistake. The paper called it a technical error, by which they mean human. They write these things in advance. But it was pulled the same day. You didn't see the correction?"

I shook my head, and he said, "Are you all right?"

I nodded, and he let go of me, smiling. "It feels good to know I was mourned."

Someone bumped me from behind. The bustling shoppers, who had parted to give us space for our scene, had closed back in. He said, "This time of year is awful. My wife makes me participate."

I sucked in my breath at the mention of her. "I read you and Laura married." And then, "I didn't realize you'd kept in contact."

"We struck up a friendship after I moved here. She was on the board of an arts foundation I was doing work for."

I bristled in defense of my old self who had been roaming the city looking for him, never imagining he was out dating.

He'd taken my hand in his, turning it palm up, palm down. "And what about you? Not married?"

I shook my head.

"But you're with someone, I imagine."

I smiled, but didn't answer. Rhinehart was squeezing my hand and looking at me intently. "It's so good to see you. It's been too many years. Why don't you come to dinner at our house? We can catch up."

"That would be nice." I was starting to get my bearings again. "Are all these gifts for your wife?"

He looked down at the bags forgotten near his leg. "No, no. Some other things. Speakers. Clothes for one of my stepdaughters. She lives in New Hampshire and says she misses wearing city things." He dug around in his pockets. "Let's do it on Saturday. Are you free?"

"I believe so." We exchanged numbers, Rhinehart inputting mine into his BlackBerry, while I scribbled his down on a scrap of paper. He was professing how providential our meeting was.

I had drained my conversational well and suddenly felt shy. "It was definitely unexpected." We hugged again, and I detached quicker this time. I could feel him watching me as I walked away.

All the way up Broadway, I strode along, my coat open, chest to the wind, as if it were summer. Elated. He was alive! We'd seen each other again after all! It wasn't until much later, anticipating this dinner, that I began to feel idiotic for making such a scene. I hadn't even admitted I was single, afraid of how I already looked, sobbing, walking around by myself, as if I'd been mourning not Rhinehart's death but our breakup all these years. I was also starting to remember things. For example, it hadn't been fifteen years since we'd spoken. I'd called him when I first arrived in the city to see if he'd like to meet up again, maybe for coffee? He hadn't returned my call, and I'd been devastated. But I must have gotten over it because I'd written him a letter after I'd heard he'd won the Pulitzer. I was so genuinely pleased to hear the news—I remembered when he was writing those poems! How he struggled!—the letter overflowed with good feeling, run-at-the-mouth honesty, and nostalgia. I parlayed my congratulations into a discussion about our relationship, the force of attraction that I'd found so intense those years ago. I had wanted so badly to be with him, even when we were sitting next to each other it wasn't enough, having sex wasn't close enough. I kept that memory-laced letter in my purse for three agonizing days. Instead of throwing it out, as I should have, I'd addressed it in care of his publisher, since I had no idea where he lived, and dropped it in the mail.

I received no response. Instead, a few weeks later, nosing around online, I read about his marriage to Laura. The news was old, but I was so humiliated, it seemed as if the wedding had taken place that morning, right after my letter had arrived. I searched for photos, gasping every time I found one—there they were, standing close, at formal events, fund-raisers. Laura had bright blue eyes, round as marbles and slightly too close together, so that if they were on a dog, you'd think it was a biter. She'd been a condescending and vaguely menacing presence during the time Rhinehart and I were together, and it burned me to know she was with him—this man I had believed was so much like me.

I had met her towards the end of my time with Rhinehart, when a fissure had begun to appear in our relationship. He'd been pressuring me to attend these weekly faculty parties with him, as he thought it would be good for us to "mix," as he said, not thinking there was anything suspiciously sexual about the term. I didn't want to. Even though the college turned a blind eye to the relationship, either because he was a visiting professor or because our association dated back to before he'd begun teaching there, it still made me uncomfortable. I didn't want to go to a party and awkwardly try and socialize with my other professors. What I wanted was more time alone with Rhinehart. And for him to come over to 31 Maple Street, Apt. B, the second story of a rickety frame house that I shared with Hallie and three other girls, and have dinner. He said that our apartment—with its half-finished projects from our scrap art class, including a ball of rusty nails and underwear sewn over a chicken-wire frame, our schoolbooks, flip-flops, and full ashtrays everywhere, the *Easy Rider* poster taped over a hole in the plaster, this comfortable, relaxed mess, where I felt most at home—intimidated him. He also said it fascinated him. So I tried to work both angles, describing the environment in alluring detail, while concealing what went on there. Our idea of a good time was taking bong hits and pulling out the batik things or inviting some of the neighborhood guys over to play drug dealer, a largely silent game that involved winking. I swore my roommates went to other colleges, even though Gertie was in a lecture of his that semester and would return home with detailed accounts of his behavior every Wednesday afternoon at four. Rhinehart was a popular topic of speculation at my house, and they had been harassing me for months to invite him so that they could surround him like the maenads, picking him over with intrusive questions and revealing embarrassing things about me. I wanted Rhinehart to see my life without him, which might add to my mystique, but I didn't necessarily want him interacting with my roommates. I was waiting for a school break, when the house was empty, to enact my romantic dinner. I had been waiting, it felt like, for a very long time.

We had made a pact, Rhinehart and me, that we would begin trading Thursday night plans. The faculty parties always seemed to happen on Thursday nights, but so did Battle of the Bands at the Chickenbone bar downtown—a date night event I'd been lobbying for for weeks, as it was also something I frequently did without him. He pulled the first Thursday, so I went along to this party, and right in the door, Rhinehart introduced me to a professor in the archaeology department, Dora, a thin-lipped woman with cat eyeglasses in her twenties, too, although late twenties. I was taking an archaeology class that semester and we'd been shown slides of the excavation work she'd done at the Mut Temple Precinct in Egypt. I asked her about the Sakhmet statue she'd reconstructed, how she'd managed to tip it upright without cracking it, and she was walking me through the process—the stone mason packing the statue in sand to protect it from the drill's vibration, inserting the steel rods, the tense process of lifting it, injecting epoxy into the cracks, and finally coating it with a protective glaze tinted the color of sandstone.

Most of Rhinehart's friends never knew how to behave with me. They were either embarrassingly girlish, or cold and haughty, probing me with questions without revealing any personal information. Dora was different, and I was incredibly grateful. In fact, the more animated our conversation became, the more I began spinning a fantasy future for us as friends. I liked her eyes. They were a deep and sympathetic brown, and she held a steady gaze. Mine flickered all over the place when I spoke, out of shyness and this pervasive belief I had that they emitted vulnerability.

She excused herself, and I drifted over to the fireplace, looking for another conversational circle to join. Rhinehart was nowhere in sight. Dora came back into the room, talking to another professor, and I hesitantly approached them. I heard her say, "She's sweet, you know, but I teach all day—I don't want to do it at a party."

Locked in the bathroom, I sat on the edge of the toilet seat, trying not to cry, cursing Rhinehart. And then, as if from my own thoughts, I heard him. He had a deep, sonorous voice that carried well. He had wanted to be a Shakespearean actor once and had even auditioned for a company. He was talking about how I disliked morning radio shows. Out of nearly a year's worth of material to describe me with, he was highlighting this trivial comment I'd made in the car on the way over.

A woman said, "Well, they are obnoxious."

Kneeling on the tile, I squinted through a large colonial-reproduction keyhole. I made out the red skirt of his colleague's wife, Laura, who was supposedly in the middle of a divorce. I'd complimented her on the skirt when I first arrived.

"But that's not the only reason," Rhinehart insisted. "It's because the jockeys are always nasty to the callers. She's right. Every morning people subject themselves to all sorts of humiliations for our enjoyment. There's something perverse in it."

Laura laughed. "If that's what she thinks cruelty is, she won't get very far." And then, I parsed this sentence in a lower, more flirtatious register. "I suppose you like these little lambs you can corrupt."

There was a pause, while my face flamed. "She's a remarkable young woman," Rhinehart said. "Hardly a lamb."

"You know what I mean. Some people would say you're afraid of a woman who's your intellectual equal."

"People say all sorts of things. For my own sanity, I ignore them."

And that was it! He hadn't leapt to my defense—told her I was brilliant, talented, an artist. All the things he told me in private! I stood up, the bumpy grouting imprinted on my shins, and stalked out of the bathroom into an empty hallway. Rhinehart was alone in the kitchen, making himself another whiskey and soda. I whispered fiercely in his ear, "I'm going home." He'd driven. The car keys were in the front pocket of his pants.

Smiling, he gave me a squeeze. "Oh there you are. I'd wondered where you'd disappeared to." He looked into my puffy eyes. "Oh, no."

"I want to go home," I said.

"Why?"

Tight-lipped, I crossed my arms over my chest, my favorite soft light blue sweater. Passing my reflection in the hall mirror earlier, with the two spots of color on my cheeks, I'd felt a part of this chilly spring night—of new, untouched things, like the sticky little buds on the forsythia bush that I'd pinched on my way into the house.

A beaded gold necklace reached down to my stomach, and Rhinehart extracted it from beneath my folded arms and rolled it between his fingers, saying, "Did I mention how incredibly beautiful you look tonight?"

"No." My lip trembled threateningly. "But you said I wasn't your intellectual equal. Although not to my face."

I expected him to be ashamed, to beg my forgiveness. Instead he said, "Here, let me mix you a gin and tonic, even though it's a little early in the season. And don't worry, no one will say anything." He knew I didn't like to drink in public because I was afraid someone would ask me if I was underage.

"If you can't drive me, if your *friends* prevent you—" My chin was quaking now. "Then give me the keys and I'll go home by myself."

He was touching my wrist, his fingers cool and slightly damp from the glass. "Just tell me what really happened. Not what you imagined happened. I don't even believe I'm capable of thinking you're not my equal."

"I can't tell you here," I whispered, "because you talk too loud, and you'll make a scene."

"You didn't get groped did you? Then we'll leave." One of the Classics professors was a lech. He wouldn't make eye contact with you on campus, but he'd run his hand down your ass in the café, while pretending to reach for the silverware. He felt free to do this to me, and not to the other students, because I was dating Rhinehart.

I shook my head.

"Then what's got you?" He narrowed his eyes. "Or are you just creating a little smoke because you saw me talking to Dora?"

"No! I didn't see that." I was miserable. "Dora's meaner than she looks. She's a smiling hound."

"What?" Rhinehart said.

"'A hound crouched low and smiling,'" I quoted. Rhinehart had given me a signed edition of e. e. cummings poetry for my birthday, which I loved, even though he said cummings seemed to have been awarded Poet Laureate of the dormitory.

He snuck a look at her through the doorway. "You have the most unusual comparisons."

"Thanks for setting us up," I added, nastily. "And I'm serious about leaving. I'll drive. You're too drunk. I've been insulted." I reached in his pocket for the keys. "And one of the people insulting me was you."

I could tell he was angry, but he put down his glass and gestured towards the bedroom where our coats were. We had to walk single-file down the claustrophobic hallway. Over his shoulder, Rhinehart said, "This was a cocktail party. It was supposed to be fun."

I never went to cocktail parties. My friends had parties with a keg outdoors in the dark where it didn't matter what you did or said, or were wearing, and where you didn't have to be so fucking careful all the time. You could just relax. My father never had them, with snobbish friends bad-mouthing our country's foreign aid policies, and throwing around the term "Jesus freaks." While my mother was still alive, as my father told it, they had quiet dinners at home. They had friends over for coffee and to play cards. He helped her make Christmas ornaments to sell at the church's harvest fair. My mother's always sold out first.

This nearly brought up the tears again. "It *isn't* fun, and these people are a lot older than me," I hissed.

"Well, so am I."

"I'll wait for you outside," I said.

I went out the front door, with its pretentious beveled glass, not bothering to say goodbye to anyone. On the driveway's hard, ringing blacktop, I waited for Rhinehart. Above me, the vast sky was as still as a painting, streaked with hopeful tailings of daylight. Where I stood by the locked car, it was already night. My hurt hardened into resentment.

After what seemed like half an hour, Rhinehart stepped out of the house, a burst of music and laughter behind him. I saw how unappealing I must be, standing alone in the dark, angrily clutching my handbag, shaking with anger and frustration. I was twenty and felt like an embittered woman twice my age.

Once we were safe in the car, I told him what I'd overheard Laura say. "Is that all?" he said. "You should have emerged from your hiding spot and started a conversation. You missed an opportunity to correct her." I shook my head. I hadn't told him the full story, about what Dora had said, as her comment seemed to highlight the real flaw in me—that no matter how I pretended, I was just too young. I didn't belong there, and Rhinehart should have known I'd be uncomfortable and not pressured me to come.

Over the phone, I related the Bloomingdale's encounter to Hallie, who'd deliberately misunderstood me, thinking I had experienced an "otherworldly vision." Even after I corrected her, she leaned heavily on its mystical aspects, and her role in prophetically guiding me to the store.

"It's New York," I said. "People bump into each other."

"But right after we had a conversation about it?"

"Maybe I was more alert to seeing him. We'd probably passed each other before, and I just hadn't noticed." Now it seemed strange that I'd never managed to run into him all those months when I'd been trying to.

She wanted a full account, which she kept interrupting. "Tatie? He still calls you that dog's name?"

"It was the name of an old lady on his street, growing up. You were the one who claimed to know a dog with that name." When I came to the crying part, I hedged, reducing it to a few tears. It still met with disapproving silence.

"You cry too much," she took the opportunity to tell me. "Too bad I wasn't there. He always liked me. He told me I had the facial structure of a 1940s screen star."

I remembered that. Afterwards, every time he was in a room, she'd walk in with her head tipped down, eyes wide open in feigned surprise. Then she'd sit on the edge of a chair, light a cigarette, and discuss me as if I were her younger sister.

As if hitting on a brilliant idea, she said, "You should bring me to this dinner! I'll protect you from getting too sentimental."

Besides the awkwardness of bringing her, instead of a proper date, the entire idea was bad—she would immediately get Rhinehart embroiled in a discussion about the past, and then, being thoroughly entertained by the idea of subterfuge, she'd embroider an outlandish career history for me, have me photographing the Queen or in Afghanistan in the trenches with my camera, when I'd merely asked that she downplay the fact that I was working in a portrait studio, which Rhinehart, who could only see greatness in the people he'd marked for great things, probably wouldn't care about anyway.

CHAPTER TWO

The intervening years had brought Rhinehart to Long Island, to one of a tangle of dark, labyrinthine streets that pooled into cul-de-sacs. His home was now an imposing Federal-style with long narrow windows and black shutters. I parked my Zipcar on the street in front. I hadn't realized I'd be this nervous. My pulse was racing, my tongue itched with apprehension. It seemed absurd to have come on my own. Along the flagstone walkway, antique carriage lamps sprouted from the ground like mushrooms, lighting my feet as they slowly approached the house.

Rhinehart opened the door, and internally, I jumped. It was still unreal, seeing him again.

We stood there, staring at each other. "I'm so pleased you came." He looked past me to the car. "Are you by yourself?"

I felt my face getting red. "I, uh, didn't think—"

"No, no, it's wonderful." He reached out and touched my arm. I could feel, or imagined I could, the warmth of his hand through my coat. "I'll have less competition for your attention. Come in."

I was led down a carpeted hallway flanked with glassed-in bookshelves, Rhinehart in suburban-looking wide-wale corduroys. Two other couples had been invited. "Bill and Jesper are friends of mine. Bill is a poet. Do you remember meeting him years ago?"

I shook my head.

"I don't get to see him very often. Melinda and Dan are Laura's friends. She's hoping they'll make a contribution to one of her projects. It's not the most cohesive gathering, but we'll see how it goes." He smiled at me with genuine pleasure. "It's wonderful seeing you again."

Inside the vaulted living room, a couple was sitting on an antique white couch. I was still keyed up and making rapid and inaccurate assessments about the crowd: Melinda's handshake was limp and slightly damp. Dan was someone I wouldn't be able to recognize on the street tomorrow. He had the polite, blank expression of the men who poured out of the buildings downtown at rush hour. Bill, the poet, gave off the impression of roundness, round black-rimmed glasses, a large stomach covered in a sweater vest with a row of circular buttons. He was short, perhaps five foot five, and beside him, Jesper, who was Swedish, as I learned, appeared even taller than I suspected he was. Laura was absent—my eyes darted towards the ornate velvet curtains, which I assumed hid other rooms.

When I was introduced to Bill, he remembered me. "How beautiful you've become. The last time I saw you, you couldn't have been more than twenty. I gave a reading at your college." He turned to Jesper. "This was before I met you, love. I had hair then. Shame you never saw it."

"Of course!" I said. "Black hair. I do remember."

"You were so lovely, like a little wildflower. Very, very shy. I don't think you said more than five words. And when you asked Rudy a question, you called him by his last name. I remember how charming that was."

Jesper began talking about how conservative he'd always found college campuses in the U.S. "So different from what I had imagined when I was watching images on television in the 1970s." He had an open, likable face and an encouraging way of leaning in towards you when he talked, to bring his height down. He began asking, conversationally, and somewhat circumspectly, how Rhinehart and I were able to get away with our campus romance. "Jes!" Bill said, and I laughed.

I had the sense that Rhinehart was eavesdropping—he was discreetly standing a few feet away, discussing an eighteenth-century painting with Dan.

"It was a pretty liberal campus," I said. "And I wasn't technically Rhinehart's student. I audited the one course I took of his." It had been the spring of my junior year, when our relationship had already begun to fall apart.

This seemed to satisfy them, and I was relieved. I disliked the chain of questions that Lawrence and other ex-boyfriends had asked: What was it like to be with someone I couldn't take to college parties? Wasn't I bored? Did other people stare? Then those "daddy complex" questions I hated. When I dodged those, we'd get back on to the generational difficulties. I couldn't explain these things. He was just Rhinehart, and inside we had always been the same age.

But now he did seem older than me, and I wondered how his life could be lived amid all this heavy mahogany and valuable silver. He had always been suspicious of anything too Anglo-Saxon, and during the time I knew him, he never wanted to live with antiques that reminded him of a history of inequity. Great Neck, of all places! A tony suburb of commuters and old ladies. Except for those years upstate with me, he'd spent most of his life in Brooklyn and Queens, amongst the working class, the brick apartment buildings and single-story houses with their wrought iron fences, the men mowing their lawns in their undershirts on Friday evenings, or sitting on their stoops, the Italian delis, the carpet stores, the local butcher, the sidewalks kids drew on with chalk.

I had concluded this must be Laura's life Rhinehart had stepped into, when Laura herself came breezing in as if it were summer, dressed in white sailor pants, her eyes reframed by narrow, rectangular glasses. I wanted the room to freeze so that I could stare at her without being noticed. Now in her late forties, her face was more lined, but she was still magnetic. She found my gaze, looked confrontationally into it, and said "Welcome" in an unwelcoming way. Turning to Rhinehart, she began speaking in a tight, aggrieved voice, and I was suddenly ashamed, as if I'd invited myself here. It hadn't helped that Rhinehart had just handed me a glass of chardonnay and said, "I remembered you prefer wine to cocktails."

The guests seemed relieved to divide off now that Laura had appeared. Bill had gotten Rhinehart started on a conversation about Plath and a re-edition of *Ariel* compared to the earlier version that Ted Hughes had edited. "I think in sequencing it's inferior, this 'restored' edition. Hughes gave shape to the book, no matter how conflicted the relationship."

"By conflicted, you're referring to how she hated him?" Rhinehart said.

"Either way, perhaps I'm not the best judge," said Bill. "I find her poems so claustrophobic."

"I can't imagine what it took out of him to edit. Being locked up with those poems, going over them repeatedly. He may have run away from her, but she finally got her audience with him."

"That's what bothers me—her glorified obsession with abandonment. The atrocity of being in love with someone who isn't as *feeling* as you are! Who isn't as *depressed* as you are."

"'My fat pork, my marrowy sweetheart, face-to-the-wall,'" Rhinehart said.

"'Zoo Keeper's Wife' is an exception. A brilliant poem. It has this terrifying, multiplying energy. The rhino's open mouth, 'big as a hospital sink'—what that one line calls up about the stink of hospitals, of sickness and war, and the inadequacy of medicine. Beautiful."

Jesper said to me, "In a minute the discussion will turn technical and then into an argument. This is when I begin speaking about basketball. Or suggest we go to a game? Or this past summer, every weekend, I said, Let's take the boat out and drink Budweisers and not talk at all."

I laughed. "This is common cocktail hour talk for you?"

"It's all the time. I'm a translator, so sometimes it's useful. But not on a Saturday night. Are you a poet?"

"No," I said. "But I'm enjoying listening." In fact, the pleasure in being around Rhinehart and hearing him talk was intense enough that I feared it showed on my face, and I turned towards the window. On the other side of the thick pane, the icy moon cast pale light on the lawn. The room had gotten noisier with two parties going on. I listened to Laura's conversation about arts-focused education and services for lower-income women in Chicago. Her voice was passionate, pitched towards its success.

Rhinehart noticed me peering out into the yard and asked if I'd like to see the garden. We moved into the darkened hallway, and he opened heavy French doors and stepped out onto a shallow balcony. The night had gotten colder, more biting, the sky a deep, penetrating blue. I was conscious of his body, his arm pressed against mine as we leaned over the iron railing like people watching a parade below.

Rhinehart pointed out a reflecting pool wearing a thin skin of ice. Under stark, motionless clouds, I made out the brittle little sticks of an azalea bush, rhododendrons whose leaves had curled up like piroulines. Below me, close enough to touch, was the shaggy beard of an untrimmed yew. I ran my hand over it. The shrubbery of my childhood. It had been a while since I had felt it.

He pointed to a bird feeder, a single pole in the middle of the yard. "We get a variety of wildlife here. It's not like Queens where pigeons try and pass for mourning doves."

"You used to be really interested in birds," I said in a voice that sounded tentative. I'd remembered a period of time he'd been fascinated with the peregrine falcon. He'd spent several weekends with a group researching and tracking them through the marshes of Connecticut. I came along on these trips and spent the afternoons at the inn, reading or studying. He'd come back around four, smelling of salt hay, dead leaves, and we'd make love on top of the white eyelet cover. Now, hidden in the dark, I felt my face flush.

"My idea of nature is not nearly as Emersonian as it used to be, I'm afraid. I've adjusted, or maybe just downsized." From our vantage point, we could see the back addition, the lights on in the kitchen. The house seemed more bullying from this angle.

From the other room, Laura shouted, "Is there a window open? It's freezing in here!"

Rhinehart closed the door, and we went back into the living room. "It's so ridiculous," she was saying. "He acts as if there are still things growing out there."

So as not to show favoritism I joined Laura's conversational circle where Dan, the only person in a suit jacket, was resting his hand on the head of a large brass dog as if it were living. He was discussing real estate, the subprime mortgages that were gouging the economy, and the speculators flipping houses who knew nothing about investing. He was considering buying a house in the area, he said, and wanted to know from Laura what she knew about local home sales. "I hear the market has really come down."

Laura wasn't interested in the subject, and I got the sense she didn't care all that much for Dan either. She shrugged. "The prices still seem high to me."

"But the properties are just sitting there. They aren't turning over. You see more and more For Sale signs popping up. In other suburban areas, Jersey especially. New housing, and we're talking big properties here, one-point-three, one-point-five million, sitting vacant."

I followed along with my expressions, but I was listening instead to Bill complaining to Rhinehart about how many changes *The New Yorker* forced on his last published poem. "You sound like Elizabeth Bishop," Rhinehart said.

"I don't have her clout. Or yours. You know they love you. They're waiting for you to start sending them work again."

"So I hear. I still publish with them."

"Nonfiction. And it's wonderful. But your poems were something else—from the soul's seat."

"Bill, please. That's hyperbolic even for you."

"It wasn't me, it was Susan for the *London Review of Books.* Listen, I'm editing a new anthology—we have an unusually good constellation of contributors, blessed, even: Glück, Pinsky, Billy Collins, Rita Dove. A league of Poet Laureates."

"I was never Poet Laureate."

"You would have been if you had a follow-up. Even a mediocre one."

I had also wondered why he hadn't. Was it true, as the obituary said, that he'd stopped writing poetry ten years ago? He'd published two collected volumes of poetry after *Midnight, Spring,* but as far as I could tell, nothing new.

"It still amazes me that the Laureate post pays only thirty-five grand," Rhinehart was saying. "I think the last person to live high off the hog was Nemerov."

"No one knows what the hell it means, anyway. I had no idea what I was supposed to do that year except brag. But I happened to mention to Bob that I'd talk over the anthology with you, and maybe you'd be willing, if a few others were also on board—"

"You have no claim. Might as well have offered them Monopoly money."

"I have hope, belief you may give me something," Bill said. "Just one poem or thirty poems. Or a draft of something. A shopping list."

"Please, don't ask me again," Rhinehart said, his voice strained. "It's bad enough coming from my agent."

Melinda, who had a way of pressing her lips together that made her seem slightly neurotic, was asking me about growing up on the East End. I was less musing than usual, sensing an agenda underneath, and soon she had picked up a thread of zoning laws and farmers who were selling off tracts of land to developers who were building cheap summer homes and ruining the natural tranquillity of the area. I could tell she thought she had a sympathetic audience in me, and I didn't blame her, but my feelings about the subject were complicated. I had lingering childhood prejudices against summer people who provided the structure and market for all this growth and then wanted to disassociate themselves from the results, which were inevitably going to be mixed. They were often more concerned about the disfigurement of their view than the water table. My father had been forced to sell some of his land for my college tuition. He'd felt so guilty he cried on the day the papers went through.

But to explain all of this would have taken social energy that was going elsewhere. Once I had started talking, Laura had excused herself to check on dinner. I wasn't entirely sure, but it seemed as if she had been refusing to make eye contact with me. Maybe I'd been staring at her too much.

Rhinehart's hand was on my shoulder. "Can I show you something, Tatie?"

I felt uncomfortable saying yes, in case Laura objected, but she hadn't returned. I wondered if she was still in the kitchen. Maybe she was in another room watching TV or talking on the phone, as Hallie had once done in the middle of her own dinner party, because, as she'd said, she was bored.

I followed Rhinehart through the dining room. I was now on my second glass of wine and inclined to look more generously on my surroundings. The house had great artwork—I recognized a piece by Tracey Emin, a snaky line drawing of a woman. Probably Laura's, unless Rhinehart had started collecting feminist art. We passed through a room with dark baseboards and gold silk wallpaper, reminding me of the inside of a coffin. He moved us along quickly, as if this house and its studied opulence indicated a failing in him.

His study was bare by comparison. It was as if we'd stepped into the servant's quarters, or into my past. I recognized so many things—the fat Chinese lamp painted with fish, bought during a time he'd been fascinated with Asian art, scrolls with misted mountains and shoots of bamboo, a small brass Buddha. His nicked-up desk resembled the one he'd had in his faculty office. It reminded me of the afternoon he told me he'd accepted a position at Columbia University and would be moving to New York City. We'd been separated but I hadn't fully accepted that our relationship was over until then. "It will be strange not to have you nearby," he said. I had my back to him, looking out the window, where students like myself were passing on their way to class. So many of them. Indistinguishable from each other.

I became conscious of how quiet the room was, just the two of us alone together, and the possibilities of that shared solitude, all the things we used to do with it. I said, "Is this where you're writing nowadays?"

"I have worked here," he replied neutrally. "What I wanted to show you was this, although I suppose I could have brought it out—" And he lifted a silver-framed photograph off the wall, a black-and-white of a young woman yelling into the open window of an apartment, the curtain billowing out towards her face. Mine. My building, my photograph. I had taken it with my 35mm and had lost the negative in my move to the city. The woman was in a half-crouch, shouting in anguish and frustration. I took it in both my hands, fascinated, and said, "I've all but stopped doing it, you know. I can't really call myself a photographer anymore."

Rhinehart sat down heavily, as if this were a matter to be thought over. "I'm not sure it's that easy to get rid of. You have to remember that only a portion of any artistic life is actually spent creating. The rest is spent absorbing, experiencing other people, getting to know yourself. I take comfort in Franz Wright, who was so riddled with anxieties he was unable to leave his house for two years, and yet he's said that period of his life was invaluable to his poetry."

"Does that theory apply if you've never really developed your art?"

"When I knew you, you worked very hard. You were the youngest person the jurors had ever selected for that statewide group show. You walked away with several awards. A lot of people had their eyes on you."

"I was a college student. I'm not sure that work counts."

"Everything counts if there's talent and a sense of mission behind it. Besides, thirty-five is still quite young. If B. B. King can get on stage and perform, you can pick up your camera."

He'd remembered my age so effortlessly, as if he'd been keeping up with me, too.

He asked, genuinely curious, "Why did you stop?"

I was prepared to deliver the explanation that I'd repeated to myself so many times it had toughened into a little fact. It was just too hard to make it here, and my life upstate where I had local recognition and was giving shows and had a network of professors to encourage me was vastly different from my life in the city where I was working two waitressing jobs and scrambling to pay rent and also carve out time to work on my projects. I had arrived with such crushingly high expectations that seemed so ridiculous to me now. The galleries I was going to with my little portfolio of college prints, Deitch Projects, Gagosian even! It embarrassed me to think about it.

Rhinehart, watching me struggle silently, said, "Let me rephrase—*when* did you stop?"

"For good, probably a couple of years ago. It was around the time my father died. I'm sure that has something to do with it. But I'd struggled for years before that. I just didn't feel I could make a career of it. I was afraid of continuing to try, I guess." Rhinehart was saying he was sorry about my father. They hadn't known each other—I'd kept them apart, fearing my father would disapprove.

I could sense Rhinehart wanting to comfort me, but I was grateful he didn't. Horribly, I may have begun to cry if I were hugged by him another time.

"I never realized how difficult it would be to start again." I'd just gotten the contact sheets back from the rolls I'd shot up at Columbia, as well as a roll I'd shot in Tompkins Square Park, near my apartment, the day after I'd run into him. It was dispiriting. There were only two or three decent images—the rest of the rolls looked stale and amateurish and outdated. There had been so many developments in photography recently. I was still shooting like a Photo I student in the

1990s. "New York has to be one of the most exciting cities to shoot in, and everything I'm producing makes it look boring as hell," I said. "It's crap what I'm doing now."

"So you *have* started again," he said. Smiling, he took the photograph from my hands and hung it back up on the wall. I started to protest that actually I hadn't, it was just those two days and a lot of complaining about it, and he waved me away. "It feels uncomfortable because it's new and you care. But you're going to be too stubborn to stop just because of that. I know you." He squeezed my arm encouragingly, and I felt sparks. "Welcome back."

Out again in the hallway, he asked if I had ever managed to spend time on a working nineteenth-century farm.

I laughed. Half-jokingly, I used to talk about moving to Old Bethpage Village and living there for a while. In my imaginings the 1800s houses were empty—there were no tourists poking through them. "I gave that dream up."

"Good," he said. "It always struck me as a difficult lifestyle."

Dinner was on the table when we returned, and everyone except Laura was seated, waiting for us. A cornucopia spilled lusty fat grapes, shiny apples, and sprigs of evergreen onto the lace tablecloth, which looked hand-done, Eastern European. Despite all this abundance, recrimination was in the air, as if Rhinehart and I had been off doing sexual things. I pulled out my chair and Rhinehart took the empty one next to me.

Laura, coming in, said, "That's my seat! So I have easy access to the kitchen."

"It doesn't hurt to change things around occasionally." But he got up anyway and moved to the other end of the table, directly in my line of sight. I was unable to meet his eyes. Instead I watched his reflection in the heavy mahogany mirror on the opposite wall. He had brought his scotch with him and was sipping it with a dark, preoccupied look.

I turned to Melinda and complimented her pearls. I had been too abrupt with her earlier. When she lifted her grateful, almost eager face to me, I saw how young she was—still in her twenties. The conservative and slightly matronly way she was dressed, the calf-length tan skirt and blouse, her blond hair held back with a tortoiseshell clip, made her seem older. That and her husband, who was likely approaching fifty. I wondered if this was Dan's second or even third wife.

She touched the necklace self-consciously. "They're family heirlooms," she said. "Dan's parents gave them to me after our marriage passed the three-year mark."

I smiled. "I have some that were my mother's." I had wanted to wear them tonight but had changed my mind at the last minute, afraid I'd appear too dressy.

I turned to Laura, who had been silently following this exchange, and told her the dinner was excellent.

She gave me a tight, unfriendly smile. "Thank you. I'm glad you're enjoying it."

Referring to a landscape painting in the hallway, I said the style reminded me of a show of young Catalan artists that I'd seen last month.

She was startled, as if the chair itself had put forth this opinion. "That's Francesc Rudel. He's from Barcelona."

"There's a lot of great art coming out of that city lately," I said. "Especially interactive feminist projects."

Laura was giving me a level, somewhat amused stare. "Not many people know that. It's still really underground. Have you been?"

I shook my head, and she told me, "If you go I can give you some names. A lot of artists show in temporary venues without much publicity. That bad commercial strip in L'Eixample still dominates, unfortunately." She carefully cut the slice of eggplant, still pinning me with her eyes. "I know the exhibition you were referring to in Chelsea. It was at Kinz, Tillou and Feigen. They have a feminisms show up now with a fabulous Adrian Piper piece."

"I love that piece!" I said, unintentionally gushing. "The mirror that says 'everything will be taken away.' You look into it, and the words are written across your face."

"Indeed," she said.

From across the table, Bill asked, "So how did you two reconnect?" Gesturing, not to Laura, but to Rhinehart and myself, and not entirely innocently.

"We ran into each other. I actually thought he'd died, because I read an obituary—"

"Oh, that!" Laura said. "He's talked about nothing else!"

"It's incredibly jarring to see yourself laid out dead in a major newspaper," Rhinehart said. "It made a strong impression on me. Understandably."

"I still can't believe that it happened in the *Times*," Jesper said. "The smaller papers, on the other hand, will print anything. In Gotland a few years ago, a group of students submitted my colleague's memorial to the local paper as a hoax. It was heartwarming, actually, they told of how inspiring he was, and how he'd made a difference in their lives."

"Every time you tell this story, I find it unsatisfying," Bill said. "How macabre, all of them plotting it out. You couldn't pay me enough to go back in front of the classroom after that. And it's very different from Rudy's case—an impartial person composed it, an obituary maker, or whatever they're called. Not a eulogist."

Dan and Melinda didn't know about Rhinehart's obituary and had to be filled in. "It was only released online, not in the print version," Rhinehart said, "so it was easy enough to retract. Still it's amazing how many people saw it in the short time it was up on the site."

Bill said, "Remember when CNN released all those draft obituaries with the wrong information? Dick Cheney described as the 'UK's favorite grandmother'?"

"There's so much competition to be the first to release news now, mistakes happen," said Dan. "Servicemen are often reported dead when they're not. I remember seeing an announcement on television that the White House press secretary James Brady had died, when he hadn't."

"Yes, but he'd been shot in the head," Rhinehart said. "He was in critical condition. There was no precipitating cause for releasing my obituary. And I found it unnerving that they'd had it prepared already. I'm still in my fifties. In good health, I thought. I should check with my doctor to see what he's been saying around town."

"What I find more interesting are the cases in which the people are actually thought to have died," Bill said. "My grandmother used to tell a story about a neighbor who'd drowned. In the middle of the wake, she sat up in her coffin and asked for a glass of whiskey. The entire room was overjoyed, except for her husband. He dropped dead of a heart attack on the spot. My grandmother claims he died of guilt since he was having an affair with a young girl in the next county. Wanted to marry her."

I felt my face turning red and instinctively put my hands over my cheeks to hide it.

"Well, this is a morbid conversation!" Laura said. "And, Rudy isn't dead. He's sitting right there."

"I could have been though," Rhinehart said. "Marcus Garvey had a second stroke after reading of his death in the paper, which described him as 'broke and friendless.'"

"Yes, but yours was impressive," said Bill. "You should tell them not to change anything. And you were headlining. You got the verb."

"What's that?" Melinda asked me.

Laura rolled her eyes. "Evidently they only put the headline in present tense for the most important person who kicked off that day. Per page, or something like that. A minor point since he's alive."

"Laura's right," Rhinehart said. "I've been talking about it too much. I've been *thinking* about it too much. You know what bothers me the most is how it said I'd never known much about my family. It's true! My mother died when I was young and all of our history went with her, the five years I spent over in Ukraine that I can't remember, the only link to my father. Why didn't I ever try and trace my background?"

"I agree," Laura said. "You should know more. But why begin researching it now, when we have a major fund-raiser coming up that I need your help on." She turned to Melinda. "This is what I was discussing before, the Chicago Women's Art Fund. We're having it at the Carlyle. It's a bit stuffy for me—I wanted to use this new event space in Tribeca with absolutely stunning views, but Belinda said that since it was a cocktail event, it was better to do it uptown. The traffic near the tunnel might be a problem at that hour."

"I won't be involved this year," Rhinehart said. "I've already told you."

"Tell me again," Laura said, putting down her fork. It rang against the side of her plate. She turned to Melinda. "You need to hear this—the blast of hot air will take the curl out of your bangs."

"I think there are some pitfalls in making philanthropy into a series of high-end parties for the donors and corporations. I think it potentially—" I could feel him being cautious with Dan at his side, "could be reinforcing the class mentality that has provided the conditions for economic inequity in this country. I prefer a more hands-on approach."

Laura was about to respond, but Dan was quicker. "But let's be realistic. We can't all quit our jobs and start volunteering. Someone needs to make the money to fund these programs."

"I believe there are ways of contributing that are more valuable than writing a check," Rhinehart said. I remembered the years he spent doing job training in low-income neighborhoods in the Midwest just before I met him. "Tatie, would you still agree with this assessment? We used to talk about it."

"Yes," I said. I realized that I'd slipped into the old habit of being quiet in a group discussion.

"I believe in changing policy," Bill said. "I always admired the poets I knew who were activists. Muriel Rukeyser was in Spain at the outbreak of the Civil War, and then in Vietnam protesting, and then in Korea campaigning on behalf of a jailed writer there. And she's a fine poet. That to me is the perfect use of a life."

"Except you're no longer the frontline type," said Jesper.

"I'm not the frontline type anymore. It's true," said Bill. "I prefer to fight injustice from the chair in my study. I'm the petition-signing type."

Laura said to Rhinehart, "How can you say chairing these foundations isn't compassionate? Do you realize how much time and effort goes *into* that work? Why would people do that if they didn't care? If they could just spend the afternoon at Neiman's?"

"Laura, we're having a discussion. Please don't take it personally. I'm not criticizing your level of commitment."

"Really, because it seems to me that you are." She stood up and started collecting the plates, banging them together. Melinda half-rose to help her, but sat down when Laura spoke again, harshly. "It's just so *easy* to sit there and cast judgment."

Rhinehart said, "I'll clean up."

She ignored him, and I tensed.

"I didn't mean to offend you," Rhinehart said, and I was ashamed of the placating tone in his voice. "We disagree on this, passionately," he told the room, "but we're still having a wonderful night." He turned to Bill, and said heartily, "It's great to see you again."

"Same here," Bill said warmly, reaching out and squeezing Rhinehart's forearm.

All of a sudden Laura did sit down, creating an unexpected movement of air between us. The dirty plates that she'd collected were stacked in front of her in an unstable, ominous-looking pile.

Laura gestured, with a magisterial little wave of her hand, to Rhinehart. "Well. Get to it."

Rhinehart remained seated. He was breathing heavily through his nostrils like a horse that's just been run. It was as if all of us had dropped away, and there was only Rhinehart and Laura fiercely staring at each other across the chasm of the table, until they, too, no longer existed, and there was nothing except this strong, sour disagreement pressing them into their seats. Rhinehart broke it by standing and reaching for the dishes. After a nudge from Bill, Jesper also stood up to help. Taking away my plate, Rhinehart averted his eyes.

Once Rhinehart's back was turned, Laura said to me, "I'd be feeling pretty good, too, if I'd had six scotches and sat on my ass all afternoon." I flinched. Rhinehart had paused in the doorway.

"Not my father," Bill said. "That's about the time he got out the belt."

CHAPTER THREE

I'd almost succeeded in putting the memory of that dinner party out of my mind when a week later I received a note from Rhinehart. He'd either looked up my address or still had it from years ago, when I'd sent him that congratulatory letter.

> *Tatie, I'm sorry. I'm still ashamed about the way the night turned out. Laura and I have separated—things have not been good between us for a while, as you may have guessed. I'm going to Italy for a couple of weeks, but I'd like to be in touch when I get back. —R.*

I read it quickly and left it on the side table, as I was late for work. When I got back home, Hallie was there. Rhinehart's note had been moved to the kitchen counter where she'd presumably read it before rooting through my refrigerator.

This was one of those times I was tempted to ask for my keys back. I'd thought now that she had two residences—the apartment in midtown that she had first lived in with Adán and a new house in Jersey—she wouldn't feel as compelled to spend time at my place, the small and somewhat dark one-bedroom in the East Village that we'd shared for the majority of our twenties, longer than either of us had expected we'd be able to tolerate living together.

She had a strange affection for it. Before she'd moved out, she requested I keep her bed around for a while in case she wanted to sleep over, and even though I refused, she still expected me, as the keeper of the rent-stabilized domicile, to preserve it as some sort of mausoleum of her single life, resenting my redecorating and calling me at work to accuse me of getting rid of the green velour couch, "the pregnant lady couch," that sagged so deep in the middle you had to hoist yourself up by gripping the back.

In truth, my best years in the apartment were when we were still new to the city, heated up with enthusiasm that made everything seem decadent, our minuscule kitchen, the back bedroom with its air shaft windows ("It's perfect for sleeping—no outside light," Hallie had said) that we'd shared initially to preserve the living room for socializing before we decided we didn't care about inviting people to dinner and wanted our own bedrooms, the pipe heating in the bathroom that burned you if you bumped into it, the fire escape where we grew tomato plants in the summer and sat out in the evenings, smoking cigarettes, watching people walk down Fourth Street, and discussing things that seemed very important at the time.

I knew some tenants who reinvested the rent they saved into renovating the kitchen, buying a new stove, or redoing the floors. In the years I'd lived here alone, I'd done considerably less than that, but I had upgraded the furniture, and hung artwork and antiques that I imagined created a friendly, warm, cared-for environment. Yet, lately I'd begun to feel trapped by my good deal, which, as the rent went up, seemed less and less worth the sacrifice. I couldn't shake the feeling that this narrow walk-up with its tilted stairway, the dark stained carpet in the hall, the small, low-ceilinged rooms and leaky bathroom fixtures and missing tiles and temperamental gas stove with its worn knobs, stubbornly asserted an identity that dwarfed mine, preceding me by many years. It was if I were caught inside the building's interminable aging process, surrounded by all my nice little things. I felt myself aging along with it, never being able to change. Hallie insisted it was "perfect for one person. Very cozy." I suspected she just enjoyed the luxury of being able to visit both the apartment and herself at twenty-three.

Gesturing to Rhinehart's note, she said, "How come he didn't just email?"

"I don't think he has my email address. And he always liked to write by hand, so it makes sense."

"That so? Since when do you know so much? I hope you're not getting hung up on him again. I thought we'd seen the last act."

I'd been behaving oddly enough this afternoon that my boss, Marty, had approached me in that tiny studio crammed with portraits and promotional cardboard displays and an elaborate gold-lettered sign "Photography by Martin" that he had feared would get stolen if he hung it outside, to ask me if I was upset about the raise I'd just received—if I thought it was too low. "You've been staring off into space all day," he said. "You're reminding me of my Aunt Rosie whenever she was listening to her saints." I'd been thinking about the deep, open look Rhinehart had given me when he passed me my photograph in the library, how he'd laid his hand on my back instinctively to lead me into the dining room. I had started to think that we could spend time together, just as friends. Maybe, in being around me, he would be reminded of the time he was writing poetry and be inspired. We could go to a reading together. Or to the Lucian Freud show at the Neue Galerie. We both loved the way Freud painted feet, as expressive as a face.

Hallie took my silence as a self-indictment. She had one pointy elbow on the counter and was preparing to lecture me. For someone who claimed to live in the present, she enthusiastically borrowed from more than thirty years of our shared experience to build arguments.

"Even if he is suddenly free that shouldn't have anything to do with you. Up until recently, you hadn't seen him in *decades.*"

"It's been less than that."

"You haven't *been* with him since we were in college. I remember. I had box seats to that tragedy."

There had been many breakups during that spring semester. I'd always gone back with renewed optimism that I'd worked through things by crying. I was prone to unhealthy, near-manic states of jealousy with him—a pattern that had never been repeated with the same intensity since. Hallie was reminding me of a time, soon after Rhinehart and I had split up, when I suspected him of dating a Russian girl named Natasha. She was in my World Literature and Civilizations class. I sat near her, in whichever seat afforded the best view for spying. She had a much older woman's way of settling herself into her desk, and her hair always looked unwashed; she used to wear it in a short ponytail, like a gymnast. She wasn't pretty, but I knew Rhinehart didn't care about that. In fact, he probably liked the shadowy sideburns and heavy brows—he had once mentioned a preference for hairy girls. Although we'd split up, I still saw him twice a week in the poetry class he taught that I was auditing. I attended, sitting resentfully in back, refusing eye contact. He had pressured me to drop the course, but I was running on a lunatic's mix of fear and stubbornness, and had refused.

Natasha was also in his poetry class, but not in the same section as me. She was with me in World Lit, though, making it the second most interesting class of the week. I'd show up ten minutes early so I could watch her as she came in. Under her heavy coat, I made out the bulge of her hips. "It's so warm today," I said to a girl next to me. "I don't know how people can still be wearing winter stuff. It's kind of depressing." Other days, I'd sit in the desk alongside her and make rapid movements, attempting to catch her attention. She never let her eyes rest on me for more than a split second.

"Paranoid speculation," Hallie had said. "Give me some proof if you want me to listen to this."

"All of a sudden he's really into painting. She's a painter." He'd started this before he ended our relationship. Abstract things with triangles. Smeary apparitional figures without any faces.

"So what?" Hallie said. "Maybe he's with that art professor Hotten. She just got divorced."

"She's not his type." Meaning, Professor Hotten was nothing like me. She had dyed red hair and a flat butt, and wore heavy eyeliner. Her body was shaped like an ant's, all the bulk in the middle.

"You have to let go," Hallie said. "I'm starting to think I should be making an appointment for you at the counseling center."

Two days later I saw Rhinehart and the Russian together. It was pure accident. I'd been shadowing him around campus for weeks, but I wasn't doing it at that particular moment. I was coming out of Brighton Hall, thinking about whether I should have my hair cut in one of those short, choppy styles that Hallie was pushing me to get. I suspected she just wanted to see how it looked on me before she got it done.

From across the lawn, I saw him. He was listening to something Natasha was saying, his hand on her upper arm. Was he stroking it? He smiled indulgently. Lovingly, almost. I stood there, transfixed, paralyzed by terror, revulsion, and excited vindication, like at a beheading. She was bent over with laughter, her nose grazing his coat. It was this, the graceful movement, the sight of her happy little teeth, like milk teeth, that got me. I'd never seen her smile before. So it was true! My legs, my whole body started vibrating like a struck tuning fork. I ran into the building, down the hallway, and out the double doors behind. Sprinting, I reached the apartment in minutes, sweaty and panting. No one was home. The bright yellow sun poured onto the kitchen floor, where I lay, wailing like a speared animal. Later I locked myself in my room. I stayed in there all night, drinking vodka and crying, looking through old letters Rhinehart had written me—how he'd changed! I fell asleep, the letters underneath me.

It was late afternoon when I went downstairs. Hallie was flipping through a magazine at the kitchen table. She started when she saw me. "Jesus."

I'd seen myself in the bathroom mirror. My eyes were swollen like an ornamental goldfish's. My upper lip was puffy and raw. I hadn't showered, and my hair was matted in back. I was listless and weak from not eating.

"I didn't even know you were here." She sniffed. "You smell like a bar. Have you been drinking in *bed*?" She made me a cheese sandwich, while I sat at the table crying into my folded arms and choking out the story of Natasha. He was with her! When the entire time I'd just assumed he needed to concentrate on his work. That I was irreplaceable!

"Every woman's got a story like yours," she said. "You need to be more proactive. Remember how you said this separation was a good thing?"

"That was before he replaced me. Like I was *nothing.*"

"I'll invite Rick and Nosh over—those idiots will distract you. Don't take any bong hits."

"I wish he knew what this felt like!" I looked up from the table. "Maybe he thinks I don't care because I haven't been showing it. Maybe I should ask him to meet me—"

"Oh, no," Hallie said. "*No.* Believe me—he knows you care. He knows you better than you think. Cry as much as you want but stay away from him."

She went to the phone. By the time the guys showed up, I was back in my room. They called to me, but I refused to come downstairs.

The next night, after thinking it over, I decided to go to Rhinehart's house. I waited until Hallie went into the bathroom, and then, my pulse beating wildly, I snuck out. Manic energy carried me all the way to the edge of his lawn. The lights were on, curtain drawn. That's when I started to have doubts. What if he was in there with her? I ducked over to the garage and peeped in the double-paned window. His car was next to the mower and the gasoline containers. Trampling his ivy, I made my way over to the living room window and peered through the open sliver between the curtains. My breath caught. He was alone, sitting in the armchair in the corner, reading, one pinkie against the wing of his nose, as when he was deep in thought. Relaxed. Peaceful, almost. I was suddenly furious. I tore around to the side door and slammed into the living room.

He jerked, dropping his book. "Tatie! You scared the crap out of me."

I was unable to move from the doorway. He took off his reading glasses, while I watched his hands.

"You look a little wild. You haven't come to kill me have you?" He hesitated. "Is that my shirt you have on?"

I hadn't even thought about my clothes. I was still in the Carhartts

I'd been wearing for several days, and an old shirt of Rhinehart's. Hoping, in a vague voodoo way, that it would make him long for me.

"I want the things I gave you back," I blurted out.

"What things?"

"My book of Renaissance paintings."

"Have you been wandering about in the yard? You have something stuck in your hair, a leaf."

When he stood up, I instinctively jerked forward to return the hug. He didn't move, and I stopped mid-motion. I began to sob, taking air in big, gulping breaths.

"Oh, Tatie."

"I saw you today," I choked out. "I saw you with someone. On campus."

"One of my students?"

"It wasn't just a student! I know who she is."

I waited for his eyes to shuttle around as he came up with an excuse. His face looked naked without its glasses. But instead he looked at me with something like pity. "You can't be making yourself ill over this. I get jealous of you, too, but I try and understand that you need to live your life independent of mine."

My heart surged to hear he was jealous, and to cover it I said, "Fuck that. You have no respect for me."

"I do, and I'm sensitive to your feelings, trust me." He sighed. "I sometimes forget how young you are."

"What does that mean?"

"It's just that these situations feel completely overwhelming before we get better trained in heartache."

I lost my mother I wanted to shout at him, what could be a bigger grief than that? But I didn't want to get us off track. "Natasha's not even pretty! She smells like cabbage. I can't believe you!"

My hands over my face, I bent towards him. He didn't touch me. Instead, he said, almost to himself, "I'd thought you'd held this theory for weeks now."

"Why? Who'd you hear it from?"

He winced slightly. "Natasha had mentioned that you glare at her. In class. I said that couldn't be—it's so unlike you, but I had wondered about it."

The horror of my situation hit me. They had discussed me! Probably in bed! I started crying again.

Rhinehart patted my tangled hair. I hated myself for letting him. After a while, he said, "Your outfit reminds me of something. Summer, maybe, or backwoods camping. It's very endearing."

He led me over to the striped couch and sat me down on the cushion with the squeaky spring. "I'll get you something to drink. Alcohol probably isn't a good idea."

He brought me orange juice in a glass from a set I'd bought him that had been similar to his mother's long lost ones. "Where did you find these?" he'd said that day, looking as pleased as a little boy.

"Try to calm down," Rhinehart was saying, and I thought of Hallie back in our snug place, watching a movie on the papasan chair, assuming I was in my room sleeping. Or maybe she'd found me out. She was right. I shouldn't have come.

I felt a rush of anger. I hated him and was on the verge of saying so, but the thought of it brought on another wave of tears. "You're such an asshole."

He let go of me, and I sat down on the couch, still huffing.

He said, "How did we get here, you and me? You never think a relationship will get to this place and then it does. Listen, forget Natasha—"

Even the mention of her name stung. "I can't forget her. The scene keeps replaying itself in my head over and over."

"Suspend the movie for minute."

This gave me a glimmer of hope. "So you're not seeing her?"

"No. I'm not. You're the only person I've been with since I arrived here. And you are more than enough for one man."

I squinted at him to see if he was lying.

"But the relationship between us isn't healthy anymore. Tatie—" He grabbed my knees. "You must see that. You must see how miserable you are with me."

But I was miserable apart from him, too. That was the problem. I started to say that if we got back together but were more careful, maybe seeing each other only a few times a week, not overdoing it like we usually did.

He was shaking his head. "It's a trick to think we can change it. Every time it gets worse. It's excruciating to keep trying. It's pathological."

"But I love you," I said, choking it out. "I never loved anyone as much as I love you. I don't want to be unhappy with you. Why are we?"

He didn't say anything, although I knew he had theories. I had theories. He retreated into his work, abandoning me. He made me jealous. I cried all the time and felt inferior. We separated, ostensibly for my good, but he was the one who became more productive, while I skipped class to listen to sad music and write in my journal about him. I didn't want to discuss these things again. He put his arms around me, and I leaned into his chest and breathed in his cologne, trying to pretend none of what had happened over the past two months had happened at all.

The rest of the evening I remember as a nauseating daze, lying like that for a while, then kissing, then him pulling back, another argument after he said that we'd done the right thing by splitting up and that we needed to move on.

"I just need to feel better," I said, trying to crawl into his bed. The sheet was too tight, and I had to jerk it back. "I just want to go to sleep and wake up again and feel better." I wanted him to join me, but he stayed on the other side of the room, arms crossed. Then he left. The light clicked off. I stayed behind, holding myself in his bed.

Hallie remembered this story. She also remembered how, after graduation, suddenly I was interested in moving to New York City with her when originally I'd wanted to go to Seattle. "And then you get here, and he can't even make time to meet you for a cup of coffee."

I felt the need to defend our relationship. Its significance. "It's difficult when there's so much emotion and intensity. We were incredibly close."

"This is what I was afraid of!" she said. "The rewriting of history. You were together for less than a year—and most of the time, you didn't even seem like you were enjoying yourself! If you'd had a therapist back then, which you should have, she would have told you that you 'modulated yourself around him.'"

"I was twenty. What girl doesn't do that at that age?"

"Plenty. There were those bossy girls that made their boyfriends buy them Monistat. Remember Gertie? Her boyfriend used to vacuum our place. She used to yell at him, 'Mark! *Mark!*'"

"Gertie was a hysteric. She made us take her to the emergency room for menstrual cramps."

She waved this away. "Ever since that dinner party, the old man's been coming up in conversation. Select cameos. As if you're thinking about him a lot more than you're saying. You're not going to see him, are you?"

"I don't know," I said, nonchalantly. "Maybe. I don't have to make that decision yet. He's not even in the country."

She looked at me again, in that annoying, deliberately penetrating way. "You know that 'separated' is different from 'divorced.'"

"I'm not looking to move in on him."

"So you say now. Anyway, I'm glad I didn't go to that party. I hate couples who fight in public. It's not good energy for me to be around. Already I'm aware that Adán and I used to have a hell of a lot more fun when we were dating."

"I don't know how you could have sustained that momentum." The two of them had been crazy about each other and just wild in general—at a corporate party at the Gansevoort they'd been caught having sex in the rooftop pool. And then they tried it again, two weeks later. Adán made a lot of money, so their partying hit a level of extremism that I, and even Hallie, were unfamiliar with. He was from Madrid, and slightly older than us, with thick black hair and hooded eyes that when he got drunk made him look a little wicked, like a satyr. What I found attractive about him was his vitality, not just sexual, which Hallie loved to boast about, but life vitality—the loud, warm laugh, a love of sharing, and a real interest in people and their ideas, even if, at times, his intensity had brought out the worst in Hallie, who hated to be shown up.

Hallie had moved on to a subject she liked. Adultery. She had a wealth of examples. "Did I tell you about my friend Dawn? The one whose husband was cheating on her and she got—hey, you remember her, you met her at a cocktail party at my house. Her husband's from Guyana."

"Vaguely."

"Well, she gets it into her head that he could disappear. Disappear! Like a fucking elf. Because every time she thought she saw him out with another woman, she'd look again, and he'd be gone. He was probably ducking behind a car."

My house phone rang. It was Adán. "Guapa, I am sorry to disrupt you, but my wife is missing. I have tried calling her phone three times. Before I make a missing persons poster I thought I should check at your house?"

I laughed and passed the phone to Hallie, who took it lazily, and I suspected that she knew Adán had been calling her and had chosen not to answer so that he'd have to track her down.

Even though it was freezing outside, she wore a silk dress with wide sleeves, an intoxicating pattern of black orchids that set off her white skin, the big green eyes and black hair. She resembled a burlesque dancer off-hours. Curled up on the couch, she murmured into the receiver. This was one of her mother's gestures; Constance had had a range of movements and expressions that infused a sexy mystery into anything she did—it was part of her professional allure. In the 1960s, she had been considered a very promising film star and was often compared to Sharon Tate.

This was what I had heard, at any rate. By the time I knew her, Constance was spending the majority of her day in her bed, always made up as if going somewhere for the evening, her hair waved, her valentine mouth painted a bright red, her deep-set eyes, which were seductively half-closed from the tranquilizers, done in neutral grays. In that light-filled bedroom, Constance reclined against her satin pillows like a gorgeous doll, indulging us with compliments and speaking offhandedly about her affairs with various directors and other screen personalities. We'd be over at her vanity, putting on her makeup and making pucker faces into one of the three mirrors that were adjustable to show every angle of the face.

"Darling, not so much on both the lips and eyes," Constance would call over. "Choose one feature to accent—a man can be frightened by too much beauty." Standing there, in the heavy Payless shoes my father accidentally bought a size too big, I was in awe of her. Everything about her. Her warm, sweet scent, her languid movements and throaty voice.

The year I turned eleven, I began imitating her heavy-lidded gaze and way of speaking at a three-quarter profile. Although I'd never seen Constance outside the house, not even in the yard, I imagined us out doing mother-daughter things together, like shopping for bras, and eating ice cream on those benches by the harbor, and having our nails done at the salon I always passed on my way to school. "This must be your daughter," the manicurist would say. "I can see the resemblance." This part of the vision felt a little far-fetched to me. I looked nothing like Constance, although she had said to me once, "I used to have lovely legs like yours when I was young."

I should have been Constance's daughter. We got along much better than she and Hallie did. Hallie was rude and gave one-word answers and said her mother's room smelled like a nursing home, while I could sit on the edge of the bed for hours listening to Constance, watching her dab her lips carefully with a napkin, then tip her plate to let the cat lick quiche crumbs from it. When Constance said, "Terry, tell me *all* about your week," I gave the most minute details, anything I thought she would find diverting or amusing. Mr. Feinberg and his car breaking down so we all had to push it. How some kids had been busted for drinking beers and smoking cigarettes behind the town gazebo. Hallie glared at me—she had been behind the gazebo that day. After several of Hallie's interruptions: "this is so boring," "this is stupid," Constance said to her, "Darling, fetch my purse and take out a ten and run down to Mr. Stevens's. I need a new pair of eyelashes. Ask him to get them for you, he'll know which ones. You can spend the change on whatever you like." After she was gone, Constance and I exchanged glances. Both of us relieved.

It was shortly after the eyelashes errand that Hallie decided she no longer wanted me to come over. "We all feel you've been hanging around too much. Like a stray." She and I could still hang out, she said, just not at her house. Which suited her, since her favorite activity at this time was either stealing or standing by the road, flashing her new boobs at cars. I knew within a week she'd be over it, but still it stung that when I rang for her, she had her visiting cousin come down and guard the door to prevent me from entering, while she cheerily called out Constance's window, "Just a moment. My mom and I are talking."

I wanted to cry out to Constance to let me in, tell her how horrible Hallie was, but of course I didn't. I just waited on the porch, dreaming of my own mother. She was fiercely protective, to the point of holding grudges. If Hallie tried to come to my house, weeping out her apologies, my mother would slam the door in her face. Would she though? Or would she be charmed by Hallie, let her in, maybe even take her side against me?

It was frustrating how little I knew about her. There was a photograph that had been on the mantel ever since I could remember, and in it she was standing next to a horse, and so I had always thought of her as a great horsewoman, although my father said that was just for the photo—she'd never ridden one. Throughout the course of my childhood, I had asked my father what she was like, particularly when he pointed out a resemblance between us, but his descriptive skills weren't very good, and he would often fall back on "she was a great woman. One of the best. And that's not just me being biased. Everyone who met her thought so." Then he'd tell me about the Christmas ornaments, and how hers would sell out first.

* * *

Hallie didn't like to talk about Constance, but when she got off the phone, I hazarded a comparison. "The way you move is like her."

"I've been thinking about her lately," she said carefully. "I just hope she never knew my dad cheated on her. It really fucked me up. I still can't get over that he did that."

I had never really taken the infidelity seriously. I had the impression it only happened once, if at all, and not until Constance was starting to lose it, which was what Hallie should have been afraid of emulating—the painkiller addiction. When I was growing up, I saw Hallie's dad as way below Constance's level. He looked like a short and rather fat bird with an overbite I was certain he must be ashamed of, and he had some nondescript office job in New York City. Constance belonged with a movie star husband. I pictured her kissing Robert Redford in the theater—their faces blown up to gigantic proportions on the screen in front of them. Yet, amazingly enough, it had been this ordinary businessman whose life had wandered into the crosshairs of Constance's and all her private demons. He'd put up with it, and so if years after his wife's death he wanted to move to New Mexico and take up watercolor painting and open a Navajo jewelry store with a loud, brassy woman who fussed over him and called him her "bubbalou," who the hell could blame him?

But this wasn't a subject I was allowed to have an opinion on, and so I said, "It's strange, isn't it, that a lot of men can't stand to be alone? They go from relationship to relationship." Except for my father, who'd been a widower for life and had a perverse pride about it, the way some military people claimed "Vet." "Why is this bothering you now?"

"I don't know. These things just rise to the surface sometimes." She bit her thumb. "Adán's not happy in Jersey. He always wanted a house and now he says it's so quiet, it feels like when he was a little boy and he was punished by having to go sit somewhere by himself.

He's been talking about Spain incessantly. I think he wants to bring over some relatives."

"What would you do? You hate strangers poking around."

"I'm trying to talk him out of it, but I know it would make him happy, so I feel guilty about it. It kind of sucks. I like having the house to ourselves. But if I say no, he'll hold it against me."

How difficult marriage seemed with those sorts of emotional contracts and obligations. I thought of Rhinehart. How free we were. We could just get to know each other again, if we chose.

CHAPTER FOUR

Marty was standing in the doorway of the weedy back lot we shared with the hair salon next door, smoking, since I told him it was bad for business to do it inside, even in his office, even when we had no customers. He bent down and stuck his finger in the spider plant to see if it needed more water, and then pointed to the shared wall, hoping to coax me into conversation. "Shani asked about you. She's been braiding this woman's hair for two hours and she's not even a quarter of the way done." He shook his head, women's hair being a perpetual mystery to him. "She wants you to come over and keep her company."

"I'll go over there later. I need to talk to her about redoing her head shots, anyway." Shani had been acting in theater for years. Her last play at Cherry Lane, in which she played a blind woman, had been widely reviewed, and it was leading to more auditions. "She didn't want me to show you her current set, since she knows what you'll say about the lighting."

As a photographer, Marty favored realism—there were no country accessories, fake flowers, or Communion altars in the studio. He was a perfectionist about technique, and we took honest portraits. I handled most of the in-house photography, and he did the events. He had a genial, middle-aged-bachelor love for bar mitzvahs, anniversary parties—anything requiring his blue suit and tie and that came with a complimentary plate of food. I used to go with him, but Marty behaved like an invited guest, often sitting down at the grandparents' table and striking up conversation peppered with examples of his life philosophy: "Some people are real bastards but most of us try and do good." People often mistook me for his date, or his wife, or his wife–business partner. With the studio, it was too much work for both of us anyway, so I now had him hire out.

"Don't charge Shani for anything, not even the processing," Marty said. "I'll handle it."

"She's already forced me into a barter, you know. A full makeover. Since you're paying, maybe you can get one, too."

I reviewed the day's list. There were two family portraits and a third-grader's retake of his school pictures scheduled. I disliked photographing children. "You have to relax, Terry," Marty said. "Kids pick up on your attitude. You should be telling them nothing bad's gonna happen instead of getting all hunched up like that."

Secretly I believed I worked best on days when I was in an awful mood. My theory was that a low-grade bad humor made me more intimidating, and even though the child sometimes had a worried look that showed up on film, a wary one-eyed squint, tantrums were rare. I dreaded tantrums. Seeing the kid's face crumple, reddening above his knotted tie, I immediately started pleading, "don't cry," before the crying began, which would cause him to break down completely, kicking his heels against the stumpy white stool. "Why don't you use the lollys?" Marty said, referring to the bowl of cheap, cellophane-wrapped lollipops he kept beneath the counter. But I felt I should be able to handle the situation without resorting to bribery. Such was the case today. The eight-year-old, a little man, came in wearing a bow tie and a cape, which Marty was able to persuade him to remove. His teenage baby-sitter stood near the entrance, staring into her phone while we worked. The boy had several stock expressions, two of which were smiles that were effective, and we were done pretty quickly. He thanked me, shaking my hand in a way that reminded me of the kind that contains a few bills. I was irrationally pleased. Marty was teasing me, saying he was going to start signing contracts with local elementary schools.

It was an abruptly sunny afternoon, and in my heightened mood I wanted to be outside shooting, and I asked Marty for the rest of the day off. I'd been going out in the mornings before work doing some street photography, whatever compelled me that day. The results were mixed, but I had promised myself not to be too critical. Then, two days ago, I'd had a breakthrough, when I realized I should be shooting in color, similar to Helen Levitt's saturated portraits of the late '70s and '80s, where every day seemed like midsummer in that dirty city with its park bench graffiti and garish plastic signs and souped-up red Novas parked along the curb, while a man, dressed in tight yellow shorts and a sweatband, stood sweltering by a phone booth, waiting for his turn. New York, cast in these tones, had always been an exciting place to me, and even though it was the dead of winter, I could feel the bumping, kinetic, sexualized energy of mid-July. In my own work, I was most interested in capturing the relationships between people, the often split-second eye contact that held implicit agreements, impressions, fears, or desires.

I wandered over to the Metropolitan Museum of Art following an urge to photograph the vendors selling knockoff artwork and mass-produced photographs of Times Square, signed and framed to look like originals. Observing a group of teenagers hesitating at a table of fake African sculptures, I felt a surge of pleasure. For the past week, this had been happening to me. I'd be walking along and suddenly feel overcome with joy. I wasn't sure if it was because I was photographing again or because I'd begun anticipating Rhinehart's return.

I'd also recently made the decision not to renew my lease. The rent was going up again, and there'd been a rumor going around the building that the landlord's son was filing for destabilization based on a tax abatement that had expired. It hadn't happened yet, but the possibility had frozen me with fear several months ago, when suddenly the rider I'd been signing all those years appeared ominous. There was a lot of nervous talk amongst my neighbors, and I became jittery every time I received a letter from the building, until I decided I didn't need to stay in the apartment and be at the mercy of it. Once I'd made the commitment, even privately, I felt freer. Maybe, for the first time, I was learning to trust my instincts.

I'd delayed telling Hallie, until she asked about it over the phone. She always remembered when the lease was up.

"Are you crazy?" she said. "Why would you move?"

"No matter how many times I paint the bedroom ceiling the paint peels because there's a leak somewhere in there. Two weeks ago, I was taking a shower and all these tiles fell off the wall and shattered in the tub. I've been calling Tony twice a day to come fix it, and he didn't show up until yesterday and then he said he didn't have the right tools." Tony was our super, who was aging along with the building. "I'm really excited about moving, actually." Looking around, I already saw myself walking away from some of the apartment's unsolvable problems that I'd learned to tolerate, how the pipes clanged when the heat came up and made the living room stiflingly hot, the grime on the outside of the air shaft window that I'd never been able to figure out a way to clean.

"Do you know how expensive the city's gotten? You're not going to be able to find the same deal."

"I don't need to live in the East Village anymore. I'm not twenty-two. All the noise and the kids hanging out in front of the bars is starting to get to me. I'm thinking of further uptown where rents are cheaper. I've been looking online."

"Craig's List? Land of false promises? Have you checked out any of those places?"

"I'll find something. It's time for me to stop being so scared of change and just take a leap."

I had budgeted $1,500 a month, which was manageable with my recent raise, and I could also take off-site jobs, possibly weddings, although I was wary of cutting into the time I'd set aside to do my own projects. After having two Realtors tell me I would be unable to find a decent studio, or even a share at that price, I increased it by $100 and then by another $100. For one of the first times in my life, I felt acutely cramped by my income and even began to resent my salary, although I'd seen the books, and I knew Marty was paying me more than he should have given what he took in. My father had left me money in his will, but not much, the farm had been heavily mortgaged by the time we'd sold. I was reluctant to dip into it, since he envisioned me buying a little house with it. A practical little house, like the one I'd grown up in. It was something I'd always expected I'd have, but later, when I was older. When I was settled.

I checked out tiny commuter apartments, two hundred square feet that only fit a bed and a kitchenette. Windowless studios, or ones where the only window faced an air shaft. I spent an entire Saturday afternoon walking in the West 30s, trying to locate a handwritten rent sign I'd seen a few days before. The sun glittered off the distant Hudson. I stepped around iridescent puddles from leaking cars. All my free hours were bound up in the fruitless search. I didn't have the energy or desire to take pictures, and I constantly worried that although it seemed temporary, I'd stopped for good.

I gave up, the only thing on this desolate stretch between the ferry and Penn Station were city auto body shops and the Central Park carriages. Horses stood out in the street in their blinders, waiting to be taken in. I thought of what Rhinehart used to say, *Illegitimos non carborumdem*. "Don't let the bastards get you down."

It had been more than a month since his note. A week ago, around the time I'd internally decided he was back in New York, a familiar feeling had begun to creep up on me. Impatience. At first an exhilarated impatience, like anticipation, and then, the more I obsessively checked my silent phone—irritation, depression. This was ridiculous, I thought. I wasn't in my twenties anymore. If I wanted to speak to him, I should just call his cell. So I did. Listening to his recorded message, I began to get nervous—it didn't say he was out of the country. I attempted to sound cheery, casual and upbeat. I waited a day, two days, before it became clear that he wasn't going to return my call. Maybe he'd reunited with Laura. Maybe he'd just had second thoughts about me. That refracted image of myself that I'd been holding on to—that confident, creative, sweet young woman—evaporated. Why the hell had he come back into my life? Just to reject me again? Make it clear that I would always feel more for him than he would for me? I had an inextinguishable loyalty, like a dog had.

Harlem was above my price range, and I began searching even farther up, in Washington Heights. In desperation, I agreed to a one-bedroom on 181st even though the hallway was strewn with trash, and I heard a cooing that I thought came from pigeons outside and turned out to be doves the woman next door kept. But it was large and bright and the building manager said there wasn't anything that size for the price, and it would go fast. I was an easy target, as desperate and unaccustomed to apartment shopping as a greenhorn.

I went back uptown the following night to hand in my security deposit and first month's rent in bank checks. Half a block short of my new building, I passed an empty storefront with the lights on inside. Even with the door closed, I could hear the music blasting. A group of men were standing in a circle around a blanket—a woman was on it, reaching under her dress, doing something. Feeling sick, I turned around and walked back to the subway.

In tears, I phoned Hallie, who said, "Call the landlord! Tell him you want to stay."

"I did already. He's rented the place for more than I was paying."

"Did you sign anything? A termination notice?"

"No, but I didn't renew in time. And he has it on email."

"Let me talk to Adán. He knows lots of lawyers. You can fight this."

"And how much is that going to cost? All that money just to stay in an apartment I want to leave. I really thought this was going to work out. I thought I was doing the right thing."

Lying in bed that night, it occurred to me that if I wasn't able to find something within the next week, I would have to start looking at shares. I felt my face flush with anxiety and shame. I was thirty-five years old, and I knew most of the people who shared apartments were younger than me, and they would think it was pathetic once they saw me show up for the interview. Women my age weren't supposed to sit on old couches that no one could remember who bought, and use a bathroom in the hall, and check off on a chart whether they'd cleaned the kitchen. I would have no privacy, have to go out on nights when my roommates wanted to have a party. How could it have come to this? Why hadn't I gotten further by now? Why was I still struggling alone with no one to help me or even to share my life? I thought angrily of Rhinehart, and then, despairingly, about myself and my inability to progress. How small my problems were, an apartment and my own self-image, and yet the fear was palpable that night. It felt real. It felt like a failing in me, and as I lay there, getting myself more and more worked up, my failures seemed the only truth.

I was so alone. I wondered if my father ever felt this way. He used to pray for my mother every night before bed, even though she'd been dead for thirty years. He'd been mostly quiet about his faith, although he'd attended the Presbyterian church in town and insisted that I go to Sunday school up until sixth grade. Whenever I was struggling, he'd use a firm tone I found comforting. "If you want to talk to God, He's always listening. He can fix anything." I never did, and the problems always resolved themselves on their own. That night, though, I got out of bed and slid down to the floor and began talking, my hands clasped together so hard my knuckles ached. I started with a long description of my problem followed by a lot of equivocation and backtracking. Then I began speaking directly, as if my father had asked me, "What do you need?" I remembered a time in junior high school when I'd accidentally offended a girl in my math class by whispering about her failing grade, and afterwards she had scrawled the word "bitch" on my locker and was threatening to beat me up. After I'd told him about it, my father stayed up half the night writing a list of solutions that ranged from him visiting the principal to things I could say to the girl to diffuse the situation. He handed it to me in the morning, and I'd angrily rejected it. He'd scrambled to come up with something more, scratching his head underneath his cap, saying "Gosh, honey. Maybe we should call your Aunt Maryanne. Maybe she's had an experience like this one." Neither of us liked Aunt Maryanne—she had objected to my mother's marrying him, a farmer, and had tried to get custody of me after she died, but he called her in Florida whenever he felt he needed a woman's advice on a problem. What I'd done was just apologize to the girl when I saw her in class, which had been the first suggestion on my father's list, and she'd acted like she'd already forgotten about it. I came home and told my father, and he'd said, "See—we shouldn't have worried so much." How blessed I'd been to have him. Maybe he was even still out there watching over me. In the end, what difference did it make if I had to share an apartment temporarily?

Marty, who was most eager to solve my problem, had mentioned my situation to his sister, who had six kids and owned a house in Staten Island with an illegal basement apartment. "Only a microwave and one of those mini-fridges, but she's real nice and a lot of times, if everyone gets along, the tenant is invited to have dinner with the family. You may even be able to earn a little more baby-sitting." I wondered if this arrangement, which sounded terrible to me, was my sign. Baby-sitting? Perhaps I should have been more specific. But I had seen a place on the Internet this morning that looked great—in Manhattan even, on the Upper West Side. Even though they hadn't

gotten back to me yet, I was feeling optimistic. So optimistic that I decided to cancel an appointment to see a studio in Brooklyn on the border of Bed-Stuy. It was a great price, lower than my range, but I wasn't so sure about the neighborhood.

"Just go," Marty said.

"I don't know if I feel like going all the way out there to be disappointed."

"What else are you going to do this afternoon—we're dead here. And if it doesn't look good, there's always my sister's place."

So I went, then got lost, and was so late meeting the agent, I debated whether it was worth showing up at all. But as I came down the block I saw her there, huddled in a down coat, waiting for me. The building was near the projects, and it was nowhere that Hallie would ever live, but I liked it. On the way over, I had passed two old women trundling their shopping carts, reminding me of how the East Village used to be.

We walked into the studio, and immediately I was hit in the face by sun streaming through an enormous arched window. I was in a large, high-ceilinged space. There was an alcove for my bed like in my childhood room and the same glass doorknobs on the closet. A deep clawfoot tub in the bathroom was on the same level as windows that had a view of a huge oak tree. I wandered around, stunned. I knew. This was where I would live.

As it turned out, I was almost outbid and spent two frantic days back and forth with the agent before signing the lease. But the lease was signed, and I moved on an overcast day in March. Stripped of all my things, my little East Village apartment looked forlorn, as if it knew it was going to be demolished and had given up all pretense of being a home. I thought about when I first arrived, before Hallie and I had bought any furniture, how I used to lie on my twin bed, staring up

at the cracked ceiling, imagining previous tenants, years of them, in their undershirts and housedresses, who drank and fought under the fluorescent lights in the kitchen, and read the newspaper at night, and cooked on a hot plate to save the gas.

The truck was packed outside, but I was reluctant to leave. I checked the narrow bedroom closet again to make sure I hadn't left anything behind on its high shelf that you could never see to the back of. It was a terrible closet but the only one in the apartment, and when Hallie and I had tried to share it, it became so jammed with our clothes, you couldn't move the hangers and had to pull out each individual item to figure out what it was. "This sucks," she said. "It's like the Loehmann's sales rack." Hallie tried to buy closet rights off me for fifty bucks, and then, when I refused out of principle, she spent an entire Saturday creating a "boudoir" out of a clothes rack and a glued-together pyramid of empty shoeboxes with a sheer blue fabric draped tentlike from above "for privacy." She even hung a full-length mirror. It had a piece of notebook paper taped to it that said, "You're sexy."

"For your confidence," she said. "Imagine a man saying it to you."

But it was in her handwriting, so all I could hear was her saying it. "And sometimes it sounds sarcastic," I told her. Within a day, the fabric had snagged on the hangers, pulling out the tacks that connected it to the ceiling, and floating down in a suffocating tangle cloud while I was inside changing. We finally repurposed it as a tablecloth, and I accepted the "porta-closet" as it came to be known, in exchange for unlimited borrowing rights to Hallie's clothes and a future date with someone from her office. She'd just gotten a paid internship in the publicity department of a men's lifestyle magazine. I was waiting tables at a crêpe place down by NYU. We both agreed her connections were better than mine.

What I wanted, more than anything, was entry into the invisible New York that I had heard about—restaurants with communal bathrooms and reverse mirror windows and Julian Schnabel art on the walls, places where celebrities had lunch with their pets, and

twelve-course meals of all desserts, and saw old-fashioned vaudeville acts and carney shows in restored theaters like where Lincoln was shot, and where you had to know someone to buy a $200 seat. The closest I'd come, would ever really come, were the nights that Hallie and I decided to splurge, and dressing up in our best clothes, went to a fancy restaurant uptown and sat at the bar, our high, elegant chairs turned outward, nursing our pricey drinks and looking around hopefully for someone to come buy us the next round. Those nights, even if they resulted in nothing, as they often did, always seemed seductively full of potential.

At my new apartment my possessions looked small and scattered, but they fit with the high tin ceilings and the old-fashioned glass-front cupboards. I had gotten rid of many things, keeping my two African violets, my mother's milk glass lamp, a wooden table. I put up a few of my photographs and hung long transparent curtains over the windows, which billowed out from the radiators' heat. My first night, steam coming off me from a bath, I put on my robe and sat at the kitchen table in my one little wooden chair with a glass of wine, and listened to kids throwing snowballs under the street lamp, shouting into the dark. I was deliriously happy. I felt as I had all those years ago, when I first moved to New York, and all I could see, all around me, were things that were beginning.

CHAPTER FIVE

I was sitting in one of the hair salon chairs, kicking my leg around. How comfortable an environment it was—its confusion of bottles and sprays, the smell of chemicals, light reflecting off the mirrors, the schefflera in the corner named Steve. The salon had no particular focus, it catered to whatever hair type you had, and like a nail place, it always seemed busy, women sitting at the entrance, flipping through magazines.

I was talking to Shani about Brooklyn where the light had a paler, more muted quality, reflecting off the brownstones. Down the block from my building, there were basketball courts behind a high chain link fence, a single-story branch library with construction paper decorations in the window. The parks with their scrub grass and oak trees and old swing sets and stone animals. There were so few people on the streets in the middle of the day. I was roaming with my camera to see what I could capture, sometimes taking the subway above ground to stations farther south, and returning, waiting on a cold, exposed platform, watching plumes of smoke from the buildings below. I was happy to be shooting again, but it seemed a bit aimless. "I feel like I haven't found my focus still," I told her. "I need a project—a series." Watching her, I had an idea. "Maybe I should shoot what I know. Like you, here, working." I was envisioning it, the grayish early daylight, and Shani sitting in her chair, maybe holding the smock she used when she was doing color, and all the pink bottles and combs and hair pieces dangling behind her. Or sitting in the chair, legs crossed, staring directly at the lens.

"Not at the theater?" she asked.

"But I don't really know you at the theater. This is the environment that's familiar. If I get this idea together will you sit for me? That can be our trade for the head shots."

"I still think you're crazy not to take a makeup consultation with Nicole. Do you know how booked she gets?" She took up the comb again, using the pointy end to separate strands of hair. The woman in the chair was talking on her cell phone.

I took a piece of paper from behind the register and began sketching, pointing out the placement of things behind her. We'd bring over the cart of bottles, and I could take a couple of shots. I needed a lot of background.

Returning to Marty's I had an illumination—what if I did a series of people in their daily environments, shooting Marty, too, in his office, hunched over, his chin disappearing into his brown shirt, a cigarette in his mouth, fiddling with his camera, the little barred window and his desk with its piles and piles of yellow papers and receipts and proofs behind him? I was eager to start framing out the idea before it disappeared in the onslaught of customers. I'd gotten out my sketchbook and was making notes, when Rhinehart called my cell phone, shocking me into silence.

He talked, filling up the space. "I'm back from Italy, and I've taken an apartment in Manhattan. Near Central Park. It's so good to be in the city again. I'm sorry I'm late returning your message. It was a bit chaotic when I first returned."

While I was groping around for a response, he said, "Would you rather I didn't call you? I can hang up, or we both can."

"No, I just wasn't expecting you."

"It seems to be our way of things, lately. How have you been?"

I stuttered. I wasn't able to condense the past few months into a response. He seemed to belong to another scenario, one in which it was early winter, and I still lived in my old apartment. Sometime after moving, I realized that I had been attaching way too much importance to Rhinehart's reappearance in my life. My thoughts had a delusional quality. I had so many expectations, as if we'd just begin building a new, healthy relationship. Enough time away from him, and I'd understood the true purpose of our running into each other—to propel me to a new stage after I'd been stagnant for so long. Now here he was, saying, "Are you up for an outing?"

He was going to Queens to visit an elderly aunt and wanted me to come with my camera equipment to take photographs of her neighbors. He had already mentioned me to her. He was still talking, referencing a series of Diane Arbus's photos, natural setting, no need to bring a backdrop.

"The nudists? This is what they want?"

"No, no. They haven't mentioned anything. I was just imagining the style of photography. Not the nudity."

I asked a series of questions about what type of lights to bring, who was driving, how long we were going to be there, and he interrupted, "Do you no longer trust my judgment because I invited you to that terrible dinner?"

"Not just that." I was also nervous to spend an afternoon with him, and the fact that I was nervous seemed to signal the danger in it. Even now my entire body was on high alert.

He was still focused on apologizing for that night. "I really do believe in philanthropic organizations and I came off as an academic and a snob, and destructively unhappy. I am no longer unhappy. Traveling is a fool's paradise, Emerson was right, but all that newness can also be incredibly therapeutic. It was very good for me while it lasted."

I wanted to know then when he'd returned, and presumably heard my message, but an old self-protectiveness prevailed. I was afraid of hurt feelings that could lead to stiltedness in the conversation. Instead we talked plans. We would meet at the train station the following Sunday. Rhinehart would help me carry my equipment.

I hung up, my heart still hammering. Why this day? Why today?

* * *

In the thrash of people at Penn Station, I spotted Rhinehart immediately—he was flipping through a magazine by the ticket window. Fifteen years ago if he was expecting you, he'd size you up from a distance. I'd always been slightly self-conscious approaching him. So much of our relationship I had played out alone on my shifting mental terrain.

He was in a sport coat with jeans and a pair of white loafers that looked Italian, and he seemed expensive—like a patron of the arts. The minute I got within sight range, he stuck his ankle out and twisted it admiringly in the dirty yellow light. "What do you think of these shoes?"

He was trying to dispel the awkwardness between us. It was something he did, took my nervousness from me as if taking a heavy package, and I was grateful and said, "They look like they'll get marks."

"You've always been so practical, Tatie. A Depression kid who grew up in the Reagan era." He looked up at the board. "Would you like to get a cup of coffee, or should we catch the 11:15?"

"11:15." I was anxious to be out again into the cold afternoon, and not in Penn Station's poorly lit interior. How many times, waiting for a train, had I sat at one of the Starbucks café tables, looking out on the bustling underground passageway as if it were the street.

Maybe because I was so quiet, Rhinehart was filling our wait time with talk. About a man in a cowboy hat, wearing a chain of MetroCards around his neck, he said, "The mentally ill have such penetrating eyes. Such a strong desire to convey things to you." About the young woman standing behind me: "Brightly colored outfits really are cheering."

And on and on, until our platform was announced, and we shouldered our way down the stairs and onto the train. Rhinehart suggested we take seats facing each other, "stagecoach-style."

Now that the trip had begun, I felt more at ease. The conductor came by clicking his puncher, and Rhinehart started patting down his pockets. "Did you forget to buy one?" I asked him as I handed mine over. He seemed jittery and I wondered if he was uncomfortable being alone with me.

Still rustling around in his clothes, he said, "I can't seem to find it. Do you think I dropped it in the station?"

"You can punch my round-trip for his one-way," I said to the conductor, and Rhinehart gave me an appreciative look.

We were riding in the head car, where you had the best sense you were going somewhere important. I liked the train, the uniforms, the politeness and patience and kindness of the conductors. At seventeen I used to take the two-hour ride into the city, dressed up for some party or a date, bringing a thin paperback along with a wallet full of money I'd saved selling flowers. I kept my purse between my knees so that it couldn't be whisked off the seat by someone passing, as it was rumored happened. One of the girls at school had chased a man through the cars, but he had hopped off at the next stop. She'd had no choice but to stay on the train all the way into the city, trying not to cry, and then, once in the station, beg for change to use the pay phone. These stories made an impression on me as I tended to worry anyway, and sometimes felt a little sick to my stomach, going in. I took the most pleasure on the return trip, lying back against the seat, mulling over all the funny things that had been said, the teasing, the kissing, if there had been any.

We emerged from the tunnel into the bright morning. Sun glinted off the metal roofs of the warehouses and trash swirled near the tracks. I felt a sudden, exhilarating rush of happiness and looked over at Rhinehart, who was staring out the fingerprint-smeared window, sun on his face. He was smiling distantly.

During the daylight hours, you were given a peep show from the train, a split-second view of people crouched in parking lots and along the backsides of buildings, an overturned shopping cart, garbage stuck in the fence links. Even people's yards were littered with trash, slack pool covers with newspapers floating in the rainwater, splayed out like dead birds. We passed a schoolyard with a fleet of yellow mini-buses, one lone albino parked in a distant lot.

"Tell me about your aunt again," I said to Rhinehart, who was eyeing a woman in the next aisle, clipping her fingernails. Elderly people were my favorite to photograph, the trapped histories of what mannerisms, clothes, and expressions used to be in vogue. "I thought you didn't have any living relatives."

Rhinehart smoothed the crease in his pants. "I use the term loosely. I'm not even sure why I call her Chechna. Just something I made up as a kid, I guess, and the name stuck. She was from the same oblast as my mother and took care of me after she died. I'm grateful to her—she made sure I was fed and went to school—but I also spent a lot of time sitting outside my old apartment, wishing everything was different."

There had been a time when I had known about Rhinehart's past, but it had been so many years that it had broken into fragments and mixed with my own memories of where we were at the time the story was told. I remembered his mother putting a board in between the mattress and box spring to keep her back from giving out. She died when he was ten, two weeks before Easter, and he'd left a colored egg and a glass of vodka at her graveside. His caretaker, or someone, used to make latkes, and nail the Christmas tree to the living room wall to keep it up. Was this Chechna? His mother gave him a brown sweater that he wore for a month, the tags tucked into the sleeve, before she sent it over to the old country. "I never liked that sweater and was happy to see it go."

"How old is your aunt now?"

"She turned ninety this year. I'm glad we're talking again. After she got stuck in the tub and I saw her naked, she didn't want to see me for a while. That was a few summers ago."

"What? How did she get stuck?"

He sighed. "She has one of those deep tubs with the high sides and that day she just didn't have the arm strength to hoist herself out—this was before the hand bars. Hours she was in there. I climbed up the fire escape to the window, which was open a crack and tried to force it, but it had these little locks on the sides. The entire time she's screaming, 'Don't come in! I have no clothes on! Call Jean!'—a lady as old as she was, who lived across the hall. I finally got a piece of plywood and was able to leverage the window open. I came in with my eyes shut, groping around for the towel, while she's screaming at me, 'Left, left.' It was over a hundred degrees in there—it's lucky she didn't pass out. I slipped on a puddle, and by reflex, I opened my eyes, only for a split second, but I saw her and she saw me. Her arms were black-and-blue. I threw the towel over her, and lifted her out. After that she told me she wanted nothing to do with me. Then, a couple of months ago, she called me again. She didn't mention it, so I assume it's forgiven."

We walked the three blocks from the station, lugging the lights, my camera and tripod, a small screen I had insisted on bringing, and presents. Rhinehart had brought two bottles of liqueur, which seemed excessive for someone in her nineties.

"Here we are!" he said, in front of a stooped four-story brick apartment building. The fire escape from the bathtub story snaked up one side. Rhinehart rang the buzzer, and almost instantly the lace curtains in a window two flights up parted. She buzzed us in.

"She's a quick one," he said.

Chechna Olesky was about four feet tall with a small sharp face hidden by enormous plastic-framed glasses and a brown coiffed hairdo that was obviously a wig. Her hand, as we shook, reminded me of a sparrow's hard little feet. From behind the thick lenses, her magnified eyes looked me over. She didn't seem all that pleased to see either of us.

"Here. Give—" She reached for the lights I'd borrowed from Marty.

"No, no, Chechna," Rhinehart said, pulling the case away. "This is very heavy."

"Put them in the bedroom." She pointed back into the dim apartment, and Rhinehart took my purse and walked down the low-ceilinged hallway that seemed, through a trick of perspective, to narrow. Chechna and I went into the living room, which was crowded with heavy furniture and had figurines, plastic plants, and little dishes covering every surface, the end tables, the old TV set with the large console, the coffee table. It was like a junk shop upstate. My fingers itched to start shooting.

"This is very pretty." I gestured to a display shelf that held two porcelain spaniels and a vivid red-and-yellow wooden egg.

Chechna stuck her nose within a half an inch of it. "Which?"

"The egg"—I hesitated—it looked Ukrainian, but I didn't want to hazard a guess.

"Oh, that. No. That's junk. It's there for color." She pointed to the plastic-covered couch. Needlepoint pillows were trapped underneath as if they were being asphyxiated. I sat down and she said, "No! Over in the middle. That cushion is the firmest."

Rhinehart appeared in the doorway. He looked enormous in here. "I love your new bedspread, Chechna. It must be hand-done."

In a voice that was several notches too loud, Chechna said, "My neighbor buys these things for me real cheap. A handmade bedspread! Nobody makes things by hand no more. Now sit." She pointed to the armchair. It emitted an unpleasant synthetic creak as he sat. Chechna went into the kitchen and returned with a tin of Danish butter cookies. I took one to be polite; it was very soft, the consistency of liverwurst, but with a vague dusty taste. I had trouble swallowing, and afterwards kept trying to sneak looks at the tin's side to see the expiration date.

"How are you? Are you eating good?" she asked Rhinehart.

"Yes," he said.

"Like what?"

"Sometimes a piece of meat, or some fish, vegetables. That sort of thing. Very balanced. I try and eat early."

"What kind of vegetables?"

"Beans. Cauliflower."

She sniffed in approval. "You should brown it in the bacon fat. That makes it taste the best. But not too much, just a little. Take care of yourself. You get to be my age, and you'll see the truth in that."

She did look as if she were going to last forever.

Rhinehart's eyes were coasting around the room. "The place looks great. I don't know how you're able to keep it so clean."

Chechna took this to mean he thought she was taking shortcuts. "I get down on my knees and scrub! Me."

Rhinehart smiled. "Well, you're doing a bang-up job."

"Have you lived here long?" I asked.

"Too long! If I was smart I would have bought the lot next door. I would have made a fortune with it! But we didn't know then. People didn't buy things like that."

Rhinehart was telling me about his childhood apartment in Greenpoint, Brooklyn, maybe thinking I had forgotten. But I remembered the story, as well as the café upstate where we'd been having breakfast, still rumpled from his bed, when he told me. "The couple that lived downstairs, in back of the hardware store, owned the building. Yushef and Esther. They were nice, used to invite me in for cocoa and that sort of thing."

"They always thought they were better than us," Chechna said. "Once they moved to Saddle River they were ashamed of Greenpoint and didn't want anyone to know. They said they were from Manhattan!"

I thought of my father's house with the clapboard siding and the crab apple tree that spit its hard green fruit onto the cracked patio every other year. "I couldn't imagine growing up in an apartment."

"A railroad apartment, no less. It used to have coal heat. In those old places, you brought the coal up on a dumbwaiter, and in the hallway was a little gate I used to swing on." He flapped his hand back and forth. "How I loved it! The kitchen had a cutout so that you could see down the length of it, through the bedroom and into the living room. I slept in there on a foldout. Chechna used to cup her hands and make the sound of a fire truck on Sunday mornings."

Chechna said, "He never wanted to go out and play! Wanted to sit around all day and help me make kielbasa. A boy! Eh." She waved her hand front of her face. "Maybe something happened when his mother was struck by lightning. To her eggs."

Rhinehart said, "I never knew she was hit by lightning!"

Chechna, sensing she had him on the hook, spoke to me. "Back in those days, after the lightning hit you, they buried you in dirt up to your neck to let all the energy seep out." Her eyes glittered, and she dipped her head in a deceitful way when she talked.

I was touched by Rhinehart's eagerness, like a boy's. He was shaking his head. "Amazing! Was this when Mama was a girl?"

"It's all gone now, Rudy. Dead and in the ground. Who cares?" To me, she said, "He always loved the past." She was gripping my knee, and I could feel her fingernails through the fabric. "You're going to take the pictures of my neighbors, right?"

"Yes. Are they coming here?"

"Yeah, yeah. They're putting their faces on. Sue thinks she's a beauty, even though she's got two hairs left on her head."

Rhinehart had extracted a photograph from his wallet and was flicking it with his thumb, waiting for Chechna to finish advising me on how to position the two fake poinsettias she had bought at a large store she couldn't remember the name of. It sounded like a Walmart, even though she insisted it wasn't. "Target?"

"No, no! It looked like Krone's Department Store but with an Oriental name."

I had no idea, and she was the type of person that got angry if you guessed wrong.

I started taking what I told Chechna were "test shots," but really I wanted to capture the long windowsill crammed with fake plants still wearing their bows. I took a few candids of Rhinehart and Chechna on the couch as he passed her a photo of a woman in a long-sleeved black dress. It looked like it was taken in the 1940s. "Do you recognize her?" he asked.

Chechna seemed alarmed. "Why would I know this person? Where did you get this?"

Rhinehart ran his finger under his watchband—a sign that he was uncomfortable. All the years we'd been separated, and I still retained the ability to decode his gestures.

"Well," he said, slowly. "I found her address recently with some of my mother's things. I wrote her to see if maybe she knew us from Ukraine. She sent this photo of her mother."

"Really?" I said. He hadn't mentioned this on the train.

Chechna's eyes were open, incredulous, or maybe it was just the trouble with her eyesight. She squinted, pretending to study the photo, which she probably couldn't see that well. "I don't know this woman. She looks like she's at a graveside. Give me another picture to see."

"I don't have any others," Rhinehart said.

"What's her name?"

"Marta. I think she might have been one of my mother's sisters. Her daughter's name is Lyuba."

"Lyuba! I know Lyuba," she said to me. She generally avoided eye contact with Rhinehart, or maybe it was just that I was new. "Lyuba was a loose woman. She bedded all the men in the town."

"Was she a prostitute?" I asked.

She ignored me. "She was sleeping with the seamstress's husband and he killed himself with liquor. A lot of men did in those days. Lyuba drove him to it, pestering for gifts. Here—I'll show you a real picture." Suddenly excited, she went over to the corner hutch and from behind a row of ornamental eggcups carefully extracted a framed wedding photo. She handed it to me. A small squat woman held a ribbonny bouquet; there were ribbons woven into a crown on her head and in the bosom of her dress. She had heavy features and thick ankles. Next to her was a boy her same height, but skinny, his dark hair oiled and combed close to the skull. There were several other girls and boys in white. Everyone looked about fourteen.

"Who's getting married?"

"That's me!" Chechna said. "What a beauty I was." She pointed to the nervous-looking man. "That was my husband, God rest. The patience of a saint. All he wanted was to eat his varenyky with the brown sauerkraut and read the evening paper. Never ran around. Never in his life touched a drop of liquor." She went down the list of bridesmaids. "This one moved away. This one had an abortion. This one killed herself with liquor. This one you couldn't trust, she'd steal out of her own mother's coffin." Her eyes were glistening with the old offenses. "After my dear aunt died, she snuck down into our apartment and helped herself to the best things, the lacework, everything. That's Lyuba there, you can tell by that whorish eye. She's looking at Alexey. On his wedding day!"

Rhinehart said, "Lyuba would be my age, not yours. What I showed you was a photo of her mother, Marta."

"I didn't have no Martas at my wedding. I would have remembered that!"

"You got married in Brooklyn," he said, pointing to the inscription on the matting. "Marta and her daughter never left Ukraine. What I was wondering was whether you knew my mother's sisters. Back in the old country."

"Your mother had sisters, sure. Three of them."

Rhinehart shifted his weight to the edge of the chair. "What happened to them?"

"What happens to all of us. They died."

"Did any of them have children? Was one of the sisters named Marta?"

"Maybe. I can't remember no more." The effort looked painful, and she stood up and carefully returned the photo to its original place. "This Lyuba ask you for anything? Money, gifts?"

"No. Nothing."

"I'd be careful, a soft-headed boy like you. There are a lot of people out there who'll be more than happy to help you part with your money. The other day a colored boy came here selling candy. I saw him peeping around the door. I slammed it in his face!"

I cringed. "Okay—we ready for the portrait session?"

Chechna picked up the heavy phone alongside the couch and dialed the neighbors. I watched Rhinehart wander over to the bookcase, reading the spines of the *Reader's Digest Condensed Books.* He was nibbling a Danish butter cookie. I signaled to him that they were old.

"Sue," Chechna shouted into the receiver. "The girl's here to take your snapshot."

Sue was also yelling. I could hear her voice from across the room questioning my credentials.

Chechna seemed to forget I was standing there. "How do I know? She says she's done it before."

They arrived three minutes later. Sue, who really was bald, and Harold, who had dressed in a brown suit jacket and yellow tie. Below the waist, he had on sweatpants and vinyl slippers.

"What're you wearing that for?" Chechna said.

"Why do I need to get all dressed up? Only the top half is going to show."

Chechna turned to me. "You're only taking pictures of the top half?"

"I hadn't planned on it, but I can."

Sue said, "That's what I told him! But did he listen? No." In the light I could see thin filaments of white hair covering a very pink skull. It looked delicate and vulnerable, like an infant's. She'd lost most of her eyebrows, too, which she'd redrawn with blue pencil.

Harold said, "What does Mimi want with a picture of our lower parts?" He'd already seated himself on the couch, while Sue was giving me instructions. "We want something nice. Classy, you know, like at one of those portrait places. We're sending it to our daughter in Florida."

Aside from Harold's outfit, and being this close to Rhinehart and his past, it was a relatively standard job for me. I let Rhinehart explain my credentials. With all these people and their directives, Chechna's apartment was even more cramped, and I was having difficulty figuring out how to set up. Rhinehart moved the armchair into the dining area to give us more space and said, in a lowered voice that startled me with its sudden intimacy, "I'll bring your lights in. Tell me what you need." Chechna shadowed him back and forth to the bedroom to make sure nothing got knocked over.

The first few shots I took were in front of the fake fireplace. Sue used to be a floor model at Harrods, and she was a natural at posing—legs crossed at the ankles, back straight, chin up slightly, with a pleasant but slightly vacant smile. In her expression, you could see the vestiges of her young, vain self.

Harold's smile, on the other hand, seemed aggressive, like he wanted to bite you, and it didn't help that his dentures didn't fit his jaw. I suggested he keep his mouth closed.

"Not smile! Who ever heard of this?" Chechna said. She was at my elbow, holding a Hummel figurine that she planned to swap out for the candlesticks so that we could have several different backgrounds. I longed to take a few shots of her.

"My daughter likes it when I smile," Harold said.

"Then think of something that makes you happy, so it appears more genuine."

"I'll think about my Jets."

"Tatie likes football," Rhinehart said. I felt him near me, the heat coming off his body.

"And this makes you want to smile?" I said. "Did you watch any of the games last season?"

"We had a bad run. Some bad decisions on offense. But that Schottenheimer knows what he's doing."

"Yeah, everyone knew what he was doing. A four-year-old could read those plays."

Harold laughed, and I took a few quick shots. I liked to talk to the people I was shooting. When Marty was around, he always wanted to talk to them, too, and I found the chatter outside my field of vision distracting.

I'm sure I caught Harold with his mouth open, but most of the shots were good once his face had relaxed. "Okay," I said. "I think we got what we needed."

I turned around and saw Rhinehart watching me with an expression I couldn't quite decipher—appreciation, awe? It was a quiet look but intense and determined—it was sexual, and suddenly the air, in Chechna's little apartment, seemed charged with it. I held his eyes, and we stared at each other. It was the look he used to give me in bed.

"If you had one of those digital cameras, we could see if they were any good right now," Sue was saying. "My daughter has one."

I turned back to her. "Film is much better quality. That's why I use it."

"She's right," Harold said. "Those electronic pictures are junk. There are grainy spots on the ones Mimi sends."

"I explained that to you six times! It's where she had to get it developed that once. At the CVS."

"All her pictures look like that, not just the batch from Thanksgiving."

As I loaded the black-and-white film, I was conscious of Rhinehart standing up, moving around. All at once, he was behind me, and still looking down at the camera, I leaned back slightly, my shoulders resting against his chest. I told him what I planned on shooting, and we whispered conspiratorially, low enough so Harold and Sue couldn't hear. He had his hand on my upper arm, radiating energy, and when he removed it, it felt as if it had left a mark.

I was wired from being so close to him, and went into the bedroom to get another light and to calm down. There I found Chechna. She was sitting on the edge of the bed, her small, bent back half-facing me. A bottle of beer was on the night table. On her lap was my purse, and she was digging through it. My lipstick, eyeshadow, and keys were out on the bedspread. My face burning, I went back into the living room and whispered to Rhinehart, "Chechna's picking through my *bag*!"

He seemed amused. "Just let her be. She'll put everything back. It's worse when you interrupt. She accuses you of spying."

"But why is she doing that? Does she not trust me?"

Mentally I was running through the contents, birth control, no, incriminating slips of paper? I probably had a bank statement. Would she be able to make sense of the numbers?

"Don't worry about it. She does it to everyone."

Harold and Sue were still standing by the mantel as I readjusted the lights and folded up the reflector. I was proud of being able to light better than the majority of photographers and lighting assistants working, thanks to Marty. It had been to the benefit of Sue and Harold, whom I'd given a much softer look.

"I'll be old by the time we finish this," Harold said. "You'll have nothing to take a picture of." I'd accidentally been shining the strobe in his eyes, and he blinked like a cornered raccoon.

Sue said, "When I was modeling I would have to stand for hours. Even when it was cold or what. I didn't make a peep."

I took the camera off the tripod. "Okay, let me just get a few more shots. These are for my portfolio." I wanted to take a full-length picture of Harold half-dressed, next to the Russian plates. I directed him to rest his hand on the back of a chair, a heavy Ethan Allen knockoff that was pulled up alongside Chechna's dining table. He was surprisingly pliant, and when I directed him to gaze out the window, I got a man lost in familiar surroundings. Excited, I asked him to think of a memory he had of himself when he was in his thirties. He began describing Christmases when his daughter was young, and I was able to see a low-ceilinged living room almost identical to this one, a tree completely covered in tinsel, a gray carpet turned nicotine beige from all the cigarettes smoked there. Harold was in plaid pants, his thick brown hair brushed back from his skull. Now he was standing here, an old man remembering, and it was as if I were fusing his memory with my own vision. It came flooding in on me, this odd, familiar sensation, and I couldn't believe there was ever a time when I wasn't creating, or that I had thought for years that it wasn't worth doing.

As soon as that door opened, it shut again, and Chechna came back into the room, saying, "Why're you sitting in my good chair?"

"This crazy girl is taking pictures of Harold," Sue said. "She says she doesn't want me in them. Can you believe that?"

Chechna was twisting her wedding ring. "It's already half past four. I didn't expect everyone to stay so late. I only have enough dinner for one person."

Rhinehart said, "Tatie's just wrapping up."

I took a few more shots of the apartment and then, reluctantly, went back to the bedroom to retrieve my purse. It looked as if it had never been touched. I thumbed through the cash.

At the door, Chechna got emotional, hugging Rhinehart forcefully. She reached up and held his face in her hands. Tears came into her eyes, "If this is the last time I see you . . ."

"Don't say that, Chechna. You're healthier than I am."

"Promise me to take good care of yourself. We don't know how much time is left us. And after I'm gone you will have no one. No wife now, no one. All alone."

I wouldn't have expected Rhinehart to tell Chechna of his split with Laura. She seemed a woman to keep things from. There was something slightly manipulative about this scene, but Rhinehart was deeply affected. "I'll call you the minute I get back to the city," he said.

The express train sped down the tracks, tossing us in our seats. Alone together again, we were both quiet, shy. Rhinehart was staring out the window. When he began talking, it was about the carpet runner in Chechna's hallway, a blue one with red markings like upside-down pinecones. I hadn't noticed it. It came from one of the Pullman cars, he said, when Chechna was working on the trains after she first immigrated.

"Did they give the rug to her after they took the train out of service?"

"No, no. The railroad barely paid them. She stole it, most likely. The employees took everything—pillowcases, sheets. They bartered with the kitchen staff, who were smuggling out the food. For a week, I ate figs traded for a bunch of towels." He smiled, but he looked tired as he pressed the bridge of his nose with his thumb and forefinger.

I said, "You've started looking for your family? Do you think the woman you got in touch with is your cousin?"

"I think she may be. She said she had letters from my mother to hers. I would give anything to see them! I don't have anything written from my mother. I think she was embarrassed of her English spelling."

I asked him to tell me about his mother again and then leaned my head back against the seat, as if settling in. He looked over at me and smiled. "You've always been an encouraging listener."

"She was pretty, wasn't she?"

"Very pretty. Dark hair, a slight figure. Very affectionate. At times she could be abrupt with people, but with me she wasn't like that. She babied me, called me her 'little prince'—Rudolf isn't a Ukranian name, you know. She'd heard it somewhere and liked it, thought it sounded foreign and regal. I played the part when we were out, holding her arm and opening the door and negotiating everything with the store clerks. The neighbors used to compliment her on my politeness and maturity. It pleased her."

"Did she like books, too? Did she read to you?"

"Not so much. But she told stories, usually set in Ukraine. I think she may have been inventing as she went along, she paused a lot. I wish she had written them down. It would be nice to have something in her own hand."

I knew what he meant. I had saved all the letters and cards my father had written me, even those from elementary school, notes jotted down on a napkin wishing me luck on a test or to remind me of something to ask the teacher. It was the most exhilarating thing about school lunch period, which seemed a confusing block of unstructured time at a long table with the smell of food garbage and the complexity of playground dynamics. To open up the lunchbox and see the napkin signed off "Dad"—it was like he had appeared next to me.

"Your mother died of lung cancer, didn't she?" I asked.

"That's where they think it started. She'd had breathing problems before. She covered them up with whistling. It took me years before I figured that out. I used to sing along with her, not knowing anything was wrong. Chechna's right, I was a soft-headed boy." He sighed. "My mother didn't get a doctor until she was in a tremendous amount of pain. By then it had spread everywhere."

We were pulling into Woodside station, the sky an uncommitted color edged by streetlights. I remembered Rhinehart telling me about his mother's death. The day she became too sick to stand and lay in the bed, raving and running a high fever. How he stood nearby, pale and nervous, covering her with blankets, which she kept ripping off. There were neighbors there, drinking coffee in the kitchen, and he was worried they would come in and see her trying to pull off her nightgown.

I was holding his hand. The feel of it, the wide, warm fingers, was familiar. Almost instinctively, absentmindedly, he began circling the joint of my thumb.

"It was a hard adjustment living with Chechna. She wasn't accustomed to children and thought I should be more independent than I was. She worked long hours, and I was alone a lot. I got myself ready for school. I was always afraid of oversleeping. On the day I had my trumpet recital, I was so excited I slept in my suit, on top of my sheets, like a vampire. So I wouldn't have to waste any time getting ready in the morning, in case I was late.

"On Sundays, though, we'd take the bus together out to that crowded cemetery visible from the Queens-Midtown Expressway. It's where my mother's buried. We'd spend the day out there, bring a picnic lunch and a blanket." I felt him beginning to pull away from the story, describing Russian Easter, when the priest went around blessing the graves, and how he'd try and leave a piece of candy for his mother. He laughed, but it sounded hollow. "I was so sad during that time. It's hard to believe you can be that sad and still get through it." He squeezed my hand and then released it. "I'm sorry, Tatie. Too much past. It's seeing Chechna again that's brought it up. You'd think after a number of years you'd forget these things. Maybe it's just the nature of pain to stay put, lodged somewhere deep inside."

I repressed the desire to put my arms around him, imagining the great, confused outpouring it would turn into, tender, consoling, inappropriate. I wanted to comfort him, to climb on top of him.

"Let's talk about you," he said. "What have you been doing these past months?"

I told him about my move to Brooklyn. The new series I was working on of people in their environments, which, after the visit to Chechna's, felt like it was taking shape. "Of course, it's mostly just an idea at this point. I'll need to see if I can bring it all together." For some reason, as comfortable as I'd felt, I hadn't talked much about myself.

He was listening intently. "Why don't you come upstate with me on Tuesday? If you can get the morning off. I'm going to see a genealogist—he works out of his home. It should be a fascinating environment to photograph. I'll ask him, but I'm sure it would be fine."

At Penn Station, Rhinehart insisted on helping me carry my things onto the subway platform, since I had turned down the offer of a cab. I felt the pressing need to sum up the afternoon, everything that I'd felt pass between us, and it came out in a stuttered rush. He nodded, as if he understood. But even after I stopped talking, he was looking at me, expectantly, as if there were more that was supposed to happen. "I'll see you on Tuesday then," he said for the second time. The train arrived with its blast of warm air and squealing, and I hugged him spontaneously. He embraced me and held on, as if like me, he had been wanting to do that all day.

CHAPTER SIX

Before picking me up in Brooklyn, a significant detour, Rhinehart had stopped to get sandwiches from one deli and knishes from another—he must have left his house at 6 a.m. to make that happen. I loaded three camera bags into the car, which impressed him. I'd gone to Adorama the day before to rent two different lenses that I wanted to try out—a high-end portrait and a 45mm wide-angle. Riding up the tiny elevator with four guys, weary photo assistants returning the gear from a commercial shoot, I remembered my days assisting, before I started working for Marty, and realized that I had actually made progress in all the years I'd been living in the city.

I was wearing a light floral skirt and tights, a little cool for the weather, but I was enjoying the sight of my knees, exposed after a dry and difficult winter. Rhinehart looked at them, too, and then pretended to be concerned with a rattling noise coming from the passenger door, making me smile into the window. It felt as if he and I weren't merely headed out of town, but to a country I'd never been. I often got this feeling around him, an ebullient bubble in my chest that made me want to laugh or run around.

He clicked on the radio, and we listened to faint jazz as we nosed our way out of the Bronx. His phone was ringing, and he excused himself as he answered it. I listened while pretending not to. It started with an article he was doing and turned into a discussion about a prize jury he was on. The schedule of meetings. I used to follow all these details. Although I wouldn't have admitted it back then, his connections had probably contributed to the intensity of my desire for him, and also, in my lesser moments, made me feel twice as insecure. He was asking who else was on the panel. I recognized the name of a famous film director. I hadn't realized Rhinehart was still leading a life with these sorts of high-profile obligations. When we were at Chechna's, he'd seemed to have nothing but time.

The phone rang again, and he shut it off. I smiled at him but his eyes were back on the road, all business. He was explaining that the genealogist he'd chosen had come recommended by his friend, a Boston neurologist who'd found Vichy survivor relatives in France and even a tenuous link to the Louis XVI throne.

We were passing the heavy brown co-ops that reminded me of 1970s TV shows like *Welcome Back, Kotter,* when I confessed that I found genealogy boring.

"Boring!" Rhinehart said, as if I'd proclaimed I didn't like music.

I flipped through the book he'd brought along, as he reached over and tapped the pages, explaining the different mapping systems, and why he favored the drop-line pedigree chart, which was neatly labeled with shorthand annotations: GC for grandchild, CA for common ancestor, reminding me of the chess moves printed in the newspaper and how they seemed to suck all the life out of the game so that I no longer wanted to play. In one diagram, a stick figure labeled "Me" was at the bottom, the massive triangular weight of his entire family history sprung from the top of his head, which, I explained to Rhinehart, seemed to accurately illustrate the egotism I had always associated with this undertaking.

"Are you doing this to find out whether this woman Lyuba really is your cousin? The one who says she has your mother's letters?"

"Exactly. As well as to learn more about my roots. A good genealogist can work wonders. A poet friend of mine claimed to have traced her family line back to the Jamestown settlement with a link to Thomas Jefferson. He was a libidinous man, but still."

Genealogical research was heavy on the procedurals. The first was to sketch a family tree of known relations. His notepad showed that he had stopped at his mother: Anna Golovnya, bn 1928, Lviv, Ukraine, one sister, Marta, with a question mark next to it, and one great-uncle.

"You don't know anyone else?"

"There are those other sisters Chechna had heard of. The surname keeps changing, which makes them difficult to trace." He took his eyes off the road to look at me. "You never had the desire to investigate your family history?"

I thought of my father, sitting in a lawn chair at the end of the driveway, buckets of zinnias at his feet to sell to the tourists coming down Route 25. On Fridays, Hallie would help out with the weekend traffic, attempting to set up dates for us when my dad was out of earshot. I'd stand behind her, cutting bouquets in my mother's old straw visor. "Lose the hat," she'd whisper every time a car pulled up. At the end of the day, my dad would bring out sun tea and let Hallie count up the cash box, always giving us a bigger cut than we deserved. Even then he seemed old, sitting beneath his striped umbrella, his rough, knobby hands on his work pants. When I tried to give him back some of the money, he'd say, "No, no. With you two gals working so hard today, there'll be no wives crying into their pillows tonight." It was a marginally profitable business, but my father understood it as a public service.

Entire summers stretched out this way. This seemed to be my history, just as removed from me as the dead relations Rhinehart was searching for. If I could, this would be what I'd revisit—the tough feel of the zinnia stems as I sawed through them, the dry fields behind me, the sound of the screen door slamming as my dad came out to join us.

The genealogist worked out of a basement apartment in a middle-class development of ranch houses with scrubby lawns and yew bushes. A small, hand-lettered sign hanging off the mailbox signaled his office, and we made a sharp right onto the sloping drive.

Rhinehart had dressed in a collared shirt, his papers in a manila folder, as if he were going to see his lawyer. He patted his breast pocket reassuringly.

"What's in your pocket?" I asked him as we went around to the back of the house. I had to watch my footing as the railroad ties that were supposed to pass for stairs were loose.

He smiled. "You'll see."

We opened the screen door and a little bell dinged. A cat shot past my legs into the yard.

The "office" looked like a rec room where Starsky and Hutch would relax with women. There was a rust-colored carpet and pine-paneled walls that made it dark for midday. The starburst clock said half-past two. Books were stacked under chairs—research, I guessed, until I saw that many were crime fiction hardcovers. The genealogist, whose name was Gerald, sat at a large, messy desk. He had an outmoded computer with a boxy monitor as big as an old TV set.

I had envisioned a thin man with a nervous tic and maybe a little pencil mustache, but Gerald was heavy-faced, with bulldoggish jowls and big plastic-frame eyeglasses, the lenses yellowed. He mistook me for Rhinehart's wife, despite the age difference. I began setting up my tripod.

They sat in a couple of cracked easy chairs while Rhinehart laid out the details of his search for his mother's relatives and Gerald took notes on a legal pad. "And your father?"

"His name was Yosyp, and his last name may have been either Romanchuk or Rudnitsky. Our last name was changed when my mother and I came over. He never emigrated with us. His mother was ill, and he stayed on with her in Ukraine. He died a couple of years after we arrived. My memory of his death is very faint, and I'm mostly dating it by a memory of my mother locking herself in the bathroom and wailing after she received the news. She couldn't bear to talk about him after and so I never found out how he died—I assume sickness. There aren't any letters between them, but I do have this—" He showed Gerald a photo, one I had seen before, of his father as a young man, not very tall, in uniform on a barren field, squinting into the sun. It had been on Rhinehart's desk when I had known him.

"Do you have any records for your father?" Gerald asked.

"No, I know so little about him. We may have to work forward to the present on his side."

From behind the lens, I cut in, "How is it possible to work forward from hypothetical ancestors?"

Rhinehart was making a motion to me to be quiet, but I ignored him. He was always overly deferential to people he hired, as if they were volunteering help.

Gerald said, "Good question. Like all detective work, it takes a little fact, speculation, and inquiry. In theory, if you put together the genealogies of everyone in the world, they would fit together like a giant jigsaw puzzle. Twenty-five years to a generation, roughly, and each of us had more than a million ancestors in the fifteenth century and more than a billion in the thirteenth. Although that number reflects a tremendous amount of overlapping, the same people popping up on the tree dozens of times."

"Just think, Tatie," Rhinehart said. "We could even be related."

I frowned. Was he serious? He was giving me a polite but closed look that discouraged intimacy. I'd noticed it earlier in the car when he dove into genealogy, a one-way topic. It reminded me of how he used to withdraw, right in front of me, if I wasn't giving him enough space. But he had invited me to come with him today. I hadn't forced it.

"It's an exciting process," Gerald continued. "I found out I was related to Don Rickles, the artist Jasper Johns, and Helen Sobel—one of the best bridge players in the world."

From behind the camera I spied on Rhinehart, staring at his hands, his lips. I was starting to wonder if all my desire—even the image of him sliding his hand up my thigh that I'd been half-willing to happen in the car—was the fantasy by-product of a hugely misinformed person. But I had felt the energy pass between us at Chechna's. Or thought I had. He'd held my hand on the train.

I was having trouble shooting here, despite the initial potential of the place. Everything I framed was too candid, as if I'd been brought in as Rhinehart's documentarian. He was looking inquiringly at Gerald, a customer intent on a purchase. How foolish I'd been to think that I'd inspire him to start writing poetry again. He wasn't lost. As usual, he already had a project.

From his manila folder, Rhinehart had removed photocopies of his mother's birth certificate, her passport and bank statements, a birthday card she had received from someone in the U.S., and a short letter that Lyuba had written and her son had translated. The originals were in a fireproof box. Rhinehart read us Lyuba's letter out loud. She was recounting one of the times she'd seen Rhinehart, "a fat little boy with a big nose" and had taken him outside to play while the two mothers talked in the kitchen. Lyuba had been enthralled with the idea that this boy was going to America where there were trains, and car traffic, and big puffs of smoke, and tall buildings. Did he remember the chickens? the letter asked. That one had pecked him and he'd been scared? Rhinehart lifted his head to interject here. He did have a dim memory of a chicken pecking him, and he'd always had a mild phobia of them. The story ended ominously. Lyuba's mother had looked into her tea cup after the visit and started crying, saying that there was a lot of bad in the world.

Despite myself, I was intrigued. "I don't get the ending. What a strange thing to say about your sister leaving for a better life."

"She was looking into her cup, so maybe she was reading the tea leaves. That was common then—my mother did it occasionally in New York, for a neighbor or sometimes for me." Rhinehart looked to Gerald, who nodded in confirmation. "If so, Marta may have seen my mother's death after leaving for America. Lyuba also sent this." He handed me a photo of a chubby little boy in short pants, standing in front of a wood-sided row house, holding a ball with both hands.

"This is you! You're so blond!" I'd never seen a childhood photo of him before. I had searched for one at Chechna's but there had been none. "It looks like it was taken in Brooklyn. How did Lyuba have it?"

"My mother must have sent it to her mother in Ukraine."

"I wish you had the other part of the correspondence—the letters Marta wrote to your mother. You'd know so much more."

"My mother wasn't a sentimental person. She probably threw them away. I recently found this, though, between the leaves of an old book." He carefully reached into his shirt pocket and removed a wax paper packet; inside were three round cutouts, black-and-white heads, which Gerald took over to the drafting table and looked at with an old-fashioned magnifying glass. Rhinehart said, "I don't know for sure, but I'm guessing these are likely my mother's three sisters. She'd tell me about how they used to brush her hair and tell her stories. I believe two may have died while in their twenties, one when my mother was still a girl." He pointed to the youngest-looking one with dark hair and a shy smile. "I think this must be Marta."

"These remembrances were common," Gerald said. "The father usually kept them."

"My grandfather must have given them to her, although by rights they should have been passed down to the eldest, and according to Lyuba, her mother was older than mine. I think I should start with her side of the family."

"Whatever you find, email to me, and I'll start plugging the information into a tree. The history is out there, we just have to discover it."

Back in the car, Rhinehart said, "He's right. I do need to center my investigation on Ukraine."

"He seemed sort of knowledgeable, despite the look of that office."

"He's one of the best," Rhinehart said, giving me an amused look out of the corner of his eye.

"Did Lyuba tell you that Marta and your mother were sisters?"

"Like me, she's trying to piece it together. But if she is my cousin, she can tell me about my grandfather and my other aunts and cousins—maybe even my father since he stayed behind in Ukraine."

"But wouldn't this information be in those letters from your mother? Did you ask her about that?"

"I did but she hasn't replied yet. The mail is very slow going back and forth. Things take forever."

"What things? Gifts?"

He took his eyes off the road to give me a scolding look. "Nothing expensive. Don't fault me my generosity."

"I just don't think it's a good idea to jump in with presents. It sends the wrong message. Remember the candidate with the pro-union platform?" Rhinehart had backed him, even stuffing envelopes and stumping, and the guy had turned out to not even have a college degree. The closest he'd gotten to unions was a summer job doing carpentry.

"That was a long time ago, Saint Peter."

I loved mysteries and had already figured out the process for solving this one. "What you need is for Lyuba to send over those letters your mother wrote her. You can see if you recognize her handwriting and then figure everything out. Have them translated over here. You don't need her son for that."

"She's nervous to send them in case they get lost."

"How about photocopies then?"

"Tatie, this is Ukraine. They don't have easy access to modern conveniences."

Already we had hit a snag. "Something seems off here."

"I'm sure it will become clear eventually. I'm just beginning the research."

We were already on the FDR, which was moving. I rapidly saw the day coming to a close, Rhinehart dropping me off at my building, with me having no clear idea of the meaning of this trip, how he felt about me, or when I would ever see him again. I sat brooding out the window, and he said, "You're quiet."

"Can I ask you something?"

I saw him almost imperceptibly tighten up. He suspected I was going to demand an emotional revelation. His eyes still on the road, he said, nonchalantly, "Sure."

"After you won the Pulitzer—" I was drawing out my sentence, maybe unfairly, but I was also watching him. He seemed frozen, a painting of a man driving a car. "I sent you a letter. Did you ever receive it?"

"Yes. I did." He gave me a serious look. "It was a beautiful letter. I saved it. I still have it."

"But you never responded."

"It was a difficult time," he said. "The phone kept ringing. I talked and talked about myself until I was thoroughly sick." He gripped the wheel. "No one prepares you for how terrifying success is. How strong the pressure is to enjoy it. Because if you're not happy then, during the high point in your life, when will you ever be?"

We were nearing the exit for the Manhattan Bridge. "I started a letter to you many times," he said. "I just wasn't able to finish it."

"And what about before that? When I'd first moved to the city and I wanted to just get a cup of coffee and I called you and you never called me back?"

"Tatie," he said, shaking his head. "Even you must have felt at the time that wasn't a good idea."

Getting out of the car in front of my building, I said, "I should be able to get you the prints for Harold and Sue this week." I'd been able to cull about ten shots I thought Sue would find acceptable. I jotted down the numbers of six of them to be made into 8 x 10s—I wasn't about to show her the contact sheets and have her choose, especially as there were some of Harold that she'd find distressing, his dull eyes and mouth hanging loose like a stroke victim's.

Rhinehart was standing awkwardly by the car, gazing up at my building. "Would you like to drop them off, maybe come over for dinner at my apartment?"

I was feeling almost physically worn down by my own circling thoughts and confusion. How could he spend an entire day with me and not want to touch me, or even ask me about myself? I was merely a witness to his research. "I'm not sure what I have going on this week," I said.

"Okay," he said, carefully. "Would you like help bringing up the bags?"

I shook my head.

"I'll call you," he said. "About dinner."

In the other two rolls from Chechna's, the ones for me, there were a few images that were so good I got chills, especially the portraits of Harold that I shot at F16, with a large depth of field, so that all the knickknacks behind him were in sharp relief. A few others were also worth making into prints—one of the living room in which I'd been able to capture the late afternoon sun glinting off the old-fashioned radiator, the dusty collection of vases casting shadows on the dresser, a candid of Sue standing next to my commercial lights, sneaking a look into her compact, and another of Chechna absentmindedly petting one of her porcelain spaniels, the light from the window washing over her hands.

I hoped to sequence these with a few I'd taken of Marty in his office. I also had some strong shots of Shani in the salon. She'd borrowed some props from the theater to make her role as hairdresser look more authentic. She also felt she needed an elaborate hairstyle, and had woven her own hair and extensions around a support so that it looked like a beehive, a couple of braided tendrils venturing out. She put on the smock and gloves she used for coloring and stood next to her chair, one hand resting on it, and looked into the camera with an open expression, then defiant, then amused, as if she had a secret with herself. In another pose she was sitting in the chair in a long black dress, legs crossed, staring out the front door of the shop with a restrained, expectant expression.

I felt I'd taken this idea as far as I could, and I was longing to do something more experimental and surreal. When I was younger I'd had a recurring dream that still had a powerful grip on my memory. I was sitting in an enormous bed, amazed and frightened, watching large-winged birds fly around the room. I thought I might be able to re-create the vision by layering separate images on top of each other, which I'd never done before. I needed to photograph the birds first. Hallie volunteered to take me to a sanctuary that she donated to—there were falcons there.

She picked me up wearing oversized dark sunglasses and red lipstick, a 1950s seductress sent out on a kill. She claimed to visit the refuge often, but I couldn't picture it. She didn't even have the proper footwear. We picked our way through the muddy puddles, past the high grunting of Canadian geese, and back into the scrubby woods, both cooler and darker, where the birds' cages were. Downy underfeathers were stuck in the fence links. "Be prepared," Hallie told me. "This is going to break your heart."

I had some trouble locating the red-tailed hawk; he was watching me with quizzical, geometric movements of his head from a swing made of PVC pipe, an old carpet wrapped around it. A staff member let us inside, and then went back to scrubbing down a neighboring cage. I checked the light meter—it was darker here than I'd expected. I loaded the 800 film, set up the tripod, and shot part of a roll. As I looked up from the camera, he flew at me, and I had to move quickly to capture it. That majestic ease birds have in their own bodies. He landed, and with his big-shouldered, old man's gait, lumbered over to his dog dish of water. His naked legs, in their feathered shorts, looked human.

"What's wrong with him? He doesn't seem maimed." He looked

up warily. I was suddenly conscious of the screeching and huffing of birds in other cages.

"He had a broken wing, and he's healed, but it's difficult to reintroduce them into the wild. You have to reteach them how to hunt." We left the cage and walked down the wood chip path. Behind us, the hawk cried, a high-pitched scream that faded off at the end, sounding more prey than predator.

As I was photographing a blind seagull, Hallie asked whether I was sleeping with Rhinehart.

"Of course not. I would have told you."

"The machinery doesn't work?"

"I have no idea—I haven't tested it."

"But you want to."

I did. The annoyance I'd felt after our trip upstate had vanished by the next day. But I wanted him to want me, too, and I suspected I would have gotten a clearer sign if the desire was mutual. I told her he'd invited me over to his house for dinner. "Maybe something will happen then."

"I'd give it the green light, except then you're going to get attached, and I'm not sure he's changed all that much. It seems like he's still really into his own thing. If anything, his issues probably have solidified."

"But I've changed. I don't think it would bother me as much now. I'm more independent."

Hallie was shaking her head. "It always feels like that before you have sex. Are you dating other people? You've got to balance it out."

"No. But if someone came along I would."

Hallie snorted. "*Came along.* At your age! Who's going to just show up? You have to work at these things."

"Love happens. It always has before when I'm least expecting it."

"After you hit thirty that magic rule doesn't apply." She took a Ziploc bag of dried corn from her handbag and spread it on the ground for the ducks. "Don't you want to get married?"

"I'm not sure. It's not the only possible relationship model."

"Name another."

"Common law partners. Sisters who live together. Grandmothers who raise children. Women who set up families with each other."

"Lesbians. That's a domestic partnership—same thing as marriage. They need to make that legal everywhere."

"No, I mean straight women."

She narrowed her eyes. "You must've read that in a novel or something. No one we know does it."

I couldn't remember where I read it, although it may have been in a bell hooks essay.

Hallie went on, "I couldn't stand to have a woman breathing down my neck all the time. We're trained to notice any change in patterns. Even *I* do it. With Adán. I think he may be considering having an affair."

I was skeptical. "How do you know?"

"Things he says. It's like he's comparing me to someone and can't decide who's better. He says to me the other day, 'You have a nice nose, actually.' *Actually!* As if someone had claimed otherwise."

"That's not evidence. It doesn't mean anything."

"There are other things, too, that I don't want to say."

Sexual things? We watched the ducks walk across the yard. Hallie was biting on her cuticle, and I was worried she was going to tell me her eating disorder had come back; she always claimed it was a signal that something was happening beneath the surface of her life, like people who can tell a storm is approaching because of an aching knee. Her bulimia had gotten very bad in college, around the time her father was coming for a visit with the woman, Margie, whom he would eventually marry. Hallie was binging and taking laxatives. She was forced to tell me after she overdosed on them and had an accident in her bed. We went to the school counseling center after that, but she still got weird about food sometimes when she was stressed, refusing to eat carbohydrates or doing juice fasts.

She seemed to guess what I was thinking. "Not that. I've been crying!"

"Really?" She hadn't even cried at her mother's funeral. I remembered her staring angrily at the coffin.

"It's starting to freak me out. Usually it's in the car. I'll be going along, doing my thing, and then all of a sudden I'm screaming and pounding on the steering wheel like a maniac." She gripped my arm. "It's crazy, right? The other day, I was on the way to the post office, and I had to pull over because I couldn't see the road I was crying so hard."

"What are you upset about? Adán?"

"I don't know."

I was concerned but trying not to show it, as I could already sense her regretting telling me. It was a thing with her, she couldn't stand to have anyone feel sorry for her. Usually the less I asked, the more she'd reveal, which required an annoying passivity on my part.

"It's fucked up, I know, but there's something kind of exciting about suspecting him. I've gotten sort of addicted to it. And it feels real, like I'm on to something." We walked back to the rutted lot. Her silver Jaguar, parked between a beat-up Toyota and the staff pickup truck, glimmered like a giant fish.

"Maybe you need to be putting this energy somewhere else. Working."

"Doing what? PR? I'd have to start at the bottom again. And I'd make so little compared to Adán. No, I had those career dreams once, but I had to let them go."

"You talk as if you married into the royal family. Lots of women work."

"Not the women I know. Not women with money." I was about to tell her that those women were also raising children, but she was on to some story about a career woman who had been "sold out by '80s feminism," had decided to work her way up the corporate ladder instead of getting married, and now found herself in her late forties, expected to work like a man for much less money, while fighting for attention in a city that was obsessed with youth and looks. "Now, to the younger men she's a cougar, and the older men don't give a shit about how she's independent."

"That's one really cynical example."

"It's real. I know other women who it happened to. And anyway, it's not like I do nothing. I have the fund-raising work for PETA. Hey"—she pulled on me—"why don't you come back to the house and talk to Adán, draw him out. Tell me if I'm crazy."

I refused.

"I'm not asking you to extract a confession. Just get him talking and see if you can read anything in his attitude."

"That's so awkward. He's going to know what's up."

"But you're so good at these things. Just come over for a drink. He likes you, you're such an audience. Don't let him talk too much about Spain. He's nuts on that topic, lately." She was leaning against her car, smiling at me. I recognized that expression. She knew, like when we were kids, that I'd just give in.

It was midday, loose shadows across the lawn. Inside the quiet expanse of steel and blond wood were six bedrooms hidden off hallways and sliding doors, a built-in speaker system, soft imported carpet. As if still outside, we walked through stretches of sun that poured in from floor-to-ceiling windows that faced the marsh. When she was in college, Hallie would always burn through her allowance weeks before the end of the semester, and she never wanted to ask her dad for more money. There was one time she was so broke we'd shared my meal card. Her favorite dish was baked ziti, and when it was my turn to go to the dining hall, I'd take along a handful of Ziploc bags to fill up on the all-you-can-eat buffet and smuggle them back under my coat. "Don't forget the parmie," she'd say, waving. Coming back across the campus in the early winter dark, trees casting shadows on the snow, I could see her waiting, backlit in the window, smoking a cigarette.

* * *

Adán came home shortly after we did. How handsome he was, with his dark, liquid eyes and hair gone silvery at the temples. Even more so than usual. I wondered if Hallie's adulterous suspicions were influencing me.

He spread his arms when he saw me. "A visit! You are never here. Mi mujer always is at your house."

"Not that much since I moved to Brooklyn."

"I don't do Brooklyn," said Hallie. "What do you want to drink?"

I asked for seltzer, and she told Adán to make us both martinis. "So," he said to me, "I hear you are with an older man now. A professor."

It always annoyed me how much couples gossiped, how unwittingly exposed you were when you sat down with one of them. Later they would discuss your reactions and postulate that you were lying, or still attached, or who would be good for you instead. I switched the topic to the injured birds we'd seen, how they shuffled around the cages like mammals. "I want to go back and shoot them as the sun's setting. When the light is more melancholy."

"Light is very important to a photographer." Adán had a way of saying things so that they were both statements and questions.

"Especially late afternoon light at certain times of the year. It's my favorite."

He took both my hands in his. They were dry and slightly warm, as if he'd been holding them up in front of a fire. "Go to Spain and visit Madrid and then after go to a little town in the north. Its name is Collbató. There I have some family, the little part that is Catalan, and you can stay with them in their house and make pictures. The light is like nothing you have seen. September it is best because the sky is very, very blue, more blue than water."

"Is this close to Barcelona?" I said, thinking of Laura and her gallery recommendations, which led me to wonder whether Rhinehart was upset about the separation. Or if he even had any contact with her.

Adán nodded. "Only an hour away but it is very different looking. All around there is not much, just farms for the olives, and also the tree for almonds, so the dirt, it is very dry and with many rocks, you know, but a beautiful pink color, like the sun has rubbed his face in it."

I could feel Hallie at my elbow, anxious to move the conversation in a more productive direction. I said, "I've never seen an almond tree."

"Very delicious, the nuts, but it is work to break the shells. No, no, if you want to pick and eat something, better the figs, they are very good, and there is another fruit, I don't know what it is called in English. And there is honey, too, from the bees. My uncle he had a big piece of this honey, the honeycomb, it was taken out of his furnace."

"Chimney," Hallie said.

"Chimney, his friends they wear those masks so as not to get bit, and they removed it, the comb, and that night we passed it all around and took a piece. You chew it and then you spit it out. The taste is very sweet. Here, you don't have those types of things, everything it comes from a store, and nobody is sharing with neighbors—"

"We all know European culture is better than ours," Hallie said. "No one is going to argue with you."

"I'm sorry," Adán said. "Am I making you bored, Terry?"

"No, no. Not at all."

"I talk too much about these things. It is too exciting for me—when I talk I remember. It is like I am again sitting there."

"So what did you do earlier?" Hallie asked him. "While we were out?"

"I went for a walk. People they don't do that here, but I like it still." He smiled at me. "Even if the cars try and hit me." He made a little swerving motion with his hands, and I laughed.

Hallie gave me a warning look, as if to say don't encourage him. "But where did you walk? In which park?"

"That one we went to that other day. By the river."

"That's funny. We passed by there. We didn't see your car."

His face was turning red, and I became uncomfortable. I didn't want to watch him lie. I was also remembering a story he'd told once about an affair he'd had with his roommate's girlfriend when he was in business school. It had been incredibly difficult, as sometimes the girlfriend would want to stay over with him and so he'd had to put a lock on his door, inventing a "new, very shy" girlfriend for himself to throw his roommate off. All his movements had to be planned in advance, but he and the girl had managed to carry on the relationship for several months without the roommate finding out. At the time, we'd thought the story hysterical, but now it seemed ominous.

"I went to eat something," he said. "After. I was hungry from all the walking."

"Where? We have food here."

"Mi amor, it doesn't matter. Our friend is here—let us discuss things that she would like to talk about."

"I'm just asking you where you went. It seems strange that you would go off and eat somewhere by yourself when I've heard you say a million times you hate diners and there's nothing else—"

Adán's face had grown red down to his neck. "All these questions!"

"Sorry, am I interrupting your Spanish reverie? Should I not talk about our real life here?"

He was shaking his head vigorously, and I was both nervous and fascinated. I'd seen him worked up before, but never this genuinely angry at her.

"I told you I do not like it! And still you persists with these questions, this checking on me, testing, and now—in front of others! What a message to send about us and our home!"

"I'll go," I said and already I had stood up. My leaving alarmed Adán, who was saying, "No, no, it was just a storm. It's passed. Please sit down again. Please continue your visit." I looked over to Hallie, who was staring frozenly out at the yard.

I asked carefully, "Is everything all right with both of you?"

Hallie turned from the window, her face clouded, still in the middle of a private argument. She laughed. "Are you afraid we're going to split up? Adán, tell her we're not going to split up."

Adán didn't deny the possibility. Instead he said, "Terry should be used to all our fire by now."

I was used to their craziness, but this exchange had been different. Adán offered me another drink, which I refused.

CHAPTER SEVEN

I'd watched my expectation level rise during the week before dinner at Rhinehart's and so, partially in self-protection, I asked if I could bring my camera and photograph his bed, if he still had it. He'd once owned an antique mahogany sleigh bed, a formidable piece of furniture, which he'd been very attached to. It was what I'd been envisioning in my new work, the birds circling it, alighting on the footboard.

Meeting me at the door, he said, "I have something for you." He produced a large black camera bag. "A friend of mine knows a photographer who was looking to let go of this one. It's in very good shape, he said. Barely used. He has more cameras than one person will ever need, it seems."

I had unzipped the bag. "But this is a Hasselblad." And a V-system, a medium-format camera that I'd been wanting for a long time. "This is an expensive camera."

"Not too expensive."

"But how did you know I wanted this one?"

"You mentioned it. At Chechna's. When you talk about equipment, you get a bit technical, but I caught some identifiable phrases."

"This is too big a gift," I said. "I can't accept it."

"Why don't you try it out, and if you still feel that way I'll take it back."

"It's such a great camera." I pointed out the features to Rhinehart, the top viewfinder, the Zeiss lens, "best lenses ever made. This is a fixed-set lens, eighty millimeter. A very good portrait lens, and versatile." I handed it to him. "Feel the weight of it."

He cradled it in his hands. "What's the crank for?"

"To advance the film," I said. "You can buy an automatic winder to replace it, but they've been making them like this for so many years, it's tradition." I took it back from him, smiling. "You even got me film. It's bigger, six by six square." I made my fingers into a little box to show him.

"I received a lot of direction."

"How can I thank you for this? Thank you so much." I was too stunned, still, to say more.

"I'm happy to do it," he said.

I wandered off about the apartment, focusing test shots. He was renting a two-bedroom on West 75th near the park, although he said he preferred the East Village. He wanted to buy an apartment in one of those old tenements with the narrow dark hallways and bathtub in the kitchen, but so far he hadn't been able to find anything he liked. "You'll have to buy out someone very elderly," I told him. "Even ten years ago, a lot of those places had already been renovated."

His current rental, despite its impersonal layout, was stamped with his presence—stacks of books and newspapers in an old firewood box, his Barcelona chairs and braided rugs, the animal sculptures he bought the year he spent in Botswana, fragile bird skeletons, turtle shells, and Long Island beach rocks on shelves, and a heavy Spanish sideboard he'd had as long as I'd known him. Lamps, made out of pottery jugs, cast yellow pools of light on the floor.

He had converted one of the bedrooms into an office with a narrow studio bed for guests. The big college desk from Laura's house had been replaced with a small oak one with curved legs and little claw feet. It was catty-corner on the room's windowless side. On the wall above, he'd tacked up a picture of a skier, which looked as if it'd been ripped from a vintage magazine. The caption read: Downhill Slalom Ukrainian Wins the Gold.

"Why don't you have any books in here?" An empty bookcase was within arm's reach, a potted fern on one of the shelves. "Isn't this your study?"

"They were too seductive so I moved them. I need to focus on genealogy. Otherwise I start reading and can't stop." He was unrolling a long off-white scroll of paper like you'd find at an art store. "Foolscap. It's archival."

"But I thought the genealogist said he'd just plug everything into the computer."

"I want to keep a copy for myself—or for one of my younger relatives."

He had no younger relatives, unless he was referring to this new family of cousins he'd yet to meet. He stood admiring the blank paper with the splay-legged stance of a ship captain charting the route. I stood back and took a couple of quick shots of him.

"Do you need me in the pictures you're going to take?" he asked.

I smiled. I'd forgotten how much he liked to model. "I don't think so. I'll be photographing myself. I have a cable release that should work."

We went into his bedroom, cleaner than the guest room, with several imposing pieces of furniture, including a large early American dresser with a monogrammed silver tray for his wristwatch. The ceiling fan and dark wood reminded me of Vietnam War movies. In the center of the room was the enormous sleigh bed that I wanted to photograph so badly, probably because it brought back memories of spending hours, entire days, working, lying around, eating Chinese food there. Slovenly. Sloppy with love. The late day sun slanting in through the window, lighting up our naked bodies before slipping to the floor.

He'd left me alone "to work" and gone into the kitchen to prepare dinner. I stripped the bed of its blankets, set up the tripod, and shot two rolls of film as the slatted light was dying through the blinds, and then afterwards, with a slow shutter speed, once the room had gone partially dark—a disorienting, anxiety-producing time of day when afternoon and evening responsibilities overlapped. Although I was still getting used to it, the camera already felt like mine. I set up lights and shot myself knees up in bed, as the large imaginary birds gathered on the dresser, on the trunk, and flew around the room, spreading their dusty wings. I'd brought a blue cooling filter in an attempt to reproduce the silvery color moonlight sheds.

Afterwards I lay there listening to Rhinehart clattering in the kitchen. On another night he'd made me dinner, he'd picked me up outside my classroom first. I'd been wearing a dress and sneakers. On my wrist was a knotted strip of leather strung with glass beads. We'd cooked steaks in a skillet like my father used to, and sat on the couch after dinner, drinking beer, the dim lamps casting light over his books and pillows. I put my feet up on his lap. I wanted to discuss a reading he'd given, an event I'd looked forward to for weeks. I was trying to convey the odd high of being in the auditorium, the mixture of vulnerability and power at seeing the person you love, who is as familiar as your own body—as a celebrity. I spent most of the time watching the audience as they listened, or scribbled down something he'd said, raising their hands with questions that would impress this man who had, just that morning, rested his head on my trembling thighs. He began rattling off anecdotes about Robert Lowell and Theodore Roethke as if he'd just remembered them. Maybe he had. His gaze, moving around, skated over my face, then locked on me in recognition. The exhilaration of being singled out by him.

"All finished?" he asked when I appeared in the kitchen. He was frying Italian sausages with peppers and onions, a dish towel draped over his shoulder.

I sat down. A chipped piece of Brown Brothers pottery held a few daisies, their heads drooping to the table. "Yes."

"Did it go well?"

"I really love the Hasselblad. Even if I wanted to give it back, I don't think I could. You'd have to pry it out of my hands."

I was so touched that he'd given me such a gift, it was making me feel vulnerable around him, even a little sad. Or maybe it was just that after taking pictures, I sometimes felt emptied out, like I no longer belonged to myself. I had to transition back into my own life from the idea I'd been swimming in for the past hour. "It's strange that I'm shooting myself. I don't know if I've ever done that. I wonder if these will be any good. I thought so but now I have doubts. Actually, I feel that way about almost everything I've been shooting lately."

"Have you shown your new work to anyone? Gallery owners, curators?"

"No, it's too early for that. My portfolio isn't strong enough."

I thought back to when I first arrived in the city and would visit galleries, my heart skittering around in my throat, pretending to be seriously evaluating the art with my portfolio clutched in my sweaty palms, waiting for the place to clear out so that I could approach the desk. I was dreading, all these years later, of coming up with the same result. The same locked doors and refusals.

"I'm not eager to start showing the work again. Maybe it's fear. I just find the self-marketing part of things really difficult."

"That's the Janus-like nature of making art, I would guess. It doesn't seem right that something held so closely should be shoved out onto the auction block. It can be a painful process."

"But there's no way around it, is there?"

"No. But it helps to focus on what you're contributing to, as Susan Sontag used to say. You have to love the world enough to fight to be good and then fight to be heard."

We had finished dinner—a meal he'd prepared for me many times before. Everything in this house was reminding me of the past causing me to evaluate the gap between then and now, filled with the results of choices I didn't even know I'd been making, and I said, "What if I don't have the courage to fight? So many times I think I've done myself and my work a real disservice by being afraid. And yet I can't help it."

"You can't be that afraid. You're actually working. That's the only hurdle that matters."

I shook my head, and he smiled. "You think you have more fears than other people?"

"I'm easily intimidated. You know that."

He laughed. "No, I don't."

We moved into the living room. Rhinehart reached over and turned on the lamp next to the sofa. It was a soft evening, and the air from the open window stirred the loose strands that had fallen from my tied hair, tickling my neck. Almost May already. Rhinehart got up to make me hot chocolate with brandy, which he remembered I liked.

From the kitchen, he called out, "Why don't you make a list."

"Of what?"

"Of the things that have intimidated you." He appeared in the doorway and handed me a notepad that had been sitting on the telescope chair in the corner. "Write down people, too, and their relationship to you. I'll make my own list of fears so you're not lonely."

I made a few lopsided circles on the page, then I wrote my third-grade teacher's name, a bouncer at a bar who'd caught me smoking pot, a downstairs neighbor who used to complain about the noise when I was just walking around, Hallie's uncle who'd hired me to do yardwork for him one summer, the guy who owned the laundromat, Laura—I filled two pages with neat columns.

Rhinehart returned, carrying a mug for me and a brandy snifter for himself. I handed him the pad. He put on his reading glasses and peered at it. "Wow." He pointed to the unnamed man who had mugged me when I was seventeen. "This is understandable."

Rhinehart was the only person who knew all the details of that story, how I was at a deli getting a sandwich and was so scared when the man came in with a gun, I'd peed on the floor. Right next to the bread aisle. When I had recounted it for him, breathlessly, in bed, two years after it had happened, I'd felt the incident shrink to the proportions of an anecdote. I had been nineteen, but I'd also been in love—a sweetness that devoured all events, even traumatic ones.

"But nothing happened to me," I insisted to him now. "I feel like I should be over it."

"You give yourself too hard a time. You're one of the loveliest people I know. This list is too long." He handed it back to me. "And there isn't even one person on here associated with photography, fine arts, or any of the private aspirations you hold for yourself."

I read it over. He was right.

"These people are from years ago. Maybe it isn't as much of a problem, as it is a remembered problem." He scanned the second sheet. "What are all these first names?"

"They were kids I used to baby-sit for. You told me to write down whoever came to mind."

"But did they intimidate you?"

"Yes, I think so. I was really put off by the experience." The quietness of the house in the middle of the day when the baby was sleeping, the smell of something sweet, Desitin for diaper rash. I watched TV with the volume so low I couldn't hear it. "If I was hungry, I was never sure whether I should take some crackers the mom said I could have. I was really careful not to make any noise because I didn't want the baby to wake up. He was always crying, and I was never confident that I could get him to stop. I used to worry he would cry all day. Sometimes the mother was in the next room, and I was always self-conscious about whether I was holding the baby correctly, supporting the neck. What if he choked on something because I didn't know what I was doing?"

"It sounds like it wasn't the child who was intimidating you but the mother."

I'd never put that together before. "They were always summer people with a lot of money. And they were really critical—I felt like they were going to find me out. That I really didn't know what I was doing."

"Do you still feel this way about children?"

"I'm not sure." I hesitated. "Sometimes I think I want a child. There are so many things I'd like another person to know." Did I want this as much as I wanted to do my art? They were two separate desires, revolving like planets, controlled by the same underlying creative force.

I was afraid Rhinehart was going to tell me he couldn't see me as a mother, but instead he said, "I'd be surprised to hear otherwise."

The brandy had loosened my tongue and head, and I reached for his hand. "Let me see your list."

On it, he'd written "Mental illness," "Death."

"There are no people on here."

"Compared to those things, people are rather tame."

"What type of mental illness?"

"Different types of mania, like Robert Lowell had, where he stripped his clothes off and went down by the river, 'a man-aping balloon.' That was probably the fun part, actually, it was the depression that was awful. The type of despair that drugs you, makes you believe you'll never be happy again. I had it in my twenties, and then again recently before I stopped writing poetry. Actually, I should update this list—I'm more afraid of Alzheimer's now." He took back his list, added "Alzheimer's" and "the absolute cruelty people have the capacity to show to each other, to wildlife, to their land." And then, "how invisible that cruelty often is."

"You were depressed? I've never seen you like that."

"It involves sleeping and a lot of negativity."

"And it was because you stopped writing poetry?" I said carefully.

"It was related. That feeling of ineffectualness. In poetry I had keys that were in tune with something much greater than myself. It gave me a sense of purpose to play them."

"But if poetry is spiritual work, and it's been given to you to benefit the world, couldn't you ask for it back?"

He was swirling the brandy in the bottom of his glass and smiling at me, maybe at my earnestness. He came over and joined me on the couch, pulling me against him, my head now resting on his chest. I smiled involuntarily, with pleasure.

He said, "How much you care. I wish I could give you an answer. Maybe it was never meant to be my life's mission. Maybe I've been pulled off one job so that I can make progress in another. Maybe I'll write something tomorrow. 'Seek out the attitude which makes you feel most vitally alive,' William James said, and so for now, I do my best to concentrate on the present. That myopia has saved me on more than one occasion."

There was something forced in his voice. Was this truly how he felt or how he most wanted to feel? Behind us, the shade banged with the breeze. It had become night. I had a weird sensation of time suspended before us, stretching out in all directions, like a flat, dark sea, and this couch a little rowboat that we were snugly on, drifting.

I could feel him smile against the top of my head. "You always gave me more credit than I deserve, thinking I'm wise. Little did you know that around you I always felt so boyish. You make me want to shout and misbehave."

He was running two fingers, very slowly, from the top of my shoulder, down over the ridge of my elbow, to the sensitive hollow of my wrist, and back up. I had my eyes half-closed in pleasure, like a cat. I knew he was watching his hand, my skin respond.

"Is that why you wanted to be with me?" I asked. "Because I made you feel young?"

"It was your adorableness, your insight. Your talent," he said, his hand drifting to the side of my neck. "Many other things. But love only writes itself down as a reason."

I felt us getting close to the cliff edge and was very quiet. I could hear his breath going quicker. I turned around and found his face and kissed him. For a blissful moment I wondered why we hadn't done this earlier. It was so simple. And then, his hand in my hair, he shifted, hesitated, and very gently moved me to the side. The warmth of him was gone. He was now holding my hand in an encouraging, comforting way, like you would for someone who'd just told you a distressing story. "It's after two," he said.

I was confused and looked over at the clock, as if the alarm had gone off. "Should I go?"

"To Brooklyn? At this hour?"

But he wasn't inviting me to spend the night with him. His expression made that clear.

I stood up, the dreaminess draining out through my feet. I felt the room rapidly cooling as both of us retreated from each other.

"There's a spare bed in the study," he said. "I'll put fresh sheets on it."

I was conscious, internally, of an indignant pricking pain—rejection. Still I lingered, unsure of what to do.

"You'll be comfortable here, I promise," he said. "Otherwise I'll worry about you."

He led me down the hall and clicked on the light. On his desk, a mess of papers. The roll of foolscap. His movements were quick and nervous as he stripped the mattress, fetched the sheets from the hall closet, returned, made the bed, shuffled some writings around on the desk, then gathered the dirty laundry in a bundle, grasping it to his chest. "This is where I take naps—the air must be rich with unused ideas."

I stared at the bunched-up sheets in his arms. Neither of us moved.

"Sleep well, sweet," he said finally, shutting the door with a click, this old-fashioned door with its many layers of paint and its round brass knob. I lay down on the bed, clutching the pillow.

I woke up at five, in the same position, my face to the ceiling, as if sleep had never happened. I stayed in bed until slivers of light began streaming in from the sides of the window where the shade had curled. Seven.

Rhinehart was already up, shaven and dressed, sitting at the kitchen table with a glass of orange juice. The hard morning light was on the linoleum. He used to stay in bed until mid-morning, and I'd been thinking I'd go and find him there, and in that more intimate space, we could discuss what had happened the night before.

"Did you sleep okay?" he asked.

I'd had tangled dreams about him. The bed had been hard and narrow and too close to the wall, and throwing my leg out in sleep, I had accidentally kneed the corner of the windowsill and given myself a bruise. "Yes," I said.

He was reading an art book. "Vasilkivsky," he said, showing me the cover. "The Cossacks were quite remarkable how they managed to kick the Tartars around. And they did it by mobilizing the peasants, who didn't want to fight during harvesting or planting." He pointed to a watery earth-tone painting of a heavily mustached man, resting against his shotgun, staring into the distance, his horse behind him. "I love this picture. *Cossack on the Steppe*. The pose, the quiet dignity, everything. It's the Ukrainian equivalent of *The Thinker*."

Whatever had transpired between us last night was gone. I poured myself a cup of coffee. "I thought you told me the Cossacks hated the Jews. That they led pogroms against them."

"In the seventeenth century, yes. Their history was far from spotless—it's why I won't have a reproduction of this done." He flipped through the book. "Here's the sculpture of Saint Peter in Kiev Square."

"Why so much Ukraine this morning?"

Rhinehart had gotten up to cook, eggs fried inside slices of bread, the middles torn out.

Watching him at the stove, I felt the heat cascading from my chest, down through my arms. How I could see all these things—his rumpled sweater and drooping khakis, and white hair mussed in the back, and yet have the pieces assemble into something else—a rush of love and desire. I was trying not to react as I'd had in the past whenever he'd withdraw from me, offended and showing it. Maybe he'd just gotten nervous. If I had pushed it last night, I would have succeeded in sleeping with him—I could feel he wanted to, but he probably wasn't ready for that yet. Maybe I wasn't ready, either, although looking at him I realized I would have done it anyway, despite the potential emotional cost. But it would have been a mistake. So, instead, I'd let him go at his own pace and not take it personally. Hallie was wrong, I'd changed.

His back still to me, he said. "I'm going there."

"Going where?"

"Ukraine." He turned around. "It's become too difficult to get the answers I need being so far away. I want to talk to Lyuba in person and see my mother's letters. I'm also contracted with *The Atlantic* for an essay about the legacy of perestroika."

I felt betrayed. With all the talking I'd done last night, yammering on about myself, he hadn't mentioned this at all. Which made me suspicious it wasn't a short trip. "How long are you going for?"

He slid the eggs onto a blue flowered plate and brought it over to me. "I'm not sure yet."

"You're not going to move there are you?"

To my horror, he hesitated. "It's where I used to live. I don't know how I'll feel when I'm there again. I want to give myself a few months to see." His speech had slowed down, and he was talking to me as you would to an animal you were afraid might bite you.

"I feel a pull to the place," he said. "Either that pull will get stronger or it will dissipate. New York, you know, sometimes you stay here because it seems like everyone else does. But it would be nice to have a little house somewhere."

"I just . . . I had no idea you were thinking this. Of leaving like this. Why didn't you tell me last night?"

Again, Rhinehart slid his hands over to the middle of the table. They lay there, supplicating. I didn't want to look into his face and see the guilty sheepish look. "I don't know," he said. "It just didn't seem to fit with anything else." He hesitated. "I'm not going into exile. I haven't even booked the tickets yet. It's just a research trip. One stage of a quest."

That's what I was afraid of—the lure of the quest. My eggs getting cold on the plate, I launched into a story of Pizarro's search for El Dorado, the city of gold. In that bright kitchen, I went on talking about greedy Pizarro, and how the gold probably didn't even exist, and how he kept on searching and searching, even as they ran out of food. Rhinehart leaving—I couldn't imagine it. And how foolish I was, thinking I had unlimited time with him, assuming he'd changed and was no longer restless. He could be so selfish. I recalled the hours I'd once spent planning a vacation at a bed-and-breakfast in Nova Scotia just to hear he'd decided to speak at a poetry conference that same weekend. Why had he invited me over here last night? Given me the camera?

I'd gotten around to the part where the convoy had eaten the saddles and were now hacking off part of the horses' haunches on the trail, letting the blood, and then plastering the wounds up with river clay, when I caught Rhinehart looking at me with a mixture of sympathy and horror. "I researched it for a photo series I was thinking of doing," I said defensively. "Before he died, Pizarro had a dream that a dragon tore out his heart. The dragon had his own face. The moral is that sometimes you can chase around blindly for something and you aren't the only one who suffers."

I felt I'd finally hit on the brilliant, cold truth of us.

From across the table, Rhinehart had taken my hands. "It's just a trip. No one will get hurt. I promise."

I should have left at that point. Spent the day in the Strand, looking for a bargain on the photography books upstairs, poking through Brassaï and Henri Cartier-Bresson, gradually unhitching my perception of myself from Rhinehart. He was interviewing a translator today, yet another thing he hadn't told me, and I wondered what else was going to come out of this mountain of concealment. When he asked me if I wanted to join him, I should have said no, but already I was aware of our time together growing short, and so I said yes.

We were meeting Fedir at Union Square Park at one. The sun was heating up the afternoon, women were out in their sundresses, there was an undercurrent of excitement and restlessness, a warm spring day in New York. I was dressed in yesterday's black pants and felt hot and anxious, a live wire of dissatisfaction. No matter how well this day went, I would be unhappy.

We sat on a bench by the dog run, Rhinehart looking leisurely in his aviator sunglasses, reminding me of those half-blind men in front of the rest home in Chelsea, playing chess with the nurse calling out the moves. We were early, and Rhinehart was enjoying sitting there, so I went over to the Strand without him. But I was overly conscious of the time and left empty-handed. When I got back to the park, Rhinehart was talking to someone on a neighboring bench—he talked to everyone. Passing a homeless person, he would ask him where he was from, or what he used to do for a living. Once, many years ago upstate, he had invited two local vagrants into a bar to talk about New York City in the 1960s. They were loudly discussing the Mets and a place called Andy's Coffee Shop that no longer existed. Rhinehart offered to put one of them, Frank, up for the night, but he'd refused. They sat there drinking for another hour, Rhinehart buying the rounds.

Out on the street, I chastised Rhinehart for enabling Frank's alcoholism. "If you really care about him, why don't you get him into a shelter, AA, or something?"

Rhinehart said, "That man's been living on the street for close to fifty years—it's his choice. He wouldn't even take me up on my offer of a bed. No need to worry." This last part was said for my benefit. He often quoted Auden to me, "In headaches and worry, vaguely life slips away," as if I were the only one to whom this applied.

There was something strange about the conversation Rhinehart was having with the man in the green army jacket and cap, but I couldn't put my finger on it until I got closer and saw that they were talking simultaneously, as if they were reciting lines from a play. Rhinehart was gazing in the direction of 16th Street, while the other man was staring down at his shoe.

Rhinehart waved as he saw me approach. Was this the translator? He was much younger than I'd imagined, seemed to be in his twenties. He had slightly concave shoulders, as if he hadn't quite grown into his frame yet, and a spotty complexion. Something about his face, the cruel, thin lips maybe, instantly reminded me of my long-dead great-uncle, who had once called me a piglet when I'd reached across the table to get a roll from the bread basket.

Rhinehart slapped the man on the back, as if they'd been friends forever. "This is Fedir. He's going to be my guide to Ukraine."

Fedir grinned and enthusiastically shook my hand so maybe the cruel mouth was an accident. Rhinehart, who most likely had already decided where we were going for lunch, said, "Let's just wander along and see what we find."

On the street, Fedir lagged behind half a step. I slowed down so that he could walk beside us. Every time I slowed, he slowed.

Rhinehart took my elbow. "Don't worry about him."

Behind us, Fedir said something.

I turned around. "Excuse me?"

Fedir looked down at the ground, and repeated it. He was mumbling, but I caught the word "idiot." I stopped dead under the construction overhang, so that people had to squeeze around us. The traffic roared past on 14th Street.

"What did you just say?"

Rhinehart said, "It's Ukrainian, Tatie. He's translating." Half a beat later, Fedir clamored in gruffly. Rhinehart raised his own voice, so he was practically shouting. "It's so that I can get accustomed to hearing the language again. I remember some words from when I was younger, but I've forgotten most of it."

"He's translating everything?"

"Yes."

I turned back to Fedir, who met my eyes and said, *"Tak."*

Rhinehart had chosen his favorite overpriced deli restaurant on Second Avenue, which he claimed was his favorite.

While Fedir was over at the coat rack, carefully hanging up his jacket, Rhinehart whispered, "I haven't quite got him figured out. He's a circumspect man. Ukrainians tend to be rather open but he—"

"That's going to drive me crazy, you know. That constant talking."

He frowned. "I keep tuning it out, unconsciously. A bad habit. Comes from living in the city."

"Everyone within three blocks can hear him. Do you know how loud he is?"

He opened the menu and glanced through it, even though, as he said, he'd been coming here for more than twenty years. Fedir returned from the restroom and slid into Rhinehart's side of the booth, so I was looking at both of them. He was very tall. His beanstalk legs extended into the aisle.

The waitress appeared, a cute blonde, younger than me, who'd done her hair in a bouffant that made her look both retro and stylish. She greeted Rhinehart warmly, calling him Rudy.

He asked what was good today and then ordered the pastrami. I suspected the portions were enormous, and I offered to split it, but he waved me away. I looked for something small and light and settled for a Caesar salad. Fedir pointed to the matzo ball soup, which made me wonder if he'd been able to read the menu.

I excused myself to go to the bathroom, but the women's room had an "out of order" sign. I didn't have to go that badly, but still it was annoying. I had wanted to go to one of the cute little French bistros along the way. Walking by, I was envious of the couples sitting in the warm light inside. Rhinehart said he preferred no European to fake European, and since 1992 it had bothered him that Starbucks had the audacity to sully the Italian espresso culture with its use of the word "venti." He always did that, annexed one grievance to another to build a case. What was I doing here, not even his lover—a resentful sidekick, another stray he'd picked up, like Frank.

When I returned to the table, Rhinehart said, "So quick?"

I took a sip of coffee that had appeared even though I hadn't asked for it. "The ladies' room is broken," I informed him.

"So use the men's. They're single-person restrooms."

"I don't like the men's room." I glanced at Fedir, who grinned—it had sounded like he was translating me in a slightly higher-pitched voice.

"So what are you going to do then?" After another minute, Fedir grumblingly stopped. They both sat looking at me.

"Why do you need to be worried about it? It has nothing to do with you. Worry about yourself."

I could tell he was miffed. He said stiffly, "You shouldn't let your fears restrict you."

It annoyed me how he was echoing my language from last night. "It's not a fear, it's a preference! Last I knew, you wouldn't go into drugstores!"

"That's an ideological stance. There are too many of them, one on every corner—it's an indicator of how we're being railroaded into pharmacology. They used to serve ice cream sodas and headache medicine."

"You'd feel differently if you actually had a medical condition that needed treatment." I looked across the street. Inside the Chinese restaurant, one of the cooks was slumped in the window, his uniform creased against the glass. I identified with the silent defeat in his posture.

The food arrived, Rhinehart's piled high on his plate. The sight of this excess made me lose my appetite.

"I don't know if I *would* take pills if I were sick," Rhinehart was saying. "No point in gilding the lily."

"That's such an antiquated expression. I'm not even sure what it means."

He turned to Fedir. "I talk too much in aphorisms—I'm going to have to stop that."

Fedir put down his spoon to translate. "It's okay," I said. "You can take a break to eat."

"My own mouth dates me," Rhinehart said. "It's funny how we get stuck in one time and place like that. I knew a man on the block, an old guy, who had stopped buying clothes thirty years back. Why not? He took care of them, and his body wasn't going to change drastically. I'll be like that. People will talk about how wide ties used to be in style when they see me coming down the street . . ."

All this talk about old men—I wondered if he was feeling sensitive about his age. Maybe afraid to sleep with me because of it? But I'd pulled this mental trick before, ascribing phantom emotional motives to him. Most likely he didn't want to get too close because he was leaving. He was leaving me, yet again—his feelings should be ranked at a lower priority than mine. I cut him off. "You're digressing."

"Yeah, so? We're just sitting here. What else do we have to do?"

"*I* have things to do."

"What things? Tell me about them." I searched his face, but it was all innocence.

Instead I redirected us to the one topic I was beginning to resent. "How's the family research coming?"

"Not bad. I'm doing it mostly on my side for now."

"Did Lyuba ever meet your maternal grandparents? That could be helpful."

"I asked her that. She said no. I don't think my aunt had contact with them."

"There seems to have been a lot of fallouts in your family. Your aunt must have been a difficult person."

"Actually Lyuba speaks about her as if she were a pushover. My mama, on the other hand, was very sensitive and tended to cling to old hurts, even if it hurt her double." He gave me a meaningful look.

"What about Lyuba's father? What was he like?"

"She said he was a very gentle man, affectionate. He was the one she'd go to with her problems. But sometimes he could be withdrawn. He suffered from depression was my guess. But again, I'm reading into that. She in no way suggested it. At any rate he outlived my aunt, who died before my mother did. He only passed away about ten years ago, I hear."

"It'll be interesting to see those letters back and forth with your mother. To see the connection." And verify it.

Rhinehart nodded, motioning to Fedir to let him out of the booth.

"I'm going to the restroom now." He turned to me. "Do you want to go first?"

"No, thanks." I wanted to get Fedir alone to see how competent his English was. I'd been watching that churlish upper lip, which had started bothering me again. There was something lazy and yet cunning about his face that I couldn't quite pin down. This was the person Rhinehart would be traveling with, depending on, and I needed to know he'd be with someone reliable.

Alone with me Fedir was shy. He tapped one knuckle nervously against the table rim.

"So how long have you lived here in the U.S.?" I asked.

He seemed confused about whether to answer or translate.

"English," I said.

"Six years."

"Wow," I said. "You must miss the Ukraine."

He nodded.

"Do you have family there?"

He looked past my shoulder to the door. "Yes, a wife and three children. A house and farm with two horses. The whole thing mine." He smiled, revealing surprisingly small teeth. The front incisor was gray, the root dead.

"You must want to be with them," I said, and he shrugged.

"I need to send the money. I make better here, a little this, a little this, I send. My wife likes that I am not always under her footsteps."

I wasn't sure how to take this—I would assume, with three children, she'd want him present. In my purse next to me, my phone buzzed. I unzipped the bag and looked down to see who it was. Manhattan number. I didn't recognize it.

Rhinehart came back to the table. As I got out of the booth, he said, "It was really very clean in there, Tatie."

As Fedir was getting up, he bumped me by accident, and said, "Excuse me, Teresa." He gave my name, my grandmother's name, a heavy Eastern European inflection that I preferred to my own pronounciation.

Back out on Second Avenue, we passed a bookstore and Rhinehart lifted his hand in greeting to a dark-haired girl waving passionately from behind the register. I felt another skip of jealousy. Rhinehart was talking about Ukrainian art. One of the few types of art I knew nothing about. To Fedir he said the Met's Ukrainian collection was embarrassingly poor. There was a pause, then the translating began. I was dying to be free of them.

Rhinehart, still talking, asked a blind man if he'd like assistance crossing. The man accepted, and we crossed together. Rhinehart walked with him to the bus stop on the corner while I checked my voicemail. It was a friend of the painter who lived in my building. She was organizing a group show of New York photographs at a temporary exhibition space in midtown, heard my work was good, and wanted to know if I'd like to put in a couple of prints. She bartended at the Otheroom, and I could come by any time tonight or tomorrow to discuss.

Rhinehart had stopped in front of the Ukrainian museum.

"I have to go back to Brooklyn," I told him.

"Why now? There's a great Archipenko exhibit here that I want you to see."

I was curious, but resisted. "Another time. I just got invited to be in a group show. I need to get my portfolio together to meet the curator." Rhinehart started to respond too enthusiastically, so I had to explain that she hadn't even seen my work yet.

He was hailing me a cab. "This is great, great news. I told you, didn't I? Just a matter of time."

He was so genuinely pleased for me, I felt guilty for tainting the afternoon. "I'm sorry if I seemed upset today. This morning, I was—"

"You were fine. Go home. Get your work together. We'll talk later this week."

In the cab, I had the feeling that we wouldn't be discussing that night again.

CHAPTER EIGHT

Rhinehart didn't call me later that week, and I was hurt and had too much pride to call him. What was there to say? If he hadn't wanted to be with me then, when I was sitting right in front of him, why would he want me now, a week later? It was as if all the warmth and desire I'd been sending in his direction had been blocked by something, a sheet of metal he was holding up, and so it boomeranged back with doubled force to burn up inside of me, pointlessly.

Since I couldn't prevent myself from thinking about him, and knew little about his trip, I researched it on my own. I read about the country's political structure, "constitutional democracy that regained independence in 1991. Twenty-four oblasts each with a capital"; the country's size "slightly larger than France but smaller than Texas"; I corrected my previous mistake ("Ukraine," not "the Ukraine"), heard about the famine from 1932 to '33 when the inconceivable number of six million people starved. I flipped through photos of the lovely old chestnuts along the Dnieper River. In the *Times* I read about Viktor Yushchenko, who had been poisoned with dioxin by the rival Yanukovych's party during the election. It was really the photograph of Yushchenko's face, a grayish color and broken out in pustules, that had stuck in my memory, the fact that an ingested poison could do this. From guidebooks, I learned about the major sightseeing spots that I assumed Rhinehart would be hitting: Shevchenko's grave, as well as Rabbi Nachman's—the founder of the Breslov Hasidic movement—before a final destination of Lyuba's house. I imagined his excitement at the prospect of meeting her and reading the correspondence that would cause his mother, fifty years dead, to chimerically appear, revealing the secrets of his past.

Eventually I did call him, and he answered as if he'd been expecting me. We talked about his trip preparations, the research he was doing, far more advanced than mine, for the essay he was writing about Ukraine. I largely concealed my new knowledge of the country. It was hard talking to him without being able to see his face.

He asked about my group show, which I honestly said I had misgivings about. It would open next month. I'd met with the organizer, bringing along the most professional body of work I could pull together. She'd quickly invited me after flipping through my prints and exclaiming at almost every one, which pleased but also concerned me—she'd seemed a little too impressed. Despite that, I'd still harbored high hopes for the show. I'd had to scale them back when I saw the space, an anonymous office building in the West 30s, next to the cheap wholesale clothing stores, a vacant stretch in the evening. There was gray carpet and the room's lighting consisted of fluorescents and makeshift spots that illuminated the marked-up walls, dirt shadows of where cubicles had once been, old nails and installation pegs, badly done graffiti. When I had gone to drop off my work, I had looked through some of the other photographs that lay on a folding table, and my heart sank. Concepts I'd seen many times before, and worse, the evidence of poor technical skills being passed off as "artistic," when I knew it was sloppiness, or laziness, or just ignorance about lighting. I was embarrassed, a prickly sensation in my face, retelling the story to Rhinehart. The implication was that this was the class I was in; people would see the show and know I wasn't going anywhere.

He said, "Your work is what it is. Where it's hanging doesn't change that. The person with the ability to recognize it—will."

"Are you able to come to the opening? Remind me of that?"

"I wish I could, but I'll be away. I'd like to see you before I leave, though. Can you come to the airport with me? I hired a car that can take you back after."

I was hurt. I'd hoped that we could have dinner again before he left. "When is your flight?"

"Next Saturday. In the morning."

I hadn't realized he was leaving so soon.

"At this point I think you should just go for it," Hallie said. "You're obviously thinking about it all the time. Why not invite him over and try again? Then you'll know for sure."

We were back at the refuge where I'd taken more shots of the falcons on their perches, this time with the Hasselblad. If they looked good, I was ready to layer them onto the images of Rhinehart's bed, so it appeared the birds were actually sitting on his headboard. Removing my camera from the tripod, I remembered the night he'd given it to me.

"This time you should be a little more aggressive," Hallie said. "Maybe take some clothes off. See how he reacts. To him, you're still a juicy young piece of flesh."

"I can't."

"Since when are you so shy? You did it once."

In my inept way, I had been the one to seduce Rhinehart. Once the semester had begun, he said we shouldn't see each other. This was stupid, I told him. It was clear we enjoyed being together. So I asked him to a lecture. Then to lunch off-campus. Then to an Antonioni revival showing at a nearby theater. Whenever he demurred, usually on the nighttime activities, I'd wait a week, then suggest something else. I had the sexual confidence of the young. And I knew he wanted to have sex with me—I could feel it. It was merely a fussy sense of propriety that was holding him back, which annoyed me. Even in the dorms sex hadn't been that big a deal—who wasn't sleeping with somebody? We were in college—it's what everybody did.

Still, with Rhinehart, I didn't seem to be getting anywhere fast. "Maybe it's what you're wearing," Gertie said. I had on blue corduroys and sneakers, a vintage Mr. Bubble T-shirt, and a silver bracelet made from an old spoon—it was one of my favorite outfits. "Older men like sexier clothes. That's what my sister says." I went out and bought a pair of high brown boots and a jean skirt. On my way to campus, I'd passed Hallie, who was hanging out on our neighbor's porch. She whistled. "Whoa, momma! Going out to make the rent?" I ignored her. I was headed to the class Rhinehart taught, and which I hadn't had the courage to sign up for. As it was letting out, I went into the room, ostensibly to ask Tim, who I knew had a crush on me, a question about a party that weekend. I saw several heads turn and consider me. Our friend Nosh joined us, saying I should dress like that more often. I watched Rhinehart watch me out of the corner of his eye, dawdling, pretending to gather his notes. I carefully reached down and hooked my thumb into the leather boot and pulled it up. The next day Rhinehart called to ask me to dinner. For weeks, he did no more than hold my hand across the table, gently, as if it were a little dove. But it had begun.

I was battling a bigger fear at this point. What if Rhinehart was no longer attracted to me? Or had realized that he was unable to fall in love with me again? I knew what it was to kiss a man I liked but could never love, not because of anything he'd done, or bad timing, but just because he was unable to call it up in me. If that was how Rhinehart felt, I'd prefer not to know.

Hallie thought that theory was ridiculous. "You're thinking like a woman. Men aren't so emotionally choosy. Especially men his age. They *want* companionship and affection and sex. It distracts them from thinking about getting old and sick."

But Rhinehart was picky and changeable still, and I knew he had a great capacity for solitude. "He's like one of those animals that would just go off alone into the forest to die."

"I don't know," Hallie said. "That breaks all precedent. Maybe there's another woman in the picture. Like the ex-wife. Or someone else. This is New York. No shortage of available women."

We were crossing the field to the parking lot. The sky stretched out in front, bright and clear. Free birds swarmed like bats, settling in clumps high in the tree branches. I thought of the smiling girl in the bookstore. I thought of Laura, who'd won him from me before. Had he been out on Long Island again?

"If so, then there's nothing I can do about it," I said. "I'm just going to have to wait until he comes back. I'll have a better sense of where we stand then." But this sounded doubtful even to my ears. I worried that we'd spin in this cyclone forever, like Rodin's Paolo and Francesca in *The Gates of Hell*, always reaching but never embracing, never fulfilled.

I was ten minutes early getting to Rhinehart's, and he was already waiting by the door with his packed bags. Behind him, splayed out on the living room couch, was a green 1960s hard-backed suitcase with a textured surface that reminded me of a toilet seat cover. This was most likely the suitcase Rhinehart wanted to bring because of sentimentality or superstition, and which common sense had forced him to abandon. Instinctively, I reached out and grasped his arm. "It's so good to see you." I handed him a bag with a cup of coffee and crullers.

"You brought me breakfast. That's so thoughtful." He did a final check of the rooms, while I waited, looking around.

"Who's going to take care of your plants?" I asked him.

From the kitchen, he said, "I know, I forgot. I was going to bring them downstairs, maybe the doorman wouldn't mind. He's picking up the mail."

"I'll do it," I said. "I can get the mail, too."

Coming back into the room, he said, "Would you? It wouldn't require much. I can give you my keys. Feel free to stay whenever you like. On the days you don't want to go all the way back to Brooklyn."

My stomach felt hollow and unsettled, jouncing around in the hired car's plush backseat. I watched the clusters of buildings pass by, the washed-out terrain of early morning. The city seemed a shimmery hallucination, a paler, weaker version of itself. Next to me Rhinehart was also staring out the window, clutching his untouched breakfast. It hadn't occurred to me that he'd be nervous, and reaching across the seat, I took his hand and held it.

At JFK, the boyish-looking driver unloaded the bags from the trunk. Rhinehart had tied a red scarf around the handle of his suitcase so that it could be easily identified on the airport carousel. A small leather carry-on hung from his shoulder. That was all.

"You sure you have everything?" I asked. Fedir had gone ahead a week earlier and was meeting him at the airport on the other side. He nodded and rolled his bag through the pneumatic sliding doors. Already I felt him moving out of reach.

Standing in line, I attempted to be brave and unfeeling, to make my heart into a little stone. He had on jeans and a black sweater. After patting down his pockets, he unzipped the bag and extracted his passport, which shook slightly in his hand. I suddenly saw his sleepless, unshaven face, and it looked vulnerable to me. This wasn't like the other times I'd seen him off at the airport, when he'd been younger, more impatient. What if something happened to him there? My heart, now a wet living thing, lurched towards him. I was uncertain what I would do if I continued to stand there, so instead I went to wait by the monitors. Yards away from me, in the vast, blue-tinted airport, he looked small and helpless. Maybe, from his vantage point, I looked the same.

He joined me eventually and as we walked towards the gate he pointed to a row of chairs bolted down near the security check-in. "Let's sit."

From his bag, he pulled out a folded piece of tissue paper and handed it to me. Inside was a silver necklace with a square mirrored pendant. "It's Ukrainian. To protect you from the evil eye while I'm away." He clasped it on me and I felt the cool skin of his forearm against my neck.

"Just be careful," I said.

"It's more dangerous in New York," he said. "You know, I'd feel better if I knew you weren't fretting about me."

I tried to smile. "Enjoy the *mlyntsi*."

"*Mlyntsi!* How did you know that word?" He pulled a strand of hair from my face, letting his fingers drift down to my chin and pause there. "Have you been studying?"

"A little. I was curious."

"Enjoy your show. Keep your mind open—you don't know what it will lead to. I'll come see it as soon as I get back." He got up and began heading to the security gate. I followed.

"Wait," I said, and then stood there, breathing shallowly.

He smiled at me but looked confused.

I wanted to tell him I loved him. I didn't even care if he didn't feel the same. I wanted him to know. "I just, I just care about you so much."

I saw the old expression in his face, like the sky changing, clouds passing over the sun. He held my arms. "I'll be thinking about you, too. I won't be gone long. Take care of yourself, okay? Promise me."

He gave my arms a final squeeze before getting on the line for security. When he bent over to untie his shoes, I turned away and walked towards the escalator.

I missed Rhinehart. I missed hearing him say my name, I missed the night we'd sat in this kitchen together. I missed the way he used to cup the soles of my feet in his palms when I was about to get up off the couch and said, "These pigs don't want to go to market."

I'd never been a caretaker for someone's plants before, and he always claimed I held grievances against indoor vegetation. It was true, in my house growing up, all the plants had been outside, with the exception of a couple African violets. I brought over some clothes so that I could spend a few nights there. But his apartment was strange and vacant without him. I couldn't decide whether it was better to stay or leave.

Hallie called, and once she heard I was in Manhattan, started pressuring me to go out for cocktails. "Do something normal thirtyish women do. If I were you, I'd take the opportunity to flirt with men my own age."

On the stereo speaker was a hopeful pot of chrysanthemums. They'd gone spindly, shedding some of their spiky petals. Fall flowers, but fall seemed a long way off. "What if he decides to stay?" I'd been fighting a sinking feeling that once he was there, he'd immediately start putting down roots and not want to return.

"Why would he do that? People want to flee that country." She paused as if trying to listen through the phone to hear what was happening in the background. "I hope you're not moping. Crying into his underpants."

Once, after our breakup, I'd let myself into Rhinehart's apartment when I knew he'd be at class and spent an hour in his closet, inhaling the sweet scent of his dry-cleaned dress shirts. Later, I'd dumped his hamper out onto the bed and rolled around in the dirty laundry, smelling the cologne he wore when we went out to restaurants, his sour used socks on the mornings he'd get back into bed after a run without showering. I'd made the mistake of telling Hallie this story once when I was drunk.

She was saying to me now, "You should be trying to find someone you can procreate with. What else are we on this earth for?" This from a person who disliked children so much, she refused to baby-sit even back when that's what everyone our age did.

My other secret fear was that something would happen to Rhinehart. I had been reading a lot about the Colombia-Venezuela hostage negotiations recently. The guerrillas would kidnap someone, usually by hijacking a car that was being driven through a dangerous area, and take him or her to a remote area of the jungle. Once they had the person's papers, they would create a financial profile—family, job, assets, relative's assets—and from that they would come up with a ransom figure that was exorbitant, but feasible given the numbers for that particular person. Then they'd contact the kidnapped's family with a suggested payment plan, as well as instructions for liquidating—sell tío Pedro's car first, then abuela's farm to make payment number one. Payments were made on a regular basis and could stretch on for several years, like buying something on layaway.

"What does this have to do with Ukraine?" Hallie said. "It's not even in the same area of the world. And who do you think they're going to get this ransom from? You? Even with the exchange rate, it wouldn't be worth it."

Gradually, I began spending nights at his apartment, especially if I had to be at Marty's early the next morning. I'd been taking more photographs of Rhinehart's bed, from different angles, for the bird series that I was still obsessed with. In sketching out the idea, it still seemed to be lacking something at the compositional level, so I'd gone back to Renaissance portraiture for help.

I'd grown comfortable at the apartment and left my clothes around. I even finished off his lemon hand cream, which I liked so much I went out to get more, as well as buy a soap dish. He had the bad habit of leaving bars of soap disintegrating on windowsills and counters.

The lotion came from L'Occitane, and I suspected he'd bought it for himself, even though it didn't seem all that masculine. He could be very particular about scents and complained about Sevilla, the entire city, because of a cheap orange-scented cleanser the majority of restaurants and hotels used. As I was going through the glass doors of the store, a blond woman coming out grabbed my arm. "Terry, right? You're my husband's friend. The one that came to dinner at my house."

Laura. She had lost weight, deepening the lines in her throat and around her eyes, and I hadn't immediately recognized her.

She quickly maneuvered our initial exchange into a question of whether I'd seen him recently. The way it was phrased made it seem as if she hadn't. I wanted to be cautious. I sensed an aggressive neediness in her that was reminding me of the addicts that hung around the Catholic ministries building across from my apartment. I told her he'd gone abroad.

She pulled me from the doorway into the store, and I was hit with the scent of lavender, which now seemed ominous.

"Ukraine." So, he'd told her. "He's gotten it into his head he's an immigrant. Ha! He's only lived in New York his entire life." She freed my arm, although she kept her eyes on it. Looking at her watch, she said, "It's only one. Let me take you to lunch."

This was so intensely something I didn't want to do that I was overly apologetic in turning her down, professing shopping, then an imaginary evening meeting with a friend. My voice sounded faint and weak. "Thank you, though."

She was staring at me with those small eyes. "Come on! It's just lunch." And before I had processed it, we were out on the street and into a cab, heading uptown. I had the sensation of being shepherded along by the Mafia.

She took me to Le Cirque, which I'd always associated with wealthy out-of-towners and flagrant corporate expense accounts. The place was half-empty, and with the soaring ceilings, and gold fabric draped in a vaguely circus-tent way, and the dizzying red carpet, it seemed desperately vacant.

I was intimidated anyway, and the last thing I felt like doing was eating a hot meal. We took a table by the window, also draped in fabric, and Laura ordered a bottle of prosecco. She was much more at ease here than she'd been in her own home last December. Self-consciously, I touched the small coffee stain on the bottom of my shirt.

She was asking me how he was. I couldn't figure out the amount of contact she had with him. Far less than me, it seemed, and I hadn't had much recently. I'd missed the call from him two weeks ago, telling me he'd arrived safely. I checked my email incessantly, and even the mailbox, since I knew he preferred sending letters, but he still hadn't written. "I believe he's okay," I said.

Laura's gold bracelets clinked against the table as she leaned in to study me. Her skin had a clean, waxy pallor that I attributed to anti-aging cream. She didn't look friendly, but she didn't look particularly unfriendly either. More curious than anything, like a bird investigating a crumb on the ground.

"Forgive me for being rude," she said, "but how old are you?"

"Thirty-five."

"We met years ago, didn't we? When I was still married to Charley and you were dating Rudy? I was in my early thirties, and you must have been very young, eighteen or something like that."

"I was twenty," I confessed.

She squinted, tapping her index finger on the table. That was Rhinehart's gesture. "I remember now," she said. "Jacob Fishburn's house. He had that colonial that was like a rabbit warren, all the strange little hallways and doors—terrible architecture. I knew we had met then, Rudy always denied it."

I stiffened. I didn't want to hear what he had or hadn't said about me. I doubted she'd filter it to take my feelings into account.

"Maybe it's seeing you at my own age then that's brought it back." She smiled. "But you and I are very different people."

"Yes. We are." So different that, sitting here, I wondered at the complex psychology of one man that could find love in both these forms. My instinct was to dismiss her as the aberrancy.

"I think I may have underestimated you, though. The shy, deferential thing. You know Rudy and I aren't divorced."

This news settled coldly into my stomach. No, I didn't know that. "Rhinehart hasn't discussed your marriage or your separation with me. It's none of my business."

Laura made eye contact with the waiter. It was so subtle that until he showed up at my elbow, I'd thought she'd glanced at the door. I ordered the salmon confit, at her suggestion, and she had the lamb. Through my blouse, I fingered the mirrored necklace, directing it at her.

After passing over the menu, she switched moods, or maybe tactics. It was tiring trying to follow her—the game seemed far too complicated for the prize confession she was after. I hadn't even seen Rhinehart naked in more than a decade.

She said, "I was being a bit misleading. He did put through the papers recently. As if it does me any favors. It's not like I'll be getting a big settlement."

"Oh?" I tried to disguise my relief. So, it wasn't a lingering attachment to Laura that had been holding him back. Maybe he had wanted to officially be a free man before becoming involved with me. Although that, too, seemed unlikely. In truth, I had no idea what the hell he was thinking, besides that I made a good house-sitter.

She was laughing, I wasn't sure at what, and the sound seemed to crumble in her mouth. She'd switched to confessional, chummy. "You can't blame me for being curious. Running into you was just my good fortune. Then again, you ran into him, didn't you? In a department store. There's some symmetry to this." She finished her glass and poured us some more before the waiter could even cross the room. "You haven't bothered to set me straight about your relationship."

"That's because there isn't one. In the sense you mean."

She went on as if she hadn't heard me. "Women make such fools of themselves over men. It's as if we need to build them up to believe in them, or perhaps in ourselves. Stupid, but inborn." She put her glass down hard and said, "You know he can be a greedy man, a taker."

I was mesmerized and wondered if she were mentally ill. Or just drunk? There was a bungled trickiness to this conversation, as if traps were being laid out way in front of me so that I could neatly step around them.

The food had arrived, intricate little portions arranged vertically on a lake of sauce. I was no longer nervous and eating heartily—this was probably the most expensive lunch I'd ever been served.

I did feel the need to contradict her. Rhinehart didn't care much about money and thought it gave a false sense of security.

"It's not a *priority* for him," she corrected me, "but he's not afraid of spending it. Anyway, that wasn't what I was referring to. What he really sucks out of you is something else. Your attention. Your emotions. Your support. He does it while pretending to do nothing at all.

To be following his own star. But all the time he asks so much. More than any man I know. He ropes you in, and before you know it, you are only concerned about him, his plans, his life, and your own has slipped away."

The blood rushed to my face. I pictured my clothes spread out all over Rhinehart's bedroom. How I'd picked up a photo on his dresser three times this morning, trying to figure out who the two women in it were. I made some vague gesture, indicating my desire to leave the table. She reached out to detain me, and I said, "I don't want to be having this conversation with you. I'm not enjoying it."

She was apologetic but didn't let go of my arm right away. "My daughters tell me I go off the deep end when I start talking about him. Blame the therapy—it makes me share too much. But I didn't invite you here to bitch. Honestly. Let's talk about something else."

My pulse was still racing. It was a bad sign that his ex-wife took this opinion of him, even if she was loose in the head.

"You're a photographer, aren't you?" Laura asked.

I nodded.

"Rudy used to have one of your prints in his study. The one of the girl screaming at someone in an apartment building."

I hadn't realized Laura had known it was mine. "That's an older shot."

"I was always enchanted with it. It's emotional but it has a sense of mystery. Now that I don't have it to look at, I miss it." She cut off a sliver of the blood-red lamb. "Where have you shown?"

I fielded this quickly, figuring she hadn't seen the current exhibition. I hadn't even seen it yet. I was too sick on the night of the opening to attend, the flu or maybe some psychologically induced illness brought on by the fear of seeing my work up in public. "I have a couple of pieces in an exhibition at the Hoffman building on 33rd. Race and class in New York."

"That's so odd—I saw that show by accident. Which ones were yours?"

I was embarrassed but I described them. A teenager on the subway looking apathetically at her newborn with his heavy head of hair, crying in his stroller. The other, taken in a bar in my neighborhood, was of two big women in fancy dresses and elaborate hairdos, watching the dance floor hopefully.

Laura put her fork down. "Those were *good.* I couldn't believe they were even there. A lot of crap in that show, to be honest. I don't know who the curator was, but to do yet another photography-in-New-York thing, and to include what looked like Pratt freshman work? No wonder no one wants to fund temporary venue shows, indulging whatever garbage someone without any experience thinks is worthy of an audience . . ."

I cringed, but Laura went on eating. "I'd like to see your portfolio," she said.

I smiled faintly.

She didn't. "I'm not being coy. I mean to buy something."

"I'm not adverse to showing it, of course. I just don't think—"

"Rudy must have told you I collect art. And I love discovering younger artists. I usually go through galleries, but sometimes they're the ones contacting me to bring them someone new. This isn't personal. It's work. Do you have a card?"

I didn't want to give her one of Marty's business cards, and the ones I'd ordered for myself over the Internet were thinner stock than I expected and looked cheap, so I didn't like to give those out either.

"What's your email?" She reached into her bag and got out her BlackBerry.

I gave it to her, and she said, "I'm sending you my number now. Let's set it up." She smiled at me in a way that was almost friendly. "Maybe something productive can come out of this meeting instead of getting into a fight over my husband."

I noticed that she hadn't said "ex."

CHAPTER NINE

Maybe she's luring you there to kill you," Hallie said, looking down at the prints that were spread over Rhinehart's multicolored rugs. I'd lugged a box of them on the subway from Brooklyn several days ago, since I needed Hallie to help me decide.

After Laura called to reiterate her invitation, I had made the colossal mistake of Googling her. Her face showed up all over the place, being honored at an ArtTable luncheon, in a photo with Gloria Steinem, profile articles in *Ms.* and *Art in America*. For years she had owned a gallery in Chelsea, which she'd let go of in favor of private consulting and managing her own collection, much of which had either been loaned or given to MoMA and the Whitney, as well as to Tate Modern and several smaller institutions in Europe. Rhinehart hadn't mentioned any of this!

When I looked through my prints after, everything seemed art-school-ish, deliberately tendentious in evoking a mood. Why on earth did she want to meet? To complain about Rhinehart some more? Or was this part of an elaborate setup to humiliate me?

Hallie was not helpful. She had spent the first half-hour nosing through Rhinehart's drawers and closets, calling out whatever she found—"What are these things? They look like mini-condoms"—while I was on my knees, shuffling through the images.

"I always liked this shot," she said, looking over my shoulder. She was referring to a photograph of herself at seventeen, standing by the road to Montauk in jean cutoffs that were far too short. She had one thin hip thrust out and was pretending to hitchhike, while smoking a cigarette. The sky was big and troubled behind her. It wasn't something I included in my portfolio.

"You can have that one," I said. I flipped through contact sheets of photographs I'd taken around the city and some shadowy abstracts at a graveyard upstate. "What if she's just buying something so she can throw it away?"

"Price it too high. Then she's the idiot for wasting money."

I could feel the tension gathering underneath my skin. Except for that initial phone call, I still hadn't heard from Rhinehart, and it had been almost a month. I'd assumed he'd get in touch while he was away, although he hadn't said so. I regretted my emotional airport declaration, which had forced him into saying he'd be thinking of me, too. Maybe it had scared him off. Maybe he'd met someone. I'd read an article recently about American businessmen who went there to find wives. The women, beautiful, young, dressed in short spangled skirts, would compete ferociously for these men—men who had trouble even landing a date in the U.S. What would they do for Rhinehart, who was actually famous? I decided to take all my things back to Brooklyn. I shouldn't have been staying here.

Hallie left with a plastic folder of photographs, as if she'd been to a sale, and I sorted through and selected the ones I wanted to get reprinted. I was trying to figure out how to sequence them so my portfolio seemed cohesive. Although I'd included older work, I had little interest in anything except the most recent images. New work was like that, glimmering seductively on the horizon, until you came on it, passed it, and began focusing on something else. I was putting everything back in the box when the phone rang—the sound was assertive and proprietary. I'd always known when it was him calling. My heart started beating heavily, like a woman running in thick shoes. I was breathless when I picked up.

There was some static, an operator speaking in a foreign language, and then Rhinehart asking in English if the call went through.

I shouted, "Hello, it's me. It's Tatie." With a click the operator was gone. We were both silent and then spoke at once. He sounded tinny and distant, as if he were miniaturized. I couldn't believe the phone lines were this bad.

"How are you? Where are you? I knew it was you calling, I can always—"

"How are things? How was your show?"

"It's open. The work's up. How are you?"

The line went quiet, and I thought for a minute we'd been disconnected. "I don't seem to remember much, Tatie."

"You were so young."

"Maybe." His voice sounded far away and plaintive, I wondered if I was just a faint little wisp, too. "I expected not to in Kiev. It's post-Soviet and I'd only been there once according to Mama. But my own birth city? I did live here until I was five."

"I'm sure it will come back to you eventually. Give it time."

"You would love to be photographing here. The trees are all shaggy and puffed up, like sick birds. Which I guess isn't the most appealing image." He laughed.

"How is your cousin? And the rest of your family? What are they like?"

He hesitated, and at first I wasn't sure if he heard me, then he said, "If it wasn't for my birth certificate, I'd believe I was born in Queens. I'll tell you about it when I get home. I couldn't even express it well in the letters. My heart can't withstand it yet. You got the letters?"

"No. You sent me a letter? A real letter or email?"

"A real letter. I only use email for business. I have to go now—I'm sorry, love. That's Fedir waving to me. He's bleeding."

"Bleeding!"

"Get the tire first!" he yelled. He kissed the receiver. "Nothing, just a little fender bender. But I wanted to hear your voice so badly. Take care of yourself. I'll see you before you know it."

There was a click, and he hung up.

* * *

I got on the subway and went back to my apartment and checked my mailbox, which I hadn't done in more than a week—there were two letters. I had been assuming he would write to me at his own address, knowing I was picking up his mail.

The first was dated his second day there, although it had been mailed a couple of weeks ago, and it shone with exhilarated metaphors and hyperbole. He compared himself to a fly with a "multiprismatic view of the world." Two paragraphs later there was a reference to Dante.

From Boryspil Airport we took a paved eight-lane highway, through a forest of pencil thin birches, a true birchy copse. I was told that during the day it is filled with the melodies of songbirds. Billboards, satellite dishes, the sign "Welcome to Kiev" was even in English. The roads have wide shoulders where people and even horse carts go.

One page was devoted to describing the trains, which "ran with surgical efficiency," but which he hadn't taken. Two pages devoted to what he saw from the car window "countryside resembling Michigan" that he imagined me photographing. I was combing the letters for references to myself. There were "elderly women selling various things, like sunflower seeds, along the side of the road, and some old men dragging pickaxes," and a short meditation on his age, and his luck in having emigrated, if this would have been his fate.

I got a sense of him bounding all over the place, heartily trying to engage. But otherwise, there wasn't a lot of introspection, mostly surface description. He enclosed a photograph of himself wearing what he said was an "authentic beaver hat." It was taken at a distance of about fifteen feet. A reference: *Dostoevsky's wicked man borrowing against his salary to buy one to snub his neighbor.* He continued, *There are wild cherry and walnut trees and so much fresh air. You don't realize how deadening New York is to the senses—you must come out and see it someday, Tatie. And of course everything is colored by my emotional state—I can't wait to re-meet my cousin. When you don't have any family, it's such an intense experience.*

Over the next couple of days, more letters arrived, catching up to the Rhinehart I'd spoken to on the phone.

My dear Tatie, he began in a letter dated several days after his arrival at Lyuba's, *I'm writing you from the upstairs bedroom like Richardson's Pamela, watching the door the entire time to make sure I am not interrupted. I share this room with an old man, older than I. I'm not sure if he is related or if he works for them.*

I was foolishly overprepared, as it turned out. In addition to the American gifts, I brought a local bouquet. Even numbers of flowers are bad luck, so I counted them in the car and threw one out! My mother was an incredibly superstitious person. I don't know whether these things even mean anything to anyone anymore. Never shake hands through a doorway. Don't look babies in the eye. Sit down before a journey. Don't whistle indoors. The old man does. I really dislike the sound of whistling.

Lyuba came out to meet me and brought with her a tall thin boy, the elderly man (who shares the room), and a couple of dogs. It seemed an effort for her—she's very stout and was perspiring. Tears were streaming down her face. I was moved and recited a sentence in Ukrainian that I'd been practicing for days, which means, in short, "I have traveled many miles and waited many years for this moment and now that it's here, I am speechless, but my heart is singing." To that I added a phrase of good fortune, "May your wheat grow so thick that even a snake can't pass through it." I must have done a decent job with the accent—at any rate she began speaking to me in very rapid Ukrainian of which I understood nothing. Fedir was busy getting the bags out of the car so no translation, but the intent was welcoming.

The house is very modest, but nice, clean, two-story. Very spare inside. Just a wooden table. I was instantly mortified by my ostentatious gifts. But I brought them out anyway, in their garish wrap and ribbons. I felt conflicted, like the rich uncle who suspects everyone secretly resents him, but Lyuba was thrilled with her scarf—Hermès of all things! Although the name meant nothing to her, she kept rubbing it against her cheek and against the old man's cheek to feel how soft it was.

Everything was going wonderfully and really the comfort of being in a family again, combined with the excitement of a new place, and thoughts of my mother, was indescribable. I thought of how proud she'd be if she could see me sitting here after all these years, having reunited with her sister's child. Lyuba inquired about my trip and introduced me to her son, Lazar, who seemed to be about seventeen or so—young to be her son. I inquired about this, delicately of course—although who knows what Fedir does to my politely turned phrasing on the other end—it seems Lazar was a "surprise baby," when she was in her forties. I don't know who his father is. He doesn't seem in the picture. I'm always on the lookout for more family—it's never enough. I was also told the dogs' names, which I promptly forgot.

For dinner she served mamaliga, a traditional cornmeal and cottage cheese dish that has fried pork rinds on top. She asked me if I was Jewish, using a word I won't repeat here. It was as if a gun appeared at the table. I didn't know what to do with any of this, the question itself—did she think I'd converted?—the way it was expressed, etc.

The letter picked up again several days later. *This may not be the best time to write. Travel morale, spirits—very low. It is hard to constantly not know what's going on—I feel like someone's grandfather, half-blind, hard of hearing, who is parked in the corner of the living room and discussed. I'm also starting to be concerned that my kindness and American-sized wealth is getting taken advantage of. I'm spending much of my day fielding business proposals. Import/Export, sunflower seed oil processing, something involving maids that sounds illegal. Fedir does the translating when I can find him. These men come in as if it's a genuine social call, have a drink, take me aside and show me a business card—then the business card goes right back in the pocket. Many of these people seem to be related to Lyuba or friendly with her. The way she has scheduled these meetings, greeting the men and bringing them to see me in a back room, makes me feel like the main attraction at a whorehouse. I've tried to explain that I'm the furthest thing from a businessman, but still they persist. And there is a lot of competitive toasting here so by the middle of the afternoon, I am completely looped and have to say* do pobachennya *and go upstairs to take a nap.*

* * *

A new letter.

There is something wrong with Lyuba, and the dinner hour is very strained. Sometimes she turns her body sideways from the table, takes her bowl, and eats from her lap, so as not to face us. At dinner, I brought up my mother—how pleased she would be to see us all together. Lyuba turned to me with such a look of revulsion, I immediately accused Fedir of mangling the translation. But he was as alarmed as I was. Finally she said something that Fedir translated as "I did not know your mother," takes her bowl, and goes off. Didn't know my mother! I'm very upset.

I started a letter to him, even though I didn't have a postal address. I felt the need to tell him that nothing meets our expectations, but if he stayed on for a while I was sure the mystery would be cleared up. I filled three pages with these thoughts.

A week passed. Then another letter.

Lyuba is a hard woman to know. She's carrying a grudge that I'm attributing to my presence in the house. What is she like typically? I've seen her kick the dogs, and she berates the old man on a fairly regular basis until he cowers. He seems to be a stable hand for the pony and two goats. Fedir came up to me yesterday carrying the message that Lyuba expected me to be paying a daily rate for my room and board, which I have not been paying. I was instantly ashamed that she should think I'd been taking advantage—but a daily rate? Like at a hostel? It isn't much, the equivalent of 35 dollars a day, but that is an incredible sum here, especially for the worn mattress I have in the stable man's room. The fact that she is giving me what she thinks is an extortionist's rate is really troubling. It feels deliberate.

Perhaps she isn't my cousin. Maybe I made up the entire thing in my desire to be related to someone in the world. There are definite physical inconsistencies between us—her heavy jaw doesn't resemble any one of my mother's sisters in those photos. My mother was also very lithe. I hate to play the Hardy Boy here, but I can't find one picture of her mother, my supposed aunt, or her father in the house—it's as if they were all removed before I came. And at times I've caught her looking at me with suspicion, as if I wasn't a long-lost cousin, but a partner she suspected of double-crossing her. It's actually this look, and the extreme way she reacts to any mention of my mother, that disturbs me. She looks like she wants to spit fire. Maybe there was some falling out? More to the story than I know.

I have a sinking feeling that the entire purpose of the trip, to see these letters of my mother's, will end in failure. That's what torments me—the idea of returning to the U.S. with the mystery still hanging open. Lyuba flat-out refuses to show me the letters. She stood there in the kitchen, her arms folded over that enormous bosom that also doesn't run in the family, and shook her head emphatically no. I asked several times, reasoning, cajoling, arguing, even pleading, which anyone can decipher from an expression, even without a translator. I'm feeling, irrationally, as if she is denying me my mother, and it makes me dislike her.

I am homesick tonight, heavy-hearted, and wish we were sitting in my living room playing a game of chess and drinking bourbon. To think that I was so careful not to get involved with you before I left, as if it would distract me from this fruitless trip. I am an enormous fool. And I have gotten myself involved regardless because I miss you more than I ever thought possible. More than when we first separated.

I'm aware this is a coward's confession, shielded by distance and one-way communication, and that I'm doing it on my own time, when you would've liked to have discussed it the morning after you stayed at my apartment. You would have been understanding, but I wasn't ready for your understanding, or to talk about anything. Now that I'm feeling very far away, and torn up with disappointment, it seems time to talk.

Here's what I haven't said. It's devastating to me that my marriage failed. Before it failed I stopped writing poetry, the one thing I'd always been able to rely on, that had given a sense of structure to my life. This isn't Laura's fault, nor is it the marriage's, although I believe the marriage took the poetry in the process of eating itself.

So, although I may seem the same to you, I'm not. I'm older, my battles with Laura have left me weary, and I don't feel like I used to—

my dry spell with poetry has eroded me. I try not to linger too long on this subject as it's terrifying to remember that space from where all those words and thoughts and feelings used to emerge. Despair grows in this sort of mental activity, and in the poisonous quiet here, I feel it growing. If I have been trying to cover that hole with the dead leaves of my genealogical research, as you intimated, then I've been tragically stupid.

There is another problem and that has to do with us, and the intensity of what we generate. We have, in the past, suffered for it. You've always been more fearless, willing to leap into things, but do you remember the unhappiness? I do. I remember you crying all the time. I still feel responsible, but I don't know how I could have prevented it then or how I would now. I'm still making mistakes, leaving you standing in the airport with your heartfelt declaration in your hands.

I'd love to hear your voice, but there's no phone here. I have to imagine it, the flat way you say "door" with your old Eastern accent. My artist.

He'd included a post office address I could write in care of, and I immediately started a response, and then another, and then I rewrote it, but my letter always became too long, and too seeped in memory, with convoluted psychological rationales. I kept finding ways to deny my own suffering, to provide a safe space in which to coax him out of his resistance, and this seemed a very bad way to go. I was responding to the intimacy of his confession. But the more times I read the letter over in its entirety, the more it seemed not a love note but an extension of the general confusion I'd been on the receiving end of in New York. Maybe he was right. Maybe our problem wasn't so easily solved.

I finally mailed a short response saying we should wait until he got back to discuss it. As it was, our letters crossed paths. He had sent me another, which arrived two days later. It began by filling me in on Lyuba, who had stopped making eye contact with him a couple of weeks before and now couldn't stand to be in the same room with him. He would come in, she would exit. Even the business proposals had stopped. *I've been tempted to leave but stubbornness is keeping me here. That and I've struck up a real friendship with Lazar, Lyuba's son, who has been advising me about his mother. He's very shy, but his*

English is impeccable, and once I started encouraging him, he was excited to use it. He's become my de facto translator and intermediary, and although I don't see much improvement in relations with Lyuba, he has managed to sneak out one of my mother's letters. It's her, Tatie! It's her signature. I feel as if she has risen up, alive again, in front of me. It's in Ukrainian, but Lazar did a rough on-the-spot translation for me—she's describing our apartment in New York! Everything, things I had forgotten, the playground around the corner with a fountain shaped like an elephant. I can't tell you how exciting this is. He is going to get them all for me—there are about twelve, I believe—do the translations and send them. Finally I feel at peace. Finally I can come home. My flight is set for September 8, 3:10 p.m. arrival at JFK.

I searched the letter again for any mention of us, but there was none. It was as if the topic had never come up. I was so frustrated, I wanted to cry. I knew then that I had reached my own internal limit. I waited two days, the unspoken words burning in my throat. Then I sent him an email, because, in a sense, this was business. It said:

> I need to know whether you are interested in a relationship with me. I'm going to feel about you the way I do, regardless, and we will always be connected, but I need someone who wants me as badly as I want him and is able to go there with me. By now you're aware if you're capable of this, or if you even want it, and you need to let me know one way or the other. Before you get on that plane. T.

I'd been shot through with adrenaline writing it, and after I sent it, I felt calmer than I had in months. Twenty-four hours passed, during which I could hear him thinking. Then, an email. I steeled myself and opened it.

> Tatie, I think it's time for us again. I will see you at the airport. —R.R.

CHAPTER TEN

After a lot of stalling on my part, and her persistent emails "checking in," I had set a date for the last week of August to meet Laura at her SoHo apartment, which she'd bought after selling the Long Island house, and show her my portfolio. Now I powerfully wanted to cancel, and I wavered, but in the end found myself standing in front of a large white building on Prince Street, at the appointed time, ringing her buzzer.

None of the Great Neck furniture seemed to have migrated with her to this new apartment, which had white carpets and white walls and delicate glass bulbs that hung from the ceiling. It was as if an entirely different person lived here, and yet there was a polished, faithful adherence to style that made me suspect she'd used a decorator, and the same one.

In the living room were several intimidating modernist paintings. One was particularly arresting, sleeping women were sewn into the canvas, the loose threads dangled, obscuring the scene. I got up closer—the women weren't sleeping, but engaging in oral sex.

Behind me, Laura said, "Beautiful, isn't it? That's Ghada Amer. I was lucky to pick it up years ago. Her work tends to be a little one-note—anything commenting on the Muslims is very heavy-handed—standing in front of the Eiffel Tower with a burkha on, gimme me a break. But her work appreciated well, and I just love that canvas."

She directed me to the sofa, low-backed with white cushions, and asked if I'd like a glass of wine. What I really wanted was tea, but I accepted the wine anyway, and when she returned, we opened my portfolio.

Looking over Laura's shoulder, I saw an impressive, professional body of work. I had included some older photographs and made prints from a few of the best images in the bird series, which I was still completing. It had taken much longer than I'd projected to create the composites—it was painstaking work compared to shooting. I'd been spending nights at the digital lab, slowly going through the entire process of cleaning the negatives with compressed air and then mounting and carefully feeding them into the drum scanner, which looked like a little tower. They gave me a good rate and so I'd stayed on and used their computers to layer the images in Photoshop. One of the professional retouchers, Big Mike, stopped by occasionally to give me advice on the color balance. Some of the images were eerie, the bedroom looked like a forest on a night with a full moon, the birds more at home there than I was. I looked as frightened as I had been in my childhood nightmare.

Laura flipped through the book, hesitating momentarily on a photo of Chechna looking weak-eyed and incredulous at someone out of the frame. "I know her," Laura said, tapping the plastic with her nail. I had debated not including photographs that could be linked to him, but a stubborn sense of artistic integrity prevented me. Rhinehart. I wanted not to think about him while in Laura's house, to remain professional—but in the moment before repressing the thought, I felt an excited shiver of anticipation run through my stomach. He would be home in less than two weeks.

Lingering over the images taken in his bedroom, she said, "These remind me of one of Tolkien's watercolors. A black wing emerging from a closet—it was a nightmare of his. They're very good, but it seems as if the series isn't fully worked out yet."

"It's not. I'm still playing with the progression of it."

"I wouldn't want to break it up anyway—it has the potential to make an ambitious show."

I tried to suppress my exhilaration with a serious look.

"These shots are interesting." She was referring to a series of black-and-white photos I'd taken when I'd first arrived in New York that I'd recently reworked at the lab, digitally removing the focal point. The car everyone was pointing to or one person in a conversation. "They remind me of Páez and Consuegra's work. They did a series of storage facilities around Brooklyn, which were whited-out. It was a commentary on the American habit of hiding personal belongings in public space. I should have bought up some of that work when I had my chance."

We had reached the end of my portfolio, and it didn't seem as if she was interested in anything. She pulled the contact sheets out of the sleeve.

"That stuff's really new," I said. "It's not finished." I'd been photographing a lot recently. I needed to get rid of some of the nervous energy I was storing, anticipating Rhinehart's arrival. More shots of New York. A photograph of a woman my age, linking arms with her mother in Central Park, stridently trying to explain something to her. Children hyperactive from neglect, crawling over the seats on the subway and facing out the window into the dark tunnel. They were all active scenes, scenes of impatience.

Laura made a dismissive motion with her fingers. "Now this is good stuff. More refined than the older work but not too slick. It's still got that odd edginess to it. You have more confidence here, I can tell." She brought the sheets over to a drafting table that stood inches from the dizzying floor-to-ceiling window and held up a red marker. "You mind?"

"Go ahead."

Squinting at the page, she circled three images: two were black-and-whites—the children on the subway and a woman crying in Tompkins Square Park. The other was a color image of a couple fighting outside a Senegalese restaurant in Washington Heights. "Can you make me prints of these? Large, like thirty by forty. Or even larger. The way you are technically, I can tell they'll work. I'd like to buy them. On a limited edition of no more than five. I'm sure that will determine the price."

Before I had come, I had asked around to see what I should charge. I had researched prices based on the photographer's name, the number in the edition, and the print size. I was still incredibly uncertain. I quickly calculated printing costs. She was looking at me expectantly and I was tempted to ask her what she felt she should pay if I wasn't convinced she'd lose respect for me. "I have them priced at two thousand each, framed."

"I'll give you thirty-two hundred for all three, unframed."

I was suddenly irritated, being low-balled. "For a limited run, I can't let them go for less than forty-five hundred."

"Okay." She put on the dark-framed glasses that hung around her neck and wrote a check. Tearing it off and handing it to me, she smiled. "I would have gone up higher, but as one of your first collectors, I expect a hefty discount." She stood up. "You should really finish that surrealist series with the birds. I will kick myself later for not getting it at basement price."

I was thrilled with the entire swift, clean transaction, and the money, by far the most I'd ever made off my own work, and Hallie said, "That's great, but keep smart. She wouldn't have bought them if she didn't think she was getting something important. I know you—you think people who have money are better than you."

Was she referring to herself, growing up? Frequently when Hallie made these confident assessments about me, she was close enough to the truth to fool me at first with what seemed like a brilliant insight.

We'd met on the East Side after her salon appointment to go have lunch. I insisted on walking since it wasn't too brutally hot a day. I didn't feel like being cooped up in a cab.

"I actually feel sorry for Laura," I said.

"Why? She's a shark."

"I don't know. There was just something a little sad about her, alone in that lavish apartment way above the street." Her life with Rhinehart had ended and mine was beginning again, and for a moment, sitting there, I wanted to apologize to her—my former rival.

Hallie had turned bright red. "It's because she's divorced, you think that."

"Not just because she's divorced." Hallie knew Rhinehart was returning soon, but I hadn't told her about his email. I didn't want her in there, analyzing, spoiling it.

"Anyway, this is probably the last I'll see of Laura," I said. "I'm pleased she thought the work was good, if nothing else. Maybe it will lead to something. Maybe not—you know New York."

"You seem awfully blasé about this all of sudden." I sensed her on the verge of questioning me about Rhinehart, so I redirected the discussion to Adán. She hadn't mentioned her adulterous suspicions in months.

"It's because I can't find anything. I keep checking his credit cards, email account, cell phone—nothing. Don't give me that look."

I disapproved of spying. I didn't like the rush Hallie got off of it, like a hit of coke. Even if, as she claimed, it enabled her to trust him again.

"The important thing is that I've found a Buddhist practice I like. My calm state is influencing my environment in a positive way. At home and here." She gestured with a Vanna White sweep of the arm to indicate all of East 28th, the honking traffic, harried pedestrians, storefronts of handbags, and a garbage can.

At one time she'd been into mysticism, had studied metaphysics and Reiki and borrowed heavily from the Kabbalah, blending these with her own ideas. In her definition of the afterlife, souls, in a cosmic lottery, were seeded out into other living forms postmortem. It was a brand of reincarnation that was more wily and unpredictable than most Buddhist beliefs. You didn't move steadily up the ranks from mineral to human, you could jump around—man to rock to horse. Rhinehart loved discussing this as well, and I remembered an entire afternoon at a sidewalk café with the two of them guessing what type of people various passing dogs and children were in previous lifetimes. I was uncomfortable, as I couldn't tell how much of the discussion was meant to be in jest. They had gotten into a heated argument over a stocky dachshund who had failed to make eye contact with Hallie. She had called the dog a pickpocket, while Rhinehart had claimed the dog's "deep, suffering eyes show he's a survivor of some national tragedy."

Her new Buddhist practice was much more structured, chanting twice a day to develop compassion and to open herself up to the rhythm of events. God's plans, I assumed, but Hallie used the word "universe."

"That's wonderful," I said, genuinely pleased. I had a lot of extra pleasure to spare lately. It was almost embarrassing how upbeat I was. "You do seem happier," I said. "And you look great."

After lunch, I was anxious to leave her so that I could think about Rhinehart undisturbed. As the 4 train train pulled into Borough Hall, I was thinking about sex. What would it be like now? What would his body be like? His flat, sensitive nipples, the erotically charged place below his jaw line, more so on the right side than the left. The thick head of his penis, which turned an alarmed red when he became excited. At one time, he'd known a lot of technique, and kept his sexual books in the bathroom next to the medical texts.

I remembered what it felt like to be lying in bed naked and hopeful. I was always hopeful that Rhinehart and I would have sex. It was the time when I felt us most alone together, all his focus on me. For a period he was studying tantra and the channeling of energy. He'd lay a warm hand on top of my inner thigh. "Now concentrate all your energy here. Every molecule." I felt a rush of sexual heat in my lower abdomen, maybe because he was using that deep voice I associated with lovemaking. He moved his hand to my wrist. I turned over to embrace him, and he said in that maddeningly low voice, "Concentrate on the forearm. Focus all your energy there like a laser beam."

I did feel a shimmying under the skin, which was increasing. I craned my neck up and kissed him under the chin. It was like kissing the statue of the college founder that stood outside my English classroom. With clinical precision he moved the hand to a spot underneath my left shoulder blade. He pressed it with the upper phalanges of his three middle fingers. "Now here. What does that feel like?"

I tried to focus but all I could feel was the wetness between my legs. I suspected this lesson was meant to tease me. Sometimes he would do that. "But I get turned on when you touch me here." I moved his hand to my breast, and then slipped it down between my legs. "That gets me wet."

"Not so fast. You can train your body to have an orgasm when you're touched anywhere." He pressed the back of my neck.

I thought of the part in *Sleepers* when they get in the orgasmatron. I started to tell him this—it was Rhinehart who had introduced me to Woody Allen—which made me start laughing, until finally he gave up on me, and we went at it the typical way. For me, that alone was almost too much fun, an overwhelming series of moods and complex positions, directions, rump slapping, and shouted encouragements. The mossy smells of semen and sweat. And sometimes, I would go somewhere else in my mind, be teleported to a modish living room in London, to the back of a galloping stallion with glistening flanks, then I was the stallion. Afterwards I lay on my back, my breasts sloping to the sides, and smoked a Camel Light, dazed with visions of myself as a great artist. Sunlight on the grass, a glass-walled studio by a river. All mine.

CHAPTER ELEVEN

Monday. I was waiting for Rhinehart outside Customs, empty-handed, without even a purse, my fists thrust in my pockets.

In the swarm of people rushing through the doors I saw him before he saw me—he was in the same jeans he'd left in but he was tan, leaner, unshaven, as if he had spent months trekking across difficult country. He was searching the faces around him, cautiously smiling, and I saw the deep creases under his eyes that appeared when he was overtired. I thought, "how handsome he is," and went up to him, and before he could focus on me, kissed him on the mouth. He took my face in both his hands and said, "Here you are." He filled the entire frame, and behind him, distantly, I heard the sounds of the airport, rattling baggage carts and the squeal of taxi brakes, announcements.

He was smiling. "I'm so glad you came."

"I emailed you to say I would." I put my arm around his waist, and we walked through the sliding glass doors to the car.

"Yes, but it was so short. I wasn't sure if you'd change your mind. I became less certain the longer the flight was in the air. I tried to call you during the layover, but I couldn't reach you."

"You did?" I looked up at him. "I think I like being the mysterious one."

"It's agony putting your feelings out there. I checked my email more in the last two weeks than I have all year."

I laughed and he kissed me again. "We're in for it now, aren't we?"

"Yes," I said. "But we're ready."

I thought I remembered what it had been like to have sex with Rhinehart but I'd gotten everything rearranged. There had been other men in the way, and I had been different back then, inexperienced and shy. Before Rhinehart, there'd been college boys, still in their teens, with awkward, overly wet or hard-lipped ways of kissing. One used to get so excited during sex, it was if he were pumping away on a swing, trying to lift off into the air without me, his head buried in the pillow next to my ear.

Perhaps I had changed. With Lawrence I was always dominant, using tricks Rhinehart had most likely taught me, and which I later incorporated into my routine. How to pulsate the tongue when giving a blow job, or to make a C-curve with my spine while I was on top, so I caught the head of his penis on a ring of slipping muscle, and with an ecstatic squeeze, released it.

But Rhinehart was still the one in control here, although it seemed for a while we were competing until I yielded. His focus, his warm grip on my wrists, turning me over, leading me. How quiet he was, only the sound of his concentration, his breathing. And I was cut loose of any responsibility, free to swim around near the ocean floor. Because he was new to me again, I was watching him, my eyes as big as dinner plates, he said. He had caught me looking and was smiling. His body was different, but not in the way I expected—he just seemed larger, a more solid presence against me. But I didn't come. Even as I felt him searching his memory for the way to angle me, slightly to the right, hands lifting my pelvis to hit the G-spot. Still I didn't. On some level I was holding back.

He was languid and serene afterwards, looking over at me. I was high off the entire experience, as if everything in me had been knocked loose, and in a disconnected jumble of talk, I was rattling on about all that had occurred during the months he'd been away—the show, the dirty walls, finally going to see it, people peering at my piece, overheard comments, tangling that up with future photography ideas, circling back to Hallie and her Buddhism, my own ideas about God, rambling, rambling, but still aware, skirting around the subject of Laura and my meetings with her. I felt, during this stream of talk, an enormous freedom, as if I were running around naked with the sprinkler on.

The next day I was up early. As I started to get out of bed he threw his warm body over mine, while pretending to be asleep. Every time he'd relax into real sleep, I'd start to disentangle myself, and he'd tighten his grip. One eye open.

I struggled, giggling. "I have to go downtown and meet the retoucher on some prints I'm getting done." I would usually do the retouching myself, but I wasn't as good as a professional, and these were Laura's images—I wanted them to be perfect. Once I'd made the break from the seductive warmth of the bed, I was eager to be out in the bright fall morning, to complete the task, be done with it.

When I got out of the shower, he was sitting up, his arms folded behind his head, smiling contentedly like some sort of prince. I laughed. Everything struck me as funny this morning.

"Don't you have any work to do today?" I said.

"No one knows I'm back in town except you. They think I'm returning next week. It's like a holiday. Let's walk in the park together."

We agreed to meet at 6:30 at Amy's Bread on Ninth and 46th, where he would be having coffee and reading, and I left, as if flung out into the day. The September sun splashing across the sidewalk, my cotton dress and clinking bracelets, the roar of the bus pulling up—all of this made me happy. The world seemed plastered with my happiness.

The retoucher, Evelyn, worked out of a spare Ikea-furnished office that she shared with her girlfriend, a graphic designer. We had made drum scans of the images; she had already dropped them into Photoshop and was finishing cleaning up the dust and scratches when I arrived. We worked on the two black-and-whites first, adjusting so I was privy to everything. Every day, same time, he'd hold up a sign asking if she wanted to meet by the pay phone. This went on for weeks. The girl—she was probably thirteen or fourteen, a latchkey kid, her dad worked sanitation for the city—she was inviting her friends over to taunt him, and they must have been holding up messages, too. I saw the guy scribble out what he wrote and replace it with 'Why?' in big letters.

"I didn't want to get involved, but things were escalating and I was worried about the girl, so I finally called the cops to see if they could clear out that building. They laughed. No one would come into the neighborhood for something like that. I called again when I saw the guy remove his pants. I suspect the girls were egging him on. She was a scrawny kid, had this long blond hair that always looked unwashed. I used to see her smoking cigarettes behind the building in that hunched-over self-conscious way. Eventually her old man found out. Someone must have tipped him off—I doubt the girl said anything. But he went over there one afternoon with some of his buddies and beat the shit out of the guy. I never saw him after that."

"Wow. That's really fucked up."

"I feel sorry for the girl—this was what she had for fun. Laura grew up like that, in the projects around Coney Island."

"Laura?"

"Until she was fifteen. Then she moved out to the suburbs to live with her grandmother. She had similar stories, guys hanging around. Most people think I'm crazy, but I believe a lot of them were harmless, really. Alcoholics or just down on their luck."

I was frozen, wondering if now was the time to reveal I'd seen her. I hesitated and the moment passed.

With the construction and pedestrian detours, it took us a while to get to the park. We arrived as the street lamps were coming on. Above us, the sky was gathering all the light from between the trees. Rhinehart held my hand, and we took the path to the restaurant that overlooked the pond, a chain of small white lightbulbs glowed in the distance, marking the destination. I pictured us as we must have looked from above, two dark little figures winding our way through a the gradation and adding a little grain; I wanted her to bring up tl contrast on the subway shot. The image of the couple outside tl restaurant took longer, as she had to balance the color. I was lookir for a more heightened, almost surreal look, and was uncertain ho tight I wanted to bring in the crop. We spent over an hour playin with it, and in the end I left a lot of visual material around the coupl so that they seemed, even in the private world of their emotions, t be at the mercy of their environment. I was lost in the images mos of the day, although occasionally I'd glance up at the clock, sunligh gathering in my chest.

I was a few minutes late meeting Rhinehart, who was standing outside the café, waiting for me. He handed me a cup of coffee, and we walked up Ninth Avenue against traffic, the late day sun slanting along the buildings. I was watching him out of the corner of my eye—his entire body was infused with mystery. The tailored dark blue shirt he had on that I thought made him look like an intellectual. His rectangular black-rimmed glasses. He'd shaved and been to his stylist, and his white hair was back in its choppy cut. His New York self. Except he had the fascination of a tourist, and we kept stopping so that he could look into the windows of the thrift shop with its dusty clutter of religious icons, or a ground-floor apartment where an overweight man was watching TV, or an English/Spanish insurance company whose rattan chairs and orange-flowered cushions reminded me of the genealogist's.

We passed a butcher and Rhinehart read "pig's knuckles" out loud.

"You act as if you've never been on this street before."

"Things seem different when you go away and come back."

He took my hand, content, and gestured to the apartment on 52nd where he'd lived in the 1980s, when Hell's Kitchen was a rough neighborhood. "Across the air shaft, there was an abandoned building with squatters, one of whom was trying to communicate with the teenage girl who lived on the floor below me. I was around in the afternoons, nest of black leaves. We took a table on the water, I pulled on a light sweater, and Rhinehart ordered a bottle of wine.

I was dying to know what happened in Ukraine, but Rhinehart wanted to hear about me first. We were halfway through dinner when he began talking about it, and then he started by telling me about Fedir, whose mother and wife lived two towns over from Lyuba, and who were constantly feuding, jealous of each other. Fedir had to be peacemaker. "He's a very mild-mannered person and refused to get involved. Instead he would drink heavily. He gets that hazy unfocused look that some drunks get. Even when he was sober, though, he was a terrible driver. We had a black Lada, a little two-door. From a distance, I'd see him coming, it looked like a tick on the countryside. He crashed it twice."

"Jesus. You should have brought someone else."

"No, no, I was happy he was there. He's a very loyal man. He seemed to take Lyuba's behavior personally and bought me locks for my suitcase. He didn't trust her after her request for rent money."

"It's terrible that someone you hardly know had to protect you from your own cousin."

"Lyuba's not my cousin."

I felt a surge of vindication. "I knew there was something off about this! She's not even related to you, is she?"

He took a knowing sip from his glass. "She's my sister."

"Your sister!" I couldn't envision Rhinehart with a sibling. "Why didn't your mother ever say anything?"

"Lyuba wasn't my mother's child. She's my father's daughter. My half-sister." He was frowning. "I have a feeling that when my father found out he wasn't going to be able to join us in the U.S., he started another family with his childhood sweetheart, Marta, who was Lyuba's mother. It's unclear. And it's upsetting. My mother would have been devastated if she'd known. She kept holding out for him to join us and then he died. My poor mother!"

"So those letters your mother wrote weren't addressed to Marta, then. They were to your father!"

"Not all of them. Marta was evidently a friend of hers, so she was writing to both of them separately. My poor mother!" he said again. "To get duped like that."

I wasn't entirely convinced that Rhinehart's mother hadn't known her husband had taken up with Marta. Someone, surely, would have tipped her off. "Where is your information coming from? Have you read her letters?"

"No, Lazar is having trouble getting his hands on them. Lyuba rehid them after she noticed one missing. But Lazar and I have begun piecing it together from fragments Lyuba has told him about her own past, and what my mother had told me. Finally things are beginning to connect! Of course, Lyuba was upset! She was *jealous*—threatened by my father's rightful family. I still don't know how he could have done it, knowing we were waiting for him."

There were pieces floating around that *I* couldn't connect, and I had a feeling that Rhinehart, with all his emotionalism, was drawing the wrong conclusions. "I thought Lyuba was older than you. Remember that story with the chickens and the tea leaves? How could she have been born *after* you then, at least six years after—when you were in the U.S.?"

I sensed resistance from Rhinehart, as if he wanted to attach himself to whatever version of events he and Lazar had already cooked up. The swelling of affection and enthusiasm in his voice reminded me of other impulsive heart-based decisions he'd made in the past. A lot of good Genealogist Gerald did with his mystery books and thick glasses.

"Perhaps Lyuba fabricated that story or it was something that had been told to her. We'll know for sure when the letters are translated," he said. He put his hand around my wrist, lightly exploring the bones with his fingers. We sat listening to the hollow sound of the water lapping against the pay boats, the rustling leaves, the scraping of chairs. Distant music. I was mesmerized by the feel of his fingers, until he took his hand away and signaled to the waiter for the check. "Let's go back to bed," he told me.

* * *

We stayed in that bed for three days, leaving it only briefly to find food or a shower. Every time it was me that left, Rhinehart would wish me a "speedy return."

On the second day, even if he was still supposedly in Ukraine, Rhinehart's cell phone began to ring. He silenced it. It rang again. He handed it to me, asking me to shut it off. "Here is where I need to be until we decide otherwise."

From the angle of the bed I saw part of a red building, one window with an air-conditioning unit, and a very small piece of sky, through which, sometimes, a cloud would move. This was "my view." On the other side of the bed, he had his, and we lay back to back and described what we saw. Leaning over the sill, I spoke about the people below, heading in the direction of the park, who they were and where they were going and how they were feeling that day.

Time became a liquid thing, and sleeping and waking and lovemaking less distinguishable, and I thought of those long couches in Ottoman-era homes, where people lounged and conversed and dozed. I knew afternoon by the pattern of sun on the headboard, the richness of its color. That triangle of light, the sheet grazing my bare back, Rhinehart looking at me, as if his entire self was concentrated into the pinprick of his gaze. Light fell across my toes. His eyes half-shut, he said, "There is lovemaking that feels as if it's doing tremendous good for everyone."

We talked. We sat up in bed, eating Malaysian delivery out of cartons. I was reminiscing about my first years in my college town, how I used to walk everywhere, and in every other house someone I knew lived, and I could drop in to have coffee or pancakes or to smoke weed and play Yahtzee on a cold winter afternoon, and then walk home, a sheen on the snow like glass, the pale sun hiding behind the trees. That time now seemed irrecoverable to me, all its pleasures and gratifications bound up with my younger self—also gone. I had loved that town, loved being a student, sitting in an overheated classroom or lying out on the lawn in front, gossiping, watching the guys playing hacky sack. I thought about teaching, once I had done enough shows to get hired at a university, but wondered if I would find standing in front of the classroom as pleasurable as sitting in the back, daydreaming about the night before.

"Do you ever miss teaching?" I asked Rhinehart. I was cross-legged, naked, facing him, clicking the chopsticks together, and looking out at a sand-colored building, the multiple black-rimmed rectangles of glass that constituted his view.

His gaze had wandered down between my legs but now he was eyeing me, trying to ascertain where I was going with this. "Sometimes. I enjoyed it, even when I was stomping around like a lunatic to try and engage them. Like Ezra Pound. You know it was capitalism that drove him mad."

"I'm sure it had nothing to do with that cage in Italy he was locked up in."

"He was a raving fascist before then. Hemingway claimed he was a stand-up fellow, if you trust Papa's ability to judge character. He mostly liked people who flattered him. At any rate, I was always very conflicted about Pound. I found him difficult to teach, but at his best, he could be a brilliant poet."

"That's all you miss? The difficulty teaching Pound?"

"Not only. I miss the environment, too. Especially the end of the semester. I enjoyed seeing the library with so many bodies camped out in it. All that thinking and whispering and small movements and the sour smell of unwashed students sneaking bags of chips under their books. How they'd be sleeping across the chairs. Sometimes even under the tables."

"I never really used the library." I couldn't remember where I studied, actually. It wasn't in the dorm, with Hallie constantly bugging me and friends stopping in every two minutes.

"What a serious-looking girl you were. Not studious looking, exactly. Just serious. Serious about the world."

"Do you remember the class I took of yours? The spring semester? That I was forced to audit."

"Of course I do. You sat in the front row."

"I wasn't always up front. A lot of times I was in the back."

"You changed seats midway through the semester to have a better view of anyone I might want to date." Rhinehart was smiling. "Sometimes when I look at you, I see that young woman with something stuck in her hair from creeping around the yard, bursting into my study to accuse me of cheating."

"With Natasha. Were you sleeping with her? I was never entirely convinced you told me the truth back then."

"No, no—you invented that. I wasn't interested in students. They were at a completely different stage of their lives, so sheltered and self-concerned. They didn't even remind me of myself at that age. The kids I was similar to were the ones working in the dining hall. Especially one girl, who tried to dress up her uniform with hoop earrings and bracelets. It's so hard to work for people your own age. She was always alone. Used to eat her free sandwich at a table by herself. I tried to slip her a couple of bucks but she wouldn't take it. She was an honest girl." He smiled. "Not that I wanted to date her."

I didn't know who Rhinehart was talking about. I didn't remember anyone who worked at the dining hall. "But you were interested in me."

"Who knows where you came from with your old-lady soul—an aberrancy. It's remarkable that you and I had a relationship. If you remember, I resisted for a long time. I wasn't comfortable with the idea of myself as one of those men."

"You were even resistant to get involved recently," I said.

"Until I received an ultimatum. I don't think you've ever spoken to me like that before. I sort of liked it."

"I'd had enough of the confusion."

"I know and I'm sorry. But I would have come back to you anyway. I missed you so much in Ukraine. I was ready to take the risk."

"So it wasn't until Ukraine that you discovered you wanted a relationship with me?"

He smiled. "No, it was months before."

"At Chechna's, even? Or that night that I came for dinner, and you pushed me off you? You wanted one then?"

"I didn't push you off—I was trying to slow things down. You were very quick to take offense. That night could have gone differently."

I thought about this. "No. I could sense you were holding back. But why? If you knew you wanted to be with me?"

"Tatie, you think you're the only one who has fear?"

Later that night, lying wrapped around each other like cats for warmth, I asked Rhinehart to talk to me about poetry. He was quiet for so long, I said, "Or your other writing. The essay you're doing about the older workforce in Ukraine." The topic had shifted slightly after he'd conducted a series of interviews during his trip.

"That type of writing is different from poetry. There are auxiliary materials to support you, you rev the engine, and you begin. Once you've started, you can always return to the material to read it over and get more ideas."

"What is poetry like?"

He rolled away from me, onto his back, considering. "Otherworldly. A poem is a burst, an orgasm—unexpected and closed. It happens, you rework it or you don't, and that's it."

I thought about photography and that indescribable spiritual feeling that came over me, tracking a vision that had the power to crack the world open like a nut, light streaming from its center. All these experiences, falling in love, making photographs, experiencing God, grouped together for me under the same heading, and were equally elusive, as if I would need an entire lifetime to hunt them down.

Outside my window the moon had moved to skulk over the top of the building. Rhinehart said, "I stopped writing well after the Pulitzer. I spent two years furiously composing, only to throw most of it away, then more time sitting blankly, looking at the wall, wondering what the point of anything was. That feeling grew into a creeping fear that grew into aversion."

"Did Laura know how you felt?" I asked carefully.

He paused. "Some. We didn't talk about things like that. She had her gallery and her foundations and I had my work with the NEA, and we were constantly socializing. Poets need solitude and self-governance and downtime to think. At first I didn't have it, and then I didn't want it. The network of friends and parties started to feel more rewarding than struggling alone, staring into a gaping cave."

I'd never heard him talk this way about poetry, and felt myself resisting the deflated voice he was using. "Did it even bother you that much back then? If it was so gradual, and you were socializing so much? Did you think you'd pick it up again later when you had more time?"

"No. And it wasn't gradual. The day I stopped writing was a Wednesday. I was lying on the study couch at the house in Great Neck, waiting for inspiration. At the end of the day, it came down to this, this waiting, except this time there was nothing there. Nothing. No energy even. It was the feeling you have when someone you love has left, and you know they won't return. I had that feeling, so I stopped. Stopping something is much easier than anyone thinks. It's the struggle before you give it up that's difficult." He rolled over to me again and was tracing the line of my hip where it met the crease of my leg. "The funny thing is that writing always came easy for me, almost too easy. Especially that time when we were together, the words raced forth, so fast and uncontrolled—it felt as if I were constantly saddling steeds."

"And now? Are you writing anything?"

"Scratchings, scribblings, but nothing of substance. No."

I wanted to convince him that it would come back, but what did I know? At thirty-five, he had already published three books and was known internationally. Twenty years from now, colleges would still be teaching his poems—there would be dissertations written on him, biographies. Odds were I would never be half as successful. But I still had the illusion of youth and young dreams, strong ambitious visions I'd yet to realize. And I was shooting. The future, for me, seemed limitless.

He said, "It would take a cataclysmic event to bring it back. Or maybe poetry's return would be the cataclysmic event. What I write, if I ever do again, will have no resemblance to what I've written before." He smiled valiantly, either for my sake or to punctuate the optimism of his statement. "I hope it's just rearranging itself in my subconscious somewhere. It feels that way, especially recently. It feels as if now would be the right time for its return."

He began kissing me behind the ear, which sent shivers down my neck, and I made my body flat and pulled him on top of me, tangling my legs up in his, longing to have him inside of me, to transfer some of this youthful ambition that felt, at times, like such a burden.

On the morning of the third day, Rhinehart and I woke up together, and after we made love, we began talking about outside things, restaurants and films and my photo studio, and he was resting his hand on my face, and smiling at me in a kind but somewhat distracted way, and I knew the time had come for us to get up. Rhinehart left the bed first to take a shower. I lay there, watching the bathroom door, my entire body curved in his direction as if with some heliotropic need. When I finally stood, weak-legged, and began to dress, I was thinking about how illogical, supreme attachments could form from the eruption of such bliss. And how crazed the craving to return to that place could make you, if you weren't careful.

CHAPTER TWELVE

In the quickly darkening evenings of late October, I would walk with my camera, hoping to capture something. If I got out early enough, I could see the light fade against the buildings. The street lamps came on at five o'clock. These were usually my hours alone, in between work and my evenings with Rhinehart, cooking dinner, or going to see a film down at the Angelika, or jazz farther uptown if one of his friends was playing. Turning the familiar corner of his block, I felt the old rush of pleasure, anticipating our night together.

He heard me come in, and called out, "How was it?" I said that this time of year made the city look orphaned.

He quoted Emerson. "Nature wears the colors of the spirit."

"But I'm not feeling orphaned. I'm happy." Although just then I had been thinking about my Brooklyn apartment. I'd only been back there a few times in the past month, mainly to pick up the mail or retrieve something, and I would need to go there tomorrow to look through my closet and see what I had for cocktail attire.

Laura had called me this morning—I hadn't heard from her since delivering the prints, which she had pronounced "magnificent." She was inviting me to a feminist art event being held at MoMA. The Guerrilla Girls were speaking. "It's more of a monthly networking thing for artists and curators, but newcomers are welcome as long as they have something to bring to the table. Imagine Naomi Wolf throwing a party, and you'll get the picture. It'll be good for you. Your generation is so decentralized. And I can introduce you to some curators. Those photographs of yours need a wider audience than I can give them in my foyer." I didn't even hesitate before saying I would be there.

Rhinehart was in the living room. He had set up a folding card table with scarred legs, the one he'd used when learning how to play bridge for an article he'd been writing. I sat down on the stool next to it. "Why's this out?"

He was rifling through a stack of pictures from the trip, a mixture of ones I had and hadn't seen. There were close-ups of Lazar, who I'd originally envisioned as an awkward-looking teenager, someone out of a comic strip, with jug ears, acne, and a flop of black hair over his face. But he was actually a good-looking young man with thin, defined features and dark intelligent brows. His lips were parted, as if Rhinehart had caught him in the middle of speech. "Do you have another picture? One that's clearer? What's this black spot?"

He handed me several others. Lazar on the side of the road. Lazar near an ox cart. Lazar in front of a cottage. Shot after shot was of Lazar. The boy was very tall. In each he stood by himself, arms hanging limply from the sockets, waiting to be photographed. There was something very confident and slightly sexual about his gaze, which was at odds with the self-conscious impression his body made. They were magnetic, those eyes with their heavy brows. On the distance shots, you couldn't see it, but up close—there it was. Rhinehart was staring at the one of Lazar with the cart, taken from at least six feet away. "He has those big, feeling eyes. And he tilts his head exactly like I do."

There were very few photos of Lyuba. In the clearest one, she stood with one hand on her lower back, squinting into the sun, her face partially averted. An undernourished dog stood nearby. She bore a slight resemblance to Rhinehart in the wide bridge of her nose. I pointed it out, and Rhinehart took the photo and scrutinized it. There were a few pictures of the town, but not many.

I noticed, above the sideboard, that he'd hung a new picture—a circus performer with an elaborate jeweled headpiece and delicate white slippers in the precarious act of walking across a tightrope. I commented on it, and Rhinehart, who was writing something in his loopy scrawl, said, "That's what Lazar does now."

"He joined the circus?"

"He's in the circus *school*," he corrected me. "In Kiev. Although he has doubts about it. His mother probably thinks it's a cash cow."

"What's he going to do there?"

"High wire, flying trapeze work." Rhinehart frowned. "Already he's being pushed into partnering with the aerial tissues girl. It's worse than having a wife."

"From what I've heard it can be a pretty prestigious profession in Eastern Europe. Like acting here. Those schools are hard to get into."

"I suspect because he won a couple of local competitions, he now feels it's the only thing he's good at. But he's a wonderful poet. And he's still young. He shouldn't feel pressured to choose yet."

I was starting to wonder whether Rhinehart was the one exerting pressure. He liked to mentor. At my college, he'd had a student following; he even had a fan club of young intellectuals, mostly male writers, that would get together at a local pub off-hours and discuss his poetry, along with the poetry of Merrill, Walcott, Wright, and Pinsky. He would often drop in for the discussion and to help some of the students find writing residencies or with connections in publishing.

On the table was a list of Ukrainian names bisected by lines. Lazar's was included. "You're making charts again?" I asked.

"I'm still interested in genealogy." He patted my butt. "Now get up. That's the translator's stool." He shook his wrist and looked at his watch. "She's already five minutes late."

"I thought we were going to dinner at Dino's. Who's this translator?"

"We can go after. I want to interview this woman first. My editor sent over her name. She'll be translating some of my poetry into Ukrainian."

"I thought it already had been translated?"

"One of the books hasn't. And this is a dual-purpose project. I'm relying on my own obsessiveness with my poetry to help me with my Ukrainian. It's difficult to learn a language at my age, even to relearn it."

I didn't like the turn this project seemed to signal. We'd spoken last week about doing a collaboration based loosely on a New York City photo assignment *Esquire* had sent Diane Arbus on in the 1960s—a series of images that they couldn't print, photographs of Russian bathhouses and the hot dog stands and peep shows on 42nd Street, a man feeding his flea circus on his forearm while he read the paper, the morgue at Bellevue. I was excited to try an updated version with the elliptical, journalistic feel of some of Nan Goldin's work. Rhinehart had mentioned that he'd like to write about New York's long-standing history of bizarreness and hidden vices in the advancing age of its gentrification. We could pair images with short essays, I suggested, and I suspected Rhinehart could get it placed for us fairly easily, maybe even in *The New York Times Magazine.* But he seemed wary of collaborating. "We have a lovely mutual admiration that I don't want to disrupt," he'd said. "I'm a different man on deadline. Less congenial." In the end, he'd said we'd keep it in mind for the future—I still considered the possibility live.

On the table was my heavily bound copy of *The Oxford Companion to Western Art*. I flipped through the glossy pages. I had the urge to tell him about Laura's phone call, but it felt like the wrong time.

"This being used to test their descriptive skills?" I asked.

Rhinehart, I knew, liked to start this way. I pointed hopefully to Artemisia Gentileschi's *Judith Beheading Holofernes*. "How about you use this one?"

"Too bloody. I'm having these people come to my house, I don't want to scare them."

"But it's the best example of immediacy. Her expression is so hard and clean. Only a woman could have painted this version. Caravaggio's is a lot less emotional."

He came over and kissed my neck. "You're perfect. Too bad you don't know Ukrainian."

* * *

The woman who showed up was in her late sixties with thick legs and streaky graying hair pulled into a bun. She had a large round face and big earnest blue eyes. I could tell Rhinehart approved of her appearance—the flowered housedress and support hose. She didn't look like anyone I'd ever known in publishing. I took her coat, which felt scratchy in my hands, like a pig's bristles.

There was some introductory chitchat on her background—she'd been working for a long time, translating indiscriminately it seemed to me, whatever she could get her hands on. She'd done a book of poems by another poet represented at the house, so her résumé had been sent over in a stack of four, and I guessed Rhinehart chose her because of her age. The woman spoke with a heavy accent compared to Fedir, whose voice in my memory now seemed light and flickering. He wasn't called in for this project, although Rhinehart said he would bring him in as a consultant on yet another round of interviews.

I suspected Rhinehart was being so cautious because he'd been burned before when a book of his poetry was translated into German. The book had sold early through the foreign rights agent, and when the original German translator had stepped off the project midway, the house had quickly brought in a less experienced translator without closely scrutinizing his work. It received such shockingly awful reviews in Germany, where he was well known, that it had fueled a debate over the demise of lyricism in American poetry. Rhinehart, after hearing about it, asked a colleague in the German language department to translate the translation back into English so that he could hear what the Germans were reading. The professor wrote it out for him, awful clunky rhythms, mixed-up words, and arbitrary rhymes. Rhinehart was so depressed, he canceled classes for a week and spent the time in his room with German-English dictionaries and phrase books, trying to translate the poems himself. He was on the phone with Germany all day, trying to get the book pulled. Eventually the administration told him they were getting in an adjunct to cover his course load if he didn't come back, and he abandoned the project. It was still a sore point, and he believed it greatly hurt sales abroad.

For this interview, Rhinehart had settled on an inoffensive Turner painting of a field at dawn. He asked the translator what she saw. She put on her glasses and was grasping the book with both hands. "Corn. No, maybe this is wheat. Wheat."

Rhinehart wasn't satisfied with the response. "But how would you describe it?"

"It's a field, of course. And there is sky there." She pointed at the page, as if illustrating the idiocy of the question. Standing next to her, I, too, was starting to wonder how relevant this visual exercise was.

Rhinehart was bending in so they were both shadowing the pages. "But detail. Detail. What does the image feel like, smell like?"

She leaned away from him. "Smell? It's paper. It smell like book." She pushed it away, as if it were distasteful. "An old book. Left in closet."

The woman took off her glasses and looked at me crossly as if I were responsible. Individual hairs stuck out above her puckered lips. "Do you have something for me to translate? Words? A poem?"

"No," he said, stubbornly.

The woman stood up. "If you have nothing to translate then why did I take two buses to come here?" As if to a maid, she gestured to me to fetch her coat.

She was still going on, gripping her purse by the clasp. "I'm a translator. Of *words.* Show me words, books. What do I know about paintings? That is the test? Stupid."

Rhinehart had his arms crossed, clearly annoyed. It was rare for him to be impolite with people he didn't know. There was a tense energy surrounding this project, and I wondered whether it wasn't the translation that was bothering him but his reinvolvement with his poetry.

"I'm sorry to have wasted your time," he said sternly. I handed the woman her coat and led her outside, to the elevator. She walked slowly, as if her legs were sore.

After she'd gotten in and pressed the button, she turned to me and tapped her temple. "Your father not using his brains."

When I came back, Rhinehart was sitting at the table, his forehead cradled in his hands. "Tatie, is this a bad idea?"

"No. I actually think it might get you writing again."

I was still troubled by the woman's remark, not because of what it suggested about our age difference, but what it said about me, as if I were hanging around the sidelines of this project because I had nothing better to do. I said, "I bumped into Laura while you were in Ukraine. She bought a couple of my prints and invited me to a networking event at MoMA. She's a big collector. You didn't tell me." This last part was to put him on the defensive.

He was shocked—as if I'd confessed I'd fallen in love with someone else. "Laura? My ex-wife, Laura?"

"According to her the papers still haven't been signed."

He brushed this away. "Why haven't you mentioned it until now?"

I was nervous and tried to explain how I saw the division of things. This was professional, not personal. It suddenly seemed important that I convey to him what a huge networking opportunity she was offering me. I feared he would tell me not to go. He was staring at the wall behind me with an inscrutable expression, and I had the bizarre sensation of again being caught in the middle of them as a feuding couple.

"I have no doubt it will be good for your career," he said.

Relieved, I plunged ahead, telling him about the prints and how much she paid for them and what this meant. I was full of unasked questions—who she knew, whether she was liable to offer genuine help, why she had closed her gallery. But he was just sitting there, maddeningly deep in thought.

"What did she say about—" He made a gesture that encompassed the two of us, and I cringed. I knew it showed on my face.

"I didn't tell her."

"Oh," he said, getting up.

I followed him into the kitchen, chattering. "I'm assuming she sort of knows. When we first met, she asked me about you, but there was nothing to tell, really. Now I feel it's something private between us, and not really relevant."

"Maybe to you it's not, but I believe she'd see it differently."

I didn't like all this intimacy between them—what he knew and didn't know about her. He was leaning back against the sink, a glass of tap water in his hand, considering me, as if I were a new, unexpected person that had appeared in the kitchen. Someone not to be trusted. Overcome with guilt, I embraced him and said, "I'm sorry. I should have told you I'd seen her."

"I'm just shocked. At all of this." His hands on me felt reluctant. He sighed. "I always knew you'd get your break. I just never imagined it would come from this direction."

That was the last he said about it. When I brought up Laura again he ducked the subject, as if he were actively pretending we'd never met. Still, I was dying to discuss the upcoming MoMA party with someone, so I called Hallie and invited her to lunch. We hadn't seen as much of each other since Rhinehart and I had gotten together. Although she had pleased me by officially sanctioning my "new" relationship with him. "It seems healthy," she said. "And that's taking your past into account. As well as your 'tendencies.' "

About the MoMA night, though, for which I expected an enthusiastic response, she said, "Sounds creepy."

"What's creepy? The event?"

"That. Laura's involvement."

"I thought you would find it interesting. It's like an old boys' club for women, to share resources and contacts we're often denied."

"I don't know that I believe that. And even if I did, I distrust tribes. They expect conformity. Groups of women can be worse—emotional conformity."

We were at Café Cluny, a small, yellow-walled bistro in the West Village. Hallie had just come from her Buddhist center, where she was clocking a lot of time. I had assumed that once things with Adán had righted themselves, she would give it up, but evidently she attributed the chanting at the center to the continued success at home, and, she said, she was learning a lot about herself, as well. For example, everyone on earth had a mission, I clearly had my photography, some people had their families, but what did she have? She felt she had been repressing it, her purpose, and was on the track to finding out what it was.

I used this as an example. "That's at the heart of the feminist movement, you know. Women discovering themselves. I thought you'd be behind this idea. You're a feminist."

She frowned. "Since when? I don't go in for labels."

"But how could you reject the term *feminist!*"

"The whole thing about women's equality is that we get to choose what type of woman we want to be."

"That doesn't justify being irresponsible. We need to band together to get things done."

"Says who? What about the entrepreneurial model?"

"People joined together are more effective than one person out there like a renegade, proving herself. There's strength in numbers."

"You should get a new book of slogans," she said. "Those '70s groups were rife with petty infighting, unhappiness, and dissent. Plus it sounds like your little party at MoMA is meant to be entertaining—there will be appetizers, I'm sure. I've been to events like those. It's not exactly the same thing as storming Washington."

"I don't know what it's going to be about, but I always believed in women's rights," I said stubbornly. I thought back to when we were in college and used to play our Ani DiFranco tapes, and tossed around the word "cunt" pretty freely, although always in reference to our own bodies, never as an insult.

She shifted in her seat, and I could tell she was going to start lecturing me. "You should have used the suffragettes as a model if you were going to try and win me to your side. It took those women sixty years of nagging, making those little pins, and marching around to get anything done. That's tenacity. Susan B. Anthony was already dead by the time they passed the damn amendment. Which is why all organizations need fresh blood like yours to keep the dream rolling." She narrowed her eyes. "Why are you so desperate for my approval, anyway? I feel like I'm getting a hard sell."

"What? I'm just defending my opinion, and I—"

She waved this away as if it were made of gnats. "Does your old man know you're going to be hanging out with his ex-wife?"

"Yes. He told me it would be good for my career."

"If it were me, I wouldn't like it." She frowned, sipped her tea.

"Are you saying I shouldn't go now? This isn't about Laura, or even Rhinehart! It's a chance for me to talk to gallery owners about my work. You don't know how hard it is to get those introductions in New York. I can't just pass it up because of some marital issue that has nothing to do with me. If I don't take these opportunities I'll still be doing portraits with Marty when I'm in my fifties!"

"All right, all right," Hallie said. "No need to get your panties in a twist. You must be feeling guilty—you look ready to cry." She signaled for the bill. "So go then. A real feminist doesn't need anyone's approval."

CHAPTER THIRTEEN

The event was held in one of the big blank vertiginous rooms of the museum. I disliked Taniguchi's redesign, the catwalks with their glass sides, the floor slipping dangerously away from your feet. It was a building that seemed to be trying to show you up.

I was smiling at everyone. I smiled at the woman who checked me in and gave me a program; I smiled at the caterers that came around with flutes of champagne. When I first arrived in New York, I'd been a server for events like these, and I remembered how invisible I'd felt, and what was worse, how invisible the people I served were. I would lie in bed after, smelling of cooked eggs and grease, trying to conjure up a single face in that mass of people. I couldn't. The entire operation, humans serving other humans as if they were a different species, seemed both ridiculous and sad.

Laura found me hesitating on the fringe of the crowd and brought me over to the people she was talking with, a shrill-looking woman with large Chanel eyeglasses, and a washed-out redhead, whose plainness, I suspected, belied a great deal of money. Both women were in cocktail dresses. I had been anticipating more artists, young artists like me. This event seemed more akin to a dinner party at the Kennedys' in which all the men had been removed.

Laura's introduction of me seemed over the top, but the other women received it calmly, as if they were accustomed to being introduced to accomplished people, artistic and otherwise. When it came time for me to substantiate her claims, I was struck with shyness. "Who are your influences?" One woman asked, and I couldn't think of anyone, except, bizarrely, Michelangelo, perhaps because I'd seen a photograph of *David* on the way in. In answering the question "What is your work about?" I felt as if I were describing an imaginary friend whose entire existence depended on my belief. One of the women said abruptly, "Excuse me?" either because I was speaking too low or just incomprehensibly, backtracking when I sensed resistance or when I felt myself drifting. When talking to women, I had been used to a certain conversational pattern, supportive, encouraging, and based on a desire to find parallel circumstances in which to commiserate or offer advice. There was none of that here. My dangling sentences, the "you know" gambits and other vocal gestures for help seemed weak and self-condemning. My lack of confidence a symptom of the societal problem we were here to eradicate.

The radical feminist group the Guerrilla Girls was giving a talk, and Laura and I filed up to the front row of the auditorium, to the reserved seats. As the group came on stage, wearing the signature gorilla masks, Laura whispered that she'd reveal their top secret identities to me later. "You'll never guess." There was a lot of cheering and even some catcalls, but the Girls sat down rather sedately, like guests on *Oprah*. They had a PowerPoint presentation that detailed their aim to increase the visibility of women in the arts, their formation in 1985 after they had attended an international survey at MoMA in which only 13 of 169 artists were women, their decision to remain anonymous and to take code names of dead female artists and writers, and their interventions, posters, and billboards calling attention to the underrepresentation of women in the art world. The longer I sat there I didn't see the masks anymore, I saw the women underneath, whose activist work I respected, depended on, actually, to help me expand my career, but whose individual personalities I wasn't crazy about. It was the self-aggrandizing tone of some of the women that bothered me. They seemed aggressively anonymous, their disembodied voices detailing in a very pointed way how they had shamed museum administrations, which had subsequently issued them invitations to come and speak. Applause followed.

Older women, in expensive shawls and dress pants, stood and asked questions that sounded more like statements, referencing their substantial gifts to the museum and the process by which someone can ensure money was properly earmarked for art by women. How different these women were from the female interns scurrying around in their black tights and headsets, making sure the mikes were okay, and everyone had a program and a seat they were comfortable with. Behaving like serfs.

I was deeply conflicted. Did it matter, really, if I didn't like them? What right did I have to criticize, anyway? Compared to these women I had done very little to help the feminist art movement, beyond being a woman and trying to express my own vision, however naively. And I *had* been naive, I could see that now, to have equated feminism with freedom, nudity, unbridled conversations, lack of judgment, and hand-sewn clothes. The social mores platform I had been supporting it on wholeheartedly, the illusion that feminists believed I was okay as long as I was being true to myself, that they would want the best for me—I didn't feel that here. I didn't get the sense that these women particularly cared about my success. In fact, I felt more liable to be discussed in dismissive or less generous terms in this upper-class crowd than I would have in a mixed bag of men and women from different socioeconomic backgrounds.

I was aware of what was possibly my first genuine activist impulse. I had the immediate, pressing desire to work towards creating a different model, a supportive community for women like me. For the college girls in the back of the auditorium who wanted to be here but were either too shy to ask questions or weren't called on.

Laura was breathing comfortably beside me, emitting a faint scent of perfume, an odor so delicate and unusual, I couldn't relate it to anything in the natural world. The Guerrilla Girls and then the entire audience gave her a round of applause for organizing the event, while she sat there with a patient smile, as if she would have preferred not to be singled out. I applauded, too, enthusiastically, while studying her profile, trying to imagine her as a teenager with tight jeans and sneakers, jumping turnstiles, smoking stolen cigarettes, feeling she had no future.

In the crowded reception hall, I took a glass of wine offered to me by a blond server, wondering if she would remember me later. People were gathering around us. Standing with Laura, I was with a celebrity. She was telling a lively story of bringing in a relatively unknown artist to speak at a feminist colloquium, even more conservative than this one.

"It was a very serious affair. Black-tie. We had some big-name artists and philanthropists there to discuss the future of feminism. Faith Ringgold, Judy Chicago, Gloria Steinem were all on stage. And this young woman, who certain collectors—and I will not tell you who—*assured* me was the next great thing, and who was *so* enthusiastic about being included, she comes up to the podium to give her presentation. She's dressed in jeans, which is odd, but not that odd, Leibovitz never dresses up either, but this woman is also carrying a plastic bag. In it, we discovered, was a change of clothes! She proceeds to take off her jeans—on stage—pulls on a little frilled skirt, changes from boots to heels, and gets out these two sock puppets."

"Sock puppets!" a woman said.

"She's not a performance artist, either, she's a painter. And this is the best part, the puppets, one was an elephant, I remember, start having a conversation about how they were bought by rich children, how poorly they were treated, then tossed away. It was a subversive rendition of *The Velveteen Rabbit* for art benefactors. She didn't use names, but she made strong allusions to some of the people in the crowd." Laura started laughing, so that she could barely get the words out. "You should have seen me. I was sitting there with my mouth open! Then she just walked off the stage and out of the building. She left the puppets next to the mike. No one wanted to remove them so they stayed there throughout the discussion, looking at us."

I laughed, too, but uncomfortably, as if Laura had been reading my mind in the auditorium and had decided to prove it to me. I was also digging around for the point of the story. Did she expect more obedience from the artists she had helped? Or was this tale being used to shame the other benefactors listening?

A woman with frizzy red hair, red lipstick, and a big smile had joined us, and Laura introduced me "as a great fit for T-Projects. Tunis, tell me you have some room for her. You love launching careers, and you're so damn *good* at it." I was a sucker for anyone looking out for me, and was feeling quite chummy with Laura now. Tunis owned a gallery on West 19th Street in Chelsea that handled a lot of young artists, and she had a special interest in photography. She also seemed like a genuinely kind and down-to-earth person, and for the first time that evening, I was enjoying discussing my work. "Laura has a great eye," Tunis said, handing me her card. "Why don't you bring by your portfolio, and we'll take a look."

The crowd was thinning out and by then I was less inclined to look on it ungenerously. I'd gotten further in the past half-hour than I had with all my years of intermittent self-marketing. I tried to convey my appreciation to Laura, who deflected it with a wave of her hand. "That's the purpose of networking. What did you think of tonight?"

I started stumbling around since, honestly, I would have given the event a mixed review—even with my last-minute success, I was still stubbornly clinging to my original assessments. She cut off the pleasantries. "The events downtown are much different. A lot more fun, younger artists and curators. The whole thing has grown so big, I'm happy to just be a figurehead now, thank God. I started this group, you know."

I didn't.

"After Charley and I divorced, I felt like I would go crazy if I didn't put my energy somewhere." Her face was flushed. "When we first began, it was really lowbrow—paper cups, sitting on the floor. I was living in the city full-time again and was excited to know more people. These women did all sorts of things besides make art. Some were cleaning houses or working in restaurants, and we'd brainstorm group shows. Even though I owned a gallery, I was no more important than anyone else. I was just one vote in a collective decision-making process."

"That sounds so great," I said.

"It was for me. It reminded me of who I was before, that seventeen-year-old with big plans." She spoke with real feeling, and I was fascinated.

I had forgotten about Rhinehart entirely, so when Laura mentioned him, I froze, becoming as wary as a rabbit sensing something moving in the grass. She kept chattering away, as if too drunk to notice. It didn't fool me. I'd watched her sizing up her audience when she was telling that puppet story, and she was probably doing the same now. I was careful to keep my face expressionless, a polite listener.

Evidently, Rhinehart wasn't much of a feminist, according to her.

"Not that he would ever come out and say it, but he wasn't too keen on these meetings. Maybe it's because he tends to see differences between individuals more than between genders. He's certainly not as sexist as Charley, who was one of those old school, whiskey glass in one hand, pinch your ass with the other types. I found it endearing back then, if you can believe it." We drifted off into Charley, who'd remarried soon after the divorce. He'd died from a heart attack several years ago. I kept guard, as I expected we would come back around to Rhinehart, and we did. "It's so hard to retain a social relationship with a man you were once married to. You want to and you don't because it seems such a farce. All the old grudges resurface, but I do miss talking about this stuff sometimes. He loved to discuss these people, the little intrigues of the art world."

Part of me was curious as to whom Rhinehart knew in the room, but I was leery of traveling any further down the path of this conversation. I didn't like being privy to her thoughts about him—it made me feel guilty.

When I got in, the apartment was dark, and Rhinehart was in bed, even though it was barely ten o'clock. In the bedroom, his lumped form seemed positioned to resist me. He didn't say anything, but I launched into a reiteration of the night anyway, while undressing—my timidity, my tangled thoughts about feminism and the distress that accompanied them, the pretentiousness of some of the women, Laura. It seemed as if he were listening out of politeness, responding minimally so as not to encourage me to continue. Even when I relayed Tunis's request to see my portfolio, he didn't have much of a reaction, and all the excitement I'd felt coming in the door evaporated.

Pinpointing Laura as the problem, and perhaps his concern that we were getting close, I said, "She's a strange woman."

He said nothing.

"Her gallery. What type of work did she have up there?"

I thought he wasn't going to reply to that question either, but he said, "You should have asked her. She would have talked about it."

"But I'm closer to you. And you also know the answer."

"But the difference is I don't *want* to discuss it. Even for you."

I was tempted to be rash, to flick on all the lights in a blinding show of force.

He said, "I've put those years behind me and don't want to open them up again for renewed scrutiny. I have that right."

Whose scrutiny? He had discussed Laura with me before. Did he think I would leak his comments to her? "I just thought since you were familiar with some of the people I may be showing my work to, you might be able to give me some advice. You and Laura used to talk about it."

"I'm glad you had a nice time tonight," he said.

If he'd been listening, he would have realized I never actually said that I did.

Laura called the next morning with gossip. Evidently there had been a man in the crowd, a performance artist in a gorilla mask, masquerading as one of the Guerrilla Girls. Security caught him after I'd left—he'd been posing for a photo with the museum director. He claimed it was a protest piece. "How hysterical!" Laura said. "I love it!

To think he was sneaking around like a spy. And there's no *rule* men can't attend—they just don't usually."

We were talking about galleries, when I asked her, "Do you think my portfolio is strong enough to show Tunis? Honestly."

"Well, she does prefer experimental work, it's true. We'll go through it again—I can help you tailor it. That series with the birds she'll like, I'm sure."

"I should probably check out her space and some of the other galleries nearby, to see what they have up now."

"How about tomorrow night?" Laura said. "I know Thursdays are obnoxious, but there's an opening for Ryan Tiesley—that British painter who's so hot right now. We can do some private viewings, maybe a few shows downtown, and then meet up with him and his entourage later for dinner."

I told Rhinehart about the plan after I got off the phone. He didn't respond. But then, just as I was leaving the house, after taking an agonizing amount of time deciding what to wear, he said, "So this has become a standing engagement?"

He was sitting in a corner chair, a book open on his lap, although he'd spent the last hour silently observing me rush back and forth to the closet in different combinations of earrings and necklaces.

"I'm just going to check out galleries. It's research. You should understand that."

Looking back down at his book, he said, "No one goes to Chelsea on a Thursday night to do research."

Laura and I did wind up in the 24th Street crowds, breezing through several loud, packed openings, vodka drinks in hand. The Tiesley opening was invite-only, but still a circus—he'd just gotten profiled in *The New York Times Magazine,* and he had several celebrity collectors co-chairing the reception. The gallery was jammed with models, and press photographers, and recognizable faces. We went to Cookshop for dinner—a table of twelve with the gallery owners, artist, and a few of his friends. From that chaotic light-bulb-flashing crowd, we'd distilled down to a somewhat ordinary looking group.

We were talking about what we'd managed to see tonight. Tunis's gallery was closed for installation. It would open next week with a show by a Japanese video artist. Not much else had impressed me, even the British sculptor's pieces seemed noisy and half-finished, like partially completed thoughts, and the way he was using his materials—crunched metal and tire and bright paint—was too reminiscent of 1980s pop art, which had been responding, at the time, to '80s culture. But as we were at his reception, I didn't want to be rude, even if he couldn't hear me, and spoke instead about what Chakaia Booker had managed to do with automobile tires, making wild, intricately detailed, sexualized organlike sculptures. "Beautiful how she just transformed her medium. Lately I've been really wanting to push the limits of photography," I said to Laura. "Maybe by doing a collaboration? With an installation artist." In a lowered voice, I described for her an idea that had come to me the day after the MoMA event, when I'd been trying to get my mind off Rhinehart. I wanted to reconstruct the interior of a house, complete with furniture. On the walls, I would put up portraits in heavy frames, but instead of conventional family photographs, where the people are woodenly posed, and which tell you nothing about them, these photographs would narrate the history of interactions in the room. In the bathroom, for example, above the toilet, where a man's gaze typically falls, could hang an image I held in my head of a brown-haired, acned teenager standing with his ear pressed against the bathroom door, listening. I wanted the photographs to appear candid, but also stylized, so that from a distance they could pass for portraits.

"We need to find you the right collaborator," Laura said. "Someone with the emotional sensitivity to understand the project, but who has the technical set-building skills for it. The more real the rooms seem, the more fascinating it will be to tour through them.

Your audience would be picking up information from tons of details simultaneously. After seeing the family dynamics in the photos, they'd be reconsidering objects that had seemed generic at first."

"Exactly," I said. "I want it to be an overall sensory experience."

"I wonder if Jen Marshall would be right, or maybe, oh—or D'bay. If he's still in Brooklyn."

"He moved his studio to Woodstock," the man sitting beside her said. It annoyed me to think he was listening in. He was another photographer. His first question, after we'd been introduced, was where I'd shown.

"Shame," Laura said. To me, she lowered her voice. "I'll dig up his phone number anyway. Maybe just ask him. He's a sweet person and really exacting technically."

Just as we were finishing dinner, my phone rang. I looked down, knowing it would be Rhinehart, although he'd never called to check up on me before. I sent the call to voicemail. Five minutes later, he called again, and I excused myself from the table to answer it.

"Where are you?" he said. "I was getting concerned." He didn't sound concerned. He sounded vaguely accusatory.

"At a restaurant. Having dinner."

"It's after eleven."

I was jammed in a hallway that the servers used and could barely hear him. He asked me when I would be back.

"I don't know, maybe in another hour? Should I sleep at my place tonight?"

"No, no, come here. It's all right. Did you have a nice time tonight?"

I saw Laura looking around for me, and I was impatient to get off the phone. "Yes. I'll tell you about it later."

"Okay. Make sure you take a cab." He kissed the receiver but I'd already taken it away from my ear, and heard him just as I hung up.

Back at the table, as I was sitting down, Laura said, "Boyfriend jealous?" I froze, staring at her. She seemed so calm.

Laughing, she said, "Educated guess. Few people would require

you to pick up at this hour. I thought it might be that lawyer you were talking about before."

Earlier in the evening, we'd passed one of Lawrence's favorite restaurants, and I'd mentioned we used to go there on Thursday nights. I hadn't realized Laura was paying attention—she'd been in the middle of emailing. I told her that relationship ended a while ago.

"Was it serious?"

"It was, at the time. We had discussed getting married."

"It's so hard for women your age. You have so many requirements in a partner. The late forties woman really is freer, kids are grown, we have money. We're wiser, or that's the theory. So you're coming to the afterparty?"

I was still rattled by the earlier part of the conversation. "I should really get home. I have to get up early."

"Come on," said Bruce, who ran the gallery. He leaned across the table. "It's only two blocks from here. An old Russian bathhouse. I'm not even sure it's legal, but we've brought in the booze and the music and converted the pool into a dance floor. It's going to be wild."

We went through an unmarked door and down a flight of stairs to reach an enormous underground space, like an enchanted cave, with thousands of tiny yellow bulbs flickering like fireflies. The DJ was excellent—she had a keen sense of the crowd's mood and the space. I danced and drank way too much and when I shouted at someone for the time, it was past four. I found Laura at the bar with Ryan, who was completely hammered and had both his hands on her hips, swaying. I waved goodbye. She said, "Leaving already?" Back up at street level, weaving slightly on the deserted sidewalk, I hailed a cab, and then, on an impulse that felt deeper than the drunkenness, directed the driver over the Manhattan Bridge, past the snow-covered broken-down cars, the orangey streetlights, the birds circling through the abandoned bell tower of the Guyanese Episcopal Church. My head buzzing, I stumbled up the uneven stairs to my apartment and fell into bed, relieved to be home.

* * *

I had texted Rhinehart before I went down into the party, where I had no cell reception, to tell him I would be very late, but for some reason he hadn't received the message until I went aboveground again. The next morning I had three voicemails he'd left over the course of the night. I felt bad and so didn't explain myself gracefully over the phone, and Rhinehart didn't receive my apology gracefully either. He fixated on the time in between my leaving the restaurant and arriving at the party, scolding me for not calling him. When that didn't work, he tried to make me feel guilty, recounting, in a voice heavy with self-pity, a night of waiting up and worrying. More translators were coming to the house that afternoon, and he had hoped I would be there to help him decide. I was hungover and still in the mind-set of the evening before and wanted, more than anything, to go back to bed. In the past, I had always longed to feel the authentic desire for time apart from him, believing it would make me appear more independent, and therefore, attractive. Now that I did feel it, it made me uncomfortable. I said I had too much work to do on my portfolio today. He couldn't argue, but he wasn't as encouraging as he'd been before, and we arrived at a standstill, both hanging up the phone unhappy.

Although Rhinehart later apologized for "being overbearing," he turned cold every time I said I was going out, and so eventually I stopped telling him. Laura had so many events, and the more people I knew, the more difficult it became to turn them down. We'd fallen in with a group of young artists, all of them successful—I didn't realize it was possible to make that much money off of art. "The key is in the commercial contracts," Laura said. "That cross-branding." We were joined occasionally by middle-aged artists who had work in the Whitney's and MoMA's collections, and who recounted lively anecdotes about the East Village art collectives of the 1980s, Club 57, the Fun

Gallery where Basquiat and Kenny Scharf got their first solo shows, or even about Miles Davis, when he lived down on Broadway and was making heavily shellacked paintings on burlap. The artists never picked up the tab. Instead it was usually a collector or his business associates from out of town, or one of the young crowd of actors and minor celebrities who seemed to have money to burn, or someone in the even wealthier and more indolent group that followed them.

Laura and I tended not to discuss anything outside our shared experiences—my personal life seemed largely irrelevant to our relationship, as was hers. Still, I felt it safest to keep both a psychological and physical buffer between her and Rhinehart, so on the nights I went out with her, I slept at my apartment in Brooklyn. It was also a relief not to have to rehash the evening's events when I came in, smelling of cigarettes and fruit nectar cocktails as Rhinehart lay in bed animated with resentful questions. How to explain it anyway, or what it felt like, the maniacal laughter and intense, intimate conversations about making art, interspersed with mean gossip or anecdotes about Murakami or Peter Beard, the boozy stumble into the street and general obnoxiousness of our famous and recognizable crowd, shuffling into taxis to dance in dark clubs with thumping music and $800 dollar bottle service. "I thought I'd outgrown this years ago," Laura said. "But suddenly it's fun again." I had lived more than ten years in New York, but I had never lived like this.

"I hardly see you anymore," Rhinehart complained. "It's as if you've moved back over the bridge." We still spent plenty of time together, I argued, but in truth, I was only staying at his house a few nights a week. More distressing to me was that on the evenings we did spend together, he didn't even seem to enjoy my company. We had less and less to say to each other, and instead of going out, he preferred to sit in his study and peruse documents. I grew antsy and then angry, and it took a Herculean effort of patience for me not to check my phone every five minutes to hear what I was missing.

He had latched on to a new idea. He'd convinced Lazar to apply for a visa to the U.S., and was acting as his sponsor, also offering him a job ostensibly to translate some poems and the essay on the Ukrainian workforce. In preparation for Lazar's visa interview, Rhinehart had been in contact with the U.S. Citizenship and Immigration Services and was mailing a dossier on himself over to Ukraine that was complete with letters of invitation (including those he'd solicited from his agent and his publisher), documents showing his income and detailing his familial relationship with Lazar, including color photographs of him and Lazar together in Ukraine to demonstrate his familiarity with his relation's economic status. To hear Rhinehart tell it, Lazar was anxious to come to New York, probably high off the glitzy lights-on-Broadway stories Rhinehart had been feeding him.

The stool and card table were back in the center of the floor with my Meatyard book splayed open to a photograph from the 1950s—a huge sky looking ready to devour the barn and the child standing alongside it. All this meant a translator had yet to be selected. I had missed another round of interviews that Fedir had judged, quite stringently, even getting into a finicky lexical debate with one woman. He'd won. That woman wasn't called back.

"Why do you still need a translator if Lazar's coming?" I said.

"Different type of work. And I'm not sure Lazar's going to want to be in all day doing this. He may want to sightsee."

"Where's he going to stay?"

"Here, of course." Still beaming with the plan. He was far more excited talking about this potential guest than he ever seemed when I came in the door. "At least initially. If it's longer, we'll have to work something out."

I was annoyed. "Doesn't he have school? What about the circus?"

"He has a break coming up for vacations. They have them in that type of school, too."

Something had shifted during the course of their correspondence—Rhinehart was now proud of Lazar's circus career. There was no more mention of his emerging talent as a poet—the translation idea had been dropped. Instead, Rhinehart began educating me about aerialists, who had the most physically demanding role in the circus, one needing impeccable timing and judgment. You had to have complete control of your body, even as it was coasting through the air. And you had to have acting skills as well, as everything had a story. Even the trapeze, which could articulate a complex narrative of two lovers caught in a betrayal.

Despite myself, I was curious as to what, specifically, Lazar's signature moves were. He seemed too tall and gawky to be a gymnast.

Rhinehart told me, "He's trained in many forms, which adds to his portfolio. He can do bareback acrobatics, balancing on his head on the trapeze, complicated trampoline maneuvers, which are lead-ups to trapeze work . . ."

"He can balance on his head on the bar? While it's swinging?"

"Well, there's a cup, but still it's very difficult. He keeps his arms and legs out for balance. He's very good. His teacher wrote me, saying he's one of the best students he's seen in his career. And he works very hard. Ten hours a day sometimes." Rhinehart was looking for something, maybe this letter, to show me as proof. I wasn't interested.

"How long is he going to stay?"

"As long as he can get a visa for, Tatie. I'm not going to invite him over here and then send him to an overpriced hotel!"

"But how long are we talking? Two weeks, a year?" I pictured the three of us cooped up here together and felt suffocated.

"I can't answer that! It depends on him, whether he likes it and wants to stay. Whether he can."

"But what about school? You're going to ask him to give up his career for the chance to see a couple of musicals and drink with you down at the pub?"

Rhinehart turned away from me and said, "We have aerialist programs in the U.S., too."

"They can't be on par with what he's in now. You said his school was one of the best in the world."

"The New York Circus Arts Academy is quite good. And it's in Queens. I'm going to take him on a campus visit when he comes."

"Never heard of it."

I picked up a circus book that had been lying on the coffee table, or maybe he'd always had it out and I'd never noticed. On the cover was a top-hatted MC, the mike being lowered into his expectant hands. The dark vertiginous slant of the stadium, the dizzying crisscross of ropes and cables overhead. A dusty circular arena, same format as when a chained lion and bear were pitted against each other. To some of the glossy pages, Rhinehart had attached Post-it notes: "Full-twisting layout salto," "Clown being used to distract us from equipment getting dismantled."

I said, "Are you aware how they treat the animals in the circus? How they abuse them? That's what I think of first—the smell of piss and misery."

"I was going to get us tickets to Ringling Brothers. But now that doesn't seem like such a good idea." He had his back to me. The conversation was over. "It's been an exhausting day. Probably be better if you went to Brooklyn tonight."

As if I did anything different anymore. As I was unlocking the door, he said, "Maybe I should have done that photo project with you when you asked."

It wasn't so long ago that I believed we'd be able to inspire each other. Rhinehart had always been my model for artistic success, but was that even true anymore? He hadn't really demonstrated his creativity in years. Once I had that thought I was ashamed of it.

He turned around in his chair to look at me. "I can't imagine collaborating now. Can you?"

I was sad when I left his apartment that night. Two days later, I was enraged. How thoroughly unenjoyable all of this was to me—Lazar's tourist visit, Rhinehart's inviting me to the circus. The *circus*! As if this was something I'd be interested in! They wouldn't even allow me to photograph in there without elaborate permits. Why not invite me for a trip upstate to Dia:Beacon—how many times had I mentioned I wanted to go but didn't have a car. He didn't give a shit about what I cared about.

For Hallie, I spared no details in outlining Rhinehart's plans for taking me to the circus, the same circus she had wanted to picket three years running because they had elephants and a lion. I was too angry to try and protect him from her judgment, and I ranted for a good twenty minutes. On the other end of the line was dead silence. I thought we'd been disconnected, and said, "Hello?"

She said, "I don't blame him. You've been running around like a fucking eighteen-year-old away from home for the first time. Are you doing coke?"

I had actually been tempted to last night. Hallie had an uncanny way of guessing these things. "No," I said.

"Well, you sound hopped up. Either high or hungover every time I see you. If I were him, I'd be annoyed, too. I'm annoyed right now, just listening to this."

I tried to explain his plan to have Lazar come over here, and how we'd never have any time alone together, and how he was obsessed with Lazar, obsessed with Ukraine, still, and she said, "You act as if all this is new to you. When you've been supporting him, giving him lots of feedback and whatever since last summer. And now you're off around town, and so he's focusing on this relative. Shit, what man doesn't withdraw when he's angry. They *all* do. I thought you and I had agreed on that."

I protested. "I've always been there for him! And now when things are actually going well for me, and he's in a position to support me or at least talk to me about it, he refuses to."

"You're out with his ex-wife! Of course he's going to avoid that situation. That's *normal.* What's weird is how much time you're spending with her. There's a big ball of deceit in that relationship."

"Listen to you, as if you're some kind of prophet, a Buddha now."

She handled this calmly, as if speaking to an ignorant person. "And bullshit she doesn't suspect you have contact with him. She's just not talking about it because like you, she doesn't want to end the party. She's dependent on you—you're her little buddy, willing to go out *every* night. And let me ask you something, what kind of woman in her late forties is out partying like this, clubs and whatever, who isn't a cokehead or going through some midlife crisis."

This called up an image of Laura, her sweaty forehead with strands of blond hair stuck to it, hunched over the table, doing a line. Her pupils were so dilated, the blue in her eyes was gone. She was pulling on my arm to tell me something, going too hard to form the words.

I was quiet, and Hallie said, "I could give a shit about her, except in some sort of abstract way. There's your Buddhism for you. But what's going to happen is you're going to come down off this, get bored or start feeling dirty, or whatever. As much as you think you can hang, I know this lifestyle, and it's not for you. It's going to run its course, and you're going to have one major fucking hangover, and I just hope you don't do too much damage in between. You always think you're the only one who gets hurt—that mind-set is really dangerous. You have the power to hurt people, too."

It did come to an end one bitter cold night when I watched a friend of Dash Snow's do so much meth he went into a seizure sitting next to me and the paramedics had to come. After the ambulance left, everyone went back inside to get high, and I thought, "What am I doing here?" Less than an hour later I was home, staring at myself in the mirror—there were dark circles under my eyes where the mascara had run. I still heard my bar voice, insistent and obnoxious, going on and on about this collaboration I wanted to do. It had become my "signature idea," and I'd whore it out for anyone who'd listen. I'd yet to find a collaborator. It was already March and what did I have to show for anything? I'd barely been shooting these past weeks. The most valuable gallery connection remained the one I'd made with Tunis at the MoMA event, and she was booked up for the next two years.

I spent the next few days reading, rearranging my apartment, and sketching out ideas. Laura called me incessantly, trying to get me to go out, even after I explained to her why I wanted to stay in. I realized how little she knew me. Eventually, I started screening her calls, recalling the neediness that had put me off when we'd met months before.

I was ashamed to call Rhinehart. I also didn't know what to say. We hadn't spoken in nearly two weeks, since our argument about Lazar. He had phoned me once but hadn't left a message, and I hadn't returned the call. I'd been afraid of us sniping at each other one too many times, so that it pushed us to do something drastic.

Two nights later, I woke up at 3 a.m. with the acute sense that I'd let something very important die through neglect, and the thought was so frightening that I picked up the phone and called him. I hung up and called again, and again he didn't answer, and I slept fitfully for the rest of the night. The next morning I left a message. "I'm so sorry. If you only knew how bad I feel. Can't we just get together and talk? Try and mend this?" By one that afternoon, he hadn't gotten back to me. I called again. Left another message. At 4:30, I got my spare keys and took a cab to his apartment.

CHAPTER FOURTEEN

He wasn't there. It looked as if he hadn't been there for days. Everything about the apartment signaled abandonment. The air was stale and foreboding. There were dust motes in the strip of light over the television set, and the kitchen sponge was shriveled and dry. I moved anxiously, quickly. In the bedroom, I rifled through his dresser, sliding both hands underneath the folded piles, while listening for the scrape of his key in the lock. But he didn't come home.

His passport was missing, as were some of his clothes. I went into his study, which seemed larger. It took me a second to realize furniture had been moved out, only the studio bed remained, along with a small dresser that looked new. Was this in preparation for Lazar's visit? Rhinehart hadn't told me whether he'd gotten the visa. Maybe he'd gone back to Ukraine to try and speed up the process? The pull-down desk was now in the living room. It was unlocked, and I picked through the drawers like a thief. There was far less here than there used to be, and I couldn't find any of his genealogy materials at all, except for that piece of foolscap.

In his filing cabinet I found a manila folder labeled with Lazar's name, which I pulled out in the hopes it might contain an email address. In it were visa requirements downloaded from the government website, photocopies of support letters, including a hyperbolic one from Rhinehart, which I skimmed. There were color brochures of that circus academy in Long Island City and a form from the admissions committee responding to Rhinehart's request for more information. There was an envelope from the circus school in Kiev. Inside it was a praising letter from Lazar's teacher—which was short, but did indeed say Lazar was one of the best students they'd seen there—and a printout of an email from last week. It took me a moment to process as I was also wondering how widespread the Internet was in Ukraine. Rhinehart seemed to send and receive a lot of correspondence via regular mail.

> Dear Mr. Rhinehart,
>
> I have now talked about our plans with my family, and we have made decision that I will stay in Ukraine to finish my study. Please do not be too disappoint. It is what we all think is the right choice made for me. But I am happy we completed our project together. It was much work with dictionary but worth it!
>
> Maybe one day when I am famous acrobat I come to New York and I take you to dinner at the restaurant you mention many times where there are photographs of famous people on the walls. I will bring photograph of myself to hang on wall so that you will be proud and can say, "this is Lazar, who I know."
>
> On behalf of my family, I send you all good wishes for a prosperous future.
>
> Your friend [and relation ;)],
>
> Lazar

On the second read, I became angry. How hurt Rhinehart must have been, receiving this stilted email with "my family" written all over it as if he were some foreign huckster, attempting to lure Lazar away. The hours he'd spent on the visa application! After all he'd done for this kid, and he wouldn't even address him as "uncle"!

As I was trying out different passwords to break into Rhinehart's computer to see if there was a record of a flight, Laura called. For some reason, I decided to answer. I was in a state of guilt, terrorized by flash memories of how self-absorbed I'd been, maybe I just needed to hear another person's voice. The minute I picked up, I knew it was a mistake. After chastising me for not returning her calls, she launched in with details of a benefit party in a collector's Tribeca apartment where Bono was supposed to make an appearance. She was talking at me as if I'd already agreed to go, and I eventually cut her off—"Now's not a good time."

"What could you possibly be doing that's more important than this? Have you been *listening* to me? I said Bono's going to be there. In the *room*."

"Rhinehart's disappeared, and I have no idea where he's gone, and I'm worried." I stopped, afraid to say more.

There was a calculated pause. "Where's he supposed to be?"

"At home. In his apartment." I looked around.

"Maybe he's there. Did you call?"

"I'm here right now. There's no sign of him."

"Wait. How'd you get into his apartment? He gave you keys?"

I started stuttering, but it was too late. I confessed that Rhinehart and I were in a relationship. "We're used to seeing each other every day. Until recently." It was when I said it, and heard her horrified intake of breath, that I saw just how big a deal this was, and how wrong I'd been to conceal it. In a half-whisper she was saying, "I can't believe this. I really can't believe this."

When she spoke again, her voice was icy, and I wished she'd just disappear from the other end of the line so I wouldn't be forced to hear what she was going to say.

"Do you think he's left, or do you think he's just left *you*?"

A sliver of fear streaked across my ribs. "But if it was just me, why would he leave his place?"

"Maybe he went away somewhere to think. That's not surprising. He does that, but you wouldn't know, because you were never *married* to him. What surprises *me* is how you played dumb and let me discuss my marriage with you! All those times we were out together! You never said anything! You just let me go on like an idiot."

"You never asked me," I said meekly. "I didn't think you cared."

"Not *care*! He's my husband. Who the hell do you think you are? You think you're so important that I'd support whatever selfish shit you want to do?" Her voice was frighteningly out of control. "I *knew* it was risky taking you into my confidence. I knew there was something about you that couldn't be trusted."

Internally, I protested. I always believed myself to be an honest person. But clearly I'd been deceptive—even if, as Hallie had said, Laura hadn't entirely trusted me from the beginning. Her suspicions probably made my company more exciting. To try and explain this to her would be presumptuous, and would lead us further down the road of insults, possibly about my photography, which I wouldn't be able to handle. I needed to get off the phone. "I'm really sorry. You're right. I should have said something earlier. We can meet and discuss it later if you want, but right now I have to hang up and deal with Rhinehart being missing."

I could hear her silently wrestling with herself on the other end of the line. Finally she said, "I don't want to meet with you. I hope I never see you again. Have someone call me if he's in the morgue."

I went home to wait for him to return. It was the only thing I could do.

A few days later I received a postcard. It was lucky that I even saw it as it was tangled up with the circulars, also garishly colored. On the front was a squat motel with orange awnings and a sickly looking palm tree. I flipped it over. The Frankfort Hotel, South Beach, Miami. He wrote: *I just picked up your voicemails. I'm taking some time away. I couldn't bear to be in New York. Love, R.*

Laura had been right. Maybe this was how he handled things. I hadn't known.

I was desperately lonely. I was also starting to worry that I was sick. For days, there had been something wrong with my body—I thought I was coming down with the flu, but it never progressed beyond a dull ache in my legs and sudden waves of nausea. While on the phone with Laura, I was convinced I'd gotten my period, but when I went to the bathroom there was only an insipid pinkish spotting. It had stopped by the next morning.

A week later, I decided to buy a pregnancy test. Rhinehart had never gotten a woman pregnant in his life, he said, and with his age, he doubted he was still able to. We used the withdrawal method most of the time, which wasn't even a legitimate method of birth control, but we also hadn't been having sex that much these past two months. I didn't feel pregnant, but I wasn't really sure what that felt like. Even though it seemed foolish, I brought the test home and squatted over the toilet. It was positive.

In an eerie, trancelike state, I called Hallie, who answered, saying, "Stop being a nervous Nellie, he just needs some time alone. You should—"

"I need you to come over. To Brooklyn."

"Right now?"

"Stop at the Duane Reade on your way and get two pregnancy tests." My entire body felt as if there were an electrical current running through it. I didn't trust myself to be out on the street alone.

Two hours later, standing in the bathroom doorway, watching me pee on another stick, she said, "Remember the time we were in college and Biddy Jo Jo came over, thinking she was pregnant?"

"No."

"You remember—you went to the Price Chopper for us. Gertie stayed in the bathroom with her. I evaluated the results and reported to the room. It was one of those sticks you had to dunk in the solution."

"Vaguely."

"We'd been drinking daiquiris all afternoon trying to calm ourselves. Everyone was damn near hysterical with the excitement. Nothing seemed tragic or serious back then—everything was cause for a party." She hoisted herself up with the heels of her hands, sitting on the vanity. "The first test was negative and we all toasted, and it was great. Then I said, let's do another. The second test was positive. We were like 'what the fuck?' You ran out for a third—it took you forever—we thought you'd lost your nerve at the store. That one was positive, too. And Biddy burst into tears, and we didn't know what to say. Next day, we went over to the Planned Parenthood, and she was pregnant. She had an abortion and dropped out of school."

"Jesus, Hallie. You tell me this story now?"

"No matter what happens—you'll be okay."

I handed her the stick, and she read the instructions on the package aloud for the third time. "This says you're supposed to do it in the morning for the most accurate results."

I pulled up my underwear. "You and I both know it doesn't matter."

We waited. Positive. "That's the second one," I said. "There's no point in doing another."

Hallie looked terrified, as if she were pregnant. To comfort her, I said, "Everything's fine."

I was experiencing an unearthly calm, as if someone had a grip on my shoulder and was firmly steering me to the door.

"What should we do?" she called out in a frightened little voice.

I was already in the kitchen looking for my cell phone. "I'm making an appointment with my gynecologist."

"But what are you going to do?" she said.

A baby. I couldn't even imagine it. "I don't know yet. First I need to know if I'm really pregnant. Then I'm going to find Rhinehart."

CHAPTER FIFTEEN

Tropical environments depressed me. It was only recently that I felt this way; as a child I had loved going to the beach, and Hallie and I used to spend all day there when we were teenagers, bringing an old sheet and a bunch of magazines and discussing Rob Lowe and Kirk Cameron and the best way to apply eyeliner to the bottom lid. The sand had been rocky and the sky dotted with hefty clouds, and the smell of tanning oil and seaweed very powerful. It was a public beach that smelled of humans and spills, and one that was only available a few months a year, crowded with city people out for the day or the weekend.

By contrast, the Florida beaches seemed manufactured, the flat sky and odorless light green water, the piercing sun that could give a bad burn, the silence—all this made me uneasy. The manic confidence that had carried me on the plane out of New York had dissipated to nothing.

The cab pulled up in front of the hotel, and confused, I rechecked the postcard. I'd been picturing a little boutique hotel. This building didn't even seem to be part of the same landscape we'd just passed through. The orange paint was flaking, the neon sign had two letters out. I stepped over crushed cigarette butts on the patio.

The man at the front desk was stocky with heavy apathetic eyes. He said there was no one by the name of Rhinehart there. Immediately I panicked, thinking he might have changed hotels or even left the area. I described him, white-haired, liked to talk. There was a mole on his wrist, but I doubted the desk clerk had gotten close enough to see it.

He started laughing. "Awful Spanish? He come and sit here at the bar. Always he wear this straw hat."

I didn't know the hat.

He rang up Rhinehart's room. "A woman named Tatie here for you."

I heard Rhinehart's surprised exclamation.

The man hung up, and pointed a thick finger at the stairs. "Second floor. Room 202. Elevator's broken."

"He'll be checking out," I said.

"He's paid through the week. No refunds."

Annoyed, I asked, "Did he pay in cash?"

The man gave an almost imperceptible nod.

Rhinehart was waiting with the door open, and he greeted me casually, as if I'd just dropped in from a neighboring beach hotel. Convulsingly, I hugged him and held on. I hadn't expected to feel such an upsurge of relief, and I tried to hide it.

"What's wrong?" he asked.

"I'm just so happy to see you. Why are you staying here?"

He looked down. "I'm depressed, Tatie."

I was a person holding a lot of information unsteadily in my hands, uncertain of what to put down, what to keep.

"You found me," he said, finally. I nodded, and he stepped aside to let me in.

There was an unpleasant musty smell coming either from the room or from him—both were in disarray. He'd been making use of the two beds. One was bare—the sheets had been stripped off and balled into the corner. If I had ever been concerned, I knew now no woman had been here.

He was fiddling with the mini-fridge, his back to me, I could see his unwashed hair sticking up in all directions. He had degenerated so quickly—now when he fell apart, it showed.

"I don't think this temperature's quite right," he said, his hands all over the inside of the door. A flooding of anxiety made me sit down. By his foot there was a stain the size of a dinner plate where the appliance had leaked.

On top of the cheap plywood dresser, he'd stacked his toiletries, empty Styrofoam cups, and scraps of paper. I picked up a Walgreen's receipt, on which he had scrawled, "He scat death on the beach." Another said, "I don't think I can sleep with the window open anymore."

"Let's leave here," I said. "I made a reservation for us at the Palms."

He leaned against the door frame of the bathroom. Above his head, a section of the molding was missing. "Expensive."

"Not so expensive that you can't afford it." He'd always been very open about his finances, leaving his old-fashioned bankbook out, as if he were courting my family's approval. Once I discovered I was pregnant, I'd gone back to his apartment and taken another pass through his desk, and then the file cabinets, including the folders of statements. He had far more money than I thought. Well over two million dollars in cash and assets. How did he have so much! I tracked his funds through multiple folders—it seemed he'd put the revenue from a few illustrious posts, his royalties, and international speaking fees into an investment portfolio that had multiplied it. Coming upon this information, crouching on the dusty floor amongst the files, I was shocked and then saddened—I hadn't known there was such a disparity between us. I had barely anything, less than three thousand dollars in my savings account, and some money in a CD from my father's will. Rhinehart, an immigrant's child, with no good role models, was far more savvy with finances than he'd let on.

He was now trying to convince me that there were two perfectly good beds here for us to sleep on. He would call down to housekeeping. Ask them to send up fresh sheets.

"No way. This is a place people go to drink themselves to death."

"Maybe that's what I'm here for." He was backlit against the picture window. I saw a smeary face print on the glass. Or was that from someone's ass?

"Is this because of Lazar not coming to New York? Is this why you're so upset?"

He didn't seem surprised. Maybe he assumed I'd rifle through his apartment for an answer. "I'm depressed. I told you."

To move us along, I told him I'd wait for him in the lobby. Grudgingly, he said, "If I knew you were going to come down here and start ordering me around, I would have sent a generic postcard."

"I would have found you anyway," I said. "You have five minutes."

There was a grubby bar at the foot of the stairs with no patrons and a man was passed out in the only chair in the lobby, so I stood near the rack of pamphlets and free condoms. A skinny woman, her hair knotted into an orange scarf, was stacking out slices of Wonder Bread and brown spotted bananas for the continental breakfast, although it was past noon. I felt the panic hardening in my stomach at the thought of being alone with him in this dirty, aimless city with so much unsaid between us. I wasn't sure I had the courage to say it.

The bartender with cracked lips was watching me, hoping to get my eye, and I thought of the little body forming in my uterus. Seven weeks pregnant. I turned away. On the other side of the open door was a lazy, overcast Florida afternoon. People walked by with beat-up shopping bags or transistor radios, singing to themselves. No one seemed well here, me included.

I was starting to worry Rhinehart had escaped through an alley door when I heard and then saw him coming down the stairs, dragging an army-issue duffel behind him. I went over to help. "Damn elevator was broken," he said, panting. He dropped it in the middle of the floor and turned to the bartender. "Well, Jimmy, the woman here says I need to leave. We'll have to finish our trivia session another time." He looked genuinely disappointed.

Jimmy was talking to the drunk man, who had migrated to a stool. He waved at Rhinehart, but his eyes slipped down to my breasts. "Sure, friend."

"Come on," I said, pulling on Rhinehart's arm. He looked as if he wanted to take a seat at the bar.

Out on the hot sidewalk, I hailed a cab, and Rhinehart held his hands up in a lamentation sign, refusing to get in.

"But it's several miles up!" I said.

"Then we'll walk until we get tired."

But I'm pregnant! I thought. But as the younger, healthier, and seemingly more stable person, I was left to my own devices. Together we dragged the bag, scraping along the pavement. He kept stopping at vendor tables, fingering thin silver chains, flipping through obscure beat-up paperbacks, trying to start a conversation with whoever was selling. He refused to look at me, as if I were his parole officer and he wanted to maintain the illusion he was free. The sun had come out, and sweat trickled down under his broad straw hat. A shirtless man, hanging out of a doorway, made kissing noises at me as I passed.

I was praying we weren't headed in the wrong direction, into some dirty South Beach netherworld far from the bank of hotels. But gradually the area started to improve, and I persuaded him to take a cab up Collins Avenue to our hotel. Everything got better once we entered the white-pillared lobby, the palm ceiling fans creating a gentle breeze—even the air seemed purer here. Our hotel room had large soft beds with down quilts and sliding glass doors that opened onto a balcony overlooking a breathtaking view of the ocean. "Isn't this great?" I said.

Rhinehart had laid down on top of the covers, his back to me. He had fallen asleep.

I went out for a walk on the beach, staring mournfully into the wind. Alone, fully dressed, I wound around laughing couples sitting out on their towels, drinking cocktails. This was not the place to have a breakdown. But what had I expected, that we'd just reunite as if nothing had happened?

When I returned to the hotel room, Rhinehart was no longer on the bed. The patio door was open, and my breath caught, picturing him sprawled out on the cement six flights down. But he was sitting in a chair with my laptop; he'd already established an Internet connection.

I hovered at his elbow, trying to control the self-pity that was making my voice uneven. "It's very painful for me to see you like this."

His shoulders hunched in a sulky way.

"I'm sorry we drifted apart. That I was out so much. But I came all the way down here to find you. I'm trying to make it up to you."

"Whoever tries to do good is often paid back with suffering."

I knew this line. He was paraphrasing from a Merwin poem. A stranger helps an injured snake and once the snake is free, he wraps himself around the stranger's neck, saying he will kill him. As the snake says, that is the law—good deeds are rewarded with bad. They wander around the village looking for examples of this truth.

I said, "That's bullshit, and you're confusing the ending. The dog saved the man's life, and the man rewarded him by giving him a home. Good repaid good."

He frowned. "That's a bad read of the poem." With a few key-taps, he had called it up on his screen. I leaned over his shoulder.

He said, "Look at these last lines. The dog called the man his 'friend' and in turn was treated 'the way a stranger would treat a dog,' i.e.—like shit."

I threw my arms around him. "Rudy, please, what difference does it make? Please come home. Please! We can work this out."

It was like hugging a boulder. He didn't move his arms. For a minute it seemed as if he were weakening, then he turned towards the sun-glinting ocean. He was looking at the water as if he had dropped something in it that he had no hope of retrieving.

"I'm not sure I'm going back to New York," he said.

Four, then five days passed. We cohabitated, but he hardly spoke to me. Mostly he slept. I felt under the mattress for pills, Ambien, Seconol, but found nothing. I'm not sure if that made me feel better or worse.

I spent a lot of time walking on the beach, trying to figure out what to do. Sometimes I brought my camera but I was too distracted to photograph anything. I was tragically lonely, torturing myself with the memory of receiving the news in my gynecologist's office. How bizarrely happy I'd been to hear it confirmed, as if I'd been trying to get pregnant. So eager to tell Rhinehart. This trip was quickly leaching me of those feelings.

I rented a car and drove to Boca, and became so upset I had to pull over. I called Hallie. "What if he stays like this forever? How am I going to raise a child alone?"

"He'll pull it together once he knows. You need to *tell* him."

I couldn't bring my fragile secret into this despairing environment. It would burn up on contact.

"The minute he knows, everything changes," I said. "If his reaction isn't positive, there's no way he can ever take that back. Maybe I should go home and wait for him there." The idea of leaving Rhinehart alone here was frightening. What if he returned to that seedy motel, got a monthly rate?

"Did he tell you to leave?"

"No. He acts as if I'm not here. I don't know what the hell's wrong with him. He's like a man whose entire world has fallen apart. Maybe it's Lazar? He had so much invested in that relationship, as if he was his only family."

"Even more reason to tell him. Your news *is* family."

I couldn't face going back to the hotel and so I wandered up and down Ocean Drive, which was crowded with intimidating groups of people on vacation. After passing by several times, I finally decided on a bar with pink umbrellas and a steel band that I thought might cheer me up. I ordered a Sprite and began a letter to Rhinehart telling him about the baby. That I hoped he would consider being a family with us. He had successfully avoided having children for most of his life, and there could be a reason behind it that I didn't know. Whenever we discussed babies, we'd always focused on me. But I'd changed. Underneath everything, I was still excited. What if he left me? How many times in my life had we separated? I counted. Six. I'd given him up six times, gone through all the emotions, yet here we were. But now I had a child to look out for. I started crying harder. Screw him—if I had to, I would raise the baby on my own. I finished the letter by extolling his good qualities and feeling slightly manipulative.

When I got in, he was waiting for me. "Where have you been? I was starting to worry."

I sat down on the edge of the bed. "I was writing you a letter."

The color left his face. "Please don't give it to me. I can't handle any more letters with bad news in them."

"We're going to have to discuss it."

"Let's have a conversation instead. Tell me what it said."

But I didn't want to have to say all this to his face. What I had planned was to deliver the letter and then go down to the beach while he read it, which would give him time to react without me witnessing it.

His eyes were large and forlorn. I reached my hand out, and he took it. "Why are you so against letters all of a sudden?"

He went over to his suitcase and pulled out a stack of yellowed envelopes, the cursive a faded blue, each one clipped to a blindingly white sheet of paper. It took me a moment to realize that these were Rhinehart's mother's letters to Ukraine—Lazar had managed to sneak them out after all.

I said, "This was the project Lazar said he'd finished."

Rhinehart nodded. "I received them a few days before he said he wasn't coming." He handed them to me and motioned that I go read them. I wasn't sure I wanted to, but I took them onto the balcony anyway. They were in chronological order, spanning a little over a year's time. The letters were addressed to "My darling Yosyp" or "My sunshine," according to Lazar's translation, which was more fluid than his email had been. He *had* worked hard.

In the initial letters, dated over the summer, Rhinehart's mother was chatty and rather sweet, giving details about their tiny railroad apartment in Greenpoint, the heat in the city that you could actually see rising up from the cement. Summer nights it was too hot to stay indoors and men gathered on the sidewalk to play cards, while the women stayed on the stoop to chat. Many of their neighbors were also Ukrainian, some were Russian, and a Polish woman lived next door, she'd lent them a fan. The apartment had a closet even, which the neighbors had said was a rare thing, and Rhinehart's mother had borrowed some hangers and made room in it for Yosyp's clothes. She had even bought him a cloth armchair, secondhand, from a store down the street and was now concerned because she wasn't sure how much to tip the men who would be bringing it up the stairs the following day. Tipping was very important here, she said. A neighbor, maybe Chechna, watched Rhinehart during the day, while she looked for work in Manhattan. Seamstresses were always needed, she'd heard.

At first Rhinehart was scared of the noise, but now he seemed delighted with all the trucks that came by, especially those delivering gas. There was a firehouse halfway down the block, and the kids would gather there to watch the firemen washing the trucks or going out on calls, the dog jumping on at the last moment. That past evening she'd taken him down to watch, a pair of the firemen's boots had fallen off the truck as it was pulling out, and Rhinehart had helped throw them back on. He also enjoyed watching the other kids play stickball in the street, although he was too young. *He loves to watch everything. Like an owl.* They had gone together to the Criterion Theatre in Times Square and both of them had their mouths hanging open. He was picking up English quickly, and soon would surpass her. She was being given lessons from an American woman who lived down the block in exchange for doing the woman's shopping. The woman had bursitis and it was painful for her to walk.

Over the following months, she wrote to say she now had a job and was working very long shifts, sometimes ten hours, at a factory making ladies dresses in midtown, which she talked about only briefly. For two letters, nothing was said about Yosyp's prospective arrival, and then all of a sudden she took up the subject with renewed force—*We keep your place set at the table every night. "That's Papa's chair," says your son. Why hasn't the Good Lord seen fit to send you yet! Why haven't you come!*

There was also an element of fantasy creeping in. I assumed, based on Rhinehart's memories of his childhood, that they had never lived in a doorman building. I'm not even sure there were any in Greenpoint in the mid-1950s. The doorman was mentioned in the same letter as the suitor, a man who insisted on buying Anna a mink stole, which she returned, saying her husband would be angered.

In the next letter, little Rhinehart had caught pneumonia. He was very ill and maybe wouldn't last long. Then nothing. Two months passed with no correspondence, while Rhinehart languished. From what I could infer, Yosyp had been investigating the illness story during that time with the help of a mutual acquaintance in Brooklyn. Rhinehart had been seen chasing a schoolmate on the playground with his jacket open, apparently in perfect health. Anna's reply was irate. *He was feeling better that day! The doctor said fresh air would be good. And he was* not *running around. He was sitting, taking in the sun. Your spy is a liar. If you are so concerned then why don't you come and see him for yourself!*

The next paragraph was devoted to determining who the spies were with a list of possible names, fired off, I suspected, in fear, now that she realized much of the content of her prior letters was considered suspect, too. And then this: *I told him all about you and what you did, all your lies and promises to come join us. It's been months! Why should I keep that bad agreement? Marta knows you don't love her otherwise you never would have found me, you would have stayed at home with your wife. She has family! They can help her raise Lyuba—she is nine now, almost a woman. I have been caring for our baby son alone in a strange country with a strange language for months! While you feed me promises to come! We are* alone*!*

So this was the news Rhinehart had been so anxious to uncover. He was the illegitimate child, not Lyuba.

His child voice, fabricated by his mother, was also indicting: *"I never want to see Papa again. All he does is hurt us." Your own son said that about you. What a lousy, selfish father you are. Even your own son is shamed that he came from you.*

I got the sense she regretted that letter. There were several penitent ones afterwards talking about daffodils she'd planted along the southern side of the building, a man down the street selling live chicks and ducks for Easter—the first she'd seen since leaving Ukraine, a ferry ride they'd taken, the kindness of the landlord in not increasing the rent that year, how well Rhinehart was doing in school. She referred to enclosed photographs that had been separated from the batch of letters and perhaps were tangled up with the father's things, which Lyuba now had possession of. Rhinehart's father had cut off all communication with Anna, although he continued to send money, which she thanked him for very formally, while pleading that she was "dying of the silence. A word would mean more than this pay."

Four months passed. Then she began writing to Marta. These letters were not as chatty. Rhinehart's mother, the mistress, not the dupe, was presenting herself desperately as being in the right. Proclaiming that Yosyp loved her, that Marta was trapping him, forcing him to stay. If Marta really loved him as much as she said, she would let him go to the U.S., where there was much more opportunity for him to make money. Maybe, she reasoned, he would even send many dollars back to Ukraine so that both families could prosper. As far as I could tell, Marta was not replying. But she was opening the letters. These envelopes were split neatly at the top, as if with a letter opener, whereas the father's had been torn down the side.

The worst one was right around July 4th, in which Anna began setting up a list of comparisons, something of a structured argument. Yosyp had reported to her that he was often irritated at the way Marta talked with food in her mouth. Especially when she was excited about the story, little chewed pieces would drop out and fall onto her blouse. It revolted him. Made him feel he had married a peasant. He ate less because of it, but with Anna, he always had second and third helpings. She then moved on to sexual terrain, and on to the topic of why Yosyp and Marta were no longer sleeping together: *He told me about how you are in bed, you just lie there and stare at the ceiling like a dead deer, so that he loses all his desire. And how you suck in your breath very quick without knowing you do it—it makes him very irritated. And so fat you've gotten! He used to touch my thin waist like he couldn't believe a woman could look like this. He worries that little girl will look like you. Already she is short-legged and big around the middle and shoulders like a farm laborer.*

Another woman, a more aggressive one, would have thrown these letters away, or told Rhinehart's mother to fuck off, or had her husband intervene on her behalf, but Marta had kept them, as if she could learn about a hidden dimension of herself by rereading them. The envelopes had been tied together with a pink ribbon like they'd come from a lover. There was something very wrong about that. The last one was separate from the others and addressed to Yosyp. Inside was a condolence card dated June 1958 when Rhinehart would have been seven years old. *I am sorry to hear Marta has died.*

I remained sitting in that cushioned patio chair, looking out to the whitecapped sea. I was waiting for Rhinehart to join me. He had been watching me through the sliding glass door until I finished. Minutes later, he came out and sat down. I had been thinking what a mess we can make of our lives, when we'd begun with the purest motives of love, and companionship, and the desire to make another person happy.

He began talking quickly, as if there were some personal offense he needed to smooth over. "It's hard to tell from the one-way correspondence, but I think he truly loved her once. She was a real dark-haired beauty and a spitfire, too—gave a lot of backtalk, a flirt. From what I could gather, Marta was the opposite. Very shy. One of those who always spoke in a low voice, laughed into her hands. She was my father's childhood sweetheart. He met my mother after. How carefully she rearranged those facts and then knitted a story around them to give me a sense of legitimacy."

"Do you think your mother knew he was never coming? That he was going to stay in Ukraine?"

"At some point he must have made that clear, as much as she hoped to change his mind. An affair is a hard thing to hide in a small town. That may have been one of the reasons she wanted to escape to the U.S. to begin with. She probably got tired of raising an illegitimate child there."

I thought of the photograph of Rhinehart's father inside its small silver frame, everything compact and orderly, his steel-rod posture, his clean uniform, and trimmed mustache.

He said, "It's hard to square this, Tatie. I didn't even know my mother was capable of thinking these things. She was always so morally upright and honest. She'd smacked me once, the only time she hit me, when she found out I'd stolen a pack of gum from the store, and we marched back there together so that I could return it and ask for leniency from the owner. I remember her grieving. She used to lock herself in the bathroom, crying. I was on the other side of the door, crying for my dead father, too. But instead she was in there writing those terrible letters to his wife to try and shame her into releasing him."

"Your father was the one with two families. He's more to blame than she is."

"They both are. The only one who's blameless is Marta. Lazar told me she had died suddenly. Her cause of death was unknown, maybe her heart, maybe self-inflicted. It's hard to believe that my mother had nothing to do with it. You read the letters. Did she even care? I don't remember her crying the summer of 1958."

You stare at the ceiling like a dead deer.

Rhinehart stood up and went inside. I followed. He was talking fast as if he shared the blame, too. "Lyuba was raised by my father after Marta died, not some stepfather I fabricated—my own father. No wonder she hated the sight of me."

"So your mother went a little crazy. She was suffering, too, and she let you hang on to the idea of your father. You would have lived your life believing only good things about him if you didn't start investigating recently."

"She destroyed the relationship with my father so irrevocably that I had no chance of getting to know him at all. She implicated me in her hate."

"You were a child. I'm sure he didn't blame you."

"He never sent for me after my mother died." Rhinehart was sitting on the edge of the bed, his knuckles pressed into his knees. He looked, at that moment, like a child, one whose fate was in the hands of several bad decision makers. This was *past*, I wanted to say. What difference does it make now? But of course, it made a difference. It was the past that had brought him and me to where we were.

I said, unconvincingly, "Maybe he didn't send for you because he didn't know your mother died."

Rhinehart dismissed this. "Gossip got back and forth to the old country quicker than mail. I would have gone to live with him. He was a loving man, I think, despite everything. Lazar knew him, said he had a great sense of humor. But instead I was taken in by Chechna, a woman who never liked children, and who always acted as if I were a burden."

"But this is *past. Past.* A million other decisions sprang from that one. Your life took shape. You became a poet and a teacher. You prospered here. This is where we met. You can't go back to a decision that you were completely unaware of and had no say in and hope to reconfigure it. That wasn't the way it went."

"It's just so hard to assimilate this information. To account for a door that opened and slammed shut at the same time. Turns out I've spent my life in complete ignorance about my own family. Me—a researcher, a supposed intellectual. My father died in 1995. I was in my forties. All those years! I could have traveled over there, reunited with him, something. Why didn't he ever try and contact me?"

I didn't have an answer.

"This period, when these letters were going back and forth, I'd always thought of as the happiest, purest time of my life. After my mother died, every night I'd walk myself through a memory of her to help me fall asleep. It was the only thing I had to hold on to when I was feeling so alone. This time."

I was picturing a ten-year-old boy carefully laying out his suit for a recital in which no one he knew would be in the audience. I'd never really understood Rhinehart, I realized. I'd always preferred to read my own distorted reflection on him, never fully comprehending how isolated he was or how much he relied on his independence to feel secure. How does one turn around and create a family from that place? I was paralyzed with the thought. Maybe this was why he'd never become a father. Not by any fault or lack of desire, but that in the end, he just wasn't able to open himself up that much.

For the next couple of days, I had a routine. I went out in the morning for coffee and pastries, rehearsing how I would tell him. Riding back up in the elevator, I would become increasingly nervous. I'd walk in, unpack the bag, sit down, and say nothing, the high-speed anticipation fading into depression. I half-hoped he'd ask me about the letter I'd written and never given him, but he seemed to have forgotten about it. I called Marty to say that I wanted to extend my "vacation" by another week. "You *must* be having fun," he said. "I don't blame you. Florida's terrific."

"Why the furrowed brow?" Rhinehart asked one morning. "And when did you stop drinking coffee?"

It was for the baby. Caffeine was thought to raise the incidence of miscarriages. I had this idea that I would completely change my diet, go organic, no processed foods, low sugar, but it was proving difficult to eat well down here. Just now I was helping myself to crumb cake.

"I'm trying to be healthy," I said. He was actually the one who was gaining a more robust, ruddy appearance. I asked him if he was sneaking beach walks.

He sniffed. "What an odd thing to be surreptitious about. Odd and difficult."

"It would be like you to have me think you were still unwell."

"I'm feeling better, actually. The Atlantic is restorative—all the life in it, the kelp and shuddering jellyfish."

"We might as well go for a swim," I said. "Since we're here."

He went into the bathroom to change into his swim trunks while I sat on the edge of the bed, waiting. His modesty was troubling. He didn't get naked in front of me, and when I'd undressed in front of him—hyper-aware of my stomach, even though it didn't look any different—he left the room. We slept in separate beds. I lay awake, brooding.

We headed out into a bright day with a strong wind. Rhinehart bowed forward, holding his hat down with one hand as we walked around the palm frond umbrellas, the sparkling pool. As we stepped onto the sand, he said, "How about we walk along the street instead and look in the shop windows. It might generate more lighthearted conversation."

We turned towards Washington Avenue, past the peach brick buildings with their flat roofs and glass Venetian blinds.

Rhinehart paused at the shop fronts with the gaudiest wares. "This is what I like about Florida."

"What?"

"This. These shellacked alligator heads. The canned sunshine." He pointed to the back of the display. "That candlestick holder with the seashells in it. This is how all vacations used to be. Beautiful settings, cheap trinkets to remember them by."

His face was lit from the sun bouncing off the pavement, and he seemed pleased. "I always envied those Floridian coots with the dyed hair combed back on their domes. They gave the appearance of being in the prime of their lives. If that were me, I'd wear my gold wristwatch every day, my high-belted shorts. Play golf during the week and bocce on Saturdays. I'd get a nice big car and drive it around everywhere."

This was not the vision of our future I was hoping for. He had on a white shirt that was ruffling in the wind. It was an old man's shirt, cut in a boxy style to accommodate a large stomach. Hallie was right, I never looked at him honestly. I always saw him as a creative and academic powerhouse, exactly as he was in his early forties.

He was going on, "The old guys in my neighborhood used to have those dreams. Those are immigrant dreams, paradise found in a nap and a beer. Academics don't think that way, don't retire."

We crossed the street, passed a big pink restaurant, a sushi place, and then turned back towards the beach. Palm trees were visible between the buildings and street signs.

He said, "I'm sorry I haven't been myself lately."

"Why don't you want to sleep with me?"

He had his face averted, was looking north, towards New York. "I'm afraid to."

My heart was beating at a galloping pace. "Why?"

"I'm afraid. I can't explain why. After my mother died I stopped talking for three months. I just didn't want to talk. I couldn't explain that either."

"At first I thought you were still angry at me because of Laura."

"It was wrong, how I handled that. I felt threatened. You have the right to be friends with whomever you like, and the two of you have an enormous thing in common in art."

"I'm not sure we ever were friends, in the traditional sense." Laura, who had once loomed so large, now seemed as distant as a speck on the horizon. "At any rate, we're definitely not now. I told her about us. You were right. It didn't go over well."

"Ah," he said, smiling to himself. He turned away, probably to hide it from me.

I gripped his arms, stopping him in the middle of the sidewalk.

"Does it even matter? Any of this? Me coming down here to that bad hotel, being here with you?"

"Of course it does! Talking about the letters with you changed everything. But nothing gets miraculously better overnight. Maybe it's ridiculous but I feel as if I'm mourning my mother all over again. Grief is a powerful force, Tatie. It's shallow but it has a very strong current."

I was thinking about how we're able to bear things we think we can't—losing people that mean everything. My father driving an hour in a snowstorm in the middle of the night to retrieve me from a slumber party because the girls were being mean. I had snuck away to call him. He didn't try and talk me out of it, he just got in the car.

We were on the beach, and I removed my sandals. Rhinehart took my hand. "I was *so* relieved when you showed up here. And you brought the light with you. Deep down, I knew you would. So don't worry about the intimacy. It will come back. I'm already feeling it. You're looking so fresh and fecund lately, maybe it's the sun, and the—"

"I'm pregnant. I found out while you were away. The doctor confirmed it." I paused. "The baby is due in November. November 10."

He had an astonished look, but I was unable to stop talking. "I'm going to have the baby. I know you think I'm afraid, but I'm not. This is no longer a decision I need to make—it's past that point, it's part of me. As much my future as my work." I hadn't known how forcefully I believed these things until I said them. This child, and the role I had in ushering it into the world, belonged to my purpose here. In this chaotic procession of events, accidental encounters, and fears that I'd struggled with, there had been an invisible plan. I was experiencing the rightness of my life, all of it, and it felt like lightning had hit me. I was trying to convey this, then I stopped and said, "How do you feel?"

The way he was looking at me recalled a spring afternoon. We'd just gotten back together, and it seemed we'd never be separated again. The air smelled of new grass and mud. I had finished my exams and was excited with everything—being cut free in the middle of the day, the summer spreading out in front of me, meeting up with him—and feeling silly, I linked him and proclaimed I'd ride him back on my bicycle. He could sit on the handlebars. We'd go through town, and I'd ring the bell, and tell everyone how happy we were. I'd just been fooling around, chattering to hear myself talk, but when he looked at me his eyes were full of love, and I was shocked to see myself as he did, as beautiful.

That's how he was looking at me now. He said, "I feel like I've been given an enormous gift that I don't know how to be thankful for."

"Do you mean that? Are we going to raise the baby together?"

"*Tatie*, how else would it be? Did you really think I wouldn't want to? That I'd take off like some sort of gigolo?"

My body had been gripping so much fear that when it let go, all of the happiness drained out with it, and I bent over. He held me awkwardly around the shoulders while I coughed, like someone getting sick into the sand.

He said, "I guess we both knew less about how our lives were going to turn out than we thought."

We slept in the same bed that night, and Rhinehart made love to me in a sweaty, natural way, as if in deference to my new partnership with mother nature. Afterwards we lay staring out at the milky traces of the moon, listening to the distant slap of the ocean.

Into my hair, he asked, "Why have you stuck with me through all this? I'm not even a young man anymore. You know, throughout my life, I've often doubted whether I was suited for a relationship. I worried there was something wrong with me."

When I was younger, I'd felt Rhinehart hadn't loved me as much as I loved him. Our relationship and its changing moods had bled all over my life—I thought about him in class, at parties, while studying. For him, the concept of us was so neatly packaged, something he could slide away into a desk with many small drawers. It was a quality that had seemed to empower him.

When I told him this, he said, "Maybe I was just afraid to risk that much of myself on another person after losing my mother."

I'd never felt that way. After my mother died, my father had doubled his affection and responsibilities. He hadn't wanted me to feel alone. I'd been afraid in my life, but I'd never been too afraid to love.

But I worried that Rhinehart still was. I asked and he said, "All the work I've done on myself over the years has led me here, so I must have finally gotten the internal lesson. Now I will be a father, and I will get to put my fearlessness to use in a new way."

It was as much a guarantee as I could offer at this point, myself. Quoting Rilke, I said, "for one human being to love another is the work for which all other work is mere preparation."

Rhinehart was smiling in the dark. I'd pleased him. "His marriage was more short-lived than mine. Do you want to marry?"

The question called up a vision of myself. I was wearing nicer clothes and owned a big house and drove everywhere. I was irritable with all my obligations, and spoke sharply and did no photography. Although I wanted Rhinehart as my partner, I didn't want to be a wife to anyone. But I also wasn't going to say so right then. Rhinehart seemed vulnerable, and I didn't want to hurt his feelings.

He didn't pursue it. Perhaps he understood. "What a magnificent mother you'll be. So warm and intelligent."

"Sometimes I'm a little worried I won't have the natural instinct."

"Nonsense. You're going to be knocked over by the force and the hunger of your love. Like Anna Karenina with little Seriozha, obsessed with the sound of his voice, the smell of his hair, while he was wriggling in her arms so as to touch his whole body on her. That joy."

CHAPTER SIXTEEN

Once we got back to New York, the first thing we needed to do was call Laura. She had left a message on my cell phone saying she would like an update on the search now that she was "involved against her will."

Rhinehart would do anything for me lately, looking at me with spaniel eyes as if I were the most wondrous thing he could imagine, carrying around his child. It was a new feeling of power I had—even if everyone else disappeared, my job would still be to bring this baby into the world.

Taking advantage, I said, "You be the one to call Laura."

He balked. "Do you think it's necessary? I like to keep those phone calls to a minimum."

After a little bickering, he did call her, while I made myself scarce. Twenty minutes later, he emerged from his study, frowning.

"How did she take it?"

"She was pissed."

"About us or because she was worried you were really missing."

He shook his head. "Not that. She didn't seem to care where I'd been. She was upset that you were pregnant."

"You *told* her! You didn't have to go that far!"

"I wanted to get it over with. I rarely talk to the woman. I wouldn't even be talking to her now if it weren't for you. We'd email, maybe." He smiled. "And I'm proud. A proud father-to-be."

Part of me was relieved it was out in the open, so that I didn't have to make any more confessions. "What did she say?"

"That I'm too self-absorbed to raise a child. I didn't even feel defensive. That's how sure I am that I'm going to be a great father."

I smiled.

"She also told me to tell you to call Clare Severeson. They have an opening in the schedule this summer, a cancellation or something, and she suggested you."

"Clare from George Menten? Really?" I had met her briefly when Laura was introducing me around. She'd been a curator at the Brooklyn Museum and had an intelligent, nonpretentious way of speaking about the artists the gallery represented. I'd actually just seen her picture in a profile spread for *Elle* on young, up-and-coming people in the art world—she was a short-haired African American woman, around my age. In the article, she'd talked a lot about contemporary painting, which seemed to be the gallery's focus. I'd liked her when I met her, and she'd been polite, but she'd also been a little cool to me, and I'd just assumed she wasn't interested in my work.

Rhinehart was now telling me she was. "And the two of them seem to be in agreement."

"It's hard to believe that Laura set this up. She said she was done with me."

"She's an unexpected woman," he said.

We were getting into summer, and I was growing too fat for my normal pants, although I didn't want to rush out and start buying maternity clothes. Instead I'd begun dipping into Rhinehart's closet, and he was often amused to see me walking past in one of his dress shirts, the sleeves rolled up.

Rhinehart's publisher wanted to put out a collection of selected works, and he had the idea that he'd pair the poems with revised versions, to show how years of not writing, what he called his "wordless gap," could change the way he understood poetry. He downplayed the project, calling it "revision." But one evening, as I was passing the study, I caught him at his desk with the familiar yellow notepad and pencils, and that big-eyed alarmed look he got when he was writing and writing well.

I preserved the silence around the subject for days, waiting for him to mention it. He didn't. Finally I approached him as he was doing bills and said, "You're writing poetry again."

It was a statement, not a question, and he looked up at me and laughed. "Not at this moment."

"You know what I mean."

He removed his glasses, considering this. "I guess I am, aren't I? For all the production of not doing it, the starting again was very quiet—it stole back into the room on soft little feet."

"How does it feel?"

"It feels—natural. I can't seem to remember what it was like *not* to do it. How easy it is to forget your struggles once everything's going well. What mercy there is in that."

When he wasn't writing, he was researching how to be a parent as if there were going to be a qualifying exam. I caught him drinking coffee at night, surrounded by books and notepaper, and said he was taking it too far.

"I have no frame of reference and only a few months to learn. I have to cram." He watched me pick up a plastic-sheeted library book from the stack and check the copyright date.

"Don't worry, I'm not being stingy. Whichever of these books looks good—if the philosophy's sound and the writing isn't too pedestrian, I'm going to buy. That way I can underline."

"I'm not worried about you buying." I had to stop him from buying. Near my foot, there was a miniature red plastic dinette set and chairs for six. "I hate kiddie furniture. It looks weird in here."

"What fun, though! The child can host a dinner party. That's a very New York thing I was reading in the *Times*."

"But this is preschooler stuff. Even that high chair won't be usable for a year. By the time the baby's old enough it's going to be outdated, and maybe even some kind of safety recall."

I felt a sinking mood coming on. It was like this lately—I oscillated between elation and doubt. For one, the show at George Menten wasn't as assured as I'd assumed. They were considering several artists for the slot, although Laura's recommendation had gotten me in that group. I'd also begun to have trouble sleeping, which I blamed on the cauldron of hormones. But it was more than that—I was harboring secret fears about my own ability to parent, and sometimes, about Rhinehart's abilities—also unproven. Would I even like this child? What if our personalities clashed? I couldn't stand negative people, and what if the child was narcissistic or cruel or a liar? Those types of personality traits were sometimes ingrained; there was only so much you could do.

Hallie told me I was talking about the kid as if I were going on a blind date. "It's even weirder than your baby phobia. How is that phobia?" When I brushed this off, she brought up an incident from 1991 when our hippie friend Droopy had come over to the apartment with his baby, and I had refused to hold her, and then when pressured into it, said my head felt like it was evaporating and I was losing my balance and I needed to put her down before I dropped her. "You and the baby were all red and grimacing. Both of you about to burst into tears!"

"How relevant is this—it happened so long ago. And it's not a phobia. I'm surrounded by pictures and plenty of reading material on newborns. Rhinehart keeps bringing home—"

She insisted that wasn't the same thing as holding one. To prove it, she arranged a lunch at her Manhattan apartment with her friend Veronica, a fashion editor, who had a nine-month-old. Hallie hadn't informed me of this, for fear I wouldn't show up, and so I'd arrived in a pair of Rhinehart's old khakis while the two of them were in heels. Hallie forced me to hold the baby the entire afternoon, even when it seemed he'd prefer to be sleeping, and asked me a series of questions used to diagnose anxiety attacks, which I deflected. She gave up and began interrogating Veronica about her postpartum depression.

Ricardo. He looked like a studious college boy, hair brushed back from his forehead. Veronica had dressed him in faded jeans and a button-down shirt, and he seemed generally pleased with his surroundings, making some intense eye contact with me, smiling distantly, and then making the same eye contact with the blank television set. His head wobbled. If I had ever disliked babies, I was that way no longer. Even the smell of him was sweet. He lay against my stomach like a hot water bottle, while underneath my shirt, my own baby lay.

After Veronica left, Hallie collapsed on the sofa, as if she'd been entertaining a roomful of children while serving a meal that hadn't been catered.

I was thanking her. "I got all sorts of tips—that thing about drinking ginger ale for morning sickness instead of eating saltines that can make you gain weight. And heartburn is pretty common and can last throughout the pregnancy."

"You should have asked her about her labia. Whether they're still hanging down like a bunch of blackened grapes."

"Veronica seems tireless."

"She's got a live-in nanny—she's only mothering part-time. It's a tough job if you're not suited for it, temperamentally."

"Constance did it—how bad could it be?"

"My mother didn't exactly embody the maternal role, if you remember. We never once sat together for dinner. I just ate wherever I wanted—on the damn tire swing. She told me to smoke to keep my weight down. To skip meals unless a man invited me to a restaurant."

But Constance had also been there for me when I'd first gotten my period. It was a school day, and pleading sickness, I had stayed home. My father was out in the field. Over the course of the morning, I'd been working myself into a frenzy of misinformation. The blood was brown and I was in a searing amount of pain—I was likely dying of an infection, which, in my shame, I was unable to seek medical treatment for. Finally, after writhing around on my bed for two hours, I packaged up my stained underwear in a paper bag, and ran stumbling to Hallie's, gripping my stomach the entire way. Without even knocking I burst into the house and then into Constance's room, where she was sitting on the bed, eating a slice of cheesecake and flipping through a magazine. I was bawling and waving the bag around, and I remembered her putting the plate down to look inside it. Then she patted the bed next to her, and I gratefully collapsed and curled up, moaning, while she stroked my hair, retrieved two ibuprofen from her bedside dresser, and poured me a glass of water from a pitcher. "You rest here," she said. She'd gotten up and was putting on a red felt coat with black buttons.

I was so shocked, I stopped crying. I'd never seen her in outerwear. "Where are you going?"

"To the store," she said, as if she did that every day. Then, with clicking heels—she'd also put on shoes—she went downstairs and got in the car that I didn't know she could drive and backed out, as I, amazed, watched from the upstairs window.

In less than twenty minutes she returned with what seemed like a year's supply of maxi pads and tampons. Every possible kind. "Your father's a lovely man, but I imagine he'll be completely useless in this regard. I stocked up for you."

Then we went in her bathroom together, and she taught me how to use everything. It was one of the best memories I had of Constance, her sitting on the edge of the tub, ashing into the drain, still wearing that flashy coat. I couldn't take my eyes off it. It seemed to signal everything that was unprecedented and significant about the occasion.

Hallie had never seen her mother drive and at the time had accused me of making it up. I hadn't tried very hard to defend my story, wanting to keep the intimacy of the moment to myself.

I was on the verge of defending Constance now, when Hallie blurted out, "I don't think the Buddhism is working anymore."

"What do you mean 'working'? It's a spiritual practice."

She had a very dark look and was chewing on her thumb. "For a while things were great between Adán and me but now I'm starting to lose it again. Do you know what I did the other day? I looked in Kate's car while she was in the dentist's office."

"Who's Kate?"

"She's a friend of mine—I have a weird feeling about her and Adán. I don't like how cozy they are when we go over there. She has so many kids, and he kept picking them up and playing hide-and-seek, and running around and shouting like he was at his own first-grade birthday party. It was a completely different man from the one who agreed I was going to have my tubes tied. And when he talks about her it's always with this sympathy, how hard it is for her raising the kids alone, and how sad they no longer have their father."

"How did he die?"

"He didn't die, he ran off. He's sailing his yacht somewhere in South America with a twenty-year-old, his former assistant. Sad for the kids, but Kate's not hurting for money—she seems to have more now than before. So I don't know why Adán has to take on the weight of it. She looks pretty happy to me." Hallie leaned closer. "I saw her car in the parking lot, and I pulled over to search it for evidence. Not everything—just the glove compartment, ashtray, those little pockets behind the seats. Not the trunk."

I disapproved. "Did you find anything?"

"No. But I didn't have all that much time. She's an upstater but still, I don't think she would leave the car unlocked if she was having a crown put in. Last time I cut it too close."

"How many times have you done this?"

"A couple."

It was then that I got concerned. When I asked her, half-kidding, if she'd also broken into Kate's house, she said, "Not yet."

"But that's nuts. You shouldn't be indulging this paranoia."

She brushed me off, as if my advice was no longer relevant. "I know how to settle it now. I'm going to throw a party. You're coming. And you can even bring the old man. I've invited about thirty people."

"To dinner?"

"Adán loves big parties. He's always complaining our house 'has no life.' I told him to invite whomever he wanted, people from the company, friends of friends—I drew the line at kids. Anyone above the age of fifteen is fine. The more the better. If I'm going to catch him out doing something, I need a distracting environment where he'll feel at ease. I even invited Ramón Marles."

"Ramón from the East Village? You keep in touch with him?"

"No, but he got Adán drunk once. It's this competitive Latin thing."

I hesitated. "What exactly do you have planned? Maybe you should just discuss this with him."

She got angry. "He's my husband, of course I've discussed it. All he does is get pissed and then not speak to me for days. He says I'm trying to remove his balls. Well, fine, if nothing is going on then my plan will turn up nothing and he can have them back and we can all return to normal."

I let it go, but secretly prayed she'd decide to cancel the idea before then.

Instead I received an invitation in the mail. We were to show up two Saturdays from now, wearing all white. Appropriate attire required for entry.

I told Rhinehart, who said, "A party! Sounds like fun."

"No it doesn't! It sounds dangerous and elaborate. She has some plan to catch her husband having an affair."

Rhinehart scratched his chin, where he was growing a beard "to amuse the baby." "Maybe it will turn out to be rather harmless. A big misunderstanding."

I doubted it. I was seeing this entire situation through the veil of Hallie's paranoia and general oddness and had a strong feeling the night would end badly. "I just can't believe Adán would cheat on her."

"I can. Even Ovid knew you couldn't find one man in a thousand who believed virtue was its own reward."

"I hope you're not referring to yourself. With that new translator who's been hanging around."

He had finally found a legitimate translator to work on his books of poetry, an NYU grad student with diluted blue eyes, who always wore the same thing—fitted black pants, white blouse, and black sweater—an archivist's uniform. She was slim, a little brittle looking, and serious. Her accent was barely discernible, more a slight hiss on the end of some words. They worked for hours together, three times a week, debating language choices—sometimes laughing.

Rhinehart was amused by my jealousy. He liked any emotional evidence he could relate to pregnancy hormones. "Marynia is the furthest thing from being interested in me. She's engaged to an economics professor at CUNY. They're getting married this winter. She wants to buy an apartment in Hoboken, but you can't get much for your money there."

"You seem to know a lot about her."

"We can't talk about poetry the entire time," he said.

The closer we got to this dinner party, the more I began to dread it. To distract myself I began shooting at the Botanic Garden, bundles of roses that looked like bouquets. I found if I shot at midday and lit just the flower with a strobe, while underexposing the ambient light with the shutter, I got something that looked like a nineteenth-century Dutch painting. Highly stylized flowers illuminated against a background of midnight. In retouching, Evelyn brought up the whites in the petals, giving the entire image an eerie effect. So I was still thinking about Hallie. Those artfully manipulated arrangements were similar to ones I'd seen at her house.

CHAPTER SEVENTEEN

The night of the party, we were running late. Close to six and Rhinehart was standing in his closet, still in his boxer shorts and socks. He brought out the white pants that I'd pressed, pointing at the crotch accusingly. "I forgot these were pleated! Pleats are too fey for this crowd. I'll have to wear something else—these white jeans."

"Those are too casual. It's supposed to be formal."

"Or these linen pants, then. I'll need to iron them."

"I hope you realize you're not going there as a single man." I got up from the couch, where I was sitting in my own white outfit, and followed him into the bedroom.

"I have a young, beautiful, pregnant wife. I need to look deserving." He insisted on calling me his wife, saying he used it in the "emotional sense."

I watched him remove the ironing board from the closet where I had just put it back, gently unfold it, and then return for the iron. I was getting increasingly impatient. Hallie had called me three times to tell me not to be late. "Maybe I should go, and you can meet me there," I said.

This idea was evidently too ridiculous for him to comment on. He continued pressing the pants.

Rhinehart was behind the wheel and in the mood to reminisce. He was tramping around fondly in what I recalled to be a miserable afternoon, years ago, when he, Hallie, and I wandered around town in an irritable state of indecision, searching for somewhere to have lunch. We couldn't find the place Rhinehart had suggested, she blamed him for wasting our time with his "memory restaurant," and the two of them began carping at each other so forcefully that I worried there was sexual tension between them. "If she and I were contemporaries," Rhinehart was saying now, "she would have scared me out of my wits. Those mischievous eyes! She wouldn't hesitate to pull a practical joke that would make you look foolish."

I'd been keeping the two of them apart, not entirely by accident, and the idea of them seeing each other again was making me nervous. I hoped Hallie wouldn't say anything unkind. Whenever she did, I initially dismissed it, but over time the comment worked on me with its souring strength. I had always depended on her opinion. Rhinehart's, as well. They both had such a strong and polarizing pull, Hallie and Rhinehart, that I sometimes felt like a moon trying to orbit around two planets.

Hallie opened the door in a floor-length satin dress in an arresting, liquid red color, like the inside of a pomegranate, that made a V almost to the navel—flapper style—it showed off the delicate bones of her clavicle more than her cleavage, which was minimal. She'd had her hair cut in a glossy black sheet that came to her chin, with a few longer pieces in front. Even though I'd stopped comparing us years ago, next to her tonight, I was a milkmaid, a round-faced girl in a white cotton dress she'd mistakenly thought charming.

"Wow," Rhinehart said breathlessly, clasping Hallie's hands. "Look at you. You've grown into a beautiful woman." Which made me cringe—it was something someone's father would say.

She didn't seem to notice. "I've played it up for the party." Leaning in to kiss me, she said, "Adán put up a fit because he wanted to wear his *black* tux. Nearly gave me a heart attack!"

Rhinehart said, "I think a black tux would have been perfect. The two of you set off against all the guests in wh—"

She interrupted in a cooing voice. "Come, I want to show you off. You're famous in this crowd—they like to think of themselves as intellectuals just because they read *The New Yorker.* And Adán's assistant has been dying to meet you. She's a poet, too, evidently." She linked his arm. "Terry must still be jealous over us. That's why she keeps you hidden away." I started to follow them, and she pointed to the kitchen, as you would to a dog. "Go tell Win to send around another tray of mushroom mousse." Her look said she was angry I had arrived so late.

I watched them head towards the vaulted living room, where the guests crowded like a flock of trapped doves. Staring, I tripped on the corner of a rug and almost fell down on my stomach. I'd become so clumsy lately. Something to do with the excess fluid in the joints. I repressed a wave of self-pity.

In the kitchen, Win was dressed in a lurid purple pantsuit and red apron—she was also exempt from the dress code. She was a big, coarse woman, and around her you felt crammed by her high-volume talk and the pressure to respond by laughing. She immediately got me on the subject of my pregnancy and its gastrointestinal effects. She had four children and a theory that the last boy was a depressive because she'd been going through a divorce and cried "all the damn time" while he was in utero. I didn't like hearing this and let my attention wander to the darkened patio, where a waiter slouched against the garage smoking a cigarette, or a joint.

Hallie came rushing in minutes later. "Suspect numero uno hasn't showed."

I arched my eyebrows to indicate Win, who was standing behind me.

"She's in on it," she said, steering me into the dining room.

The long table twinkled, as if dusted with frost, tiny points of light refracting off the cut crystal glassware and vases and high polished silver. For a moment I was overtaken, subsumed by that wordless excitement I'd experienced as a child when I saw delicately beautiful iridescent things: cellophane, paintings of fairy wings.

In front of each plate was a fingerbowl of pink roses and a white place card with a name. Hallie pointed to the far end of the table. "I'm sitting there." Of the nearer end: "Adán's here. I don't want to put him on guard by sitting too close. He knows I have sharp eyes." She pointed to the seat to his right. "Kate's here, next to him. Obvious, I know, but there's no other way to do it. I put suspect number two on his other side. Liza, his golfing buddy's wife. I don't think it's her—he's not into the freckly thing. But he seems to think I'm jealous of her, so he'll believe he has a buffer for Kate. If it is Kate. And if she shows up—I don't know why the hell she isn't here yet."

My place card was next to Liza's. Rhinehart's was miles away. "How come Rhinehart and I aren't sitting next to each other?"

Hallie rolled her eyes. "Couples are never seated together. It's bad etiquette. So here's how it works." She sat in Adán's seat, at the head of the table, to demonstrate. "This is the corner he'll be sharing with Kate"—she waved her hand above that area, like a magician. "If he wants to touch her in secret—and believe me, if he's fucking her, he'll want to touch her in secret—he will have to stick his hand underneath the table here, bypassing the table leg and these weird little decorative things, to get to her knee, thigh, crotch, anywhere on her lap. He will have to do this while *not looking at his hand*. So here's the genius—" In the flickering light, her eyes looked manic. "I've put a black substance, a marking oil—it took me forever to get the consistency right, it's sort of like thick ink—on the leg of the table that he shares with Kate, and underneath the table here, along the diagonal path from his body to hers. If his hand is reaching for her there's no way he can avoid brushing against the oil somewhere, and once he touches her, the evidence will be all over her *white* dress, wherever he put his hand."

She stood up, triumphant. "I even extended it over on her side in case she reaches for him. I didn't bother with Liza's side."

I was horrified. "Where did you come up with this?"

"I read about some Brazilian society women who did it with white powder to catch a man playing footsie. My idea's better."

She pointed to my seat, which was diagonally to his left. "You're there so you can overhear any conversation and watch their body language. I put a bore on your other side so you won't get distracted."

I rubbed my back, which was starting to ache. "I'm against this plan. If you're going to make me do it, then at least put Rhinehart next to me. He's the only person I know here."

"Will you stop with that? It took me over a week to come up with the seating chart!"

I crossed my arms, annoyed, and she sighed. "All right, I guess I can put him across from you, is that good enough? He doesn't know anything, does he?"

"No," I lied.

"This is better anyway," she said switching the cards. "Adán will be less suspicious of you then. And it puts that tramp Lindsay on Rhinehart's other side—he's out talking to her now. Serves you right for making such a big deal about it." She inched over the flower arrangement so that I could have a better view of Adán's seat.

Win stuck her head in the dining room and announced that dinner would be ready in ten minutes and to start getting everyone to the table. In the living room, I found Rhinehart, who was talking to a dark-haired, small-boned girl with ferrety little brows. She was in a tight white dress with lace over the cleavage. I came up to them and Rhinehart encircled my thick waist.

"We were just discussing Rimbaud. I've always thought Satie was his equivalent in the musical realm. Every art form has its mirror in another," he said to Lindsay, who nodded knowingly.

He continued, "To Neruda there is André Kertész, a mood-inflected Hungarian photographer. Very emotive work. In just the shadow of a fork against a plate, he could convey a lifetime of loneliness."

This was an almost word-for-word rip-off of what I had said two days ago, when I'd taken Rhinehart to see the exhibit at the ICP.

"Time for din-din," Hallie said, appearing next to Lindsay and taking her thin arm. Once they were out of earshot, Rhinehart said to me, "Young women are constantly touching themselves, making all these little adjustments to their clothes and hair. So distracting—I kept losing my train of thought."

"You seemed to be doing okay."

He looked expectantly around the room. "I had hoped to get one of these young fathers to discuss his methods of disciplining with me. Maybe at dinner."

We went into the dining room and Rhinehart found his place next to Lindsay, who was already seated. "Isn't this fortuitous!" he said robustly, shooting an unhappy look at me.

The man to my left, who had a rough-hewn face and a disarming way of speaking about his wife as if she wasn't sitting two seats down, was talking about his new home in Englewood Cliffs. They were going to close on it next week. The homeowner offered to pour me a glass of wine. I passed. Across from me, Rhinehart was responding to something Lindsay said with his forced laugh, "Ha, ha, ha," like clumps of snow falling off a roof.

Kate had arrived finally, a little breathless, just as we were assembling at the table. Whatever I had been expecting, it wasn't this. Everything about her seemed to indicate an average suburban mother, her thick sandy-colored hair, her sporty white ensemble that resembled a tennis dress with a long skirt. In fact, walking into this scene without prior knowledge, I'd place a bet that the seductress was Hallie, with that harlot-colored gown, and darting eyes, and loud, flirtatious talk at the end of the table.

I was trying to discreetly watch Adán, who had finally taken his seat—he'd been continuing a conversation he'd started in the other room, and once at the table, kept leaving to fetch photographs related to it. He was flush with laughter and talk, enjoying himself immensely—I wasn't sure I'd ever seen him so happy. Catching my eye, he said, "Hola, guapa! I didn't even greet you." He came around to my side of the table, kissing me on my cheeks, and reaching down to rest his hand on my stomach. "How beautiful you look—so happy and healthy looking. A very natural woman. And the father there—" He pointed across the table to Rhinehart, who looked as if he'd just been presented an award. "He is very happy, too. Muy orgulloso as we say in Spanish—" Adán swelled out his chest. "Very proud. Like a toreador."

Kate was telling the story of why she was late—the nanny had come down with the flu at the last minute, and after frantic calling around she was finally able to bribe a neighborhood girl out of her movie date to come over. "The worst is that I said, 'Don't worry, I'll feed the kids.' I'd made them spaghetti and meatballs! Which they love, they were over the moon, but when it comes time for them to eat, I'm already dressed, and I'm wearing this *white* dress"—she pointed to herself—"and two aprons, one around my hair, scrambling around trying to serve without getting near the food."

"And this little Bobby, he eats with his hands," Adán said to Rhinehart. "Like this," and he made as if he was flinging food past his mouth and behind him. He was laughing. But was this unusual? Did it indicate he'd spent time at Kate's house alone? I'd seen him looking a little distant earlier, maybe he was thinking about her, or her abandoned kids, or about sailing away on his own boat with a twenty-year-old. How the hell was I supposed to know?

And anyway, Liza seemed like the bigger problem, the way she kept pulling on Adán's arm, and flashing her tan boobs and ropey biceps and big teeth. He appeared to be enjoying that, too. I watched his hands, waiting for them to creep below deck. But they remained in sight, where they could assist him with eating the salad. We just might get through this dinner without a scene after all, I thought, relieved.

Just as the main course was being served, Rhinehart stood, presumably to go to the bathroom. Glancing over, I saw the front of his pants smeared with black. I gasped. He followed my eyes down and said, "Good Lord!"

What had Hallie used! It looked like motor oil. He was dipping his napkin in his water glass, wiping at the stain and making it worse.

I leaned across the table and said, "Maybe you should do that in the other room."

By now most of the table had noticed. Kate got up and went into the kitchen to retrieve salt and seltzer. Win came out, still carrying dinner plates, saying, "No, no. Bleach is the only thing." The man next to me agreed. "You don't know what you're talking about," his wife called down the table, "we stopped buying bleach months ago, because it yellows the fabric. We use Murphy Oil Soap," she told the woman next to her. "It's what chefs use on their whites."

"What the hell is this? Tar?" Rhinehart was running his hand under the table, where he said it felt sticky. His fingers came back coated in a viscous black fluid, so now he couldn't touch anything.

Adán was apologizing to everyone, saying "seat" instead of "sit" and "please ate your dinner." He'd gotten out the flashlight and from under the table, we heard him curse. "It's all over this legs! Everywhere!" But then he came up again, saying, "Not to worry, just a little oil in this section. The rest is fine." But many people, watching Rhinehart still struggling with his pants, remained standing, and were nibbling on bread or asparagus spears they'd taken off their plates. One man was leaning against the wall and eating, as if at a barbecue. Liza and Lindsay and a few others had left the room and could be heard laughing in the hall. Hallie had disappeared. A woman had gotten some black on her dress, even though she'd been seated by Hallie, and was saying repeatedly that it would never come out. Other women began inspecting their dresses. Kate discovered some black on her elbow and a few drops on her knee. I stood up, banging my stomach against on the table lip and gestured furiously to Rhinehart to follow. We passed Hallie standing in the hall, frozen with indecision. Her face had gone pale, all the blood drained out, like a death mask.

Locked in the bathroom together, the light bouncing metallically off the stainless steel and mirrors, Rhinehart and I assessed the damage.

"Did someone touch you?" I asked. "Did Lindsay?" But she had been sitting on the other side of him, away from the oily ink.

"Why would she touch me there? I must have brushed against something."

Eventually, we pieced it together. Leaning over to talk to Kate, he had grabbed on to the table, coming in contact with the oil under her place setting. Hallie hadn't been as precise as she thought in applying it. Rhinehart, black on his hands, and not noticing, had then smeared it while adjusting himself, as the pants he'd chosen to wear were too tight in the crotch.

We'd made a mess of his pants. The entire front was a dirty gray color. The wet linen had gone transparent and I could see the tender outline of his thigh, the white section of pocket. He shook his head. "How humiliating. How could I have been so clumsy?"

"It wasn't entirely your fault," I said. "I'll tell you the whole story when we get home."

But he wasn't that easily consoled. "How humiliating," he said again, rubbing at the stain. "At this party, of all places."

"Since when do you care so much what others think?" I said. And then it occurred to me that he'd probably been anxious to see Hallie after all these years, which is why it had taken him so long to get ready. He was also probably self-conscious in this young, affluent crowd, some of whom knew him by his work. He was no longer just a writer. I, along with the baby, had forced him into a new role and one that could be easily caricatured—an aged goat chasing after his youth.

I put my arms around him, spontaneously. I suddenly loved him so much, it felt like something I would never be able to find proper words for. I knew it only as this tenderness, a dull ache at the center of my heart.

We realized we'd ruined the towel. I folded it and set it alongside the tub, behind the shower curtain. Rhinehart wondered aloud why Adán hadn't come to check on us. "He's such a gracious host."

"I think we should try and sneak out," I said, holding his face in my hands and kissing him. He still looked upset.

"I was really enjoying myself, too." He sighed. "I hope they invite us back."

While we were in the bathroom, Hallie must have confronted Kate. A small crowd was gathered at the end of the hall and Kate was crying—another woman had retrieved Kate's purse and was arranging for people to move their cars so she could leave.

"What's going on?" Rhinehart said to me.

I saw Adán through the open door of his study, where he was smoking a cigar with his business associates—did he know what was going on? Was he pretending not to? He no longer seemed like the host, but some defamed guest, looking deflated and ridiculous in his rumpled white tux, the red bow tie that matched his wife's dress.

I walked up to Hallie and saw her eyes were still burning aggressively. In a voice high with false cheer, as if Kate hadn't just walked past her, sobbing, and out the door—she made a big, theatrical apology for Rhinehart's pants—she'd had some men come in and fix the table leg and they had probably left grease behind. I told her I was leaving. She kissed me roughly on both cheeks, her overheated face bumping mine, and signaled that she wanted to talk to me alone, but I was angry and pretended not to notice—I'd had enough for one night.

CHAPTER EIGHTEEN

I was dreading Hallie's phone call. But I didn't hear from her all day. Or the next day, or the next, and that's when I started to wonder whether she was angry with me, or with Rhinehart for screwing up her trap. I broke down and called her. Before I could even say hello, she said, "Adán's left me." Then the line disconnected. I called back several more times but there was no answer. I was getting my things together to drive to Jersey, when Rhinehart stopped me. "Give her until tomorrow, at least." And because I always seemed to be forcing people out of their shells to comfort me with assurances of their well being, I listened to him.

The next day I went to the florist and selected a large bouquet of her favorites, sunflowers and orange roses, which we used to give each other when we were down. Fresh flowers reminded us of my dad's farm. I had them sent to her house with a note telling her to call me when she was ready. I wrote six versions of that note, debating on whether I should include the line: "I'm worried about you." Protective sentimentality often annoyed her, so in the end I left it off.

The afternoon passed with no word, and I wondered if she was too sad to even appreciate flowers. I called, and she picked up on the first ring. "Those were from you? I thought this entire time they were from Adán!"

"There was a card. Didn't you see it?"

She dropped the phone, and I could hear her in the background rustling around in the cellophane and paper. Then quiet. Then her on the phone again. "Why did you *do* that? I was going to call him and thank him. I would have looked like such an *idiot*!"

I was apologizing, but she had hung up.

The following day I received a phone call from Clare Severeson. They had chosen me for the opening in the gallery's schedule. I was stunned. My own show. She wanted to meet this week and go through my portfolio again, pulling the images we thought would work best in the space, including the series with the birds in Rhinehart's bedroom that I had finally finished after we returned from Florida. I saw Rhinehart hovering in the doorway, listening. He disappeared. When I hung up, he was back with a bottle of sparkling cider he'd bought down at the corner store. "A solo show!" I said aloud, and we toasted. "It's actually coming together!"

"It was only a matter of time," he said.

I drained the glass. "I'm going to celebrate with some wine. Don't give me the scolding look. It's a special occasion. I feel like I'm at my sixth-grade graduation with this cider."

"It's appropriate," he said. "Congratulations, graduate!"

I'd imagined I'd have to select and sequence the images myself, and then present them to Clare, but she dispensed with that idea in the first five minutes. After looking through my portfolio, and asking me a series of questions about how I saw my work, she suggested an arrangement for the show, a gradual move from realism to surrealism, that had an internal logic I could never have come up with. We didn't agree on everything—I resisted including some older shots taken out east, near my father's farm, that I didn't think were strong enough, but I said I would at least get prints made, so that we could pin them up and see how they looked. The gallery, which had seemed a bit cold to me when I first went in there with my portfolio, was now a familiar, congenial space. Just walking through the heavy glass doors was uplifting, greeting the assistant, Mark, and passing behind the frosted glass that hid Clare's office. I was so appreciative, I'd sent Laura a bottle of wine along with a card, thanking her for all she'd done to make it happen.

More than a week had passed since I'd spoken to Hallie, and I was feeling incredibly guilty. She had said she wanted time alone, and in truth I'd been too busy to check up on her that frequently. I'd found someone to take over the lease on my Brooklyn apartment, and so I'd been packing my things, destined either for Rhinehart's or storage. I was also training my replacement for Marty, although we were calling it "a leave of absence," and I was often rushing from there to the photo lab or the gallery. When I finally got Hallie on the phone, I tried to break the awkward silence by apologizing for the flowers.

"What flowers?" There was a pause. "Oh, yeah. Forget about it."

"Why don't I come over there?"

She coughed a couple of times. It sounded rattly, like an old lady's cough. "Listen, now's not a good time. My show's on."

"You're watching TV? In the middle of the day?"

She sighed in annoyance, as if giving in to a telemarketer. "All right, fine, come over."

As I was leaving the house, Rhinehart suggested I bring the red plate. It was something I'd owned since childhood. My father had told me it had magical properties, putting a good mood into the meal and then into me.

"I don't think it would do anything. Look at the way the flowers went over."

"I'll eat off of it, then. I'm feeling a little low myself."

He did look pale, and there was a fine sheen of sweat on his forehead. I put my hand on it, but it was cool. "What's wrong?"

"Just sometimes I worry about the future."

"That's not like you."

It was late afternoon, and the melancholy orange light was making squares on the wall. I noticed the shadow of Rhinehart's small tree, the seated Buddha statue that he had by the window. He said, "For the first time, I really wish I were a younger man. I feel my life is just beginning now."

Hallie looked terrible, although I couldn't pinpoint exactly how, it was that indefinable thing that grief did to the posture and skin and expression. She was leaking sadness. I was alarmed. As I hugged her, she just stood there, letting me feel the bones of her spine beneath her sweatshirt.

In a clogged voice, she said, "It's a real party here, can you tell?" I followed her into the house—she'd lost weight, her jeans bagged in the rear. We passed my flowers, which were still in their wrapping, lying dead on the hallway floor. I picked them up, looking for the trash. She had already retreated into the living room.

The place smelled like an ashtray. "You're smoking again?" I called out.

She was balled up on the couch with a lit cigarette, releasing dirty trails of smoke. "You want something?"

I shook my head.

"I don't think I have anything, anyway. I stopped eating. Remember when we were young, and some guy dumped us, we'd say, hey, at least we'll get skinny. But it doesn't look so good on us anymore. Now we just look old."

I tried to inhale shallowly to avoid taking in the smoke.

"So he's gone."

I looked around the room, instinctively, as if to verify it.

"Not before telling me I was a sick person, 'mal de cabeza.' Kept shouting it. He shouted nonstop for two days and then accused *me* of trapping him inside an insane asylum. He claims he was never with Kate, although he may be now, who knows? He went somewhere. I don't know where."

"He's just angry about the party. And embarrassed. He'll come back when he calms down."

She shook her head. "No, we discussed that. He says there's something not right with me. He thought once we married, I'd settle down, but instead I've gotten crazier, and he doesn't want to spend an entire life fighting. Maybe he's right. Maybe I am sick. I may have imagined the Kate thing—how fucking sad is that? I almost wish he had been with her now."

She looked as if she was going to cry, and I made a move towards her. She put her hand up. "Don't hug me."

Her eyes had grown dark, as if her thoughts had shifted from self-pity to something malicious. "He's been wanting to go back to Spain this entire time. What would I do there? I don't speak Spanish. Anywhere outside Madrid I get bored in two days. Now he can just go—he doesn't have to worry about me."

She abruptly shifted her gaze in my direction, and I blushed, as if caught doing something wrong. "I wish I had artistic talent," she said. "Then I could turn this shit into something. A poem or a painting. Isn't that what you do?"

"Not always. I'm not sure what that word 'artist' means most of the time."

Hallie said impatiently, "But you *are* one. Walking around with that camera bag." She gestured to it. "You even brought it here. Were you going to take my picture?"

I shook my head. "I just bring it everywhere. In case."

"Exactly. What normal person does that? Your strange tastes, the weird shit you notice that no one else does. You don't wear much makeup." She smiled, or it was a pinched look around her lips that resembled a smile. "You really don't think of yourself as an artist? Is this because you haven't had a real show yet?"

I felt the ebullient rise of my news, which was in the entirely wrong key for this setting. Still, I took her question seriously. Lately, in all my dealings with the gallery, I'd been identifying more with the word "professional" than "artist." I'd thought myself an artist when I was younger, obsessively sketching the tortured workings of my heart in charcoal or pastels with the music blaring in the background. I'd felt the most genuinely artistic when I hadn't been producing anything of quality. I started to tell Hallie this, but she was staring vacantly out at the yard, so I stopped. It was a hot, humid day, and you could hear the whirring of insects, see the heat rising like a mist off the grass—it looked uncut. Had she fired the gardener? The entire place seemed to be falling apart, as if Adán had been gone for years.

I wondered if I should suggest a walk. The A/C was turned up so high, it was bone-chillingly cold in here, and awkward, like at a funeral parlor. Hallie was wrapped in a comforter, a little smoke-huffing cocoon.

The cat rubbed against my legs. I picked him up and then remembered pregnant women shouldn't handle cats—was that just an old wives' tale? I was full of dubious information lately. I put him back down with a soft plunk near where the end table used to be. Furniture was missing. The antique desk and chair that Adán had had shipped over from Spain. The lamp that was on it, as well as a tapestry by the staircase, supposedly the mate to one in the Met, and a small oil painting of Adán's grandfather. "He took the furniture?"

Hallie looked confused, as if I had pulled her away from a television show. The TV was off in this room, but I could hear it on in the bedroom and pictured the sickly blue glow on the unmade bed, the room's stale, sour smell.

Focusing on the vacant corner, she said, "He didn't take anything."

"Then where is it?" I wondered, not for the first time, if she was taking pills—she seemed so out of it. "Do you still have that storage locker?"

"I haven't had that thing in years." She ground her cigarette out in a white saucer she was using for an ashtray. Then lit another. "I put up an ad on Craig's List." Gesturing with the lighter, as if it were a magic wand, she pointed to an empty corner. "That table with the antique tiles went for thirty-five bucks. I wanted fifty, but he talked me down. I think he may have been a student at Fordham. Cute."

She was laughing in a frighteningly joyless way and then stopped. "Listen—no offense but the hostess thing is really wearing me out."

I didn't stand up right away. I needed to take her with me, but I didn't know where to bring her, or how to convince her to come. "Tell me what—"

"I don't like blubbering about my problems. I don't see the point." And then, "I hate it when you stare at your hands with that mopey look to make me feel guilty. I have a lot of rage, Terry. It's not bittersweet or sad or something you want to hug. It's ugly and dirty. I've been abandoned. The thoughts I have are sickening."

"Like what?"

"Like finding him, wherever he is, and cutting off his testicles with a pair of scissors."

I started to laugh. "I don't think he'd let you get close enough."

"I'd drug him with the pills I was prescribed after my operation last year and the tranquilizers I'm on now." She was looking at me with her large icy gaze—it was as if I could see clear through her body into the nothingness on the other side. "But I've changed my mind. Lately I've been thinking of inviting him over so that he could watch me slit my throat."

I could hear my own breathing, and she hunched up and said defensively, "You asked."

I knew that I would have to stay there for a few days, and I got up to call Rhinehart to tell him. I gave clipped instructions, the clothes he needed to bring, a detailed grocery list, but otherwise said little. It was as if Hallie and I were hostages in that house, and I didn't trust the terrible thing holding us not to make a sudden move.

I slept with her on the king-size mattress that Adán used to sleep on, with sheets damp from her night sweats and her crying, her blowing her nose in them. I found the Spanish tapestry balled up behind the couch. Frequently, in the middle of the night, she would wrap herself in it and drift out of the room, shoeless, like a ghost.

My pregnancy grogginess had burned off in this crazy house, and I got up and followed her. Sometimes she yelled at me over her shoulder, calling me her jailer. Other times she looked through me, the same way she did to the cat, who also padded behind her, hoping for a handout.

When I first arrived, I cased the house for her supply of pills, intending to monitor her intake. I found nothing, but followed the same routine daily. First the bedroom. Then I moved on to the hall bathroom, its vanity crammed with old hairbrushes and makeup samples and the cold medicine that I decided to remove just in case. I flushed the toilet to make it sound like a legitimate bathroom visit, even though she was dead asleep, having wandered the house and part of the yard all night, smoking and crying.

I opened the door, and she was standing there. I gasped.

"How come you were using this bathroom?" she said.

"It was closer to the kitchen, where I was going to have a snack."

She snorted. "Yeah, right. Don't you think if I wanted you to have my medication, I would have given it to you?"

"Medication! Who's even prescribing it? They're drugs."

"They came from a physician. I picked them up at CVS."

"But they're also lethal, and you said you were thinking about suicide."

Without taking her eyes off me, she fished her pack of cigarettes out of her robe. "Not suicide—revenge fantasies. You weren't listening." She was looking more alert, and I wondered if maybe she'd run out of the pills, or was rationing them herself. Exhaling smoke near my face, she said, "I'm not too keen on you coming over here to play house—I'm thinking about kicking you out."

"But tranquilizers! Hallie! After what happened to Constance!"

She looked at me, horrified. "Why are you bringing that up?"

"Why? *Why?"* It seemed tremendously important that she see the connection. As it was, we barely discussed it—all those years together in college, thousands of conversations we'd had lying in our beds in the East Village apartment, and we'd only made passing references to that afternoon. It was like we'd silently agreed to erase it. "Tell me you're not thinking about it right now!"

Hallie turned, walked back into her bedroom, and shut the door. I heard the click of the lock. Never before had she locked me out of a room she was in.

It was near the end of our senior year of high school, and we were walking back to her house. Hallie was jealous because the day before we'd all been together in her mother's bedroom, and I was talking about Todd, who was the closest I'd ever come to having a boyfriend, although we hadn't really done anything except kiss and stare at each other. I was describing him for Constance in minute detail—she was a great audience—the blond hair that curled around his ears, the way he held my hand, two fingers dangling out to stroke mine, his likes and dislikes: strawberry ice cream, no okra. Hallie was standing nearby, ready to correct me if I strayed even fractionally from the truth. Sexually, she had gone much further than me, had given a blow job, even, which she boasted about to me in lurid detail, but she didn't have a proper boyfriend and so was limited as to the amount of information she could disclose about any one person to her family.

Constance, having had many lovers, was well versed on the subject of boyfriends. "Playing hard to get is for women who have no confidence. Those not sophisticated in love. There are many ways to seduce a man, a million and one, but they all involve showing and eliciting desire. Once you're at the stage where you have him in your pocket, do whatever you wish. Everything you do will have his knees turn to water."

I was thinking she should drill that into her daughter, who lived by the rule of never letting a guy think you were interested, even if you were half-undressed in the backseat of his car.

"You're going to have to give him up soon anyway," Hallie said, and then informed her mother, "He's going to the University of Colorado." We'd accepted offers from the same college upstate. At that moment, I wished I never had to see her again, and I already regretted the fact that we'd even applied to the same schools.

"I wouldn't worry about the distance," Constance said to me. "It can be an aphrodisiac for two people meant to be in love." And she proceeded to tell us a racy story that didn't involve Hallie's father even marginally. It concerned an affair she'd had with a foreign director, back when she was sixteen and acting in plays in New York. I was sitting on the edge of her bed, transfixed, and imagining an older and worldlier version of Todd taking me to dinner at a little Italian restaurant and then undressing me in a boutique hotel in the theater district.

The next day, a Friday, Hallie claimed to have seen Todd in the parking lot of the TCBY, in a car with this girl Mona—an obvious lie meant to cut me. So on the walk home, I was giving her the silent treatment. I would have ditched her entirely and headed back to my house except I wanted to ask Constance's advice. Todd had invited me to dinner on Saturday night, and I was uncertain how to behave once the check came. Should I offer to pay my portion? Two blocks from her house, Hallie began coaxing me to talk to her, she couldn't stand being ignored, and was alternately insulting and flattering me, until we arrived at her front door and opened it.

I was the one who saw Constance first, sprawled out facedown on the stair landing. My first thought was that this was a practical joke she was playing on us, although I couldn't figure out what it was. Her legs were spread open, and her crotch was visible to anyone walking in. It was the first thing you saw, that dark space between her legs where the nightgown had ridden up. Next you saw the carcass of a cooked chicken, which was on the bottom step. Hallie ran over to her and began straightening her clothes. "We have to call 911," I said, and since I was the only one there to do it, I went into the kitchen and called. When I came back into the room, Hallie was trying to wake her up. "She's breathing," she said hopefully to me.

"Okay, good, just leave her. Stop shaking her. She's going to be okay. They're coming." I kept repeating this. An overturned bottle of Perrier had made a small waterfall down the stairs, and I picked it up and clutched it to my chest. I didn't want to go near Constance. Hallie had arranged her mother over her lap like a giant doll and was stroking her hair, saying, "Don't worry, it's just Terry here. She doesn't care if your mouth's open." I nodded foolishly in agreement.

It seemed like we were there forever, just the three of us. It was so quiet, we could hear each other breathing. Then there was confusion and noise and blaring lights and the paramedics came in with a stretcher and machines, and moved us away to the periphery, and Hallie called her father. Or maybe he was already there. They all went off in the ambulance together. I stayed behind, and instinctively, maybe inappropriately, went up to Constance's room to wait. I ran my hand over the bedspread and dresser, over the perfume in antique bottles with pump sprays. The scent of her. Constance believed that perfume should be worn in the hot spots, on the wrists, behind the ears and knees. Every time I visited, she squirted a fine, elegant mist on me, and all the way home I would discreetly sniff at myself, pretending to rub an itch above my lips. For Christmas that past year, she'd bought me my own bottle, and I was rationing it to last me through college. I was thinking these things. I was thinking of how Constance had pulled me aside a few weeks ago and told me how much she was going to miss me when I was away at school.

The phone rang. Constance's ivory phone, with a dial, where she took all her calls. The receiver smelled like her. I hesitated before saying hello.

It was Hallie. Constance had died twenty minutes after they got to the hospital.

Hallie and her father returned dazed and tearless and strangely intact, as if they'd been out somewhere else, to a movie. I was standing in the foyer waiting for them, a tissue balled up in my hand, bawling, and it was as if everything had been turned inside out, and I was the bearer of this horrifying news. I didn't want to go home and was afraid they would ask me to leave. But instead Hallie's father excused himself very politely to me, as if I were his guest, and went up to bed. Hallie was in the mud room, rummaging around for the flashlight. The cat was missing and she was going to look for it. I thought it had been scared off by the paramedics, and would come home eventually, but I was in no state to argue, or to do anything. I went into the living room and curled up in a fetal position on the couch. For hours, I listened to her outside, calling for Pooky. At times, I also heard Hallie's father crying upstairs, a terrible, frighteningly intimate sound, like hearing him have sex. I covered my ears. Hallie called for that cat. I dozed in and out of sleep, as the beam of her searchlight scrolled past the windows.

We found the cat in the refrigerator the next day. By some miracle, he was still alive, a cold, balled-up body of fur. He'd eaten everything on his shelf, even the tofu, and had furiously clawed the doors. It was months before it occurred to me that Constance, high on pills, was probably carrying him when she went to the fridge for the chicken, and had set him down in the most convenient place.

Sitting on the floor outside Hallie's bedroom, I decided it was time to talk about it. Everything I could remember. I could hear Hallie crying on the other side of the door. "Maybe it was an accident. Or she was just so focused on her own pain, but it was the worst thing that's ever happened to us, and if she had known that, she never would have done it. You need to think about the people who love you. Because we both wanted her not to have been so selfish. We loved her. I loved her, too. She was really good to me. There were times when I used to pretend she was my mother." Even as I said that I felt a tremor of the old fear of being laughed at. "I know that sounds stupid, but I'd imagine what it would be like."

From the other side of the door came Hallie's choked voice, "She used to say the same thing. Really pissed me off." I heard the click of the lighter, her inhaling. "You're lucky you weren't though, Terry. You were shielded from so much of the bullshit. Sometimes she'd throw fits in the middle of the night, wake everyone up. She'd overdosed before, you know. She even spent time in a psychiatric hospital—that summer we went to camp."

Hallie had told me her mother was suffering from exhaustion and was going to a place where celebrities went to de-stress. I had believed her, and when Constance had come back, she was in such a high mood, she'd danced around the kitchen, cooked us pancakes with rose petals scattered on top. We were in fourth grade. "How could you have kept this from me? I was at your house all the time."

"I was ashamed probably. You thought she was so great."

But I had always had a realistic view of Constance. I knew her behavior was strange. I said as much to Hallie. "I just accepted her, I guess. Maybe you're right. It was easier for me."

"Oh God, I'm exhausted. I'm so exhausted," Hallie said.

"Unlock the door," I said.

She did and then returned to the mattress and curled up. Automatically, I walked towards the chair in the corner, and she said, "Go on and get something to eat, Nancy Drew. You don't have to worry about the pills—I dumped them all two days ago."

Later that night, lying next to each other in that big marital bed, whispering as if afraid someone would overhear, Hallie added to my version of that day. She remembered looking for the cat, but could have sworn I was with her searching for most of the night. Both of us remembered the stillness of the house while we waited for the ambulance to arrive. "She was still alive then," Hallie said. "Those were her last moments." She paused. "I always wonder if she took a little too much that day because she was getting scared to lose us. Because we were going away to college."

This was too terrible for me to contemplate. I got up and opened the window. The muggy night pushed through the screen.

We were both quiet, remembering. Into the silence, Hallie said, "I wasn't honest with you. I did contemplate taking the pills."

"When? I've been with you every moment."

"Four nights ago. While you were sleeping." I was stunned, and she said, "I'm sorry I lied to you—you weren't my first priority. I dumped them out on the living room floor, who knows if it would have even been enough for a lethal dose, and just stood there, staring at them." Her eyes were shining with excitement in the retelling. "You know what was going through my head? That tree out in my backyard that we used to play on. Do you remember it?"

"Of course."

"I was sitting up there, in the branches, proclaiming that I was going to save all the animals in the world. We were nine, maybe, and I was calling down to you. You were on the swing. I just remember the excitement of describing how I'd have a big house with tons of dogs and cats and birds that no one else wanted, and they could all live there, and I'd take care of them. I never even came close to that."

"Because it's unrealistic—who do you know that's turned their house into a shelter? And Adán was allergic."

"It's just that I used to have this sense that my life was going to be special. And here I am, almost thirty years later, lying on the floor, weeping over a man. I haven't done anything with my life really, not anything significant—I've just been existing. Like Constance was. She really had talent, you know. I didn't invent that. I saw her on stage once—she was so incredible. The entire audience was electrified by her." She laughed, weakly. "Why was she so fucked up?"

I felt a tremendous surge of compassion for Constance, thinking of how she was always so carefully made up, as if waiting for that life to come back. "I don't know. But it wasn't your fault or your dad's fault. He suffered, too, you know. You give him too hard a time."

She was looking at me plaintively, like a child. "Tell me the truth. Am I that fucked up?"

"No, of course not. You're also not addicted to anything. Except maybe cigarettes again."

"I'm just feeling so lost. I've never been this lost before. And I'm so alone now that Adán's gone."

I began to protest, and she said, "He's not coming back. It's okay.

It's time for me to get my shit together. Build up my confidence again. Get a job."

"You have enough money for a while. You don't have to rush into that yet."

"But I *want* to. Even when I said it just now, I got excited. I still have some of my old PR contacts. I can make some phone calls." She rolled over. "I always liked working."

I hugged her from behind. It reminded me of the times I'd slept over as a little girl. Once the lights were out I'd leave my cot and join her in her bed with the Strawberry Shortcake sheets. In the morning, she would wake me up by sticking a feather or a piece of string up my nose to make me sneeze. There were always rainbows on her walls from the teardrop crystals Constance had hung in her windows. We were obsessed with rainbows, rainbow hairclips, stickers that we traded and stuck in our albums, metallic rainbow-colored ribbons that fluttered off the handlebars of our bikes as we circled around her backyard, shouting names to each other, "Titface," "Asshead," and laughing. She was my sister. What it would have been like to find her lying facedown on the living room rug? It chilled me to think how close we'd come. A shark skimming behind us in the dark ocean that had, just by chance, turned and slipped away.

Hallie had begun chanting again. I could hear her through the walls of her study, where she had a little cabinet, and a pillow on the floor, and a bell. I came up behind her, and she turned around and smiled. "Come chant with me. God won't be mad." She got out a pillow and threw it down next to her. "We'll chant for Constance. For her happiness. Already I'm feeling as if something big has happened. Something's changed." Later, while I was eating breakfast, she made a phone call to her old therapist, and I knew then it was finally okay for me to go home.

CHAPTER NINETEEN

Rhinehart would spend occasional evenings discussing writing and politics with his poet friends, but during the day, if he wasn't in his study, he was hanging out down the street with the owner of the dollhouse store, whom he referred to as "a fellow of the highest order." Buddy, the "true artisan," was also very accessible—he spent at least twelve hours a day in his shop, and he lived in a studio apartment above it, into which I conjured a sagging twin mattress with striped ticking and a hotplate. Although Rhinehart and I had agreed not to find out the baby's sex, he and Buddy had both decided I was having a girl, Buddy favoring the Spanish names, like María José. Rhinehart was pushing for the ridiculous name of timothy lowercased, signifying wild grass.

That's where I went to find Rhinehart, eager to see him, to touch him, after all that housebound trauma with Hallie. He wasn't in the front, although if he had been, he still wouldn't have been easy to spot. The place was jammed with forty years of Buddy's solitary business, finished and unfinished frame structures, staircases that led nowhere, miscellaneous carpentry tools, doll heads, stiff little wingback chairs, and blue china plates, sale items.

Being in here often called up a fear I had when younger that the dolls left their house and walked around my bedroom while I slept. I was afraid of getting up in the middle of the night, stepping on one, and killing it. I was often subject to visual hallucinations at Buddy's, convinced I'd seen something small moving about. Maybe because of this, I had a strong desire to shoot there, although I hadn't yet asked

Rhinehart to finesse it with Buddy, who I sensed wouldn't be that willing. I'd have to clear enough space for the lights and tripod. But I liked the idea of alternating photographs of these interiors with the highly stylized images I'd taken of the roses, as they both seemed to speak to a common theme of artifice. It was an incredible place, this shop, and all it suggested, hours of effort put into scaling down a home to a manageable, easily manipulated size. I wondered what Buddy's own family life had been like to choose this as his career.

I found Rhinehart in the sawdusty workroom, perched on a stool. "Finally! I was starting to feel abandoned!" He kissed me all over my face, and then my belly, which embarrassed me in front of Buddy. "You look like a seedpod about to burst. How is Hallie?"

"Much better. It was an intense few days." Just then, I realized how completely exhausted I was. Rhinehart fussily lowered me onto his seat.

"Will you look over the prints with me that I'm making for the show?" It was only two weeks away. I really wished I had Laura's help, but Rhinehart had an emotional response to the photographs that could be useful.

"Of course, of course. We can go right now. Buddy's doing a custom-made house for the baby, and I can show you some of the features on the way out."

I whispered, "But we don't even know it's a girl, yet."

"If it's a boy he can admire the house's craftsmanship and historical architecture like we do."

Buddy put his tar brush back in the bucket, and said in an abrupt voice. "The Tudor in front."

Again, I saw something flash out of the corner of my eye, quicker this time. Buddy stopped in front of a blue house, spinning it around on its lazy Susan contraption to show the interior—oriental carpets, glass-fronted china cabinet, even red silk wallpaper in the drawing room. These rich dolls sat stone-faced in the bedroom. Buddy pointed out the staircase with its carved newel posts and antique trim. The house had a garret with a tiny stained glass window. Inside, he poked with his beefy, stained fingers at the beds and chairs.

It took me another half an hour to get out of there, while he and Rhinehart discussed different types of crown molding and the half-timbering on the exterior. I finally squeezed Rhinehart's arm, hard, and we left.

Once outside, I said, "I now have enough material to fill up several doll-themed nightmares. I think we're having a boy, anyway, and I doubt he'll like those houses as much as you."

Rhinehart reached over and felt my stomach. "Kicking away. Like Oedipus after his father sealed up the exit. That's from a Ted Hughes poem." He recited, " 'He was a horrible fella.' "

"Have you thought about boys' names at all?" I said.

"Adam."

"Really? I was wondering if you were going to want your own name, or your father's."

"No, no. I don't believe in legacy naming. It dilutes the animus's force. And I would never saddle an American child with the name 'Yosyp.' Whereas Adam has this wonderful biblical resonance. Prefall. It suggests that God had a plan for me I didn't foresee."

"What about timothy?"

Rhinehart took me by the elbow as we crossed the street. "That's a girl's name."

After dinner, we'd walk down to the coffee shop on the corner to get malteds, which I seemed to always get a craving for around eight o'clock. He steered me as if I were an old lady. "Your tummy is getting big. If it were a package, you couldn't carry it more than a block before setting it down."

"Thanks a lot," I said. "With all the books you've been reading, didn't you see the list of what not to say to pregnant women?"

"If we didn't already know I would think it was two babies. I would have loved to have been the father of twins," he said, mournfully.

"I think one will be more than enough for us."

* * *

At other times, though, Rhinehart seemed preoccupied. More than once, I'd caught him staring out the window, not even hearing me when I came in. One night late in July, I discovered him in the kitchen, rocking, his hands over his face.

I flipped on the overhead fluorescents, and he looked up at the harsh light, his eyes black, the pupils still dilated.

"Are you sick?" I asked him. The back of his neck was clammy and cold.

He shook his head. "I don't know. I feel nauseous. My heart is racing. I took aspirin that had gotten wet. It was in the pocket with some coins. You don't think that would have caused this, do you?"

"No."

"Coins poison water. The metal releases toxins into the water."

I went soft for him. Whenever he got anxiety he became convinced he'd ingested something laced. "I'm sure that's not it." His forehead was damp, and I brushed his hair back from his face. "You're probably just feeling some fear and focusing on the physical sensation. Do you want to talk about it?"

He didn't say anything, just slumped over in the seat, his head between his hands.

"Why don't you come to bed then?"

Surprisingly, he allowed me to lead him back into the dark reaches of the bedroom, and got in obediently between the cool sheets. He closed his eyes, but when I turned over in the middle of the night, I saw they were open again. He was staring at the ceiling, as if he'd been looking at it for hours.

The next morning he felt better and so we didn't discuss it, but I was worried he was feeling trapped by the baby. It wasn't easy to read Rhinehart recently, or perhaps I hadn't been trying as hard as I had in the past. I had the upcoming show, and my own body had also become the site of so much of my attention that it was difficult, at times, to move my mind away from it.

* * *

Hallie had followed through on her PR idea soon after she'd voiced it, and had been steadily developing a list of corporate clients over the summer, some of which she'd already done freelance projects for. "I'm working on building a flashier clientele. Wealthy individuals. So I can coordinate the publicity for high-end events." During her downtime, she'd been volunteering with PETA. When I met up with her in Union Square, she had just done a zoo protest. Along with two other women, she had stripped down naked, gotten body-painted as a tiger, and hunkered down in a metal dog crate by the zoo parking lot underneath a banner that read, "Wild Animals Don't Belong in Cages."

Her face was heated, retelling the story. "One guy dumped an entire soda through the bars. What they were really pissed about was the nudity, I think. You couldn't see our nipples or anything, but you could see a lot. People were staring. I mean you really felt like a caged animal. That was the crazy part. During breaks I'd come out and put on a robe and just talk to people. I think I got through to some of them."

She got out her notepad, which I'd noticed was a constant thing with her lately, and jotted something down. "I think that campaign may be more effective if we dress in animal costumes instead of going naked—so we can relate to the kids."

"You're good at finding the most persuasive method." She'd gotten me to give up most meat, except for shellfish, and all commercial eggs, after grueling accounts of thousands of live chicks dumped on conveyor belts and into the trash. When she'd first started volunteering, about a month ago, every other story out of her mouth was an animal torture story. On a bright summer day, crossing the park, I was listening to accounts of terrified beagles being shipped to laboratories. "I can't," I finally said. "I can't. Just tell me what to buy or boycott, and I'll do that. I'll believe you."

She regarded it as her own personal accomplishment that she'd converted me.

"You know I think this is the work you're really suited for," I said.

"Yeah, but it's nonprofit. I'm not crazy about the office culture—it's so dowdy. And they don't pay jack. I like to have my own money. I don't want Adán picking up the tab for everything."

He'd moved back to Spain and was staying at his family's house temporarily. I didn't know which house that was, probably the one in Madrid, but still I envisioned him in the place he'd wanted me to visit, Collbató as he'd described it, the red soil at the foot of the mountains, the long, weathered table under the grape arbor, his aunt who'd married the Catalonian man, serving crayfish from a big paella bowl, flies buzzing around.

"Do you think you'll see him again?"

"I don't know. Whenever we talk, I get all excited and then two days later I'm miserable. He says he feels the same. With separations, sometimes there's no solution except just getting by." She smiled at me. "And I feel good lately. Better than I ever have, Terry. I mean, there are times when I get depressed, but I feel different. It's hard to explain, it feels so internal."

"I can see it," I said. "I can tell."

That night, as we were getting into bed, I repeated what Hallie had said about Adán to Rhinehart, who'd been out to dinner with his stepdaughters, drinking port wine, most likely—his special occasion drink. They'd recently reunited. Evidently they'd been upset with him after he and Laura split, which I hadn't known.

He said, "*Tout passe et s'efface dans l'espace sans trace.* It loses the assonance in English, but loosely translated it means 'everything fades eventually without leaving a trace.' It's how I felt tonight, being out with the girls. How much of their lives I get a snippet of, meant to represent the whole. In fact, I think it actually subtracts from what I know of them."

I was on my side, facing him, the only position that was comfortable anymore. Lying on my back, I felt as if my insides were being crushed. "Can you spend more time with them?"

"I would like to, but it's difficult. It's not just the distance. They satellite around a different star—they have husbands. They have Laura. I met them as independent adults, living away from home, and so the bond between us isn't as strong as I'd like."

"Sometimes I think the only real family unit is the one you have when you're a child. The one the baby will have," I told Rhinehart, who added, "The home we will make for little timothy."

The unnamed baby, this little soul, probably the same size as my soul, where did it come from? I was throwing these questions upward to circulate around us. Was the soul newly minted for every life? Or was it slightly worn, a crumpled dollar having made a series of mysterious rounds, impossible to know where it had been. Arriving with a history of lives in a dossier. Having loved others before us. Having already lived and lied and done wrong many times over?

Rhinehart thought this was a good thing. "When the body is born the soul gets another chance to make everything right, to settle any harm caused by its prior actions. Some religions believe that in each life we are given a set of challenges specific to the individual soul's path to God."

"Do you think we knew this child in its past life?"

"Probably. I always believed you and I knew each other before."

I assumed he meant we were married, or perhaps long-lost lovers who had missed the opportunity to marry, but instead, he said he thought I might have been his brother.

"Your brother!" I said.

"Don't laugh, Tatie. I'm an only child. It's no accident that you're an only child, too. The roles we take in each life are just helpful guises."

"An older or younger brother?"

"Around the same age. Maybe even a twin."

"Really!" I was flattered.

He laid his palm on my belly. "And who do you think we were?"

"I'm not sure I believe in reincarnation."

"Ah, the good Presbyterian. I've always found reincarnation a greatly reassuring philosophy, although I struggle with the idea of karma. It feels strangely unfair."

"But what you feel like to me sometimes is my mother. It's the emotional attachment, I think, the caring. And also probably this feeling of distance. That no matter how hard I try, I'll never be able to be close enough. There is an absence embedded in our relationship."

"I think that's true of most people's relationships. It's the distance between what we feel and the reality of another person, who is a collection of his or her own separate feelings and desires."

"I miss her. How can I miss someone I never knew? Is that stupid?"

"You *did* know her. The baby that was you knew her."

"I feel cheated." Tears ran over my nose onto the pillow. "I'm most worried that because I never had a role model, I won't know how to be a good mother."

With his palm he wiped my face. "I'm in the same boat, but I don't think it matters. It's something you do instinctively."

"Explain reincarnation to me." I'd had a flash of an idea that the baby could be my mother, and we could have a chance to know each other again.

"Some Buddhist traditions use the metaphor of a tree to describe the soul. Just because it has no leaves and isn't blooming at that moment, doesn't mean it lacks the potential to bloom. Death is just a dormancy period, as a tree experiences in winter. The flowers are still inside, waiting for the right conditions, like spring, rebirth, to manifest themselves."

I pictured the cherry trees in the Brooklyn Botanic Garden. "And how long does it take before someone gets reincarnated?"

"There are several different theories on this, but I believe it depends on what type of life you've had. How much of a rest you need and how enlightened you are. Some people need less time. When they went looking for the next Dalai Lama, they checked for babies that were born on the day he died."

I wondered how much time my mother would need. Would she

have needed more than thirty years, or would she have lived a life in between, a short life, and then come back into this one.

"What do you think you'll be in your next life?" I asked Rhinehart.

"A girl, probably, and you?"

"I don't know, but I'd like to try something different. See what it's like to live inside a man's body."

"Maybe you'll be my father, then."

I laughed. "Maybe. I just hope we know each other."

"I'm sure we will," he said. "I don't think we're done with each other yet."

My opening was on a Thursday. I walked alongside Rhinehart in a long dress and flats. I'd seen old ladies on the Upper East Side in trendier shoes, but my ankles were swollen, and already I was hobbled by nerves. Rhinehart hailed a cab, and then, either to calm me, or just because it occurred to him, began recounting a story about a boyhood blueberrying trip to Maine, during which he spent all day industriously stripping several bushes of unripe berries. He was under the impression that fruit ripened during shipping to the city. The proprietors had asked his chaperone very nicely that he not return. "I love Maine. The way the tidal flats rise up, changing from mud to lake. The water oozes from the ground, like a great underground spring."

I'd been thinking about Laura. Clare had mentioned that she'd be there, and I felt as uncomfortable as I would seeing an old lover. She hadn't spoken to me since that searing phone conversation months ago. But perhaps, if she was coming, it meant she had forgiven me.

In the quiet of the cab, the city glittering around us, Rhinehart asked how I was feeling.

"Excited," I said. "Part of me just can't believe this is actually happening. It's exhilarating, but also sort of odd." For so long I've been the one pushing my work along and now it felt as if it had built up its own momentum and was the one pulling me. "I'm not sure I can live up to the thing I've created."

"But you don't have to. Your job is done. For this body of work, anyway. Even if you decided not to come tonight, the photographs would still be hanging there. There would still be a crowd. Wine and cheese on the tables." He smiled. "In some ways, we're only a vehicle for the work we do. So it gets produced and then seen."

I took his hand. It was warm. "Thank you."

"Tonight we're just partygoers. And I've been looking forward to this party all summer. You're going to love it."

In my imagination, one of my fear-based imaginings, there was a thready, bored group, awkward silences, and my work on the walls, gaping nakedly at everyone. But the gallery was packed with a noisy, drinking crowd. There were so many people in there, you couldn't even see the art. I scanned the faces and recognized several women from the MoMA event, my old neighbor, a few artists I did the show in midtown with, even Marty had come along with Shani, who hugged me, saying, "I am *so* proud of you. And inspired." Marty, peering at the photographs, complimented me on my "first-rate" technique. I was soon surrounded by a congratulatory group, and the locus of a lot of heady praise.

Rhinehart had drifted off. I spotted him studying a photograph that had been taken in his apartment, when Laura appeared, smelling of Chanel No. 5, and bent in to kiss me before I'd even had the chance to focus on her face.

"Everything is perfect. What a success."

In the celebrity glow, I was thanking her for her help and advice, telling her I was sorry for our separation, and that I missed her, which, in the state I was in, seemed true, although in retrospect that period stood out as a time when I was dangerously confused and off-balance. But she had done a lot for me, and I told her so. Although she was saying little, I could tell she was affected by my impetuous feeling talk.

She looked down at me. "You're definitely pregnant."

"Did you think I wasn't?"

She laughed. "There was a period of time when I considered he was lying. I just couldn't picture it."

Behind Laura's head, Hallie was waving frantically, as if we had planned to meet up here, and she wasn't sure she'd been spotted. Laura turned her head to look, and I saw Hallie's eyes light up with interest.

"I should let you mingle and enjoy your night," Laura said. She looked as if she was going to put her hand on my stomach, and at the last moment shifted it to my arm instead. "You have no idea how this baby is going to change your life. The best thing I ever did was have those girls. It's a kind of love that's unsurpassed."

The minute she'd moved off, Hallie was on me with questions. "Was that her? I pictured her so different—older and more uptight. She's a classy-looking woman."

"She can be really graceful sometimes." It occurred to me that I hadn't been entirely fair about Laura, even in my own head. Our relationship didn't seem over, as much as transitioning.

Hallie was looking around, excited. "You're a genuine celebrity with these hoity-toity types. *You!*" She took my arm, and we walked around the room together, stopping in front of the series of the birds—she referred to them individually, by their refuge names.

On display here, my work felt so divorced from the warm intimacy of the idea, it was as if it had been done by someone else. When I'd been creating them, these photographs seemed to be sparks of what felt like God. Now they were mere shadows, castoffs of a creative process, and I had to look hard to try and see that original light. I was proud of them, but they no longer felt related to me.

I spent the rest of the evening in a babble of my own talk. I was especially keen on playing career matchmaker, resurrecting that desire I'd first felt at the Guerrilla Girls talk when I'd had so little power—would I experience it differently sitting in the audience today? Channeling Laura, but lacking as much finesse, I introduced some of the collectors to other artists I knew, young women who hadn't already made their own connections.

Later in the evening, I saw Rhinehart talking with Laura. They were behind me, and I let my attention drift from the conversation I was having to theirs, the astral redistribution the senses are able to perform. She was congratulating him, rather formally, on the coming child, and he thanked her. Information was exchanged about her daughters. A car one of them had decided to buy. The conversational tenor was one of distant relations, and I wondered if they had ever been close in the way that Rhinehart and I were. I never saw him as much as sensed him, an innate, noncerebral communication like that which animals share. It was a mystery to me that people could do it any differently, choose to combine their lives and yet still behave as if they were co-workers at a job neither of them particularly liked. I knew Laura had felt a lot for Rhinehart, but it was questionable whether her feelings bonded her to him or isolated her. As for Rhinehart, I didn't know what his love for her had felt like. On some level, I didn't want to.

As the gallery was clearing out, and we were assembling a group to go have dinner, Rhinehart came up to me, talking heatedly. "I haven't seen that woman for years—" He pointed across the room at Mrs. Bainbridge, whom I knew by sight only. "She's the real deal. A collector like Ileana Sonnabend was. I overheard her talking to the gallery owner, asking who represents you internationally." He kissed me, running his thumb down the top of my spine. "You're just glowing, as you should be. I'm so proud of you. I know how hard it was for you to get here—but you crossed a river tonight, and once it's crossed, you never go back."

CHAPTER TWENTY

The 26th of August, a brutally ordinary day, and I was almost thirty weeks pregnant. It had been a muggy afternoon, and I was in the grocery store in front of the dairy case, agonizing about whether to buy the commercial cheddar cheese. I had a craving, and they didn't have the local, humane kind. I wound up leaving it behind. It was already close to evening when I got home, and the heavy orange sun seemed to be setting inside our apartment. The chair rungs cast long shadows on the floor, like fingers. I was suddenly, foolishly, seized with panic. A tragic dangerous feeling, no reason for it, but I was electrified with nerves. Where Rhinehart usually sat, there was only his shirt, ominously draped over the back of the chair. He was in shadow, like in a Beckett play, drinking. I heard the ice cubes rattle when he took a sip.

"You should watch the drinking. You're getting a potbelly." My voice was full of false cheer.

"Tatie, there's something I have to tell you. It's best I do it all at once." He cleared his throat, my chest went cold, and I thought, But we've been so happy.

"They've discovered a tumor on my liver and believe it's cancerous."

My legs started vibrating, and I thought, if I don't sit down now I may fall. I found a chair. He didn't get up. He was talking about how he'd been concerned about his health earlier in the summer, on little evidence, really—he hadn't had much of an appetite, and had been feeling queasy, but that could have been due to anything, anticipating the baby. He'd gone in for blood work, which had picked up an abnormality, and so he went back for an ultrasound and AFP, the test for a protein that appears in the blood of 80 percent of patients with liver cancer. This was around the time of my art show. He didn't want to burden me. He felt guilty making doctor's appointments on the sly, but he was hoping he was just being overly cautious. He was testing clean for hepatitis B and C, which meant the baby and I were okay, and in that swamp of talk I was fishing for something to contradict what he had first said about cancer. To solve it. The ultrasound and blood tests indicated he should get an MRI. He'd just gotten the results that afternoon.

I didn't want to hear about the phone call. I didn't want to see the film. "So what's next?"

"A biopsy to test if it's cancerous. But Tatie, I have to warn you, it doesn't look good. It's large, and the MRI is showing other abnormalities. The cancer may have invaded the blood vessels already. It may have already spread." He began to cry, a large sound that filled up the entire room.

"You don't know it's cancer yet!" I said, coming over to him. "The imaging isn't perfect on those scans—it could be anything." I held him. I listened to myself tell him how much treatments have changed. Even if it is cancer, I said, chemotherapy has advanced so much. I sounded rational and convincing, sturdy even, but I was like a skin of ice that wouldn't be able to support anyone who dared to walk across the lake, thinking it was frozen through.

He went in to Sloan-Kettering to get a section of the tumor removed. Then we waited for the pathology report. During that time, I wouldn't let him out of my sight. I followed him from room to room, even into the bathroom, holding his hand, staring big-eyed and quiet with trembling lips, trying not to cry. His mute, distorted shadow. I needed to concentrate on seeing. I was afraid that once he moved out of my field of vision, he would be lost forever.

He didn't look sick, didn't seem sick. I'd done some research on the Internet—a manic rush of typing, freezing me with fear whenever I hit any mention of death. But also it said many people with liver cancer had pain. I asked him twice if he had pain, a dull ache below the right rib cage that perhaps had traveled to the right shoulder? He said no. Unexplained fevers. No. Well, that was a definite sign. Maybe he wasn't ill at all. The idea of this being one big, malicious mistake was delightful, like stepping into a bright expanse of field after the terrifying tangle of woods. This was what I got down on my knees and prayed for. That it wasn't true. I sustained this prayer up until the pathology report came back. Hepatocellular carcinoma, stage IV.

We were in the doctor's office, a gray-haired, wide-faced man with splayed fingertips smelling slightly of camphor, a caricature of a small-town doctor, and yet a Manhattan oncologist and a personal friend of Rhinehart's for years, typical that Rhinehart would go to him. I now knew things. I knew about this man's schooling, for example, and about his job. I knew the liver was the largest organ in the body, weighing over three pounds. It acted as a filter and made bile, greenish in color, which emptied into the intestine. Bile was what gave feces their brown color. I was listening to the doctor say that Rhinehart's tumor was inoperable because of its size and location. It was actually three tumors, one large, two smaller. One of those was pushing up against the portal vein. Why hadn't Rhinehart known about this earlier? The liver doesn't sense pain very well. Only the outside has nerve fibers. It also has a high functional reserve—even an advanced tumor may not alter normal operations or show up on blood tests. The oncologist pointed to a chart done in lurid color-pencil detail. Rhinehart didn't have cirrhosis, which was a good thing, but irrelevant, as he had developed cancer anyway. There was no good reason he had—he didn't have a metabolic disease that would have destroyed the liver, making it vulnerable, nor was he a heavy drinker. I thought briefly back to the scotch he'd been drinking that afternoon he'd told me about the MRI results. It was probably his last. The thought took my breath away. I struggled to come back, to listen. There may have been a more extensive history of cancer in his family than he knew. What family didn't have a history of cancer in it?

If the tumor couldn't be operated on, what about a transplant? This suggestion was from me. I was patiently told, as you would tell a schoolchild, that the chances were low that he'd receive one. The list was very long. Those most eligible, also ranked on a numbered system, were young with localized tumors and/or in severe stages of liver failure. If the cancer metastasized, he would become ineligible. Basically, by then, they would be throwing their precious liver in the garbage by giving it to Rhinehart, and there was no way they were going to do that. He was beside me, quiet, and I had the odd sensation that they were replaying this treatment discussion for my benefit only. Decisions had been made when I wasn't in the room. I was only here to give the scene its due, to fully enact the audience's part of outraged disbelief.

I said, "Please explain the course of chemotherapy he will have to go through. And I'm not interested in statistics," I felt pressured to add, "at this point. Just the facts. Which drugs—I've read that doxorubicin is the most common, but perhaps a combination might be better in this case."

The doctor and Rhinehart exchanged glances, a secret society energy passing between them. I could feel myself becoming hysterical.

Rhinehart took my hand. "He's discussed with me the potential benefits of chemotherapy, given my system and the stage of the cancer, versus the drawbacks of that approach. They're marginal. And you know how I feel about pharmacology. Especially when it seems unnecessary."

"So what's the treatment, then!"

The oncologist spoke up. "I'm recommending palliative care at this stage."

"What's that? What's palliative?" I was mentally searching for the definition of that word, which kept sliding from my grasp.

"Supportive care. Pain management, comfort—we'll work together on nutrition and monitoring the progression of the disease and its symptoms, so he feels the best possible."

"Feels the best! But he'll be *dying*!"

Rhinehart didn't say anything, and I started screaming, "You don't have a treatment? Just this! A special diet. What kind of doctor are you? And you're supposed to be his friend. We have a *baby* coming!"

I was crying, not looking at anyone, not even wanting to be there. Minutes passed before Rhinehart could calm me down to the point where I was no longer disruptive, so that he and his friend, the doctor, could go over the details of their course of inaction.

I was angry in the car. I was enraged, and I nourished the feeling. It seemed a more proactive response than weeping, or that useless pantomime in the office. I was demanding Rhinehart get a second opinion. He said that it likely wouldn't change anything, but he could.

"You need someone who is willing to do chemotherapy for you! Or get you into a clinical trial."

"I can do those things now. Phil would put me on chemotherapy."

"Then why don't you? Why don't you *do* something?"

He pulled the car over and looked at me in agony. "If you want me to, I will. I just didn't want to do it that way—with diarrhea and mouth sores and constant hospital visits. I discussed it extensively with Phil. There's no evidence to suggest it's going to extend my life. It may even shorten it. Tatie, what I have has *no cure*. There's no cure anymore. I just want to enjoy our time. And pray that I'll still be here to greet my little child."

"Oh my God," I said. "Oh my God." The traffic rushed by on Third Avenue, a man selling Burberry knockoffs, a man selling purses, people in light jackets, on their cell phones. How did this nightmare become so real that in the middle of the day, in the car with the man I love, such things could be said.

Within two weeks, Rhinehart had assembled a support team. He had a nutritionist, who put him on a low-salt, no alcohol, macrobiotic diet. She brought the food, which she purchased from farms upstate, into the house. He had a spiritual advisor, a Sufi master, who had him meditating two hours a day. "I should have done this years ago," he said. He joined a cancer support group, which, from what he said, felt like what he always imagined AA to be—outbursts, crying, a lot of very personal information shared in a roundtable setting, a real catharsis. We were having the birthing class at his place now to make it easier. There were so many people coming and going from the apartment, it seemed as if we were in a boom time in our lives.

His Berkeley-schooled acupuncturist gave him a list of herbs to buy, specific for liver cancer, including various mushroom extracts and milk thistle. On Grand Street, where they sold turtles, and fish crammed into tanks so they could barely wiggle to stay afloat, and other forms of cruelty, we went on a crappy morning to find these herbs that would supposedly help him. Here, where no one seemed to be living a high-quality life. If these potions did what they promised, wouldn't these people have made a bunch of money and moved away to a decent house, a more tranquil environment?

The sky was spitting rain, spreading dark, infectious puddles on the street corners. Under the sooty clouds and weak sun, I walked, angry, so angry. I was going on weeks of barely contained rage. A burning tower of anger split up through my soul, but I spoke to Rhinehart sweetly, and squeezed his hand, and he told me to deal with it however I was going to, my emotions wouldn't stay consistent anyway. The man, a Korean man, went into the back, while we waited out by a cheap plywood desk tacked up with posters showing the different reflexology zones of the foot. The place had the confusing smells of chamomile and dust, dried things, of the period after decay, when things turn brittle and disintegrate in the hand. We left, a hundred dollars later, Rhinehart clutching a plastic sack of dried plants with reputed medicinal properties.

I had little hope in that or in anything. During the day I was exhausted, wet manacles of sadness dragging me down. At night I was poisoned with insomnia. Around 2 a.m., I'd leave Rhinehart asleep in the bed, like a soul up and departing a body. I was going to watch television. Every night between two and five, I sat glued to the sickly glow of the screen and felt the toxic panic working its way through my blood. I thought about Rhinehart dying. I thought about him writhing in pain. Next month? Next week? I thought about the baby trapped inside my body, and how I no longer had a choice not to have it. I was trapped, too. The baby would have to come out. And then what? Would Rhinehart be dead by then? I was chained to these thoughts, sometimes gasping, unable to disconnect my line of vision from the screen. I no longer talked to God, who hadn't listened to me the one time it had really counted. Instead, I talked to myself. I said awful, ugly things.

"Nothing's been decided yet," Hallie said. She meant "he isn't dead yet." "Now is the time to call on your spirituality." A familiar refrain. She wanted me to come to her Buddhist center with her. She said she was chanting for us to get through this. She told me I was depressed.

"The only man I've ever loved is dying before my eyes. Just when we're going to have a baby. So, you're right! I'm depressed! Thank you for your wisdom. Would you like to tell me why this is happening? What the spiritual significance is?"

Her eyes were red. "I don't know. I don't know why."

"Then just shut up about it. I don't want to hear your Buddhist talk right now. It's hard enough even waking up in the morning. I just have to put my head down and get through it."

Once I said this, I thought, And then what? What was the end result here? Get through to the time when he dies and then get over that? Things would never get better. Rhinehart was dying. And I was unable to do anything about it. I had never felt so useless in my entire life.

But it was a quiet kind of dying, of the type that lulls you with its normalcy. Rhinehart took me to the obstetrician, to the movies, to hear Umberto Eco speak at the New School. He'd been losing weight, but he was also so upbeat and genuinely interested in the world that some days I almost managed to forget the disease gathering in his body. I was desperate to play along. For the act to be the truth.

We took a walk through Central Park. Fall would be unimpressive this year. We hadn't had enough rain, and some of the leaves had turned brown prematurely. The light struck a blighted tree near the pond, sharpening it, so that it didn't even seem like a tree, but a dead stick someone had shoved into the ground. I thought about how in moments of fear everything was intensified. The street lamps down by the Columbus Circle station were glittering spots, carved out in the sky. I looked around blankly. I wasn't fully here. I wasn't fully anywhere.

"So gorgeous," Rhinehart said, patting the gnarled trunk of an oak. "The best thing about nature is that she reminds you you're part of a cycle, yours and hers. I can remember my own tangled thoughts walking this path at another time. And yet how silly they seem."

I nodded, but I was thinking about whether I would ever be able to come back here after this day. Even enter the park. He smiled broadly at me, like a child would. He grasped my hand in his, and slightly swinging it, walked up the path. He said, "You're not handling this so well."

I was indignant. How *dare* you, I thought, which I translated to, "How should I be handling it?"

I could sense him trying to be delicate. "Tatie, this is awful, terrible, shocking news. The only thing worse would be if our situations were reversed. But this is part of life. On some level we have to accept it, and once we do, we can appreciate the time we have together. I want to do that."

I halted on the path, so he had to stop and backtrack. "I can't accept it. I'm unable to."

"My sweet, sweet baby. There's life for you still. There's life for me."

"How can you be so calm?" I pictured him in that lousy hotel room where he'd holed up after receiving his mother's letters. His hair sticking up.

He stared at me, his eyes tearing. "I'm not. I'm terrified and I'm angry and more than anything I feel guilty. I wake up at night paralyzed with it. I'm abandoning my own child. I know what that's like! I know the empty place it creates in a child's life. I swore I'd never do it, and I'm about to."

"But it's not your fault," I said.

"We don't need something to be our fault to feel shame about it." He put his arms around me, talking into my hair. "This is the cruelest thing I've ever done to you, both of you, and I'm so sorry for it. I'm so sorry I got sick."

I had started crying, and it felt like everything was coming up and out of my burning throat.

He said, "But this isn't anybody's fault. It isn't God's. So instead of acting as if we're in an emotional war, how about we try and see it differently. Because I am a very blessed man. I've led, and I'm continuing to lead, a very blessed life. I'll never want to consciously give it up, but this looks to be the way things are going, and we can't spend months angry. I don't want to. I want to love you. Even better than I have before. It's most important that I get it right now."

He asked me if I was praying, and I felt ashamed saying no, as if I wasn't availing myself of every possible means of helping him.

"You should try meditating with Hallie. You're going to need something. The road ahead is too treacherous to go alone." We were going to have to push into places we never imagined we'd be, he said, and it was best that we tried to go there together, instead of separately. I agreed because I loved him, and I wanted to please him, and because I didn't know what else to do. There was something glimmering in his words that if I could grasp it, would keep me from being swallowed alive. "We need to understand that there is a plan at work here—even if we can't see it, we trust it."

"How am I going to live without you?" I said.

"I don't have to be here to be close."

* * *

Hallie was thrilled I was finally coming to the center with her, convinced my salvation was bound up in it. Maybe I did feel calmer, more inclined to think of things I was grateful for. Maybe I had just begun the slow process of acceptance, although I struggled, the ship had begun to move. I needed it, because soon after Rhinehart was to get much more ill, and when he did, it happened quicker than I ever would have thought possible, than anyone had predicted. I didn't realize how much of his illness I'd been dealing with on a theoretical level and how little all that thinking had done to prepare me for anything.

I woke up one morning, complaining about how the baby seemed to have jammed its feet in between my ribs, when I turned over and saw Rhinehart. He stared at me with hot hollow pits of eyes.

"I don't feel so well," he said.

"I'm going to call the doctor."

"No, no. Just lie here with me." His head shook. He was shivering, even though the room was overheated, and the quilt pulled up to his chin. His face, even the whites of his eyes had a yellowish cast.

I called the hospital. They wanted me to bring him in. I went back into the room, where Rhinehart was staring out the window at nothing.

While he dressed I watched him, the hairless skin on his buttocks and the backs of his knees made me turn away. The khaki pants he preferred were almost too loose to wear, and I suddenly remembered him at Chechna's, months and months ago, and how when he leaned over in his chair, the fabric stretched tight across his thighs. I helped him with his shirt, and he stood patiently, like a child, too weak to protest.

We waited and waited. More forms. Tests. His platelet count was low, but there was little that could be done about that. The jaundice wasn't being caused by a block in the bile duct, which would have required a risky procedure to put in a stent. By itself, jaundice wasn't harmful, but it was a sign that his liver was beginning to fail. To see Rhinehart so complacent, so quiet and obedient, waiting for the doctor to write out a prescription for Benadryl in case he started to itch, broke me, and I started sobbing. Rhinehart had revived and was more spirited. He was patting my back, which was making me cry harder. I excused myself to go to the lavatory. "She's a very strong woman," I heard him tell the nurse as I left.

In the car ride home, he said, "It's strange to be out in the world," and I saw how without realizing it we'd adjusted to spending most of our time indoors.

We came back to a quiet apartment at midday. He was exhausted from the trip. His eyes kept unfocusing, and so I let him sleep for a few hours.

In the early evening I went into the darkened room to get a sweater, and saw that his eyes were open. He smiled, slowly, as if even moving his facial muscles was an effort. "How are you feeling, Tatie?"

"Fine," I said.

"How is your back? Is it bothering you?"

I shook my head silently. I leaned into the window, my forehead against the pane. A cool, wet night was pushing against the glass. The veggie burger I'd had for dinner sat heavy in my stomach. Rhinehart reached for me and fell short. He stroked the covers instead, and I climbed into the bed and curled up, my body feeling enormous next to his. I lifted his hand and put it on my ass. He squeezed it.

"My obstetrician gave me the name of a woman who can come and stay with me after the baby is born. To help. She's a retired nurse. She called while you were sleeping. I'm going to meet with her tomorrow." I now hired people for everything. A man had come in and assembled the crib. Groceries were delivered from the supermarket. I was highly organized and spent the day making lists, phone numbers, times when Rhinehart's friends were stopping by to see him, supplies

I still needed for the baby, including a sterilizer for the bottles. I had preregistered with the hospital and had already packed my bag even though my delivery date was more than a month away. I had arranged for a driver to be on call. "Do a dry run of the route to the hospital together," Rhinehart had advised me. We did. It took seven minutes.

"I think we should find out the baby's sex and not wait," I said.

"I can tell you, it's going to be a girl. I hope she has your eyes. You have beautiful eyes. They're so big and deep and loving. You know the pagans believed that love dwelled in the beams of the eyes. That you could shoot a man through with just a look."

I smiled. "Is that what happened to you?"

"Yes, and I began to keen. I had fallen in love." He stroked my hair. "I remember missing you so much when I was in Ukraine. I used to lie on that mattress, it felt like it was filled with straw, and try and conjure you up. Your smell. The feel of your plump little lips. Those hairpins you drop all over the house."

"I don't wear those hairpins anymore. I stopped in college."

"To me, you'll always wear them. I'd think about the little sighing you used to make in your sleep." He smiled to himself. "Had I known how wonderful it was going to be falling in love with you again, I would have tried to make it happen sooner."

Rhinehart didn't give any specifics about the type of burial he wanted, and I hated to bring it up. Before he got sick, he'd talked about how interesting mausoleums were—a small, heavy-hewed stone house, where your box of bones was carefully and tidily stowed in a little niche in the wall. I took this as a fleeting fascination and not a directive.

In his will, I was the sole beneficiary. He brought in his financial advisor to go over all the investments, which he had regulated so that the baby and I would have enough to live on.

"Once your photography begins to take off, you may not even need this money, but best to be safe."

The gallery show. I'd forgotten about it. It seemed to have happened years ago. The majority of my pieces had sold.

* * *

He was taken over by a new project—a scrapbook of his life. "I don't ever want my child to have to agonize over who daddy was," he said. "Here I get to document my past and also describe myself."

"Is this going to be a heroic account?"

"Perhaps. You can have your say, too, and feel free to be honest. There will be sections for our relationship as well. Parts 1 and 2. I come off better in Part 2." I brought boxes of his mementos into the bedroom. He had saved things I didn't think he would have, such as faded *New York Times* reviews of his books, both good and bad, copies of his magazine articles, and notes I had written him when I was in college. Everything in lowercase. The appropriation of his terms of endearment for me.

I've gone to class, my love. Will be back at 4. Let's go get a drink at the Briar. Will you come with me? Toby's band is playing. I want to catch the first set.

"Hey," I said to him. "You saved the note but you refused to come with me to the show."

I dragged in my box of old photographs. The bedroom was so full of our lives we had to fight a path to the door.

He wanted to cut things out, but in the kitchen all I could find were the poultry shears and a plastic pair of scissors that looked like they were from a third-grade classroom. "Check in the sewing basket," he called out.

"What sewing basket?"

"Under the leather chair."

There I found a wicker basket with several spools of thread, needles, and a sharp pair of scissors. There was also a length of raglan yarn. He'd always claimed to know how to darn. It was the reason he gave for refusing to throw away socks with holes in the big toe.

* * *

His illness was making him tired much of the time, and although his pain was still manageable he would soon need someone to administer the medication. We hired a private nurse, a young Pakistani woman with short black hair and a soft double chin. She had very smooth skin, and an elusive darkness that gathered around her eyes and lips. She was cheerful and Rhinehart seemed to like her. We had interviewed a dour Russian that I would have thought was more his type, but when I asked if he wanted her in, he shook his head mutely no.

Now that my care hours were reduced—even the term hospice bothered me, I wouldn't use it—I was encouraged to go out. Weeks in the pressing sadness of the house had left me unprepared for this pointless perambulation outdoors, and there were times I would race back after only fifteen minutes, under a mounting fear that he had died in my absence. Sometimes he would be sleeping. Sometimes I would come back to a house that seemed more cheerful than when I had left it, the hurricane lamps lit and classical music playing, Parveen reading Hafiz to Rhinehart, a favorite of his, in her lilting voice. Coming into this scene, I was a lumbering intruder of darkness with my heavy body and sodden sadness. If her job was to usher him into death, to coax him into quietly releasing his claims on the earthly world, then I was operating at cross-purposes to that. Big-bellied and stubbornly healthy, I was asking him to cling to this life. It was as if I were the source of pain in the house, reminding Rhinehart that he was about to back out on the deals we'd made.

At other times, when I could stand to be out for longer, I'd go chant at the Buddhist center, praying fervently for all of us. It became a routine, and I relied on it, as if it were the only thing propping me up. Afterwards, I'd just walk around, purposelessly. Once I wandered into a department store and around the shiny carousels of clothes until one of the clerks offered to help me. On his face I saw alarm. I looked at myself in the mirror. My eyes were vacant, as if I were staring out of the back of them, into myself.

* * *

Perhaps sensing that with the exception of the Buddhist center, my afternoons out weren't doing me much good, Rhinehart suggested I take my camera along. For a couple of days, I brought it but took no pictures. Then one afternoon, in a coffee shop, I began talking to another pregnant woman, and she let me photograph her. After that I began looking for and photographing pregnant women when I could find them. It was strange really, how often they were alone, except for the teens, who were often seen in couples. They were still at that stage of their lives where their habits and schedules mirrored each other's. Sometimes I had them pose, which they willingly did. But I was entering a phase where I was more interested in the potentials of surveillance photography than portraiture; it didn't escape me that this entire project had a strong psychological imperative. I felt like an outsider, one who was curious as to what drew people together. It was often the interracial couples that seemed best suited, their energy was more dynamic.

I began following couples I marked as mine for the afternoon, observing how they had their arms wrapped around each other's waists, or one hand tucked slyly in the back pocket of the other's jeans in a very retro sign of mutual ownership. I noted whether their fingers were entwined or whether one of the partner's hands enclosed the other's. I became a cultural anthropologist of these gestures and categorized them according to the headings I remembered: wiping something off the other's shirt was a maintenance gesture. Handholding: proprietary.

I was both conspicuous and inconspicuous because I looked so harmless in my large maternity clothes. I would wander on and off buses, watching my couple as they sat, one leg slung over the other's, rubbing each other's hands. I'd follow them right up until the point they would part, kissing goodbye in front of the subway station or building or where two streets intersected. Or if they lived together, I would follow them into the grocery store while they bickered about the produce and apathetically discussed what to make for dinner, and then back out into the dusk, into Brooklyn neighborhoods of single-family homes with metal awnings and aluminum siding and early Halloween decorations out on the stoops, where the raccoons crept along the power lines at night to travel to adjacent fenced yards, where there were more garbage cans and fewer black trash bags on the curb. I stood across the street, taking pictures and waiting for the lights to come on so that I could see the interior, the shape of the furniture, the type of lighting, harsh or dim, they spent their evenings in.

It was then that I would wake up from the trance of the spy, who without even realizing it, fuses herself with her subject so that her body and self disappear. I would sometimes be lost and have to ask for directions, feeling confused and pathetic and let down. I thought about suicide occasionally, not in any sort of constructive way, but to scare myself, or that was the result, at any rate. It also seemed the only way to avoid all the pain and misery and incomprehensible loss that was heading at me like a levy break on a hill, the debris coming down in slow motion. It bothered me to think these things with Rhinehart laboring for breath at home, and a child struggling inside of me, absorbing my confusion. At times, I rested my hand on my stomach, drawing strength from the person in there who'd yet to know this type of pain.

One evening I was returning from following a young couple in their twenties, who were angry with each other because he'd gone to help a friend in Queens with a graphic design project, and the friend was a girl, and he hadn't returned home until noon the next day. Most of their time was spent discussing the unanswered phone calls as well as free agency in a relationship and whether if the friend was a guy she'd be as upset. I found their discussion engrossing. Still, I was relieved to leave them.

I wasn't ready to go home yet and decided to visit the Ukrainian museum downtown, if they were still open. I could finally make up for the trip I hadn't taken with Rhinehart, and buy him some postcards for the scrapbook.

I was changing trains when a young woman on my side of the platform caught my eye. Or her earrings did, thick rings of amber that hung heavy in her lobes. She had long dark curly hair, pulled back, and they showed up against her slender neck. I was about to compliment her on them but hesitated when I noticed the very subtle affectionate gestures she was making to someone on the other side of the platform, who was headed uptown. With my instinct for couples, I looked across the tracks for him. It was my old boyfriend Lawrence.

I was out of his sight range, and I quickly got behind the free-standing subway map so that he couldn't see me. From there, I watched her. She had a very easy way of moving, laughing. She had on wide-legged pants and a brightly colored scarf, an outfit I admired but never felt I could pull off. Years ago, I would have assumed she was an artist, based on how she was dressed. I would have envied her.

The train came, she got on it, and I remained hidden behind the stanchion. I had dallied briefly with following her, but what would I say? What could she tell me about the beginning of their relationship, their lives spread out before them like a map? I was feeling irrational, like a spurned lover. The train pulled away. I stepped out from hiding.

Lawrence had taken out *The Economist* and was reading it. His flat black shoes, his jeans hemmed just a touch too short—all the things I had forgotten. It was the interest I was creating, standing alone on the opposite platform, staring intently at him, that caused him to look up. Even his startled expression was familiar, and I instinctively smiled and waved.

He was genuinely pleased to see me and shocked to see I was pregnant. He pointed to my belly and mouthed, "Congratulations!" I turned to the side to give him a better view.

"Thank you," I mouthed back. "You look good." He did.

"I'm doing okay. But *you*!" He leaned forward slightly, in that way he had, which meant he wanted to plug me with questions. He was grinning. "When are you due?"

"November 10th."

"How are you feeling?"

"I'm good. Okay. It's a little uncomfortable, but not too bad." It had been a while since someone had asked me this question in reference to the pregnancy.

"That's so wonderful! Is it a boy or a girl?"

"I don't know yet." I threw my hands up to enunciate. "It's a mystery!"

"Congratulations," he said again with real feeling. All this genuine pleasure and warmth and excitement for me was confusing. For several minutes, I'd forgotten Rhinehart dying in that room with Rachmaninoff playing on the stereo. I was just me, healthy and seemingly happy. I stood there like an idiot, smiling, as if I were someone to be truly envied.

Then the tone signaling his train's arrival, and he waved, almost a deferential salute, before it rushed in, he stepped on it, and was gone. I remained there, staring out onto the empty platform.

When Hallie found out I was going to my obstetrician appointments by myself, she insisted on accompanying me. She looked so uncertain and out of place in the waiting room, staring at the pregnant women when she thought they weren't looking, that I told her not to come. But she kept showing up anyway, sometimes waiting around in front of the office if I was delayed with the subway, or Rhinehart, or just my inability to leave the house. She'd fussily hold the door open, park herself in the seat where she had the best view of the room, and start flipping through parenting magazines. She had become addicted to them, I think, and was culling information, usually scatological—there was a period when she was obsessed with the best toilet training methods—that she could weave into lively, opinionated conversation for the ride home. She had asked to be my birthing partner.

"Do you realize what goes on when a baby is born?" I said. "There's blood and secretions and it's a mess."

"I know. I can handle it. I've been preparing."

"How? With those magazines in the doctor's office?"

"No," she said stubbornly. "With videos. It's not as bad as everyone says. I also learned the breathing." She panted rhythmically to show me.

"You'll be the only one in the hospital room doing that. I didn't study Lamaze."

She looked hurt. "Well, how am I supposed to know if you don't share your birth plan with me?"

"Birth plan. I see you're picking up the vocabulary." I envisioned all the passion she'd brought to animal rights advocacy diverted to my delivery. It was somewhat frightening. "We'll see."

At every appointment, I'd been putting off finding out the baby's sex, unwilling to let go of our original idea for it to be a "surprise." Finally, I did. I told Hallie in the car on the drive back. A girl. I had been wanting a boy. Someone who had Rhinehart's nose, and way of standing with his hands clasped behind him, and his laugh. I missed him already. I would have given anything to be able to go backwards, even to the worst moments, even to after we found out he was sick, that day I walked angrily alongside him in the park.

It took me a minute to realize that a persistent small coughing noise I'd been hearing was Hallie crying. It sounded awkward, as if she didn't know how to do it properly. The sound was accelerating in speed and intensity. I told her to pull the car over.

"Why are *you* so upset?" I said, and it came out harshly.

She wasn't responding so I had to wait until she had calmed down enough to whisper, "I'm just overwhelmed."

"With what? With the birthing videos?"

She shook her head. "No, no. It's just that it's a girl—it seems so right that it is. It makes so much sense. And now my whole life's going to change."

This was so unexpected, I laughed. "*Your* life! What's going to change for you?"

She turned around in her seat, sharply offended, and stared at me with her reddened eyes. "What the hell do you think I've been doing this for? Why have I been going to the damn La Leche meetings?"

"The breastfeeding organization?"

"I'm going to have to move in with you again, at least for the first month. Maybe longer, until we get a good child care schedule going. I took myself off PETA's volunteer roster. I've told my clients that my hours in November and probably December are limited."

It was strange, but it hadn't occurred to me she'd be around. I couldn't picture it. I'd always been the one to take care of her—that just seemed my role, as fixed as other things about us, the slight difference in our ages, my timidity and her outgoingness. "But I hired someone. You don't know anything about babies. You don't even like them."

"You don't get it, do you? This isn't a theoretical infant. She's a person, a little girl like we once were." Her tone rebuked me, and I felt guilty for having been initially disappointed. "*We're* going to be her family. Both of us. My role is huge. It's all my therapist and I have been working on for the past month, getting myself ready for it. My Buddhist group is chanting for us. I'm fucking terrified, but you can't care about something this much and then fail."

"I'm just . . . I had no idea you were taking it this seriously." I wasn't entirely sure I wanted her involved. Then I imagined her calling around to her friends for recommendations on schools or conferring with me about a pediatrician or just hashing out one of millions of decisions, and I was suddenly, enormously, relieved. "You mean like a co-parent?"

"Exactly," she said. "You'll have final say, obviously, but I'll be the researcher. Like a consultant, but hands-on. I've already amassed a ton of information." She had restarted the car, was pulling out into Eighth Avenue traffic. "This is going to be the greatest thing we've ever done together."

* * *

It seemed foolish, but I had hoped for Rhinehart to be alive to see the baby. It didn't appear possible now. He was on a regular regimen of pain medication and spent most of his time in bed, except for a mandatory afternoon walk that we took around the apartment together to keep his circulation up. I hadn't wanted to believe him when he'd said that what saddened him the most, besides leaving me alone, was that he wouldn't be able to see his child. I thought of how the original expectation for his own life, that he would never be a parent, had actually been right.

Standing over his bed, I said, "Your clairvoyance is impressive, Madame Blavatsky. Timothy, lowercase 't' is on the way."

He opened his eyes slowly, coming into consciousness. "A girl!"

"Hallie was pleased about it. I'm not sure she would have been so keen on a boy."

"If you don't like timothy, we can combine our mothers' names."

"Anna Lily," I said. I liked it.

He said, "I knew today would be special. I felt God with me and stronger right before you walked in the room."

I climbed into the bed knees first, like a child. "What does it feel like?"

"A source of stillness and peace. Like a woman is with me, like she will go with me. God feels like my mother and my wife today." He smiled. "Tomorrow may be different. But today the feminists were right. Will you take our picture?"

"Now? Why?"

"Because I want to capture this moment. The moment we found out about our baby girl." In a burst of effort, his dry mouth closed around the word and he smiled.

I set up the tripod and the cable release and photographed us. I was looking at him, not the camera; he looked peaceful, although I could see, in the tightening around his eyes, that he was in pain. I refocused the shot—the viewfinder was wet and my vision of him blurred. I knew it would be a very long time, decades maybe, if I lived that long, before I would ever be able to look at these photos.

Later, we lay in bed, listening to music. My arms around him. "Tatie," he said. "I want to tell you before I get too sick to say it. You have been the great event of my life."

"And you are mine."

"The baby will be yours now." I started to protest, and he said, "No, trust me. It's the one thing that helps me to understand everything else."

When Laura had been told Rhinehart was sick, she had become hysterical, saying "I want to see him! I want to see him!" This had been several weeks ago, and she had arranged numerous visits since, only to cancel an hour before she was to show up. The afternoon I took our photograph, I called her to tell her straight out that if she wanted to visit, she needed to make it soon. I had a perverse urge to add "speak now or forever hold your peace."

An hour later, she showed up red-faced as if she'd been crying all the way over. It was hard for me to look at her. She'd brought a box of chocolates, not knowing how pointless that was—he was barely eating anymore and would never have been able to swallow those anyway. She stood in the hall with her coat on, gripping the chocolates and a bouquet of flowers, looking so bewildered that I had the sudden, dynamic desire to throw her out, protect Rhinehart from her weakness, so he wouldn't have to see the horror of his own fate reflected on her face. But he was stronger than any of us, recently. Maybe he could soothe the disconsolate, maybe he could comfort even her. I pointed mutely to his closed door, and she looked at me as if I were gesturing towards the gangplank. She knocked timidly, then pushed it open. Ten minutes passed. I could hear her crying in there, and I wanted desperately to be out of the apartment. But a sense of duty restrained me. I didn't want her to have to walk into an empty living room after leaving him. So I sat with my baby, Anna, and we waited for her.

When she emerged twenty minutes later, I feared she would want to talk about how terrible he looked or her own horror. She had questioned me extensively on the phone, gasping when I said he was jaundiced, or that we had to rotate him every hour for his comfort. I had been giving her the sanitized version of what went on in this house, and it was still too much for her to handle.

"How did it go?" I asked, and she looked at me with such enormous nakedness that I thought back to something Rhinehart's Sufi spiritual advisor had said, that the entire world, all that we'd said and done and felt and seen, could, at moments, be reflected in our eyes, as the eyes were the gateway to the heart, and the heart the gateway to the soul. The soul itself could never be alone, as it was connected to everyone else's.

Laura said, "He's dying with grace."

I felt him starting to withdraw, to be relinquishing his claims on his life here, as a person moving overseas will give up his bed, and car, and house, all the things he can't bring, and no longer has use for anyway. They represent the old life, and can only be relevant to those people left behind. Sometimes he would look at me, and I would get the sense he was seeing many things simultaneously, the past, the place he was traveling to, the immediate concerns of the present. I saw Anna and myself looming large and then receding into the distance.

I sat on a chair next to his bed and fed him ice chips, as he liked the sensation. He was dehydrated—I could tell from his lips, which were dry and cracked. He took one to please me, then shook his head. Such things as thirst, too, were the concerns of the living.

While I'd been out, he'd taken a call from Chechna. She was recovering from a hip operation, unable to travel to see him. Instead they had been talking weekly by phone. This conversation, perhaps their last, had been different, and afterwards Rhinehart was very alert and struggling to convey its importance to me.

"She said it's wrong for. Her to outlive me. If she could she would. Trade her life. For mine. Sounds like. Something. A mother would say."

I was rubbing his hands. "She does love you, you know."

"Also. She said. My father. Tried to send for me. After my mother died."

"Really!"

He nodded. "Chechna was honoring. The promise. The promise she made to. My mother. To have me raised. In America." He swallowed noisily, and I offered him his water glass with the straw. He shook his head impatiently. "Chechna thought. My life would be better. Here. She was right."

"I am so thankful for her decision."

He was still smiling. "Now my. Father and I have nothing to be. Ashamed of. When we see each other. Again."

The day I thought Rhinehart was going to die, I cried for hours, convinced that I was sensing what was going to happen and preparing myself. He was slipping in and out of consciousness for most of the afternoon, talking in garbled half-sentences that I strained to make out. Then, late in the day, he rallied unexpectedly, and looking at me clear-eyed, said, "You're a wreck today."

I was so relieved I started laughing and babbling, "What if all this crying is making a melancholy baby, a little Princess of Denmark." I told him about Win's story. "There are women who say the baby is affected in utero. The ones who were happy had easygoing kids."

His eyes had been fluttering closed, and they opened again. "No, no. It has to do with the heart."

The next morning he was feeling better, and I even let the nurse take the afternoon off. It was an unseasonably warm day for the first of November, and I opened the window a crack. "Nice," he said, inhaling the air.

The baby was kicking a lot. "She's going nuts in there," I said, and put his hand on my stomach to feel.

Since he had responded so well to the breeze, I wondered if his sense of smell was more acute today, and so I decided I'd make a pumpkin pie. Rhinehart and I had always loved autumn, and the scent might even chase out the dry medicinal smell that had settled on everything. I asked him if it was all right if I disappeared for a bit to make it, just from a can, nothing fancy, and he nodded. I was gone no more than ten minutes, and when I came back into the room, he was still lying in the position I'd left him in, his hand outstretched where I'd been holding it. His eyes had rolled back into his skull, and there was a dark rattle in his throat. His breath stopped, and I froze, then he inhaled again, noisily.

"Oh no, oh no, oh no." I went back and forth to the phone and picked it up and then dropped it again, when I realized it wasn't going to do anything. My hands and then my whole body began trembling, and I climbed into the bed with him, and wrapped my arms and legs around his, which were rigid as if he were waiting motionless for what was coming. Since I could, I began talking insistently, remembering that the nurse had said he would be able to hear me up until the end. I knitted a rope between us, speaker and listener. I told him about how when I was in college I used to watch for him to come home, and then jump into a chair to make it appear I'd been doing other things, about these visions I had that took place at my elementary school and in them I was a child, and he was coming around the corner to pick me up. They were so bizarre I'd never told him. I said that with him I'd felt protected. I felt understood, as if he could see deep into what I needed, before I could even. I talked about what he had looked like at forty-one, the blond hair on his tanned, freckled forearms, and how excited he'd been when he'd finished one of his poems, we'd gotten out a bottle of champagne and started drinking even though it was only 7 a.m., and what it felt like to be twenty years old, standing next to him after one of his readings, holding his hand. I spoke of the future, of the baby so that he could see her. I told him he'd made me stronger in these past few weeks than I'd ever known I could be. His breath grew coarser and rolled on, the rattle more drawn out. "Thank you for letting me be with you," I said. "Thank you for letting me know you."

It was coming up and over us like an enormous wave, all our past, and we were together, gripping each other, rushing down this terrible chute with such speed, I became terrified—we were going too fast. I knew I needed to stop talking, but I couldn't stop. I shouted, "Stay! Stay with me!" I shouted at God for aid and in anger. I was still attached to Rhinehart, it was as if there were millions of hair-fine roots joining us, I could feel them tearing, and I clung to him. And then, all at once, I didn't need to anymore. I let him go. Tiny ripples of shivers like an electrical current raced over his body. He shuddered violently, and for a split second he felt so close to me, as when we were making love. The side of his face pressed against my pulsing temple. What's next for us? I asked him. His breath had stopped, and a dark stain spread over the sheet.

ACKNOWLEDGMENTS

I owe so much to my parents, not only for the original encouragement, but for all the years after, for having faith in me. And Graham, who I'm very lucky to have as a brother, an artistic inspiration, and a friend.

I'm very grateful for my agent, Lane Zachary, for her kindness, insight, dedication, and belief. Everything changed the day I met her. I'm also very fortunate to have been paired with the incisively bright and talented Anjali Singh, who opened the book up for me, and is also so much fun to talk to. Thank you to everyone at Simon & Schuster, especially Jon Karp, Anne Tate, Nina Pajak, Jackie Seow, Fred Chase, Gypsy da Silva, Sarah Nalle, and Jill Putorti. And especially Millicent Bennett—many thanks.

I didn't know it at the time, but this novel began at an unofficial residency in Cambridge, home of poet Mariève Rugo, whose intellect and talent continue to inspire me (not to mention that sense of humor). Many thanks to everyone at Fundación Valparaiso, Spain, where the novel was torn apart and constructed, and the International Writers and Translators' Center of Rhodes, Greece, where it was revised.

I've had the very good fortune to study with these writers and scholars: Leslie Epstein, who understood my style and helped to develop it; Ha Jin, who has been fundamental; the deeply inspiring Guinn Batten; and Marshall Klimasewiski, who first saw something in my work and advocated for me—I will always be grateful.

Thanks to my early readers: Lee and Eva Bacon (who provided a large quantity of counsel and good judgment), the insightful Coray Ames, and Doug Harrison, whose opinion I will always seek out. As well as Dr. Lorraine Burns, a generous physician and friend, for consulting on the medical facts.

I'm also very thankful to writers Adriana V. López and Andrew Lloyd-Jones for talking it over and giving sound advice, and especially artist Karrie Hovey for our long phone discussions about art and how much to give up for it.

For all their support, and for answering obscure questions or offering well-timed anecdotes or situational metaphors: Hila Katz, Kara Decas, Sophia Sinko, Nicole Caruth, Alex Ortolani, Jen and Jacob Drew, Matthew Nicholas, Lauren Haynes, Katy Brennan, Mónica Páez, Tania Kamensky, Nicholas Cohn, and Katy Acitelli. As well as my extended family for all the stories I've overheard, my grandparents, the Betschs, and Lotts, especially Susan Lott for her support (and likely influence, too).

My Cobble Hill Buddhist group (SGI) has been a constant source of encouragement, especially Deborah Goodwin, Lynne Winters, and Eduarda Rocha-Waid, my unconditionally loving friend.

And a very special thanks to my Green Street—Ellen, Meegs, and Katie—Heidi, Jeremy, and Attie, and our lives together. Back when everything came with an interesting story.

ABOUT THE AUTHOR

Jessica Lott is the author of *Osin,* winner of the 2006 Novella Award from Low Fidelity Press. Her fiction and essays have been published in the U.S. and internationally, including a monthly column, "Alchemy of Inspiration," for PBS: Art21; *NY Arts;* and *frieze,* London, where she won the 2009 Art Writer's Prize. She has an MA in Creative Writing from Boston University and an MA in English Literature from Washington University in St. Louis. Jessica lives in New York.